"How do you women want to die? How do you want your children killed?"

"Captain!"

"Abby, I've dreaded this moment but I can no longer put it off."

The color left Abby's face and she tightly gripped the arms of her chair. Blaine's eyes held hers and he spoke slowly, carefully.

"There are no fighting men left in the fort and the savages outside will soon come over the stockade. I can't leave you to that fate—it will be our last act of mercy. Please ask the ladies and let me know."

"But—can't we hold out for a little time yet?"

"Not long, Abby, and it's best I know now, to prepare the men for the task."

Abby sat unmoving. A shot sounded from the stockade but it only accented the silence and underlined the futility of the defense. She pictured row on row of waiting Indians ready for the attack. Then she saw her baby, Henri, kicking and cooing in his crib; she imagined other children and all the other women.

She closed her eyes tightly.

How could she answer Captain Blaine?

SENSATIONAL SAGAS

THE FRONTIER RAKERS   (633, $2.50)
by David Norman
With half their lives packed in their covered wagons and the other
half staked on the future of the great frontier, these brave pioneers begin their arduous journey down the Oregon Trail.

THE FRONTIER RAKERS #2: THE FORTY-NINERS
by David Norman   (634, $2.50)
Lured by the promise of gold the pioneers journeyed west, coming face to face with hardship, struggling to survive. But their
need for adventure, wide open spaces and new-found wealth led
them to meet the challenge of taming the wild frontier.

THE FRONTIER RAKERS #3: GOLD FEVER
by David Norman   (621, $2.50)
The brave and determined forty-niners are blazing their way
across the wilderness, heading toward California, the land of
gold. Neither murder, thieves nor Indian attacks can deter them
from staking their claims and fulfilling the great American dream.

WHITEWATER DYNASTY: HUDSON!   (607, $2.50)
by Helen Lee Poole
This is the first in a new historical-romantic-adventure epic that
traces the growth of America by its magnificent and powerful
waterways—and the proud, passionate people who built their
lives around them.

*Available wherever paperbacks are sold, or order direct from the
Publisher. Send cover price plus 50¢ per copy for mailing and
handling to Zebra Books, 21 East 40th Street, New York, N.Y.
10016. DO NOT SEND CASH!*

WHITEWATER DYNASTY
DYNASTY
THE OHIO!

BY HELEN LEE POOLE

ZEBRA BOOKS

KENSINGTON PUBLISHING CORP.

ZEBRA BOOKS

are published by

KENSINGTON PUBLISHING CORP.
21 East 40th Street
New York, N.Y. 10016

Dedicated to
Peg Larson

I

Long ago the Iroquois had taught Abby Forny, nee Brewster, to keep her expression impassive no matter what she felt or thought. So now she listened to the admonitions of the midwife as attentively as would any young frontier matron. Of course, the red-cheeked, gray-haired woman seated so primly on the ladder back chair knew many of the very early treatments for pregnancy that the Onondaga did not. On the other hand, Moon Willow knew of barks, leaves, roots and grasses needed for the birthing that were far beyond the ken of Madame Dean.

Abby rarely dwelled on the Indian years of her life but now she felt a touch of regret that sharp-eyed, sharp-tongued Moon Willow would not be beside her at the delivery. Those red brown hands had been so skilled at so many things!

A shadow of a smile touched Abby's lips when she made another comparison between "Mother" Dean and Major Leonidas Howard, doctor and surgeon to the British and Colonial troops of the Fort Pitt garrison. He was as old as Mother Dean but his long horse face had turned an embarrassed beet red when she told him of her need. He had stroked his chin, pushed his knuckly fingers up under his powdered wig, setting it slightly askew, and managed a quite professional "hem" and "haw." A pinch of snuff and a violent sneeze had helped somewhat but not nearly enough. He could readily cauterize a wound, extract a musket ball, amputate or treat pox as well as the supperations of the "French disease" that camp followers so readily and freely donated to soldiers everywhere. But to see a proper matron through pregnancy and delivery had obviously upset him.

Mother Dean broke in on Abby's thoughts. "Stand up, lass, and shed your dress. Let's see the shape of ye."

Abby rose, unbuttoned her blouse and pulled it and the attached skirt up over her head. She slipped off her petticoats, then turned to face the midwife.

Mother Dean nodded as she professionally studied Abby's tall, slender figure, her long legs and full, rich

8

breasts. "Ye be as pretty of body as ye be of face and hair, lass. Your husband should have pleasure of you, I'm sure."

"I hope so. He pleasures me."

"What ye carry is proof of that. Turn slowly about, if ye please."

Abby slowly turned around in place and Mother leaned forward slightly, gray eyes narrowed. She spoke in a half-whisper as though to herself. "Wide hips—they promise well. Your stomach's still flat but it'll start to bulge afore long. Tits look like they'll hold enough milk for the young'n to come. I figure your laboring 'll be fairly easy but, of course, you never can tell."

Abby shrugged. "I was once called Strong Woman."

Mother looked up at her. "Funny name for a girl." Mother chuckled. "Bet you wore out your husband and he calls you that."

"Edward can match any woman. No, it was something I did back east, just this side of the Hudson River and—"

"New York!" Mother exclaimed, then sighed longingly. "I was born near Albany. Then my folks moved down to Philadelphia and I landed out here in this wilderness. I didn't know you was from York Colony."

"Connecticut—Westover, but near the York line."

"Folks from nigh all the colonies were coming out this way until the Frenchies and Injuns started taking scalps. Now the war's over, maybe it'll all start again." Mother slapped her hands on her knees hidden by her linsey-woolsey dress. "Well, get dressed. There ain't much either of us can do for a

9

while—not until that young'n decides to pop out and that'll be months and months from now. You'll get tired of carrying it."

"No—not Edward's."

"Daft about your man, eh? Don't blame you none. Edward Forny cuts a fine figure that any woman'd look at twice. Even one as old as me."

"Why Mother Dean!"

"No mind." The old woman sniffed. "My day's over, when it comes to that. But, mind you, I had my flings in my time."

"I can tell you were a beautiful girl."

"Not as ugly as some, for sure." Mother carefully changed the subject. "Your husband, Mr. Forny. He acts and talks French sometimes."

Instantly the constant caution of the war years sent cold signals along Abby's spine. She carelessly answered as she swept a lock of auburn hair back from her high, tanned forehead and hoped her voice did not betray her. "That's because he trapped for pelt from Niagara to Detroit along the Lake of the Eries and he picked up the courier way of speech and accent."

To Abby's relief, that seemed to satisfy Mother Dean's curiosity about her husband. Abby served tea, stoutly laced with a fiery brandy that Edward used in his occasional trading to the settlers along the Allegheny and Monongahela Rivers who were beginning to trickle in from over the mountains to the east. Abby contented herself with the strength of the tea alone but Mother Dean, typical of the frontier people, downed the hot, strong drink as easily and readily as the whiskey she had known along the

Atlantic seaboard.

Mother, after more instructions and warnings as to the pregnancy period, finally picked up her huge woven cloth bag and waddled away toward the village. Abby watched her a few moments from the doorway and then, with a sweeping glance along the high-pointed stake palisade wall of Fort Pitt, closed the cabin door as she stepped back into the house.

Dressed now, she could pull the heavy drapes from across all the windows. One, like the door, gave her a restricted view of the Fort's palisade. But she could face south and look over the land to the trees that bordered the Monongahela River coursing north and westward to finally be hidden by the corner of the fort built right out at the point.

But the window across the room held her attention. She could see the south flowing water of the Allegheny, called by the Indians the Allegeway and by both the French and English soldiers and settlers, the North Fork of the Ohio. It, too, flowed in a westward direction to be finally hidden by another corner of the fort. Beyond that obstruction, it joined the Monongahela and formed the Ohio that everyone, red or white, called La Belle Rivière, the Beautiful River.

Abby walked to the window and looked the short distance she could see to the first bend of the Allegheny. High hills, tree and brush covered, hid all the rest but her imagination leaped over those rugged visual barriers to move on northward. Somewhere up its winding course, Edward would be working his way toward her with canoe paddle or rafting pole.

She closely studied the wide rocky river beach she

11

could see, the tangle of bushes on either bank and the oaks, beeches and birches towering beyond them. She did not realize how her gray eyes had narrowed, becoming hawklike, missing nothing. The Onondaga and Seneca had made all that instinctive. Her own survival had once depended on it and might easily do so again. The wilderness demanded wilderness ways and alertness, in spite of the fort and the nearby cabins of the small settlement. Relaxed vigilance had cause the attack of Westover and her own captivity.

"Be careful, darling!" she whispered and felt the warning, protecting thought speed over trees, ridges and river bends to Edward.

Lord! how she wished he was right here with her in this room! No, in the room beyond where the great, empty bed waited! Her cheeks warmed to her thoughts and then she started in surprise as a light tap sounded on the door.

She lifted the latch and opened the street door. Letitia Smith had her fist raised to tap again but she dropped her hand as Abby appeared. "I bein't turning you none?" she asked uncertainly.

"Of course not, Letty. Come in."

"I seen Mother a'leaving and I reckoned to ask how you do."

"Very well, according to Mother." Abby moved aside and her neighbor stepped into the room. "I'd feel better, of course, if Edward was home."

"Aye, a woman needs a man when she's a'carrying. I knowed I did to the point where Dick became right put out by my holding him back from plowing, hoeing and all. But I just put on my stubborn and he gave in."

Abby laughed and closed the door behind her guest. Letty Smith hardly looked old enough to be a mother of three—one in the crib and two urchin boys almost always underfoot in the village, the fort or the fields. Letty swept off her bonnet and golden, silky hair fell over her shoulders and down her back.

"Tea?" Abby asked, hospitality forcing her to put Mother Dean's many cups out of her mind.

"Reckon not. I just never worked up a like for it. But—"

Abby smiled and nodded, sparing Letty the spoken request. When she returned to the room with two small glasses of brandy, her own water-weakened, Letty smiled her thanks. Both she and Mother Dean had come from the Virginia mountains and Abby wondered sometimes at the liking of these hill people for strong drinks. Abby had known of some in Connecticut with similar tastes but nothing like what she had encountered here in Fort Pitt. Perhaps the British soldiers with their daily ration of grog had something to do with it.

Letty loudly sipped her drink, the sound conveying appreciation and approval. Maybe, Abby thought, the mountaineers had learned that custom from the Indians. Different ways for different people, she thought, and suddenly wondered if many of her mannerisms might seem strange.

"How does your family do?" she asked Letty.

"Tol'able, thank ye. Dick sold his 'taters to the sojers a few days back and that's a thing that brought me over visiting."

"But we don't need vegetables."

13

"I figured. But what with pence and shilling newly come to us, I'm thinking your Edward might git us a few things next time he's east toward Ligonier or north toward them French traders along the Lake of the Eries."

"He could . . . but I don't know what he plans until he gets back from this trip."

"Time and enough," Letty dismissed urgently. She smoothed her hand over her long rough skirt and looked longingly beyond Abby to the window. "Reckon he could get dress goods so's I could make a skirt and blouse for me and a shirt for Dick? It'd be mighty fine to be rid of the linsey-woolsey and the buckskin for Sunday meetings when they build that new church back of us. Then there's tobacco, maybe a rubber ball for them two kids and a rattle for the young'n."

"I'm sure Edward can get them for you."

"And mayhap he could find a jug of mountain whiskey somewhere?"

"I don't know. I'll ask him."

Just then a knock sounded on the door and both women started in surprise. Abby recovered her composure. "Now this is certainly a day for company! I wonder who that can be."

She crossed the room and opened the door on Major Howard. He held his tricorn hat under his arm and bobbed his head in what Abby took to be a bow. Sun glinted from the golden buttons of his red uniform coat and weskit, a bright contrast to his gray-powdered wig with its queue gathered in a watered red ribbon.

"Good day, Madam Forny."

14

"Major! A surprise."

"Not really, madam."

Abby caught up her manners and stepped aside. "You're welcome, Major. Will you come in? Mistress Smith is visiting and—"

"Then I'll not intrude."

"Nonsense, sir! Come in and welcome."

He hesitated, then surrendered. "Thank you, madam." He came into the room, merely jerked his head at Letty in acknowledgment. Abby felt a touch of pique. These stiff Britishers! Afraid they might recognize some inferior form of human life! The frontier didn't seem to change them. But Letty had hastily stood up, curtsied to the doctor and turned to the door.

"I best be getting back to my work and my kids. Them two boys is in trouble if I so much's turn my back. Good day, Major. Abby, tell your man my needs when he makes his next trip."

"I'll not forget."

Letty scurried out and Abby closed the door, turning to the doctor. "Our house is honored, Major. Is there aught I can serve you?"

"Nothing, Madam Forny. I came to see if you progress well."

"Mother Dean says I will do splendidly. But sit ye down, Major?"

He accepted the chair she indicated and placed his hat on the floor beside his feet. Then he studied her critically and nodded. "I would agree with the midwife on that score but not on her roots, bark and nostrums. Sooner or later you'll need to be purged and mayhap cupped to cleanse the blood. There'll be

15

laudanum to dull the pain of the birthing itself."

"Mother Dean—"

His raised hand stopped her. "Aye, madam, she is excellent for pregnancy but if there is need of medicine or such, then I would be delighted to make sure you are exactly, scientifically dosed instead of chancing a frontier rule of thumb."

"Thank you, sir. Edward will be pleased to learn of your concern and offer."

"I'm certain of it, madam, since I believe he's not too long from Europe and so is not fearful of doctors."

"He'll be here when the time comes on me, I'm sure, Major, and he'd be the first to call you if the need arose." Abby had seated herself in another chair so that she directly faced the doctor. She sensed his barely concealed hesitancy. "Is there aught else?"

"Your husband is up the North Fork preparing logs for our fort and the town. When will he return?"

"Even he didn't know the exact time. It depends on how well the work goes as well as how soon he finds the right timber for the purpose. So he made no guesses when he left." Her voice sharpened. "Is there bad news?"

"Of course not! I feared you might take my question amiss."

"There's something a'bother, sir."

"Nothing of immediate concern—no more than rumors as vaporous as air, I think."

"What might they be?"

He made a vague gesture, took another pinch of snuff and replaced the box in his voluminous uniform pocket. "Oh, whispers that though the

Frenchies have been beaten and have run down the Ohio or retreated to their New France, they may seek to stir up trouble. Had your husband heard of that? Perhaps he may have spoken of it to you."

"We both heard exactly the same whispers, Major. Neither he nor I know more than you. Unless—?"

"We've learned more? No, madam, just increased whispers, not about the Frenchies but the savages."

"The Indians!" She smiled in relief. "Major, this is wilderness and I've lived in it from Connecticut Colony to York Colony to here. There is always fear of Indians if a leaf in the forest so much as turns."

"I've heard as much, madam, from the Colonial militia we have at the Fort. They laugh about it."

"Then they're from the eastern colonies and the coasts—long settled and secure. The rest of us who have lived among the Indians sometimes smile and laugh at the tales but we never scoff. We know better. My own father and a man I loved years back both lost their scalps."

"I am sorry, madam."

"It's long in the past, sir. Now, what tales have you been hearing?"

"It will not upset you—in your condition?"

"As I said, I've heard whispers before, and mighty scary ones at that. But I think I'll know a rumor from the truth, or find a fact in a whisper if there is one."

Major Howard looked relieved and came directly to the point. "The French soldiers have left but still their couriers or *voyageurs* travel the country round-about in search of pelts. They speak of the rumors."

"They'd know, if any white face would."

"White face? That is an uncommon phrase."

17

"I learned it from the Indians, Major. Now and then I use it. What about the *voyageurs?*"

"They say the tribal and village chiefs have suddenly disappeared into the woods and hills. They don't know why."

Abby stiffened, her instincts suddenly ringing alarm bells. "All the chiefs? Or just one or two here and there? One tribe, or many tribes?"

"Not all of them, but enough to make the *voyageurs* wonder. They say most of the tribal chiefs have gone somewhere. That worries them."

"Is there a hint of where they might have gone?"

"North—and west, but mostly north."

"What word of the Seneca?"

"They are quiet—too quiet, the Frenchies tell us."

The alarm still played along Abby's nerves but she kept it out of her voice, half shrugging. She spoke thoughtfully and calmly. "It just might be a thing to watch, Major. The Seneca are part of the Iroquois—the Six Nations—and this is their hunting and fishing ground. They are called 'Keepers of the Western Door' and that means this Ohio Country."

"Then have you heard—"

"Nothing, Major. But when my husband returns, I will ask him and send him to your commander. If something brews among the Seneca, and all the other tribes and villages send their sachems to a meeting somewhere, my Edward will have heard of it."

"I pray he has not." Major Howard picked up his hat and arose, Abby rising with him. He turned to her at the door and again bobbed his head in that distinctly arrogant English way. "I thank you to send him, madam, and I thank you for receiving me."

18

She smiled, curtsied and then closed the door when he left the cabin for the palisaded fort. She moved thoughtfully to the northern window and looked long and hard up the swiftly flowing waters of the Allegheny. Alone now, she could allow her expression to show her new concern. Then she tried to throw it off, knowing she would have to wait for Edward to tell her if he had heard any of this.

Her thoughts echoed the major's words. "I pray he has not."

II

Confident of Edward's ability to take care of himself, Abby tended to dismiss the old doctor's visit and his rumor as no more than an annoying ripple in the even, peaceful tenor of the days. She watched the northern river as it restlessly surged its bright sunlit waters out from between the wooded ridges but her eagerness was born of the need to see her husband again, not of fear.

Some of the village men fished the three rivers that joined at this point and many of them hunted game amidst the hills and valleys that lined them. Now and then they would meet with a trapper or *courier du bois* who daringly sought peltry this close to an outpost of the British enemy. So far as Abby learned, none of them had heard of Indian restlessness from the Frenchmen of the woods who ranged so far afield in all directions.

But as the days slowly dragged by and Edward did not appear, Abby began to feel a small nibble of uncertainty. She laughed it off, dismissing it as she exchanged the small, almost meaningless bits of news that came to the village. In the scattering of a dozen cabins and Edward's small trading post, unused in his absence unless Abby could supply a settler with an item of its diminishing stock, the smallest act had an importance beyond measure. When Jared Williams started clearing an acre of land of brush and saplings so he could plow and work it next year, everyone had to make profound judgments as to the wisdom of the course or muse and contend whether Jared had chosen potentially the most productive acre as compared to others.

There were discussions as to whether the French would return someday, or whether the Smith milk cow was going dry. Abby knew her own pregnancy made a delightful morsel for the other women to chew upon—of course, when she was not present. Mother Dean would have spread the word from almost the first moment she knew life had been planted and now grew in Abby's womb. That would be as certain as tomorrow's coming.

Often Abby would leave the cabin and stroll along the river bank, trying to find a spot where she could see just a few yards further around the first bend. But the dancing, rippling waters of the Allegheny seemed to give her only friendly, pixie laughter for her endeavors. So she would stroll around the Fort to a place where she could see the drill ground beyond and on out to the point of land where the two rivers joined, forming the wider, gigantic third that flowed westward into inconceivable, misty distances. She remembered how once her mother had wondered how far west the trees and the land would extend. Abby had traveled several hundred miles farther westward but still the land seemed to roll endlessly toward the sunset.

The red-coated soldiers and the blue-coated Virginia and Pennsylvania Colonial militia drilled under the barking orders of a martinet sergeant. They would all become ramrod stiff and move with extra military precision when they saw Abby and she always gave them a bright smile that they expected, a recognition of their manliness. But soon she'd look southward to the Monongahela, emerging out of the ridges down toward Virginia Colony. Not far down that way General Braddock had been killed when Frenchmen and Indians ambushed him in the woods.

But the Allegheny always called her back and, always, its flowing surface gave no hint about Edward. Now and then a subaltern or even the fort commander would come out, gallantly bow and ask permission to stroll with her. When that happened, she'd ask if they had heard more Indian rumors. But the fearful whispers had ceased as quickly as they had begun.

Two weeks passed, the days long, empty and lazy, and Abby grew more and more concerned. Edward should have been back by now. She held tightly to the thought that timber cutting, raft building or barter had delayed him. Mother Dean checked her again and left strange-looking dried leaves to be made into a tea.

"Take a cup every other day. It will strengthen the blood."

"Does Major Howard know of the potion?" Abby asked.

Mother sniffed disdainfully. "He knows nothing but dosings for the French disease should the soldiers catch it, or a blood-cupping, or a knife for bullet wounds. Woman's ills are not for his knowledge or care."

True enough, Abby thought, and, equally true, he'd be disdainful of anything he didn't know. It must be very comfortable to have a closed mind. How much worry it prevented! So she took the potion, nearly gagged on it, fighting for several minutes to hold it down. Pray God there be no more potions— and pray God Edward would soon return!

Apparently this time God listened. Late the next morning she heard shouts outside the house and the rush of feet down what passed as a street. She had just finished her morning room-dusting and she looked out the north window. Her eyes widened and her mouth formed a startled round O before she caught her breath and voice. The first raft had just turned the far bend that had been so empty up until just now.

23

Then she saw a second and third. Two men on each side of every raft used long poles to keep the clumsy crafts off rocks and from whirling about and around with each tug of the current. The man on the right side of the first raft and Edward's slender, supple figure and swift, flowing movements. Even though he was still far upstream, Abby knew every contour, muscle and shape of that beloved body. She dropped her broom and raced to the door.

For a moment the small crowd swept her along but her racing feet outstripped even the fleetest of the women and men who ran toward the wide, flat bank where the rafts would land. River water lapped at her moccasin toes and splashed against her ankles and stockings but she paid no attention, was not even aware. The rafts swiftly came down the current and she knew that Edward now saw her. She waved but he dared not return the greeting, for a split second's release of the pole would send the raft out of control.

She heard Edward's desperate shout. "Out of the way! Off the beach! Abby! All of you will be hurt."

The river's power had the rafts in its grip. Before the stream took a sudden, sharp turn and swept by the fort to become part of the Ohio, it swept the heavy log monsters directly toward the beach with battering ram force. There was no way the raftsmen could check the lashed logs. Abby saw terror for her and the others pressing close around her in his drawn, frightened face. She whipped about to add her own screaming voice to Edward's shouts.

"Back! Back!"

By some miracle the crowd dissolved as she lunged frantically toward the grass bordering the coarse gravel of the beach. She gained it, tripped and fell headlong. She heard the crashing sounds behind her. Cries and yells lifted, men shouted and there were more heavy, solid crashings. Then powerful hands grabbed her shoulders, lifted and turned her. She looked up into Edward's lean tanned face only for a second before he pulled her tightly against him and his powerful arms held her like secure steel bands.

She felt his sweaty bare skin on her cheek and she gripped his arms. His muscled chest lifted and fell with his swift, deep breaths and she heard the steady beat of his heart in her ear. It drowned out other sounds, voices, crashes. His fingers taloned into her shoulders and he held her so he could look at her, his expression still fearful.

"You are all right, *non?* There is nothing hurt?"

"Nothing."

"Merci à Dieu! It was close, that."

"Oh, Edward! You! How I love you! How I miss you!"

His fear vanished. She felt he became aglow from within from love of her. He crushed his lips against hers for a second and then broke free.

"The others, *Tonnerre!* How many are hurt or killed!"

He stood up and turned about. She saw the gravelly stretch of wide beach. Five rafts had slammed onto it. Lashing had come loose and thick, long logs lay like jackstraws where once only sand had been. Three men lay prone but each slowly lifted himself on stiff arms, head hanging as he gasped and heaved for breath.

Edward ran to the nearest and bent over him. The

25

soldiers from the fort and the people from the town stood in a tight crowd even further away from the river than Abby. She saw Major Howard race out of the stockade with more soldiers. More rafts had arrived but the polemen had been able to guide them and they had slid ashore with little damage.

Edward wildly waved Major Harris over before he turned to the second, then the third. Abby pulled herself to her feet. She felt bruised and shaken and she saw bloody marks along her calves and shins where gravel had scraped but she knew no bones were broken. A greater fear touched her—the life she carried. She sat quite still, holding her breath and, strangely, listening as though she might actually hear what might have happened within her body.

A sudden shadow made her look up. Edward towered over her, then he crouched down beside her, his fingers again on her shoulders and his concerned face close.

"L'enfant, the little one—what of him?"

She placed her hands on her stomach, fingertips gently probing. Mother Dean rushed up, tried to push Edward aside. She had turned pale and her eyes seemed great, frightened gray orbs. She grasped Abby's wrists and forced her hands away from her stomach so that she herself could gently press here and there.

Abby regained her voice. "It is all right. I'm sure it's all right."

"No pain?" Mother Dean demanded. "Not sick?"

"No, nothing."

Mother Dean sat back on her heels, studied Abby and then looked around at Edward. She gave a gusty relieved sigh. "It's not too far along. Let's hope. But we can't be sure yet. Abby, can you stand up?"

"I think so."

"Help her," Mother Dean snapped at Edward. "Take her home and put her to bed. I'll get some herbals and be right over as fast as I can make it."

"But I'm all right!" Abby tried to reassure the woman but Mother Dean looked around at Edward and pointed to Abby.

"Home and bed for her. Walk her slow and careful so she doesn't drop before she should."

He took Abby's hands and slowly, carefully pulled her to her feet. Before she could take a step, he swept her up into his arms and strode off toward the village and their home. Then he turned and called to Mother Dean.

"How about the fort surgeon?"

"Leave him to tend the soldiers so he won't have a chance to kill your wife. She carries a baby, not a musket ball."

Abby tried to protest as Edward carried her to the house but she might very well have saved her breath. He strode on, heedless of her, heedless of the excited, worried group of village women who followed him like a small maelstrom, cackling advice and warning. He kicked open the door, strode inside, kicked the door closed behind him and then carefully placed Abby on her feet.

"I'm all right, darling! Really I am! I can tell. I know."

"Stand still while I untangle this lacing and open these hooks and eyes. We take no chance—not with my wife and my son!"

She just knew there was nothing amiss, though she didn't know how she knew. But suddenly it was good to quit struggling and protesting and docilely turn and move to Edward's gruff orders. It was good to look down at his muscular back as he bent to loosen her skirt and let it drop in a heap about her ankles. How wonderful were his awkward touches and tugs and how secure she felt now that he had come back and would take care of her. He loosened the tight band about her breasts and flung the cloth away.

Mother Dean came hurrying in, carrying a little stone jug as well as her voluminous bag, both of which she placed on the floor beside the bed. She ordered Edward out of the room so fiercely that he meekly obeyed. She wheeled around to Abby who tried to protest. But Mother Dean would have none of it.

"Lay back on your pillow, young lady, spread your legs and let me have a look. No telling what can happen even as early on as you are. For that matter, you're lucky to be alive the way them rafts and logs flung around. Spread your legs, I say!"

Abby obeyed, lying back and closing her eyes, allowing the woman's fingers to search her groin, to press on her stomach and then explore her groin again.

"No blood. No sign of trouble."

"I knew there wouldn't be."

"Hmmmph! You'd know—being the first time with child and all."

"A woman knows," Abby insisted.

"For now ye might. But how about in two–three hours? the rest of the day? Sometimes trouble can

28

hold back in cases like this and then—" She stood up. "I'm to the kitchen for a cup and a dipper of water."

She swept out of the room and Abby looked up at the ceiling's rough plaster, thankful that the village carpenter had been so skilled in finishing a house as well as framing it. It would have been completely beyond Edward's ability and she giggled at the picture of a one-time Gascon gay blade and courtier even so much as shaping a hut. Then she sobered. Edward had learned so much since he had been forced to flee to New France and then to this western wilderness.

Look at what he had done so far! He could now cut trees and shape logs along with the rest of the men he had hired. He could lash the logs into a raft and pole it down a river. She caught herself up. He could then without warning smash the rafts upon a gravelly river bank.

Mother Dean returned just then, marched to the bed and held out a cup of bilious green liquid. She propped up Abby's head and pushed the cup under her nose. The contents had a heavy, medicinal smell as horrible as its appearance. Abby's nose wrinkled and she started to turn her head but Mother Dean's strong grip prevented that.

"Drink it. All of it."

Abby gagged on the first swallow of the bitter, repellent fluid. Mother Dean's grip tightened on Abby's neck and head and forced the cup to her lips. "Down with it. Would ye want to miscarry and lose the baby!"

At last Abby fell back, fighting to keep the fluid down. Major Harris's potions and powders could not

29

possibly have been worse! Mother Dean remained seated beside her until she knew the potion would not spew back up. Then she hurried to the kitchen for a cup of steaming tea that Abby gratefully gulped down. The evil taste left her mouth and her stomach stopped quivering.

"There!" Mother Dean said with satisfaction. "I think that will do the trick."

"I hope so!" Abby gasped. "I couldn't take another dosing."

"Ye will if need be and we'll see about that afore supper time. Now let's salve and unguent them cuts and bruises ye have all over."

As she worked with the cool, healing unguents, Mother Dean spoke of the accident on the river bank. "We've had rafts come down the river afore but only one or two at a time—not the dozen or more your husband had cut and lashed."

"They were for the fort by contract," Abby informed her. "There are newcomers to the village who want cabins. My Edward had logs cut for them, too."

"That's why sojers and all rushed out when they saw the rafts a'coming. He should'a had as lead poleman someone as knows the currents and eddies of the river."

"That would not be Edward's way."

"He might be fine for scouting timber and cutting it but not for river floating." Mother Dean added with justified satisfaction, "Wouldn't have been two legs broken and logs floating out of sight down the Ohio."

"He lost the rafts?"

Mother Dean pushed her back down on the bed. "Just two—his and the one following. The others knew the river and they managed to avoid a pile-up. Could'a been mighty bad, though. Anyhow, it's over and done and no real bad loss to anyone, except maybe your husband. But he can cut more logs."

"He'll not think so much on that as on the broken legs. That will vex and worry him."

The older woman sniffed in disdain. "And Major Harris will be pleased to have something more to do at last than setting bones instead of lancing boils! Anyway, it won't happen again. The commandant has ordered all sojers and townfolk not to rush down to the river's edge next time a train of rafts come swinging around the bend. They must stay well back, outa harm's way."

"You can be sure Edward has learned his lesson, too. In a week, he'll have walked up and down both banks for miles just to study the current and its speed."

Mother Dean applied ointment and salve to the last of Abby's scrapes and bruises, replaced the salves in her bag, then gave Abby a long inspecting look. She nodded.

"You'll heal now—at least your skin. Like I said, we'll have to wait to make sure about your carrying." She indicated the closed doors of a tall clothes press across the room. "Be your dresses and such in there?" A moment later she handed Abby a gown. "Git into that and then back in bed. Can your man fix sup?"

"He can but I—"

"Ye stay in bed, me lady. That's final, at least until morn after I look at you."

"But you said tonight!"

"So I did and I will, but once more tomorrow if all goes well."

Abby slowly swung out of bed, winced as one of her cuts stung her leg. She slipped the gown over her head, pulled it down to cover her and sat on the edge of the bed.

"All the way—under the covers!" Mother Dean ordered sharply.

Abby obeyed, pulled the patchwork quilt up to her shoulders and looked inquiringly at the door. "Is my husband—?"

"Waiting and worried, I reckon. I'll send him in, now I'm done until nightfall."

In a moment Edward strode in and Mother Dean closed the door behind him, leaving them alone. He sat down on the side of the bed, careful not to shake or jar her. She smiled at him.

"It's all right. I won't break. Honestly, I won't."

"Ma foi! That old woman would not have me believe it. She would have you delicate like an egg, ready to break at a look."

"Midwives are over careful, my darling. Did she tell you she forced a potion down me that was strong and bitter enough for an ox? I doubt even you could have held it long."

She pulled the covers down from her shoulders and started to sit up but he instantly held her shoulders to prevent the movement. *"Non! Non!* You are to be—"

"In your arms, *mon coeur,"* using the French

32

words he had taught her. "It's where I belong. It's what I've missed for all the time you've been gone. That's the medicine I need." She twisted out of his grasp and sat up, throwing her arms about him. "Hold me close. I can't believe you're actually back and safe."

"But—but—"

Her finger on his lips stopped his words and then she muffled further protests with her lips, warm and moving under his. How wonderful the kiss! He sat rigid for a moment, frightened for her and she knew it. Her arms increased the pressure about his shoulders and she murmured softly as her lips moved to his cheek, his temple, his eyes and back to his mouth.

The tension left him in an instant and he embraced her fiercely. She found his hand and deftly inserted it under the neck of her gown, onto her bare flesh and down to her breast. He made a hungry, guttural sound and then pulled the top of the gown to her waist in a single motion.

Her breasts sprang free, round and white and she arched up, silently begging for his kisses upon them, his lips moist around her nipples. She pulled his head down and he cupped her breasts, lifting them. Thrills coursed through her. She threw her head back and closed her eyes, feeling only an overwhelming need for him, sensing only his touch.

"But we should not—" Fear for her returned to his voice.

She tugged the bed clothing free of the weight of his body and flung them aside. She lay naked under

33

his avid eyes, longing for him. She sank her fingers in his broad, tanned and muscular shoulders and pulled him down across her.

"Darling!" She did not recognize the gusty half-moan of her own voice. "Oh, Darling! Love me. Now!"

III

They lay side by side, naked and asprawl upon the bed, the quilts and covers a wild tangle, but both were too satiated and tired to care or move. Abby didn't think—she didn't want to. It was so wonderful just to *feel*, to be fulfilled, to still have the sense of Edward alive, vibrant and overpowering, within her. He had dissolved a great hunger, a strange sort of emptiness that she had not recognized until, blessedly, it was gone.

She turned her head slowly so as not to break the wonderful, magic aura of love that was almost tangible about her, and looked at Edward. He lay with one arm thrown over his forehead, his closed eyes in shadow. She slowly drank in the high angles of his temples and jaw, the long planes of his cheeks. His dark hair lay in a tangle on his head. His strong chest rose and fell slowly with his deep breathing and she could still feel the heavy weight of its muscles and bones on her breasts, the tight grip of his arms about her, the thrust and withdrawal of his stomach and groin to meet her own archings and avid twistings. It was good just to sense these things, to know life had completion once more. No need to think, no need at all—just feel.

She suddenly realized that he was watching her from a corner of his shaded eye and that his mouth had slowly, slowly formed into a gentle, wonderful smile. It widened when he, too, became aware that she knew he covertly studied her.

"A *sou* for your thoughts, *ma cherie*."

Only the muscles of her mouth moved to form a pout and then she whispered, "Just a *sou?* They are worth far more than that."

"A dozen *louis d'or* then or a hundred pieces of eight, a thousand of your colonial shillings or a million English pounds."

She cuddled closer and sighed, "My! How valuable my brain must be!"

He turned on his side to her and traced his finger along her lips with a gentle, loving touch. "Not at all. It is your heart I value."

"You have it—always."

His kiss was as gentle as the tracing of his finger and then he dropped onto his back again, looking up at the ceiling. Abby saw that he was as dreamily content as she and she allowed her love for him to surge through her mind, heart and body. She suddenly remembered the Biblical phrase, "Blessed above all women." Her mother had used it a long time ago but now it applied to Abby.

At long last he broke the silence with a deep, sad sigh. "There are stirrings and troubles everywhere—except here. I am glad to return to you—and to peace."

"But there has been no fighting in a year or more."

His lips curled in a bitter smile. "I know. Your King drags the lilies of my country into defeat. All of New France is gone now but there is war everywhere else in the world—in Europe, and Asia. My country fights yours for its life. In Madras, in North Africa and—"

"Edward Forny! There is no more *my* country and *your* country! You are not French but American. I am not English but American. Oh, the British call us 'Colonials' but we are more than that. We are more than Pennsylvanians and Connecticuters or Virginians or Yorkers. We are *American!*"

He stared at her, surprised by her sudden vehemence. He placed his hand on her bare arm and smiled. "Eh, my little fighting bantam!"

"It's true! Mayhap we are counted part of England—and I'm not sure that's as it should be. But we *are* different, like another nation."

"And the redcoats at the Fort just beyond our

house—what of them?"

"Well—" She sought an explanation but for the moment could find none. She tossed her head in disdain. "They lord it over us. You should hear the commandant or Major Harris, the surgeon. They speak and act toward us like we are all little children that somehow grew up aforetime. None of us like it—or them—but what can we do?"

"*Vous avez raison,*" he agreed. But perhaps your new king—"

"New king! England?"

"Ah, I had not time to tell you. I heard of it at Fort Niagara. Hasn't word come to your soldiers here?"

"No. You must travel faster than official couriers."

"The waterways are faster than post roads and coach and four."

"Who is he? When did George II die?"

"I had only the bare news at Niagara. It was so slim as to be hardly more than a whisper—what you call 'rumor,' eh?" He dismissed the stunning news with a shrug. "But there is more, *ma cherie.* I heard at Niagara there is a new royal British commander and governor in New York, Lord Jeffrey Amherst."

"I never heard of him."

"Newly come from England, I'm told. Eh, perhaps he has brought news about the king and you will be hearing soon."

Abby sat frowning across the room, wondering what these great new changes would mean for her and Edward. Probably nothing, she decided after a few moments. Who in the royal palace in far distant London had ever heard of or cared about the Fornys of this far-off wilderness outpost of Fort Pitt? Suddenly she remembered the rumors Major Harris and the couriers had heard.

"Darling, have you heard of Indian unrest?"

Now Edward looked startled. "No—and I was as far as Lake of the Eries and Detroit. Is there trouble?"

"No one knows. The whisper is that all the chiefs and Sachems have vanished."

"Disappeared! Where? and why?"

"No one knows but everyone says that things are much too quiet."

"Are they?" he asked. "You've lived among Indians and should know the danger signs. I've met *les hommes rouges* along the river Allegheny and *lac des Eries.*"

"Bands of them?" she asked.

"No—one or perhaps a dozen in *batteaux,* small camps built for hunting, fishing or trapping. They travel as usual to the posts to trade. I have done some small barter with them for moccasins, fringed shirts—things I know the settlers here might need and want. I have several bundles of their trade wares."

"Then they are friendly?"

"Eh, who can tell when an Indian is truly friendly or simply wants something you have and which he can get only by barter if he can't kill first?"

"You are not fair, Edward. A war band paints fighting colors and symbols on their faces—and bodies."

"*Oui . . . vraiment . . .* that is true. But a single Indian without paint can knife and scalp as easily as one with paint, eh?"

"Generally he won't unless he's a renegade. I know

the Onondaga and Seneca do not speak with a forked tongue."

"'Forked tongue'," he repeated and laughed and kissed her as her frown deepened. "You turned Indian without warning and *très charmante*. So how can I tell about your Seneca or Erie or Shawnee?"

Mollified, she pushed him away. "Seriously, Edward, have you heard whispers or seen signs of unrest? How about the chiefs and Sachems? Have they vanished?"

"I can't answer. I have seen some chiefs at Niagara but I heard there was—what do you call it?—powwow at Fort Stanwix. Maybe they were there and that is a long, long distance away on Lake Ontario. I heard Sir William Johnson called all the tribes. It might be that the chiefs were there."

"What was the conference about?"

"*Je ne sais pas*, my heart. I don't know." His voice became more serious. "There are changes everywhere now that the war is over. Did you know the French have ceded to the Spaniards their lands west of the Mississippi as far as New Orleans and Florida?"

"The fort officers know. They say France fears England will grab that, too, if ever there's a regular peace treaty."

"They would try," he nodded.

"But no word about the chiefs?"

"No . . . No . . . unless," he hesitated.

"You've heard something," she accused.

"No more than a bird's chirp on a passing breeze."

She pretended anger as she stabbed his muscular chest with her finger to accent her demand. "Let me hear the bird, *mon ami."*

"Eh, it is foolish and no one thinks of it except to laugh. There is an Ottawa chief—oh, a very small chief that one, I hear."

"Ottawa? An Algonquin people."

"I do not know except that always they and the Huron have been friends of New France and the couriers and *voyageurs."*

"Who is he?"

"He is called Pontiac. There are greater chiefs and Sachems."

Abby searched her memory but finally shook her head. "I have never heard of him."

"C'est une bagatelle—of small matter. But let's talk about you and me and—" he stroked her stomach, "—and our son who will soon come along, eh? I have plans, *ma cherie.* I have thought much each day and night we cut logs. I have made a decision, *oui."*

"Oh?"

"Remember the sea captain who said water would always be part of my life?" He continued when she nodded, *"Eh bien,* so I think on that and I see from the time I come to New France to this moment here in this bed with *ma belle femme—"*

"Beautiful wife indeed!" she scoffed with a pleased smile.

"Vraiment! But you do not listen, eh—" He pointed to the window whose pulled curtain hid the small village and then to the wall beyond which the fort stood behind its palisade. "More people come out here now that war is over. Beyond the fort is the Ohio, *La Belle Rivière.* It flows westward to the

41

Spanish lands hundreds of miles away. Settlers will come. There are already settlements of my own countrymen out there—Vincennes, Vevay, along the Oubache River which they call 'Wabash' there are settlements—Terre Haute, Ouitenon. *Mon Dieu,* what does that mean?

"Tell me."

"It means the river is a highway long and broad that will carry canoes, great *bateaux* filled with trade goods and guns and needles and condiments and spices that people need, eh? Who will carry them? Who will sell them?" He punched his chest with his thumb. "I, Edouard de Fournet."

"You! a trader! But I didn't think that an aristocrat—"

"Aristocrat!" he exploded. "I am a fugitive from a *lettre de cachet.*"

"But the French are gone. You're safe. You can go and come as you please!"

"Go and come, *oui.* But not as I please. How do I have the *louis d'or*—pardon—the pence and pounds that will feed us, eh? I think this log cutting and rafting will do it. But—"

"It has. The Fort Commandant will pay you in the king's gold and not the paper money from the colonies."

"But, *ma belle,* the axe and the saw are not the tools for me. They are for men with strong backs, arms and thick heads, *non?* Me, I go east to Ligonier, or Lancaster mayhap even to your Philadelphia. I go down to Virginia—they also claim this land and send settlers. I bring tobacco and pipes—cotton cloth and strong broadcloth, eh? I buy down there or in

42

Pennsylvania Colony and sell here and all along the Ohio. Each settlement, each farm, each traveler I meet might see something I have that he needs and will buy, eh?"

"Merchant! You?"

"Better than empty stomachs, *ma petite!*"

"Oh, my!"

"*Pourquois pas?* Why not, my dear?" He continued excitedly. "I have good King's gold for the logs, eh? I leave enough here for you and the little one and go east with the rest. I buy trade goods cheap there, eh? I buy a cart and a horse to bring the goods here. I sell the cart and the horse and—*qui sait?*—some of the goods. I have Indians or *voyageurs* build me, oh, a very large *bateau.*"

She grasped the idea and his excitement and finished for him in a rush of words. "You go down the river—"

"—and sell buttons here, rifle there, cloth to this one, and gunpowder to that one—"

"—and come back—"

"To go east or north again to buy more!" He hugged her. "Eh, we will be the first on the river—"

"—the big Ohio and all the little rivers flowing into it."

"I will go up the Allegheny to the Lake of the Eries and from there to Fort Niagara and Fort Detroit, eh? Merchants there bring cargoes from Europe and from the Caribbean Islands both English and French."

"I will go with you!"

He had started to speak but she caught him in stunned surprise. He turned to her, mouth open. Then his jaw grew rock firm.

"No! You will stay right here. There is the baby, eh?—the one who is to come? Horse and canoe are not for a woman who is *enceinte* and you, *m'amant*, are pregnant."

"But I can't stay here alone and do nothing!" she wailed.

He kissed her. "You will stay here and bring us a son when the time comes. You will think, while I am gone, on how we keep what you call 'record' of what I buy and what I sell—how much paid and how much received, eh?"

"But—"

His hand flat against her lips muffled her words and he would not allow her to free herself from it. He smiled. "There is more you can do here for us."

She looked askance and he removed his hand. "What can I do but wait and plan the records we'll keep later!"

"I shall hire builders, *ma belle*. I buy goods and bring them here. Where do we keep them before they are in the canoes to be sold along the rivers? Where do we keep the goods I cannot take with me, eh? We will build warehouse and store. When it is finished, then you trade like me right here with all these people about us. That will not harm our son, eh?"

She digested the idea. She wanted to go with him but in all honesty she knew Edward was right. It would be a foolish risk, not for her but for the child she carried. That was more important than all the grand plans they made so quickly. She and Edward must have an heir. She wanted to see her husband in miniature in her child—their child. In that way, neither she nor Edward would ever grow old. No, she corrected herself, they need never fear growing old for the baby would be their renewal.

She looked deep into Edward's eyes and felt her own grow misty with love. She threw her arms about him and he held her secure and close.

"I'll stay."

She had no idea how many decades to come her words encompassed.

IV

A strange quiet came to the Ohio country. It was less a peace, Abby thought, than a brooding interlude, a time of waiting for something unknown. She found herself constantly searching the wooded mountain ridges or looking along the waterways for signs of unrest or trouble. Instead of lessening as the weeks slowly passed into months, the sense of pressure increased, the feel that something impended.

Mother Dean came at regular but well-spaced intervals and each time left a potion of some sort along with a pleased comment about the progress of Abby's pregnancy. She encouraged Abby to take easy walks along the river banks but always well within sight of the fort so that the sentinels at the wide gate atop the stockade walls could always see her.

That brought immediate protest from Edward, who was supported by Major Harris. Both worried that the walks might bring on premature labor or a medical complication that would cause her to lose the baby.

The major was quite emphatic. "You are in—ahem—a most delicate condition, Madam Forny. A lady in such a state should be most careful. I might say extremely careful. A sudden stumble along a rough path, an encounter with an Indian or a wild animal that might suddenly come out of the woods would frighten you badly."

"Eh, I have said that to her, *docteur!* I have said it many times. But she will not listen to me."

"Nor to you in this case, Major, as much as I respect you."

"But sound medical practice—"

"Sound for whom, Major? and where? I daresay this is the farthest wilderness outpost in America and I have lived all my life on the frontier—with my own family in Connecticut and with the Indians in New York Colony."

"What do they know of medicine and babies!" Major Harris snorted, reaching for his snuffbox.

"What do they know!" she exclaimed. "Maybe little of your military medicine but everything about babies. I vow that every girl on the frontier, if she was alone and her time came on her, could deliver herself."

"Bah!"

She laughed at him. "Major, have you ever delivered a child?"

"Well—not here, of course, nor in the colonies. But in medical school—"

"Be honest, sir. You watched midwives deliver in your school as part of your training. Perhaps afterwards you performed surgery on fine ladies if there were complications beyond the knowing of the midwives. True?"

"Yes, so far as that goes. But we attended the ladies daily up to the time of delivery. We purged and bled them if it was needed."

"But the delivery?" she insisted.

"The midwife," he conceded. "It is not counted decent that a male, even a doctor, be so intimate with a lady unless there is emergency need for the scalpel."

"We are not so squeamish—or prudish, Major. You planned to have Mother Dean attend me in any case when my son comes. Why do you object to her now?"

He answered angrily. "Because it is not yet her time to attend. But we speak of your constant walking. You should be off your feet."

Edward cut in. *"Ma petite, il a raison*—I have told you."

"My love," she answered curtly, "the more my

48

body is strengthened by sun, air and exercise, the more certain life is for our baby. We'll have no more argument."

"Well now!" Major Harris exploded. "We will see to that!"

"Indeed! How? By guard day and night? by the stocks or the post jail? Or perhaps I will be tied down in my own bed?" She became aware that all of them argued to no point, for she alone had the solution. "I will do this in my own way."

"The savage way!" the Major snapped.

"If you will, sir. I call it the way of my mother, her mother and all the Connecticut mothers before her. It is the way of the wise women of the Iroquois and the Onondaga. If you wish to see healthy babies, Major, visit any town of the Six Nations. Why, you can even step outside and visit any cabin here where children live."

Major Harris and Edward exchanged a long questioning look. "She always carries a hunting knife at her belt," Edward assured the doctor. "And a small pistol primed and loaded with lead ball."

"I can use both if need be," Abby added.

"When I peel bark and cut tough willow for the canoes I shall build, I will always be close. I shall even walk with her when my *voyageurs* work on the canoes, eh?"

Abby clapped her hands in delight. "Would you, Edward! Would you really! I would be safer," she confessed.

"Ah!" He lifted a long finger. "So there might be trouble, *non?*"

49

"Little chance. When have we last seen an Indian? But *you* beside me holding my hand! Would you really!"

He laughed, looked at Major Harris, who gave them both a sour yet understanding smile, then chuckled. "What chance has an old gray-haired soldier against young love! Go ahead. Have your walks."

Then he grimly held Abby with his stern eyes. "But if Mr. Forny is not about, you must have a soldier nearby—or a stout, armed settler from the village. Agreed?"

"Agreed," she conceded.

Each day thereafter, if it did not rain, Abby took her walk, sometimes out to the point where the two rivers met to form the Ohio. She would look along the wide westward flowing path of water that disappeared into the far, far distance. Again, she would stroll along the north fork of the Beautiful River that she always thought of by its Indian name, Allegeway. She kept to the south bank and never went beyond the first bend that would take her out of sight of the fort.

But more often, she followed the Monongahela to a point just beyond the village where Edward and his *voyageurs* built the huge canoe that he had planned. Actually, except for size, it was no different than the smaller ones the French fur trappers had used all along the stream. She watched the bearded, laughing and chattering wilderness men bend supple willow to form the light but durable frame of the craft as

50

Edward supervised and checked every inch of it.

He would always turn from the work when she approached with her stout village lad or muscular soldier escort. He dismissed her guard with a word of thanks or a small coin and strolled along with her. He told her how much the French had taught him about the river and its tributaries far to the west and how they had instructed him in the bending and shaping of the willow to form the frame, high-prowed fore and aft, and wide in the middle. He had learned to shape and polish paddles from the light wood the men brought.

"It is a whole new life, this way of the rivers," he told her one day as they stood at the point and faced westward. He chuckled. "And to think, *ma cherie*, I once thought the Rhone, the Gironde and the Seine the three greatest of all rivers. This one, *La Belle Rivière*, is like an ocean compared to them."—

"Do you wish you were back?"

"I?" His head swung around in surprise. He saw the dancing, soft lights in her eyes and he laughed again. He cupped her chin in his hand and lifted her face to kiss her. "Even if I could, I would not go without you. It would be empty for me now. I thought I had fled from the king's prison but, *ma fois!* I fled to meet my wonderful destiny on the Allegeway. The good God gave me apparent disaster in order to bring me real joy."

She held his arm tightly and he swung her about to point to the north fork of the river. "Remember how you came out of the woods up there and saved me from Seneca knives and lances?"

51

"Your *bon Dieu* put me at the right place and time," she nodded. "I have prayed my thanks for that over and over—and now I pray for our son."

He looked down at her stomach, beginning to become slightly rotund. "It will be all right?"

"Now everything is all right for us."

They had strolled without thought or plan along the Allegeway beyond the post. They could see the scatter of cabins and the narrow trail that one quite dared to call a road, leading eastward into the forest. A rider suddenly burst out of the trees and spurred to the fort. He wore the blue rough coat of the Pennsylvania troops but a broad strap across his chest bore a dispatch bag and Abby glimpsed the bright crimson of a royal seal.

Cabin doors flew open and a sentinel called a challenge from the fort's main gate. The rider raced on but pulled himself erect in the saddle. He snatched off his broad flat hat to wave it above his head. "Long live the king! News! Royal Dispatch! Long live the king!"

"That one is crazy!" Edward exclaimed. "Long live the king? The king already lives, eh?"

The rider plunged through the gate into the fort. Abby and Edward joined the gathering throng but the stockade gate closed before anyone had come within a dozen yards of it. Everyone stopped short and stared blankly at one another, at the stockade, then milled about.

Edward pointed to the flag staff that stood high above the log walls of the post. *Voyez!*

They heard a ruffle of drums and then, amazingly,

the British ensign slowly descended and disappeared. But only for a moment. It shot high again and muskets crashed a volley, crashed again. Abby heard a great shout from within the post and looked about as men, women, children, *voyageurs* from Edward's canoe and the *courieurs du bois* from their camp at the edge of the woods gathered. Questions flew back and forth in two languages and a dozen colonial dialects but no one had an answer.

Suddenly the stockade gate opened. The commandant, his officers and soldiers with their muskets, formed a somewhat crooked line. But the commandant did not notice. He stepped forward and lifted his hand, gaining instant attention.

"News has come." His harsh voice carried beyond the crowd to the edge of the forest. "We have it directly from the general commanding in New York colony. His Majesty, King George, second of that name, is dead. His Majesty, King George Third is our new monarch. The king is dead. Long live the king!"

A lieutenant at the end of the line of soldiers barked an order. Instantly muskets pointed to the sky and, at a second barked word, a volley crashed overhead. So the news of a new king ascending the throne in far-off London came to the Ohio. As the roar of the muskets ceased, the crowd answered with a shout. Hats tossed in the air and some young men grabbed hands and danced a jig.

The commandant's harsh, demanding voice cut through and subdued the hubbub. "There is more news. Major General Jeffrey Amherst announces the complete capitulation of New France. Only the royal

British flag flies over the land from the Atlantic to the Mississippi, from Hudson's Bay in the north to the borders of Spanish Florida in the south."

"Mon Dieu," Edward breathed. "New France disappeared a year or more ago. Has he not been told?"

The commandant continued his announcement. "Lord Amherst now governs in the name of the king until such time as a formal treaty is signed with the defeated enemy or His Majesty pleases to appoint another governor." The officer took a deep breath but his harsh face broke into a smile of triumph. "We are all—*all!* Englishmen, colonists, French and Indians—subjects now of our new Majesty, King George III!"

The muskets blasted another volley. The soldiers aboutfaced and marched back into the fort. The wide gate remained opened and guards were not posted. Instead, red-coated soldiers strolled around the parade ground and through the gate. The villagers sensed that the military routine in the post had been relaxed. When one of Letitia Smith's urchins streaked toward the open gate and his mother called him back in fear, one of the soldiers laughed at her.

"Blimey, ma'arm, let 'im go. We've 'ad an extra ration of rum to celebrate the new king and governor. The colonel and 'is officers be 'aving their party."

"But they've been ordered not—"

"Let 'em caper like goats as they please, ma'rm. So long they don't go near the powder magazine or the storage area. It's a great day for victory and for a new king, ma'rm. All of ye can look about if ye like."

Slowly, uncertainly, the villagers approached the

gate and looked in on the empty parade ground and the line of cabins for the common soldiers along one stockade wall, a second line of better built and more roomy officers' quarters along the other, the storage cabins and the forge far across the way.

Abby and Edward, curious as any of their neighbors, moved with them right up to the open gate. At that moment, a subaltern stepped out of the door of the largest of the officers' cabins and marched toward them. The crowd instantly grew tense and quiet.

The young man, uplifted chin and haughty demeanor accenting the contempt in his eyes and quirked lips, came on as though he alone were the whole royal army. His red and gold uniform with its high collar, and the single epaulette on one shoulder made him look slightly ridiculous rather than stern and military as he so obviously believed. He halted just a few steps within the gate as though another step or two would bring him in touch with the small crowd and contaminate him. He strove to speak sternly but his voice broke to a high youthful note, completely destroying the impression he sought to make. But his ego and arrogance would not recognize his own popinjay air.

"The commandant's orders of the day permit visitation by those who wish to enter the fort and stroll the parade ground. However, you are restricted to its boundaries." He pulled a snuff box from a wide, deep pocket of his uniform coat, delicately sniffed a pinch and haughtily stared at them as he flicked gray grains from his fingers. "You may fraternize with the soldiers."

"Ain't nothing like the king's bounty!" someone exclaimed from the rear of the crowd.

The subaltern's head jerked up and he stood stiff in anger. "Who said that?" he demanded getting no answer. His face burned as red as his coat and his jaw tightened so that a muscle jumped in his cheek. His hand fell to where his dress sword would have been but he realized he had not belted it about his waist. His face turned even more red but he gained control and stared haughtily and contemptuously about him.

"You louts!"

He turned on his heel and marched back to the commandant's large log house. Silence held until he disappeared within and the door closed. Then laughter as contemptuous as the officer's hauteur swept the crowd. Letitia Smith's husband spat through the gate, his eyes hard and angry on the officers' row of cabins.

"The likes of him! Do they think to send fools and blockheads to order us about?" He spat through the gate once more. "They can wait until hell runs water afore I gawk around their precious parade ground!"

Edward's hand on Abby's elbow turned her away from the gate toward the Allegeway path. They were almost to the first bend when Edward said soberly, "The new English king will not rule this country over long. *Certainement,* his soldiers and hirelings will see to that."

She stopped short, swung about to him, staring. "What are you saying? That's treason!"

"Pas du tout, it is prophecy, that is all. You have

said yourself, this is America, not England, and all of you are Americans, eh?" His eyes cut back to the post. "How long will you Americans allow *un imbecile* such as that one to slap you in the face?"

"We Americans? Do you count yourself with us, Edouard?" He laughed and covered her hand with his. "Of course! With your help every day and—every night, eh?"

She kissed him. "As soon as our son permits. I'll try to make him hurry."

They turned the bend and walked along the bank out of sight of the fort and the village. With Edward beside her, Abby had no fear. The sun was warm and the usual breeze from the north blew soft and cool along the river. The beach alternately widened and narrowed as trees and bushes came toward the water and then retreated only to approach again a little farther along.

They came to a finger of land pushing almost into the river, the bushes thick and high along the path. Edward led her to the tip of the point and pointed northward. "See those rocks out there in the center of the river? Eh, they nearly wrecked all of us. It took fast pole work and all our muscles to save the rafts."

She looked up at him with dancing eyes. "It prepared you for the wreck on the village beach."

"Ah, so it did!" His laugh echoed hers but instantly died in his throat the second he wheeled her about to return. Abby lost her smile.

An Indian stood in the path, blocking the way. He had notched an arrow to his bow but had not yet pulled the string back to his ear to release the deadly

57

shaft. Abby recognized his Seneca garb and she called out to him in the Onandaga tongue.

"Friends! Iroquois."

The bow quivered in the Indian's bronze hand. She saw the pressure slowly ease off the string. But the weapon remained poised, ready to launch its feathered death. The man's unpainted brown-red face remained tight, and his black eyes glittered. Abby had surprised and puzzled him.

"Iroquois? You speak the Onandaga."

"You're Seneca, a Guardian of the Western Gate. I am Strong Woman of the ouwachira of Moon Willow in the main town of the Onandaga."

The Indian lowered the bow and replaced the deadly arrow in its quiver in a single flowing movement. His hand dropped to the heavy knife at his belt and he pulled it from the sheath.

"I speak with straight tongue. The women scrubbed the white from me and my blood is mingled with the Onandaga." She held out her arms so that he could see the scars on her wrists. "See, there is the mark of the Keepers of the Faith who gave me their blood as I gave them mine."

Still holding out her arms, she stepped toward the Indian as Edward made a low, startled warning sound. She dropped one arm to make a swift signal behind her for him to remain silent and motionless and then held out her arm again. She stood within a pace of the Seneca and held up her wrists to him. He looked at the old ridged knife scars, then up at her as though to read confirmation in her eyes. His heavy deadly knife snapped into its sheath in the same flowing motion that had replaced the arrow. He slipped the cord from the bow and swung it up on his shoulder.

"You Onandaga," he conceded and then glared beyond her. "But him?"

"Friend, not enemy—my friend, your friend. He keep me safe from bad white face at the fort." She hurried on before he could decide what she meant by "bad white face." Her question accompanied a sweep of her arm around the horizon. "All chiefs and Sachems gone—where?"

"Big council called at Detroit. White chief talks to all the tribes. Bring gifts. Talk peace."

"White chief?"

"He name Johnson. What that mean?"

She didn't hesitate to speak the first thing that came to her mind that she knew an Indian would understand. "He warrior son of Mighty Sachem across the Big Water. *His* name John—Chief John. So chief at Detroit John's son."

"He speak straight tongue?"

"He speak straight." Suddenly a cramp sent a blade of pain along her back and into her stomach. She gasped, swayed, caught herself as Edward sprang to her side and held her. The Indian jumped back but now he eyed her and Edward. He spoke to Abby.

"You carry papoose. Him come soon." He pointed to Edward. "His?" When she nodded, the Indian glared at Edward. "She need wise woman at your fireside—your *ohwachira*. You fool keep her out here, eh?"

He wheeled around and disappeared into the high

59

bushes and trees. They shook and swayed a moment or two and then became motionless.

Abby gasped as another pain lanced through her. "Hurry! Soon!"

He swung her into his arms and carried her toward the post.

V

Though Edward Forny sang of the dark-haired, beautiful maidens of Marseilles and the even more beautiful, acquiescent girls of Gascony as his paddle matched stroke for stroke that of his companion in the bow, he really sang of the auburn-haired Abby, his *bonne femme*. What girl anywhere in the world could equal his good wife back at Fort Pitt, which until the ascension of the present English king had been called Fort Prince George? And what Gascon's son in all France could equal the child Abby had so recently borne him!

He broke off the song to shape his tongue to the child's wonderful, proud name. "Henri! *Eh bien*, Henri!"

"Qu'est que c'est?" his companion asked. "What do you say, my friend?"

"Henri," Edward called over his shoulder. A strong name."

"Oui. But these stupid Americans and English! They will call him 'Henry' and what kind of a sound is that?"

"Prenez garde, Old One. Take care of how you call my wife. She is American, remember?"

"You have made her French."

"Au contraire, Simeon, she has made me proud."

He heard Simeon Ridoux's warm and understanding chuckle and Edward bent over the paddle, eyes on the rippling water of the wide river, golden now with the afternoon sun. All the west is gold, he thought, golden water, gold flecks in the swinging trees on either far bank, on the open glades of grass bending and swaying to the summer breeze, golden to his plans and thoughts of the future of his small family.

His head lifted with the new thought that always amazed him since Henri—no, Henry—had come. Family—three of them—to always hold in his mind and not himself alone as it had been before he had come to this new and wonderful land. Ah, thank the good God for the anger of the wattlenecked old Duc de Verre! He had never thought, as he fled the king's catchpolls, who would have locked him away forever in the dungeons of Toulouse, that he would ever have a wife and a son. Thank the good God for all that had brought him first to New France and then, still in headlong flight from the royal governor, across Lake Erie down the Allegeway to the arms of Abby Brewster, herself a fugitive from the Iroquois.

Simeon broke in on his flow of memories. "Do not be so loudly happy, eh? You shake the trees. You frighten the animals. Worse, my friend, you could bring any passing Shawnee war band down upon us."

"Ha, my friend! on such a glorious and beautiful day even the Shawnee will be happy."

"No Indian's every happy to see white men, French, British or American, on his river—this one."

"Because he does not have a wife like mine or a son like mine, that is why. If they could only see my Abby and my Henri."

Simeon said dryly, "Don't take a Shawnee, Seneca or Cherokee home to see them, my friend. You would not have them long."

"You are always the wise one, *mon ami*. So, I sing to tell the Indians about my joy."

"Peste! but you are a likable fool," Simeon growled and then chuckled. "Please! Sing softly to the rippling water and not to the whole wide world. You and I will keep hair on our heads the longer for it."

"Wise again, Simeon. I am glad I chose you from all the *voyageurs* at the Fort; you know *La Rivière et ses habitants.* I, too, must learn of those who live out here and where they live and what they need."

"They live poorly and need little, I have told you."

"Ah, but there is powder and ball, eh? There are traps and there are the long rifles they make in Pennsylvania, no? There are hammers for the rifles and clothing and hats and needles. All Frenchmen are traders and bargainers at heart and I am French, eh? I will become the best and wealthiest of them all."

"Not if you keep bellowing. You will be the deadest of all. Look to the left, to the south bank."

"I look—and what of it?"

"No Indian tribe lives there. They come into it from north and south only to hunt and to war with one another. It is called the Dark and Bloody Ground."

"But look at the trees! and the grass so dark a green it is almost blue! and so thick, like a carpet. It is not *dark!*"

"But bloody with Indian and white gore. We are near the Great Warriors' Path, *mon ami.* The Shawnees and Seneca come down from the north and cross the river. The Cherokee, Creek and Chickasaws up from the south. They war over there among themselves. Every man, red or white, is the enemy of every other man."

Edward sobered and placed his paddle across the thwarts as he studied the passing land to the south. Simeon's skillful handling of his own paddle kept the canoe in midstream and in the firm grip of the steady current. Edward finally broke the silence.

"It is empty, that land? Always? Why?"

"*Qui sait* why? It is told that hundreds of years ago the land was filled with Indians and animals, with villages and tribes. But—poof!—something happens or something or someone comes. The Indians run, some north, some south. They leave teepees, food, fields of maize—everything—and run. And Indians, *mon ami*, are not cowards, eh?"

"Truth?" Edward asked, "Or tall stories the old ones told to frighten children, and told them so long they finally believed them?"

"Stories, *oui*. I have heard whispers of strange warriors and people with blue eyes, white skins and weapons such as had never been seen before. But they, too, left quickly, like a summer storm of thunder, lightning, rain and a great swirling wind. They were never seen again."

"But, after a time—"

"No Indian from the north or south goes there but to hunt or kill or sometimes gather salt in muddy ground where there are huge bones of animals no living man in memory has ever seen."

Edward shook himself free from the thrall the eerie tale had thrown about him and laughed. "Ah, you frighten yourself! But we will not linger, Simeon. Where there are no people I have no interest."

"*Dieu ne plais!*"

"Yes, God forbid if you forbid."

"I do."

They paddled on and gradually the shadow of Simeon's story of the Dark and Bloody Ground lifted from Edward's mind. He bent to the paddle and the canoe seemed to race the very current that carried it.

Ahead, as the sun slowly moved down the sky, the path of gold seemed to widen and increase, and the river disappeared into the very heart of it. Edward pulled his wide hat brim down to shade his eyes, already squinted against the glare. The northern bank began to lift in a series of increasingly high, rugged bluffs on which oaks, sycamores and other hardwood trees typical of the Ohio country formed thick, leafy crowns. The river made a long, curving bend south and west and suddenly Edward saw an island in the middle of the stream.

Simeon called to him. "Make for its south shore. There is a clearing and a cabin beyond the point you see."

"A settler? French?"

"The start of a farm. A man named Jonas has some corn out to grow. He rafted a cow, a trunk, supplies and wife over from the north bank."

"A wife, eh?" Edward laughed. "Then he has more than corn out to grow."

"Not planted yet that I have seen," Simeon answered in his dry way. "Haloo the cabin the moment we round the point and you see it."

"Eh, what is 'Haloo'?"

Simeon answered by example. They had swept down on the island and he and Edward swung the canoe to its southern shore. The gravelly, sandy island point seemed to rush by and suddenly the trees thinned. Edward saw a cleared field, a squat log cabin with a thin plume of smoke spiraling out of its sapling and mud chimney. He glimpsed a man in the field drop a hoe and saw a woman in a rough dress wearing a huge sunbonnet in a garden patch jerk erect, then wheel and race to the open cabin door.

"Hallooooo!" Simeon called out through hands cupped about his mouth. "Monsieur Jonas! It is Simeon Ridoux and my good friend, Edward Forny."

The man had bent to snatch up one of those long Pennsylvania rifles so common to his river country. He had leveled the weapon on them but now he slowly lowered it and his voice came clearly over the rippling waters.

"I know you, Simeon. Tie up and welcome."

"Merci," Simeon called and Edward heard his relieved sigh. "Another second and one of us would bear a bullet but would not know it. Both Jonas and his wife can shoot a squirrel from the top of a tree, and they've killed Indians trying to reach them from the south bank. Head in for the beach over there."

The canoe came to shallow water and Edward jumped out, dropping his paddle into the bottom of the boat. Simeon made one more stroke, shooting the canoe ahead and then he, too, jumped out as Edward grabbed the high, narrow prow. The river current swirled and gurgled about his ankles and water filled his moccasins as he strained to bring the canoe higher. Simeon pushed and then the keel scraped on gravel. Instantly both men lifted the craft to carry it out of danger of that rock or stone that would rip its bark covering.

Jonas came up to help and the three tipped the craft on its side. Edward and Simeon now recovered the packs and rifles they had dropped on the beach.

Simeon thanked Jonas for his help and his hospitality, then jerked a thumb at Edward as an introduction. Jonas held out his hand and Edward found the man's grip firm, muscular but pleasant.

"Forny? You're French, too?"

I have an American wife, monsieur."

"Well! So you ain't entirely heathen like Simeon here. It's Hank Jonas, case Simeon didn't tell you."

Jonas stood a head or more shorter than Edward but his wide muscular shoulders and deep powerful chest strained at the rough cloth of his shirt. His sleeves had been rolled up to his elbows and his arms were hairy, thick and as powerful as his thews that threatened to break through the rough cloth of his trousers. He had a bullet head and a rocky and protruding jaw below a long wide mouth with overly thick lips. Sun had bleached his hair and etched small wrinkles in the corners of blue eyes that met Edward's studied examination steadily and straight on.

"This one," Edward thought, "is a good, solid man. His friendship and his word must be as firm as his body, eh?"

"Hank?" the woman's sharp call swung them all around to the cabin.

"It's all right, Pearl. You know Simeon and this 'n's his friend, Edward Forny."

The woman stood framed in the doorway, her long rifle held with the hammer pulled back, ready to drop on and spark the flint into the powder pan. The huge, concealing bonnet had dropped to her shoulders and Edward could now clearly see her. She was not to his taste, he thought, even as he jerked off his hat and bobbed his head in the greeting he had learned from the settlers around the fort.

Pearl was tall and thin where her husband was short, wide and stout. She had lank, long black hair combed back over her head and pulled tightly into a knot just above her shoulders. Her jaw and nose were long, sharp and somewhat craggy. If she had breasts or legs, her shapeless coarse gray dress concealed them. Bare, dirt-stained feet protruded from under the garment and Edward saw that their soles were as hard and calloused as leather.

His eyes lifted again to her face and then he really saw her eyes. They were set well apart, framing her high-ridged nose and they were a luminous soft brown, round and truly beautiful. Though they were narrowed in frontier caution, Edward sensed they could turn warm with understanding and friendship. He suddenly wondered how they would look when she lay in the arms of a man receiving his love. Shocked by his own thought, he hastily cast out the vivid picture.

"They gonna stay a time, Hank?" she asked. Her voice sounded pleasant but was marred by a nasal, drawling twang.

"Be ye?" Hank asked. "ye're welcome."

"The night perhaps," Simeon answered, throwing a sidelong look at Edward.

"If we won't intrude," Edward added.

"What be 'intrude'?" Pearl demanded.

Edward looked blank and Simeon deftly answered. "Be it means we do not what you call 'put you out'."

Simeon's broad thumb again indicated Edward. "My friend, he is not long in this part of the country. He is from New France—Quebec, Montreal and Lake of the Eries to the north."

"Furriner," Pearl grunted.

"He has an American wife, Pearl," Hank informed her.

"American? From what colony?"

"Connecticut and York," Edward said.

"That be solid enough for me," Pearl said as she eased the hammer down and lowered the rifle. "But he talks sort of funny, Hank." She looked at Edward again and now those amazingly lovely eyes had become bright and warm as Edward knew they would.

"You ain't putting us out none. We got vittles and there be sleeping room in the loft. Hank and me been alone for a while and we've sure missed company. Have ye news of doings? Be there new folks coming in to the fort or along the river?"

"My wife and I," Edward answered with a smile and the hint of a bow that obviously pleased her.

She beamed. "Might say you do the fort a good, mister. Is your wife purty?"

"Thank you and, *oui*, she is pretty."

"Them French words! Someday maybe I'll learn 'em. But I hear you Frenchies has been beaten by the lobsterbacks."

"Pearl!" Hank remonstrated.

"Ain't no wrong if it be true! Is it, mister!" she demanded of Edward.

He shrugged. "It is true we have heard. But there is

70

yet no treaty."

"What be treaty, Hank?"

Simeon laughed. "Eh, the British and the French 'way off across the ocean do not yet smoke the peace pipe."

"Damn fools! It's over, ain't it?"

"For us out here," Hank put in. "But them bigwigs across the water have to do it all hoity-toity, Pearl."

"Well . . ." she considered a moment and then copied Edward's shrug. "Us plain folks got sense if they ain't. If war's over, war's over and we go about our business. But here we jabber and you two ain't relly lit down yet. Come on in. Stay as long as you like."

"Only the night, madame."

"Hey, hear that, Hank? You never call me such nice names like he does."

"You ain't give me no call to the way you screech and holler at me from dawn to dark."

"You give me reason enough." She turned to beam at Edward and Simeon. "But you come right in and sit. Besides vittles we might find a jug o'firewater if Hank can stir his lazy bones for it."

Since Simeon already knew these people, Edward dropped back to let him lead the way into the cabin. It was roomy and surprisingly clean for a rough frontier dwelling. In a single sweeping glance Edward saw proof that the Jonas' had come to the island to stay, to build and improve as well as farm and hunt, the activities to which most of the settlers limited their ambitions. The thick log walls had already been chinked and plastered against the winter cold and the winds that blew along the river. The floor was mostly smooth-packed, swept dirt but already a portion of it at one end was of sawed, fitted and puncheoned board. A stout heavy table dominated the center of the room and another stood against a far wall not far from a huge stone fireplace, its wide black maw broken by the bright flicker of a small fire under a heavy iron pot whose bubbling contents savored of a stew of some kind.

Hank pulled out crude but stout handmade chairs at the table. "Sit ye, Simeon and Mister Forny."

"Edward, if you please, *monsieur*. I hope we can be friends, you and I." He smiled at Mrs. Jonas. "And you also, Madame Jonas."

"Pearl—ye call me Pearl."

"Thank you."

Hank bent to reach under a long wide shelf along the wall beside the second work table. He pulled out a squat, heavy jug, its mouth stoppered by a corn cob, worn and stained by much use. He thunked it down on the table and Pearl produced rude clay mugs from a shelved cupboard, also against the far wall, and placed them before each man. Hank removed the corn cob and with a smooth, flowing movement swung the jug over one shoulder. A white liquid gurgled into the mugs.

He lifted his own in a salute to each guest. "Down your gullets to your health, gents."

Edward lifted his mug and caught a whiff of harsh liquid an instant before he took a swallow. Instantly his mouth became fire, a sheet of water flooded his eyes, blinding him. He choked and gagged as the blazing hot liquid coursed down his gullet. It exploded in his stomach like a bombshell of heat and came back up to fill his mouth and nostrils with fire.

He twisted around and beat over as the stuff spewed from his mouth in a fit of coughing and he choked, gasping for breath. He had tasted a little frontier brew before but nothing like this. He clawed at his throat as though his fingers could tear out the fire. He saw nothing, his eyes tightly closed against the flaming mist that filled them no matter what he did. Something pounded his back again and again.

At last a thin pencil of blessed air entered his mouth and throat and penetrated to his lungs. He gasped desperately for more, still bent over. The pounding on his back continued until, with a choking cry, he could straighten and at long last find air and, miraculously, breath. His chest still heaving, he tried to knuckle the water from his eyes and succeeded after a fashion.

His vision cleared. Simeon stared at him in consternation. Hank and Pearl sat to either side of him at the ends of the table and both of them had wide smiles. Pearl broke into loud laughter and Hank's cackle echoed her amusement.

"Lordy! but you ain't one to handle man-sized whiskey, be ye?"

"Jonas corn is counted the best distilled all along the river," Hank said between chuckles. "Ain't you Frenchies used to good drinkin' firewater?"

Edward still gasped for breath now and then but the spasms slowly subsided. His mug had tipped over

73

on the table and he realized his moccasins and feet were wet, the dirt floor stained beside his chair. He swallowed and gulped and gradually the flames left his lungs and stomach. He managed to speak between gasps.

"That brew—came—direct from—Hell. *Mon dieu*, was it stirred with blazing pitchforks!" He stared unbelievingly at Simeon and weakly indicated the mug the man still held. *"En vérité*, in truth, do you *really* drink of that?"

Simeon looked contrite. "I should have warned you of the river brew. I sip a drop or two, then later another drop or two. Much later I manage a full swallow. But that is all."

Edward managed a weak gesture toward Hank and Pearl. "How do they—"

"They learned long ago from their fathers and mothers. They brought the art of distilling from the Carolinas and Georgia colonies—and also Virginia's mountains."

"Le diable alone could have taught them. He should have chained them and their jugs—"

A muffled shout from outside and quite obviously from the south bank of the river galvanized them all. Hank's chair crashed over as he jumped up and Pearl leaped out of hers to the door in a twisting motion. As though by magic, they both held rifles. Simeon sprang across the room to where he and Edward had dropped their packs. Simeon swept up his own rifle and looked to the priming.

"That sounded like Injuns!" Hank snapped.

"War party!" Pearl shouted. "From the south—

74

that'd be Cherokee."

Hank dropped a heavy bar across the door and stepped to a loophole, one of many bored through the heavy logs of the cabin wall.

VI

The shouts came again as Hank peered through the loophole. Pearl found another and she snapped to Edward and Simeon, "Git to watching and if they be Injuns, shoot!"

Edward snatched up bullet pouch, powder horn and rifle, and jumped to a third loophole along the wall. He opened the metal spring gate in the butt of the weapon, pulled out wadding then reversed the weapon and poured powder into its long barrel, ramming down wadding and then a lead ball. He replaced the ramrod below the long rifle barrel and the gun was ready for use by the time he too was peering through a loophole. He saw nothing but the slope of land to the river, a wide expanse of water and the far shore. Whatever threatened over there was beyond the limits of his narrowed vision.

Then Hank said, "Four riders, white men and not Injun."

"That'n leading," Pearl said, "ain't that the Croghan feller that's been traipsing up and down these parts?"

"George Croghan," Hank confirmed after a moment. He lifted the bar from the door and threw it open. "Be your horses can swim, come on across."

"They can swim," a voice answered, the words slightly distorted by the constant rippling noise of the river.

"Eh, and who is that one?" Edward asked.

"The Britishers sent him to powwow with the Injuns and he also be land agent for Pennsylvania Colony. I reckon he's fresh up from the Cherokee country."

Pearl spat on the dirt floor in disgust. "That'n! Wonder he ain't lost his hair long afore now the way he's first north and then south of the river. How come if Shawnee or Seneca ain't captured and fried him, the Cherokee or Choctaw ain't?"

The riders, holding rifles and leather pouches high above their heads, swam their horses across the stream. Edward and Simeon followed Hank and Pearl outside as Hank answered her question.

77

"Four of 'em, woman, and you bet everyone can shoot the ass off a jaybird. Injuns leave 'em alone, that's why."

Horses and riders dripping, the four came up on the near bank, trailed a stream of water nearly to the cabin and then dismounted. They carefully put their packs far to one side to keep them safe and dry, lowered their long rifles and checked the powder pans before placing them beside the packs. They completely disregarded soaked moccasins, leggings and trousers as they turned to the cabin.

The leader pulled off his hat whose big brim had shaded his face. He was as tall and lean as his three companions and, like them, had the indelible mark of the wilderness wanderer on him. But there the similarity ended. Though his dark auburn hair was long and fell over his shoulders, it was smoothly combed and brushed and obviously had known the scissors of a barber. His forehead was high, somewhat square and blocked at the temples in contrast to his round cheeks and deep-set eyes. They were green or hazel, Edward could not decide which, alert and keen. His nose was a high rocky ridge, long and slightly tipped at the end, the nostrils somewhat flared above full, mobile lips. His jaw seemed all bone, pugnacious and square, a fighting Irish jaw if Edward ever saw one. But the man's smile belied its belligerence.

For the moment he had only a swift but all encompassing glance for Edward before his attention swung to Jonas and his wife. "How be ye, Hank? and you, Pearl? Did ye escape the misery this winter?"

"Oh, I had the ague, George," she answered, "but

78

not nearly as bad as usual."

"That's good news. We had thought to spend the night with you before we went north but you have company."

"No mind. They's the loft in the cabin and they's the barn where ye could drop your pallets. Four more's no trouble be your boys able to shoot a deer or a b'ar—maybe a mess o'wild turkey or some rabbit and squirrel."

"We'll do that, Pearl."

"Then git a'huntin afore dark sets in," she said and turned to the cabin. "I'll just add more 'taters and greens to the stew I already got a'cooking."

The man's companions did not need his orders. They swung their rifles over their shoulders and remounted, kicking the horses' ribs as they rode around a far corner of the cabin heading north. Then he turned to Edward and Simeon and smiled.

"You're new to these parts. French, I'd say. *Voyageurs* or couriers? I'm George Croghan on his Majesty's business with the Indian tribes of these parts. I'm also land agent for Pennsylvania Colony and speculate in land of my own. Do you aim to settle?"

Edward accepted his proferred hand and Simeon followed more slowly. Edward said, "We are *Français, oui.* But I am *voyageur* only long enough to see what is on the river."

"What do you seek? Land? I can offer some good locations that will make rich farming for you and your family—you have one?"

"*Oui,* my wife and my new son. But I do not seek to farm, monsieur. I seek to know the chances for trade and barter.''

Croghan's Irish face lighted. ''Ah, we have needed your kind in this country. You'll find small settlements downstream all along the river. What will you trade and barter?''

''Whatever a man or woman needs to house, clothe or feed, monsieur. I will accept coin—British or French—pelts if they are prime and well cured. I will pay in trade or in money.''

Croghan indicated Simeon. ''And what about him?''

''He is the *voyageur* and courier—my guide for this look at the river and for what business it may have to give.''

''Not much now but it will fill up with settlers as soon as everyone knows peace has really come and what kind of a peace it will be.''

''What kind? Eh, there *is* peace—what else?''

''I wish I knew. A lot depends on what our good new king does, and what he does can be decided by Sir William Pitt. There is also Lord Amherst. There are the Indians—and Sir William Johnson and myself hope we can keep them off the warpath. If we don't, I doubt you'll have much trading in these parts for a time.''

''Be ye stand out there,'' Pearl called from the cabin door, ''and jaw away the day or be ye come in and rest your bones?''

Croghan grinned at Edward. ''Ohio hospitality. It's hard to find its like anywhere else.''

When they entered, there were more chairs at the table and a second squat jug with a corn cob in its mouth. Croghan pulled off his hat and dropped it to the floor beside him when he pulled out a chair and sat down. He made no objection when Hank filled a mug with the fiery liquor and placed it before him. Hank reached for Edward's almost full mug but Pearl stopped him.

"He's right handsome, Hank, but he ain't been out here long enough to grow a man's stomach."

Croghan laughed at Edward. "So! You've tasted the brew. Your first?"

"*Oui. Mon dieu*, it was enough."

Croghan repeated Simeon's advice. "Sip it. Just enough to wet your lips and burn the tip of your tongue."

"Not even that."

Croghan shook his head. "Then you'll not go far in this country. When you deal with people on the Ohio, you do more than trade. You gain their respect."

"With this brew straight out of hell?"

"Now see here," Pearl cut in angrily. "There's a lot of things Hank don't do good, but 'stilling ain't one of 'em. Jonas corn likker is figgered the best from here to Cave-in-Rock and St. Louis."

"They have a saying out here that a man who can't handle a jug doesn't have any hair on his chest," Croghan added.

"Never knowed it to fail," Hank echoed.

"Shoo! You ain't got none and you make the stuff," Pearl scoffed and then she bobbed her head at Edward. "But this'n will learn, give him time. Go ahead, Frenchy, give it another try. Gets better as you go along."

Edward looked appealingly to Croghan who

closed the door on hope. "There you are, Mr. Forny. Don't start off on the wrong foot, as we Americans put it. Just a sip, like I said."

Edward looked around at Simeon, who nodded agreement. Reluctantly, almost fearfully, Edward inched his hand forward and slowly tightened his fingers around the mug. He hesitated to lift it and then saw Hank's narrow eyes and his lips, already curling in disdain.

"If you plan to trade—" Croghan suggested softly.

Edward lifted the mug. He caught the harsh smell of its contents and almost put the mug down again. But he took a deep breath and closed his eyes as he put the mug to his lips. They burned but he managed to get a drop or two of the brew on his tongue. He held it until he could no longer stand the burn and then swallowed.

Even the few drops seemed to set his gullet afire but he managed not to choke, though his eyes watered once more. His stomach flamed for a second and then the ordeal was over. He opened his eyes and gulped in air to cool the flame on his tongue.

"Well, now . . ." Croghan approved. "Give yourself time."

"Eons and eons, *je jure ses dieux*, I swear by all that's sacred."

"Not nearly that long," Croghan assured him then suddenly cocked his head. "Our hunters return."

One of his men stepped in the doorway. "George, we shot us a buffler."

"A buffalo!"

"So many in these parts it wasn't hard to find. We skinned and gutted him across the river. Nathan and

Dave're bringing his tongue with steaks enough to go around."

Pearl stood up. "Hank, you git over there and see if the hide is worth keeping for a robe. Throw the rest in the river afore it starts stinking."

"You and the boys help him," Croghan ordered his man. "After you give Pearl the cooking parts."

"And you, Hank, stir your bones," Pearl grunted at Hank. He started to protest but Pearl apparently anticipated him. She stood, fists on hips, towering above the table. Without another word, Hank left the cabin.

A few moments later, two of Croghan's men came with the buffalo steaks and tongue. Pearl had them dropped on the work table near the fireplace and she rolled up her sleeves as the men left to help Hank. She then looked at Edward a long moment before glancing at the others.

"You gents take the jugs and clear out while I git to the cooking and fixing. I'll be studyin' on how to bed ye for the night."

Croghan led the way outside. For the first time Edward had an idea of the extent of the river island. It was wide and very long, containing more acres than he had thought. Many a Gascon and colonial farm was smaller. He saw stout log buildings west of and behind the house—stable, barn, storage cabins, even an open-side forge. He glimpsed a field of corn and a large garden area, a beaten path wriggling westward between them to disappear into a grove of hardwood trees.

"It is an estate!" he said in surprise.

Croghan laughed. "Almost. But there are even

larger islands downstream. That's why I suggested land to you instead of trade."

"I do not know how to farm," Edward shook his head.

"Too bad. There are not only the islands but rolling fertile acres to the north belonging to my Pennsylvania Colony—acres you can file on for a very, very small fee."

"I need only just enough to hold a trading post and factory—and also enough for vegetables and camping ground for those who will come to trade for my wares."

"So little profit for me!" Croghan sighed and led the way to the shade of a huge elm tree. He dropped to a seat on the thick grass. "But I could arrange it."

"I will think on it," Edward promised.

Croghan shrugged and dropped the subject as being of no pressing nature. They lolled full length, facing the far south shore and the rolling lovely country over there. They talked idly or, rather, Croghan talked a good deal, Edward somewhat less and Simeon not at all. Croghan spoke of the country, of the war with the French and of recent events, answering the sharp questions Edward now and then put to him. Edward soon learned how little he really knew.

Croghan revealed that Fort Pitt and the settlement there were actually involved in a dispute of long standing. Pennsylvania Colony claimed it but so did Virginia Colony, the conflict starting a century or more ago because of the overlapping charters the English monarchs had given to William Penn for Pennsylvania, to a family with the French name of

Calvert for Maryland Colony and also to Virginia.

"There will be no end to the question until the boundary line between the three is surveyed and determined. I have heard that Maryland and Virginia now talk of such a survey and it just may be made. But such things take an unconscionable long time to agree upon."

"But this Virginia—have I not heard it is the most *ancien* of all?"

"The oldest—long before Massachusetts Bay where the Puritans and Pilgrims settled."

"*Eh bien*, Virginia has the claim."

Croghan laughed. "Lord Dunmore, the governor, would certainly agree with you. In fact there is a Virginia Land Company making claims out here in Ohio. They sent one Colonel Washington and Christopher Gist to explore and establish claim before we started warring with the French."

"But the Indians?" Edward suggested.

"No one considers them! We call councils of the tribes, make treaties with them as we would with a European nation to buy their land."

"*Alors*, that should be the end of it."

"Except an Indian tribe is not a European nation and a tribal chief is not a monarch. He is leader today but only a warrior tomorrow. The treaty is not binding on him. To the Indians land is not owned by any individual or any tribe. They never had that idea. Land belongs to the Great Spirit alone who allows an Indian or a tribe to use it. The tribes roam freely, hunting, warring, moving their villages now and then as they see fit. But the land is never owned."

"Then why is it you make treaties to buy it? We

French have done that in New France. Have we built Quebec, Montreal and *le bon Dieu sait* how many other towns, villages and trading posts on land that is not ours?"

"As a white man, the land is yours acquired by treaty, but to an Indian, you were a fool to pay him good trade goods for something that was not his to begin with. The Indian laughs at us, my friend."

"*Eh bien*, they laugh. But do they laugh when we drive them off? *Tonnerre!* Now I understand. They have as much right as we to stay. We rob them, eh!"

"And we believe the Indian goes back on his spoken and signed word."

"So there is war—always, eh? We kill, they kill. We burn and destroy, they burn and destroy. We are right, they are right—no one is right."

"That's right," Croghan agreed with a wry laugh at his own poor joke.

"*Le comble de la confusion*," Edward sighed. "It is confusion worse confounded."

"And will be more as time goes on," Croghan agreed.

Pearl Jonas called from the cabin, "George, you Frenchies—the vittles will soon go on the table! Best get in and sit."

They found the cabin somewhat crowded with Croghan's men, who sat against the log walls on the dirt floor, a thick platter bearing a buffalo steak before each, a mug of Hank's brew to hand. They ate swiftly, using fingers and heavy hunting knives to cut, spear and devour the meat. Edward's brow lifted as he saw the crude platters. Lighter, easier handled plates should readily replace what he saw and he made a mental note to see if such were obtainable in Pennsylvania or north in Quebec or Montreal. He should be able to turn a neat handful of *louis d'or* on such a deal. Pearl cut in on his thoughts.

"Mister Forny, you and George sit to table with me. I held out some choice buffler steaks for us."

As Edward sat down, he asked, "Where's Monsieur Jonas?"

"I sent him chasing our milk cow that found a section of fence rail down and she's strayed somewhere to hell and gone. He'll likely be hunting for her most of the day and part of the night."

"Quelle mauvais nouvelles!" Edward exclaimed.

"What'd he say, George?" she asked.

"What bad news, Pearl." But she gave her full attention to Edward and hardly heard him. Croghan pursed his lips. "Strange how easily a dumb beast can find a way to escape."

Pearl started as though she had just heard and looked around at George, back to Edward and again to George. She turned to the fireplace as though to retrieve more steaks. She spoke over her shoulder.

"Ain't it, though?"

VII

Edward had long since become accustomed to the frontiersman's way of eating a meal. He would linger over a pipe of tobacco. He would drink hard and long, but never hurriedly. He would loll on a river bank and talk lazily, exchanging news, gossip, weather and river conditions. But he ate as though the food before him must be swiftly disposed of in order to go on to more important things. He almost literally gulped it down.

So it was tonight. Edward had hardly started to eat when the men along the wall used thick hunks of bread to wipe their platters clean of the gravy and juices of the steaks. Simeon was almost as fast, while Edward had eaten no more than a few bites of his meat and some of the vegetables. Suddenly Pearl stood at his shoulder. She looked at his nearly full plate and then at him.

"Ain't the vittles good?"

"They are very good, madame. It is just that I do not have the fast way of eating. I am sorry. I delay you."

"Shoo! No mind. Them others, they're like pigs at a trough, swilling down slops. You just take your time like a gentleman should. It makes me no never mind."

The men along the wall rose, picked up their platters and turned to the door. Pearl's voice carried over the sound of their shuffling and talk. "Wash them plates clean in the river and then sand-scour 'em hard. Hear me!"

Croghan, whose platter was almost as full as Edward's, leaned across the table so the general noise of the room covered his remark. "My friend, you have charmed Mrs. Jonas."

Edward stared at Croghan and slapped his hand on his chest. "I have charmed! *Moi!*"

"Yes, you. How did you do it?"

"I had no thought to. *Vous êtes dans erreur*, you are mistaken."

"Am I? We'll see."

When the room finally emptied, Pearl filled a

89

platter for herself and came to the table. She sat down beside Croghan, facing Edward, and spoke directly to him. "Be ye mind if I sup with ye, Frenchy?"

"Pas du tout."

"What's he say?" she asked of Croghan.

"He says he'll be delighted."

She beamed and, as Edward had first thought, her eyes became beautiful and her face lost much of its angularity. He was surprised to see that she actually must be much younger than her appearance. Had the hard ways of the wilderness and a frontier farm robbed her of youth?

She ate as intently and speedily as the others. Now and then she looked up at Edward, each time her eyes gleamed but in another second they turned down to her plate. She used knife, fingers and hunks of bread as eating utensils. Though she had started long after Edward, he had barely finished his own portion when she pushed her empty platter to the center of the table and leaned back, using her apron as a napkin. She looked about the room as though measuring it, put her elbows on the table for support, then thoughtfully rubbed her hand along her jaw.

"I reckon we'd best figure how we divvy off the sleeping places tonight."

Edward gave Croghan a puzzled, questioning look which he disregarded except for an enigmatic smile. He said to Pearl, "My boys have slept everywhere and anywhere—outdoors and in."

"I figured," she nodded, shot a sidelong weighing look at Edward. "So, let's see . . . Hank and me use the sleeping loft upstairs." She pointed to a wooden ladder nailed flat against a far wall. It disappeared into an open trap door in the ceiling. "There's another loft in the barn just beyond the house. Folks have slept out there, spreading their blankets on the hay. I've used it when we've been real crowded."

"But you don't have that many tonight, Pearl," Croghan suggested.

"That's right—so there ain't no call to bunch up like we do sometimes."

Croghan leaned back in his chair, hands in his lap, twirling his thumbs. Edward thought his expression and smile grew more puzzling. Ah!—knowing, that was it, somehow certain as to what was to come and it all focused on him for some strange reason.

"Let's see now," Pearl continued, "George, your boys can roll up under the trees, what with it being warm and it ain't gonna rain."

"They'd like that better than the cabin," Croghan agreed.

"Sure they would, George. Now you—how 'bout you take the loft upstairs along with Simeon, the other Frenchy?"

"Good enough." Croghan's eyes danced as though he silently laughed. "How about you, Pearl? You've about run out of sleeping space."

"Shu! you forgetting all this room down here." She gestured about her. "I can sleep over there afore the fireplace. It'll be warm and, that way, I can be up and about starting the morning meal 'thout wakin' no one. That leaves the loft out in the barn."

"Him?" Croghan bobbed his head at Edward.

"Ain't no trouble at all. Ain't nothing to fash him out there."

"Fash?" Edward asked.

Pearl shook her head in wonder. "Ain't you heard good American words, Mr. Frenchy. It means you ain't going to be woke up by a passel stirring around like you would be with the others."

"Ah! Disturb?"

"That's right," Croghan nodded. "Not by me and my crew."

Pearl looked to the door. "Last light's not far and all of us best get settled while we can still see. George, you skin up to the loft after you show Mr. Forny where to settle out in the barn."

"I thought you'd be doing that, Pearl."

She bristled. "Ain't no call me going out there with him and causin' talk. Nope, he can gather up his rifle and belongings 'nd you can see he gets settled. Me, I got a heap to do right here. Now clear out."

At Croghan's shrug and signal, Edward picked up his gear and started to the door. He had just reached the threshold when Pearl said, "Mr. Forny, come night it gits mighty dark out there up in the loft. But it won't be no mind to you, I reckon. Too many folks 'round for them Injuns to even paddle or swim to the island let alone sneak about."

"Oh, I do not have fear, madame."

"Didn't figure it but thought I'd tell you. Oh, if you need to git up in the night—you know—there's a door cut in the logs at the west end. Just swing it open and take care of things. But watch the open trap in the floor. If'n you fall through that—"

Edward laughed. "I'll be careful, Madame Jonas."

"Can't you set your tongue to Pearl, Mr. Forny?"

"*Certainement*—if you set your tongue to Edward."

"I'd be pleasured, Mister—Edward. You're gonna be real comfortable up there once you git blanketed down in the hay."

"I'm sure. Good night, mad—Pearl."

It became her turn to chuckle approval. She turned to Croghan. "Light's going fast, George."

"So it is. Come on, Forny. Pearl will have our scalps if all of us aren't bedded down and asleep before full dark."

When Edward climbed through the trap and into the stable loft, shadows had become thick. Croghan walked to a far end, worked a small, thick wedge out of a hasp and threw open a wide door. Soft, faintly golden twilight poured in, silhouetting a heavy beam jutting far beyond the building. Edward saw a heavy wheel, a thick rope looped over it and attached to the stable wall.

"After the field grass is scythed and dried for hay," Croghan answered Edward's question, "they use the pulley to lift it up here and store for the livestock. But tonight—"

"Une pissotiere—"

"The French word has the right sound, so I'd say 'yes.' But stay clear of the far wall over there around the open trap door."

"I shall remember." He looked around. "I would not have believed so much space."

The loft was wide and long, its walls higher than Edward's head before the logs slanted in to meet the high ridgepole of thick, adzed timber. He saw the shadowy shape of handmade shingles, themselves thick enough to support the weight of deep snow or heavy ice in the winter.

"Will it do?" Croghan asked.

"*Oui!* I shall be more comfortable than I had thought."

"I believe Pearl had that in mind. Good night, Forny."

"*Bonne nuit,*" Edward answered and Croghan dropped through the trap before he could be questioned about his peculiar statement.

Edward opened his pack, removed his blankets and spread one atop the hay near the window that Croghan had left opened. He felt safe enough, as everyone had assured him he would, but his long rifle lay propped against his pack close at hand and his heavy sheathed hunting knife lay beside the rifle and his pistol. His flight from Quebec and Montreal toward Detroit, then across the Lake of the Eries, through Seneca country to Fort Pitt had taught him respect for Indian skills in avoiding the slightest sound. He did not undress but stretched out on one blanket, pulling the other over him.

For a time it seemed that the twilight would never end, the shadows thickening slowly in the loft. Edward heard birds sleepily twittering in the trees outside. Then, as though an unseen but gigantic hand erased the day, the light snuffed out. He could not even see the shape of the trees against the black sky. His eyes closed and he slept.

Something penetrated his sleep-dulled brain and his eyes snapped open. For a second he was confused. A bright silver light poured into the loft through the open door and each tree stood starkly etched as though cut from black steel. A full moon began to lift above the boughs.

He lay unmoving for moments, certain it was not the bright silver light but a small noise that had really awakened him. Then he became aware of another, near presence, a faint, soft irregular breathing. He started to turn his head at the exact moment fingers touched his hand like a caressing feather.

"Qui est—?"

A hand clamped over his mouth and Pearl's voice made a fierce, sibilant whisper in his ear. "Shush! You want all them menfolks to know I'm visiting you!"

He started to rise but she pushed him flat with surprising strength. Straw rustled and her shadow cut between him and the moonlight as she bent over him and her hand traveled down to his trousers, fumbling at his crotch. He instinctively groped to free himself and his hand touched bare, smooth flesh. She grasped his wrist, lifted his arm and his fingers covered a full, rounded breast, the nipple outstanding and hard.

"You've had women afore, Frenchy. You're married, ain't you?"

"Oui, mais—"

"No need speaking funny words. Just do to me what you was made to do to a woman. Here—"

She had found the entrance to his trousers and worked him free. She now had his other hand deep between her legs and she moved up against him as his fingers entered her body. She pulled his head down to her breast and her nipple waited his lips.

"Mon Dieu!" he thought. "I am being raped!"

His hand dropped along her bare thigh and he realized Pearl must be completely naked. She gasped as she touched his muscle, now strong. "Jehosophat! I knowed you be this big!"

"But Hank—"

She smashed her lips down against his then pulled away long enough to whisper, "Who do you think freed that cow!"

She still loomed above him and when he tried to answer, her lips again smashed against his, making his words a gurgling series of sounds. He saw moonlight on her head and shoulders for a moment and then on her bare leg as she leaned to one side. Her hand still held and stroked him and then in a quick, spasmodic move she threw her leg over and straddled him. He had also glimpsed her fullsome breasts that had been hidden by her repellent dress, which she still wore but had pulled up about her neck and shoulders.

She guided him home with frantic fingers and then dropped the full weight of her body on him. He went deep, stone hard, and she gasped, grew rigid and then became writhing, moving, avid flesh. Edward's body responded despite himself. He thrust, pulled back and thrust again, his rhythm increasing with hers.

Her nails sank into his shoulders even as he wrapped his arms about her waist. She moaned and then her hands framed his cheeks, her kisses rained over his face. He hooked his fingers in her buttocks and she arched to meet him, her breathing heavy and fast, irregular, explosive gasps interspersed with moans.

Noise! flashed through his mind. Someone . . . will hear . . . ! then her avid demands erased all his clarity, if he ever had any since she had touched him.

Suddenly she threw back her head and her body slammed against him as she cried out. He slapped his hand across her mouth to silence her and she bit him, a purely animal act without thought. He managed to cut off his yelp of pain.

She continued to clutch him, her body wholly avid motion. It flashed through his mind that Pearl was one of those insatiable women. She had a second orgasm, then a third as the pressure in his own body suddenly exploded deep within her. He became emptied but she continued to clutch and move against him. Finally he wedged his hands between them, straightened his arms and with a powerful heave threw her off and to one side.

She lay shivering, making little mewing sounds as she blindly fought him. He pushed her groping hands aside, tried to come to his feet, slipped on the straw and fell but well beyond her reaching arms. His chest heaved and he gasped for breath. The loft echoed with the ragged sounds they made. She spoke the first coherent word.

"Frenchy!"

"*Cela suffit!* Mon Dieu, that's enough!"

"Ain't," she gasped. "Ain't never! When I get back my breath again, we'll—"

"No! Your husband—"

"Hank?" She gasped for breath again but could finally speak once more. "Hank . . . he ain't . . . never been much. Not like you . . ."

"No! No! I mean, he will come back. He will find us—like this."

"He ain't got guts enough to do nothing, Frenchy." She pulled herself up to a sitting position. "But you—look, I'll send Hank packing and you . . . stay here with me."

"What!"

"Sure. No mind. There ain't been a parson this way in two years. Hank and me ain't married church-like."

He stared aghast at her faint silhouette in the darkness of the loft. She has lost her mind! he thought. He slid further away from her along the straw. His hand struck the smooth stock of his rifle and his pack. His eyes cut to the open door filled with moonlight and then to the dark oblong of the trap leading to the floor below. Pearl blocked his way to both but he had to escape. By a mighty, desperate effort he forced his thoughts into some sort of order.

"Eh, perhaps not married but would not Monsieur Jonas try to keep you? I would."

"Well, now," she almost purred. "I'd drive him off."

"But in his place, mádame, I'd come back. I would wait my chance and, *peste!* a rifle ball would take care of me, no?"

"It would," she agreed, fell silent for a second and then spoke eagerly. "I can take care of that! The first passing Indian would put an arrow in him for a bottle of Hank's own firewater—then take his hair to boot. Sure! That's easy done."

"Ah, *oui*. But not tonight, eh? Perhaps tomorrow. There are others around."

"I can send'em skeedaddling."

"What means—how you say?"

"Skeedaddle? Oh, that means running, shoo 'em off. Tell 'em all to git."

"But they can't find you here with me. If they do and then Monsieur Jonas disappears—"

"Damn! You're right. I best git back downstairs and to the house. Can't have no suspicions about us, can we?"

"*Pas un*—not one."

She sighed and pulled herself to her feet. For a moment of panic, as she hesitated, he thought she would come to him. Then she sighed again and walked to the trap.

"It's been some night, Frenchy. I ain't gonna let Hank stand in the way of you'n me having more of 'em. Won't be long 'cause there ain't a week but what an Injun paddles by or comes begging. We can wait for that, huh?"

"*Oui*, we can wait."

"Like you say, I best git back. See you tomorrow night, maybe?"

"No, we cannot be fools, eh? We be—how you say—natural, like before now, eh?"

"Reckon we better, damn it! 'Night, you French bull."

She disappeared down through the trap. Edward remained motionless, strained, until he heard the slight sounds of her departure from below. Then he expelled the air in his lungs in a long, whispered whistle and passed his hand over his face. It came away moist with sweat. He thought of Siméon and of the canoe tipped on its side near the river. Then he dismissed that idea. Pearl would be as wide awake as he and would hear the slightest sound. He had best postpone escape until morning.

He returned to his madly rumpled and twisted

blankets and, with his movement, realized his shirt and trousers clung damply to his body, dirty and clammy. But he could do nothing about it now. He straightened his blankets, stretched out, but not to sleep.

He stared into the bright moonlight and started to plan the next critical hours. He visualized the main cabin, the fireplace near which Pearl would sleep. Croghan and Simeon would be up in the loft and that posed the real problem.

He stared at the moonlight as he mulled over the puzzle but the solution would not come. Very slowly the quality of the silver light changed and he realized that the night moved into the small hours. Then it came to him—did the main cabin loft have a door like this one? Was Pearl as satiated as he? She must be after all that activity. If so, she would be sound asleep, but she might be like a cat, alert to the smallest noise in the main room. How about outside—and the chance of a loft door?

He jumped up, folded his blankets and placed them in his pack, strapping the heavy canvas cover over it. He walked to the loft door and looked out. Nothing stirred. He dropped the pack and heard it strike the ground with a dull, hardly audible thud. He shot a searching look at the main cabin but nothing moved.

He grabbed up his rifle and stepped to the dark square of the trap. He groped down with his feet from rung to rung and finally touched solid earth. In another moment he was outside, plastering himself against the wall and listening for the faintest sound of alarm.

Satisfied, he angled to the far end of the main cabin, moved several feet away from it and looked up. When he saw the black oblong shape of a door to the left, he choked down a shout of triumph. He bent, fingers groping along the ground until he found a pebble, then another. He stepped as close to the cabin wall as he could and still see the upper door. He threw a pebble through it and hissed, "Simeon!"

No answer. He held his breath, listening for sounds of disturbance on the main floor. None. He threw another pebble and again hissed. A ghostly face suddenly filled the upper black oblong.

"Who is it?" a voice called softly and Edward cursed under his breath. Croghan! But he was now committed.

"It is Edward," he whispered hoarsely. "I need Simeon. *Par le sacre nom de Dieu*, don't rouse Madame Pearl.

He heard a chuckle. "She had you, huh? I saw her sneak out to the barn."

"In the name of God, don't waken her. Can Simeon jump down here?"

Simeon himself answered so loudly to Edward's ears that he knew everyone would come wide awake.

"Peste! Silence!" Edward hissed. "Drop your pack to me. Silence, eh?"

Simeon disappeared for long, long minutes that stretched out into infinite time. Then he reappeared and Edward saw the pack in his arms. Edward caught it, nearly losing his balance with the slam of the falling weight. He stepped to the wall of the cabin.

"Now the rifle to my hand."

In a moment, he grasped the smooth stock and

stepped out into the waning moonlight. "I have it. Jump down now."

Simeon's form filled the black orifice above and then the man swung out and dropped to the ground as silent and catlike as an Indian. Edward gave swift orders. "To our canoe. Now! *en silence de mort.*"

"With the silence of the dead," Simeon repeated. "Then what?"

"Mon Dieu! We escape this island!"

He heard a low laugh from above and Croghan's carrying whisper. "And Pearl Jonas. I told you. Did she eat you alive?"

"Vraiment! Tout les cornes et la tete. Je suis devoré!"

"Devoured you head and horns," Croghan chuckled.

"Oui, et me sauve!"

"Run for your life," Croghan's whisper agreed. *"A bonne chance."*

"I need good luck. Come, Simeon. Softly! Softly!"

VIII

All that day, the canoe shot down the river like an arrow, propelled by Edward's and Simeon's flashing blades. Miles separated them from the Jonas island when at last Edward allowed Simeon to turn the craft to a stretch of beach and helped him carry it well beyond the lapping fingers of the water. Even so, Edward now and then searched back upstream, as though Pearl might shoot around a bend in her own canoe in avid pursuit.

Simeon pulled his knees up under his chin, wrapped his arms about his legs and looked long and hard at Edward. Both could now speak easily and freely in the French patois of the *voyageur*. Edward told his companion what had happened. Simeon's eyes grew rounder, his lips moved under his beard and then he broke into a roar of laughter.

"It is not all for laughter, my friend," Edward snapped. Simeon only shook his head and continued to laugh. He finally regained his breath and wiped the tears from his eyes while Edward glared. "What would you have done?"

"Exactly as you—enjoyed the woman and then run like hell. You're safe from her now so long as you never go back to that island."

"I am not so certain, my friend, when she actually began to plan to have her man murdered to clear the way for me."

Simeon commented with a note of envy, "No woman ever thought of doing that for me. But then, you must have much more than I, or most men for that matter."

"It is not to laugh nor to make wild guesses about what I have or do not have. It is time to hurry down the river now that we have rested."

"And eat," Simeon added.

"What? I have brought nothing."

"Jerky and pemmican. Every *voyageur* carries them in his pack. You will learn to do the same. We eat as we paddle."

So they were back in the stream, both of them chewing on the dried buffalo meat called "jerky" and the mixture of meat mixed with suet, raisins and sugar called pemmican. It was far from gourmet but it was food that the men of the wilderness trails and rivers knew would sustain them for days on end if need be.

Once more the river banks rapidly wheeled by and the miles increased between them and Pearl Jonas. As the sun lowered toward the west, Simeon called forward. "Best to beach, Edward. We can take the time to find fresh food while we can yet see to either fish or hunt."

"We'll round another bend, eh?"

"If you'll feel safer from your lady love," Simeon agreed.

Around the turn they found a wide and sandy beach where a small creek flowed out of the woods to join with the great river and Edward immediately turned the canoe in toward it. They soon had the canoe well up on the sand, tipped on its side. Simeon produced fishline and hooks from his packs, cut a long stick and set Edward to digging for worms. Simeon picked up his rifle and waited a few moments until Edward's hunting knife blade turned up worms from the moist black soil beneath the nearest trees. Then Simeon, with a single, silent woodsman's step vanished into the woods. Edward baited his hook, found a deep hole carved from the bank by the force of the current and set himself to the patience of the angler. But he constantly looked upstream.

The river must have been alive for within a very short time, Edward had hooked a pike, a catfish, perch and some smaller fish that he later learned the Ohio people called "sunfish." He then pulled in his

105

line and cleaned his catch at the river's edge. He built a small fire behind the tipped canoe so that its flames could not be easily seen along or across the river. He had no more than finished when he heard a shot in the woods, then a second. Shortly after, Simeon appeared with a brace of rabbits.

They ate quickly and had the fire doused by full nightfall. They divided the night into watches and Simeon rolled up on the sun-warmed sand behind the shelter of the canoe, his rifle cradled in his arms. Edward hugged his knees and watched the river darken and then disappear completely into the night. The fireflies came winking and blinking their small cold lights in an erratic but lovely dance across the beach, beneath the trees and over the water flowing eternally by. Finally, judging the time by the stars, Edward awakened Simeon and himself rolled up under the canoe to sleep.

First light found them both awake and rewarming the rabbit left from the night before over a small fire. They kept a sharp eye on the south bank but if there were Indians, they made no sound or move to reveal themselves. Edward still now and then glanced upstream but with dawn light, he had wondered wryly why he still feared the appearance of Pearl Jonas. She'd never pursue him this far. Then he had the startling, sobering thought that she stood between him and his return to Abby at Fort Pitt.

Simeon shrugged carelessly when Edward spoke of it. "We can leave the river a mile or so this side of the island and portage around it. But, most likely, we will not be on the river."

"Where then? Fort Pitt is upstream."

"But the Ohio's current is strong. We will probably take to the woodland trails. I doubt if we so much as see the island."

"There are the Indians," Edward reminded him.

"There are always Indians, everywhere in this country, *mon ami*. We stay to the north bank and avoid the Cherokee war parties to the south. Shawnee, Miami, Pottawatomie and Seneca to the north have traded time and again with courier and you must trade with them eventually. If you have an open hand, gifts and a straight tongue, there is little chance of trouble."

He had the right of it, Edward acknowledged and besides, a man was a fool to ask for trouble in his mind long before it came upon him along the trail. He wanted to know if the river trade and settlements held any future for him and here, already, he came close to allowing an over-sexed frontier woman to block even this first tentative foray. He laughed aloud at himself and Simeon looked up curiously.

"Is there something for laughter?"

"No, Simeon. I am not a grown man but a little boy afraid to step out of the house door."

Then Simeon laughed. "By the end of today, if not tomorrow, the little boy will disappear. You'll see."

They were on the river little more than two hours when Simeon called up to him, "See that trace of smoke among the trees to the north? A cabin up there, I'll bet, and we'll see the river landing before long."

He had hardly spoken when a man came out of the woods to the river bank and waved to them. Edward could not see his features at this distance but the wide-brimmed, flat hat, the rifle barrel protruding above his shoulder, the long-shirted jacket, trousers like leggings and the moccasins marked him as far from Indian. Edward turned the canoe toward the bank.

Closer up, Edward saw a man with a tanned face, square jaw, a nose flattened in some long-ago brawl and a welcoming grin that broke the solid blond bush of his thick beard. He waded several steps out into the water to meet the canoe, grabbed its high prow and, with a surge of muscular shoulders, help shoot it up on the beach.

Once the craft was safe from the river's grip, the three men took measure of one another and Edward saw the stranger's eyes darken in disappointment. "Hell! You're just *voyageurs* like all them Frenchies."

"*Oui*, I am French," Edward acknowledged. "But I am a trader. I am married to an American. *I am* American. I am Edward Forny out from Fort Pitt."

"Forny? That don't sound French. Your wife's American? Where's she from?"

"Connecticut and York Colony. Her family name is Brewster."

"Now that sounds downright American. But if'n you're a trader, where's your goods?"

"I first come to see who is on the river and who will trade with me. I discover what is wanted and needed before I bring valuable goods for nothing or perhaps for the Indians."

"That's smarter'n I'd give a Frenchy to be."

Edward bristled. "You think I am a fool, eh?"

"Now hold on!" the man quickly exclaimed. Then his broad grin broke out like the sun behind the cloud of his thick beard. "Here I be lonesome for a face and come rushing down to powwow. Instead, I pick a fight. I'm the fool, Forny." He held out his hand. "I'm Sean Cleary, ten·years out in this country from Boston town."

Edward hesitated a moment and then accepted the proffered hand. The man's clasp was firm and strong. He looked over at Simeon. "Now that one's Frenchy from the outside clean into his backbone."

"Yes. He is Simeon Ridoux, my guide and my good friend and companion."

"You both be welcome. Let's bush the canoe and you come up to the house. I reckon you could give me a deal of news about Fort Pitt and maybe even Boston town."

"And you can tell me of the river and those who live along it, eh?"

"Sure—a fair trade. But first, I'll help ye with the canoe. Ye'll want to bring your packs with you."

He and Simeon lifted the light bark craft above their heads while Edward gathered the packs and the rifles. Sean led the way along the long strip of narrow beach to a thick wall of swaying bushes. The wall proved to be deceptive for Sean pushed right through it to an open area beyond, its grassy expanse cut by a narrow brook gurgling down the hill, twisting about to join the river somewhere beyond another wall of bushes to the west. Edward saw a canoe tipped on its side beside the brook.

Sean and Simeon placed Edward's birchbark beside it, tipped it over, and then Sean turned to a faintly discernible path that paralleled the brook in a steep ascent of the hill. Trees and bushes shaded the way and the path twisted and turned so often that Edward could see but a short distance ahead. Then they suddenly broke into a clearing bounded by high, leafy trees.

A squat but long cabin of logs sat squarely in the center of the fields, the path leading straight through standing rows of Indian corn called "maize" instead of the European term "wheat" which Edward had always called the plant until he had arrived in New France—it seemed so many ages ago!

A black and yellow dog of large size but indeterminate lineage burst around a corner of the cabin, its loud, constant barking sending echoes rocketing to the sky as it came rushing at them, teeth bared.

"Pluto!" Sean yelled, "Damn you! These be friends. Down, ye dolt and mind your manners." The dog instantly subsided and Sean said apologetically, "He guards for Injuns so he has no company manners. He don't need 'em, seeing there's just him and me up here."

"You have no wife?" Edward asked.

"Ain't had time to look for one since I've been out to this country. Back in Boston Town I reckon I was too ugly for a lass to give me a second look."

On entering the cabin, Edward had the thought that Sean did not need a wife except as companion and mate, for the place was as clean and as orderly as any woman could have kept it. A large rock and clay fireplace filled the center of the far wall and to either side hung brass and copper pots, pans and skillets, each polished and burnished brightly to reflect the sun from the open doorway. A long heavy table

110

dominated the center of the floor and Edward saw, at one end of the room, a ladder leading to the dark oblong of the loft trap. He thought of the one at the Jonas cabin and quickly looked away.

Sean had built cupboards and Edward could see the man had skill as a cabinet maker and also taste in design. Sean opened one and pulled out a jug with a corncob stopper and plunked it down on the table.

"Firewater!" Edward exclaimed.

Sean's brow shot up at Edward's dismay and he laughed, "If ye be meaning the burning acid that passes for a decent drink in these parts, ye'd be mistaken. Me own father, rest his soul, taught me the trick of Auld Country distilling. It's done with potato over there and—"

"Potato!"

"That it is. Then I learned the way they distill the corn along the river. I've been trying their way, but changing it here, adding this, taking away that. I've come up with a smooth and velvet brew. A lone man has plenty of time to try first one way and then another and I think I've found a sour mash to suit me."

He filled the clay mug and extended it. "Try it, Mr. Forny."

Edward looked over at Simeon, who made a faint shrug. Sean pushed the mug at Edward. "Go on, Bucko. Ye fault me if ye don't even so much as taste it."

Edward cupped the mug in both hands and looked at Simeon as Cleary eyed him expectantly. He tipped the rim of the mug to his mouth and slowly, care-

111

fully allowed its contents to touch his lips. The brew did not have the hot, harsh smell he had encountered before. When he sipped the liquid, he found it hot, but pleasantly so. This would not peel the skin from his tongue or pull the taste buds out by main force.

He sipped again. His throat felt warm and his stomach glowed. He lowered the mug and Sean asked, "And what would ye be saying?"

"Ma foi! I am surprised. What was the word you used for this?" Edward asked raising the mug.

Sean looked puzzled, scratched his head. "Whiskey? No? Then 'sour mash'—no? Ah, velvet—smooth."

"That is it! Smooth. Have you much of this?"

"Enough for me and for folks like you that come along now and then. Oh, some of my neighbors—if ye call men forty miles away 'neighbors'—come to buy jugs now and then."

"How much could you make in—say six months?"

"None, Mr. Forny. It takes time. I have a deal on hand, though."

"After that?" Edward asked impatiently. "How long?"

"Oh, a poor batch in two–three years. Like this, though, in six to eight."

"Start making it—for me alone, monsieur. I will take it to Fort Pitt and west into Pennsylvania—up to Lake of the Eries. I want all you can brew and—"

"Distill," Sean interrupted.

"Qu'est que c'est?"

"What's that mean?"

"That's what I asked you—'distill.' What is that?"

"Oh, now I get you, Mr. Forny. Beer is brewed, like ale. Wine is aged or laid up. Whiskey like this is distilled, a process of some intricacy, me lad. Wine and smooth whiskey need age. Beer and ale—" Sean snapped his fingers—"like that, though there's some who dislike the thought."

"It is not of a consequence. I will buy all your 'distill' you have on hand now and all you can distill later, eh? Here—" He dropped coins in Sean's hands and the man stared at the gold in amazement. "That is an earnest to our bargain, *n'est pas?*"

"Well!" Sean weighed the coins with a lifting motion. "I never thought my whiskey would bring money like this."

"It is more than whiskey as they know it on the Ohio, *mon ami*. We have the bargain sealed, eh?"

"We have it sealed, begorra! And how will ye be having it delivered?"

"I'll not be. You'll store it here for me, no? Most of it will go downstream and much of it will sell in the country around here. What I need upstream and about Fort Pitt you can deliver by pack train."

"I don't have the horses."

"When I return to Fort Pitt, I will buy animals there or east in Pennsylvania Colony and send them to you."

"What about the Indians?"

"Build stables here. I will have men like Simeon and good stout couriers and colony men to guard the train. So, it is done between us, eh?"

"It is done," Sean agreed.

The next morning, Edward and Simeon continued

113

their exploratory trip downstream. Now and then they came on lone settlers like Sean Cleary. Again they'd round a bend and find a small cluster of cabins on the north bank, never the southern. These would contain French couriers and *voyageurs,* fur trappers for the most part, men who found it hard to understand that they were now subjects of a British king and not a French monarch.

There were new restrictions, Edward learned, far more stringent than the easy ones of New France. He encountered restlessness and uncertainty everywhere. Everyone disliked and even cursed Lord Jeffrey Amherst, a man whom none in the Ohio country had seen but whose words and rules had changed all their lives and even angered the Indians.

By the time Edward had come to the Falls of the Ohio, portaged them and continued on to the mouth of the Oubache, he knew beyond a doubt that the English, out of misunderstanding or sheer arrogance, unwittingly incubated the eggs of bloody revolt. The first indication came in the news that Amherst had cut off all treaty gifts to the Indian tribes and word came that Croghan was appeasing the Indians with their expected gifts out of his own pocket.

Next, word came that Lord Amherst, undoubtedly following orders from the ministry in distant London, had drawn a boundary line at the source of all rivers flowing eastward from the mountains to the Atlantic Ocean. There would be no settlement allowed from the crestline of the mountain chains westward across the empty country to the Spanish controlled Mississippi River. Only Indian tribes could hunt and trap, bringing their pelts to English factors in Detroit, Niagara and Quebec.

Edward had word of impending trouble brewing everywhere he went. The fairly large settlement of Fort Vincennes on the high east bank of the Wabash, or Ouabache, confirmed all he had heard elsewhere. The English built a fort there amidst the French cabins as part of a chain leading from Detroit to Fort Kaskaskia on the Mississippi to Vincennes itself and on to Fort Pitt—a ring of military steel to contain the Indians, force out settlers and keep the whole Ohio country securely under the British flag.

The final act made the Indians treat with factors in what had once been New France—unable to get any price for their pelts except those set by the factors under the king's law as interpreted by his Lordship, General Jeffrey Amherst. Edward began to hear of Pontiac, a chief of the Ottawas, a tribe far to the north. Once more, local tribal chieftains vanished and whispers came that they had gone northward in answer to the war calumet Pontiac had sent to them.

Edward turned to Simeon for explanation. "What is this calumet, eh?"

"A pipe. It is smoked when the tribes gather for treaties among themselves or with the white man. Then it is white and for peace. But a war calumet is a pipe of scarlet red, the color of blood."

"Indian war?"

"*Oui*—and everywhere from the Spanish lands to the eastern mountains. This whole country will be afire and running with white blood."

115

"Mon Dieu! Abby!"

"I think she will be safe at Fort Pitt," Simeon tried to reassure him but Edward shook his head.

"Non! This Pontiac will know that Fort Pitt will always be a British knife blade at his back unless it is taken. He will try to destroy it—and Abby is there. *Sacré nom!* I must be with her!"

IX

Abby missed Edward more than she believed she would ever miss anyone and sometimes she wondered at herself. The Good Lord knew that she was a woman quite capable of taking care of herself. She had only to think of the intervening period between the time Corn Dancer and his Onondaga braves had attacked and burned Westover back in Connecticut and all that she had overcome since to be sure of that. Still she wanted and needed Edward, his very presence giving her assurance of safety.

She thought of it again this bright sunny morning as she bathed and changed her infant son and placed him in the low rocking cradle that Dean Smith had so skillfully fashioned. Dean's wife, Letitia, sat in a rocker nursing her own youngest, her milk-full white breast exposed to the baby's eagerly sucking lips.

"When d'ye study on Edward being back?" she asked as though somehow she had picked up a portion of Abby's thoughts.

"There's no telling. It depends on what prospects he finds along the Ohio."

"I hear there's many and many a mile and bend to that river," Letitia commented. "Goes clean to the Spanishers on the Mississippi, and ain't telling how far that is. Injuns all along the way, too."

"You're mighty cheerful to a friend whose husband is somewhere in the middle of all that!" Abby smiled and laughed. "My Edward can take care of himself. Besides, he has Simeon with him."

"Now there's a good, dependable man," Letitia nodded. "I ain't got much truck with couriers or *voyageurs* but Simeon Ridoux is different'n most of 'em."

"That's why Edward chose him."

Abby pulled a chair alongside the crib and resumed sewing together colorful rag squares. Eventually she would have the top of a quilt for the big double bed in the next room. As she worked, she

118

heard a sergeant's shouted commands from beyond the high stockade walls of the British fort that blocked her view of the westward reach of the Ohio.

"Drill," she sighed. "Every day and all day without end they drill."

"Except for the officers," Letitia sniffed. "They're too hoity-toity good to get dust on their boots or weary their muscles."

"Oh, I imagine before they came here, they had their share of drill over in England. How else would they become officers?"

"My Dean says their families *buy* their army rank."

"I wouldn't be too sure, Letty. I know the Connecticut Colony militia elected its officers and they drilled hard and long right beside the common soldiers. The same is true of New York Colony and here in Pennsylvania."

"But we ain't got families with castles and lands. Can you name a single American Baron or Duke or something like that!"

"Well—no."

"Ever heard of one of ours being a major like the fort's surgeon? Or a colonel like the commandant over there? I mean in the British army, not our colonial militias."

"No—but surely—"

"Take that pip-squeak of an ensign, like. Give him a rifle and he'd shoot off his own ass."

"Letty!"

"It's true." Letty broke off with an exclamation and gave her baby a mock glare. "If'n ye bite down like that once more, I'll starve ye for a week, so

119

help me!"

Abby laughed and the two women grew silent, contented as good friends are with one another's company, the attention of each centered on her own baby. Abby's moccasined foot continued to rock the cradle in an easy, slumberous rhythm. She studied the boy as her fingers plied the needle. "Henri," she mentally repeated the name in something like amazed awe. How much like Edward he looked! Fair of skin and dark of hair, eyes still that indeterminate baby tone but they would probably turn Edward's color. Would he be quick of mind and agile of body as Edward? How could he help but be! she made her mental answer.

Letty broke the silence. "Dean met a man newly come from Ligonier. He aims to settle somewhere near them Dutch Moravians up near Gnadenhutten."

"That's far up the Muskingum," Abby commented, "and an Indian mission besides. What takes him there?"

"Dean don't know exactly except the man says he'd be safer to settle up that way what with Indian trouble brewing."

Abby's foot froze. "Indian trouble!"

"That Pontiac again. The man heard back east that the red devil's stirring up the tribes against the British. Seems he wants to drive 'em out and bring the Frenchies back into the country."

"Why?" Abby asked.

"Better treatment from the *voyageurs*." Letty jerked a thumb over her shoulder in the direction of the fort just beyond the cabin. "We got a sample right here of why Pontiac, whoever he is, don't like English soldiers, traders or anything British."

"They've treated us well," Abby protested.

"But how? They're always treating us like we're no older'n my two boys and with as little brains. Even Major Harris gives us purges and bloodings like he's doing us a favor. That's what this Pontiac's mad about."

Abby shrugged, admitting reluctantly, "They can be superior."

"Is that the word, Abby? That means looking down their noses at us like they do?"

"Something like that."

"Well, maybe it's just all talk again like it was a time ago. Remember when all of a sudden there wasn't a chief or Sachem to be found in this whole western country?"

"But we learned they had been called to a meeting by Sir William Johnson, nothing more."

"Sure hope it's the same this time!" Letty buttoned her blouse over her breast, put the baby over her shoulder and patted his back until he emitted a resounding burp. "That'll do ye, young'un. I best be getting home and start sup. I swear men folk, big and little, pret' nigh eat me out of house'n home!"

Abby, in the days that followed, thought little of the tale Letty had brought. There was always dire talk of Indian trouble, and that was natural on this far edge of the frontier. Just as natural was the eager gathering of news and gossip from every source and few bothered to determine what might be fact and what might be only whisper. Everyone out here felt too isolated, individually and as a group, from events in the world beyond the forks of the river or over the hills eastward to Philadelphia or Virginia or New York. Even the new young king in far-off London was hardly more than a name.

The whisper of Indians always came again and always died down again. So Abby took care of the cabin and the garden in the intervals when Henri did not need her attention. She thought wistfully of Edward each day, wondering where he was, what he did, and said a fervent prayer for him. Time moved on from sunup to sundown to sunup again and there seemed to be no change except in the always fickle weather that could bring up a shower or a thunderstorm almost without warning. Then she would imagine Edward soaked to the skin, crouched under such shelter as he could find to shiver and wait out the storm. At such times she wondered how the grand ladies in Philadelphia, New York or Hartford lived. Probably without worry for their men since in the cities everything and everyone would be neatly protected from the elements. Abby, having always lived on the frontier, could only imagine such comfort.

In the meantime the life at Fort Pitt and the small settlement about it went on at its usual slow and easy rhythm marked by the predictable bugle calls from within the post, the morning crackle of muskets as the flag was raised and the evening explosions as the standard came down for the night. French trappers came and went, now and then a family moving west drove a heavily laden wagon in from Ligonier or beyond, or a Christian Indian from the Moravian mission would appear for a day or two, vanishing back into the forest as soon as he had bartered his peltry.

No change, she often thought, a security that the fine ladies back east had in theirs.

Except of late. It was nothing tangible—just a peculiar *feel*. Abby could express it in no other way. Mayhap it had something to do with the years in Onondaga Town with Moon Willow, Corn Dancer and—yes, in a strange way—the aloof, mysterious Keepers of the Faith. Behind the calm, aloof faces of those tall, graceful priestesses of "The Great Mysterious" Abby had often sensed a secret knowledge passed in some strange fashion from one Keeper to another.

She often looked at the sun-glinting, rippling flow of the placid three rivers as she occasionally strolled around the village or the post. Or she would become aware of the low ramparts of the hills along the Allegeway, the Monongahela or the open plains north and west of the confluence of the two to form the Ohio. Sunshine, peace, trees, grass, flowers—peace, and nothing to disturb it.

Yet it seemed that her eyes looked upon a wall of illusion behind which things stirred and hidden things moved. Sometimes she had the feeling that a threatening, evil, dominating mind somewhere out in the tangle of ridges and forest concentrated on this small triangle of land. She would involuntarily look up at the sky to find it invariably clear of all but the most innocent, woolly and fleecy of benign clouds.

123

As the days and weeks passed, she felt the unseen threat approach slowly and silently. She recalled how Corn Dancer and his band had suddenly burst from the forest with war bow, tomahawk, lance, knife and musket. Westover had died within hours—her parents, the man she was to marry, her friends and neighbors murdered and she stumbling along the forest glades an Indian captive along with twenty or so other young women, most of whom did not live to reach their destination.

She tried to cast aside the dark thoughts and feelings and sometimes she would succeed for days on end. But they would return and she'd warily watch woods and streams, hover over Henri in his crib or hold him close against her if she took him out for the sun and river breezes. Now and then she would venture to the encampment of the *voyageurs*, who welcomed her because Edward was French and Simeon Ridoux one of their own.

They spoke freely to her but could tell her only that the chiefs and Sachems had left their villages to the old men or secondary chiefs and had gone on a mysterious mission to some equally mysterious place.

"I have heard," one said adding a morsel of news, "that they have gone north toward New France. But that is only talk, *vous savez*. We hear nothing *qui est de preuve materielle*."

"Nothing of substantial proof," Abby repeated and sighed. "Well, I suppose that will come in time."

"*Oui*—or not at all, madame." The man chuckled. "Eh, remember, Indians gossip like all of us."

True enough, she thought, and had to return home.

Each week or ten days a supply wagon came from Ligonier with dispatches for the fort along with powder, musket balls and other items needed by the soldiers. One Colonel Bouquet commanded at Ligonier, a Swiss professional soldier in British pay who apparently kept his ears more attuned than the English. Still, he reported no more than the absence of chiefs of the Ohio River tribes.

"It's wrong, Letty," Abby finally said to her friend.

"Sounds good to me," Letty answered carelessly. "The less Indians I see, the safer I feel."

"And that's exactly the wrong way to think. It's when you *don't* see 'em you should worry."

Letty shrugged. "Tell our commandant. His lordship just might listen to you, but I doubt it."

So did Abby but she had to warn someone who could do something to ward off disaster. That very afternoon, she sat primly in a chair across a table from Colonel Carleton, resplendent in his red and gold uniform and his newly combed and dressed wig with a watered silk ribbon about the queue. He wore a black framed monocle between cheek bone and eyebrow. It was also adorned with a watered silk ribbon attached to his red, elaborately embroidered vest.

"You are telling me, mistress, that the Indians are a threat?"

"I am, Colonel."

The officer sighed wearily and spoke with the patience he would give to a child. "But, mistress, there is no word of them. None of their chiefs are about to threaten us."

"It's *that,* Colonel, that makes me feel—or rather *know*—there is trouble brewing."

"Indeed! And pray what is your experience, since you are obviously not a soldier either of the king's army or of any of these colonial militias."

"I was forced to live with Indians, Colonel. I was taken prisoner in Connecticut Colony and adopted into the Onondaga tribe of the Iroquois Confederacy."

"Live with them!" The monocle dropped from his eye and he used the ribbon to whirl it about his finger as he stared at her with new interest. "For how long?"

"Over a year, Colonel."

He pursed his lips and she didn't like the ghost of a smile that played at the corners of his mouth. It suggested lechery lurking beneath the surface of his voice.

"Did they—ahem—molest you, mistress?"

"That is not the point, sir. We are speaking of present danger."

"Present—ah, yes. You had no danger with the Iroquois, I assume?"

"On the contrary, I would have been killed several times had it not been for a war leader. He saved me from the tomahawk and lance until we reached Onondaga Town."

"War leader?" He studied her slowly from the crown of her head to her moccasins and she felt his eyes strip her full, decorous gray dress right off her body, leaving her fully exposed. Her gorge began to

126

rise and she struggled to keep anger from showing in her face. Her knuckles grew white with the increased pressure of her clasped hands.

"War leader, Colonel. I was adopted into the *ohwachira* by a blood ceremony that made me an Onondaga. So I know Indian ways of acting and thinking."

"Indeed, I think you must. This 'war leader'—was he young and handsome? Did he make you his woman?" His smile widened and he dropped back to his chair. "Indian plaything, I take it."

She jumped to her feet, arms stiff at her sides, her hands balled into fists. "Colonel! There is no need for—"

"Close questioning? I can readily see it. And how did you swing from a savage chieftain to an almost equally savage courier, mistress?"

She took a lunging step toward him, stopped herself and drew up to her full height. "I came to give you a warning out of my own knowledge of Indian ways, Colonel. You give me insults, sneers and dirty hints in return. I have no more to say to you. Good day!"

"Mistress!" She stopped short, her hand on the door latch, and turned. Carleton lounged back in his chair, the monocle out of his eye but whirling about on its ribbon, the disdainful smile still on his lips. "Warning of your own knowledge, eh? D'ye think that a garrison of His Majesty's troops doesn't have knowledge of what goes on! Certainly ours is grounded on more than that gained in lice-infested Indian blankets, where at one time or another you obviously gained yours."

She gasped as shock ran through her. Then, her mind entirely a red haze of anger, she took two long strides to the table and leaned across it. Before Carleton could move, her palm smacked loudly across his cheek and jaw, the force of her blow snapping his head to one side.

She whipped about and was out the door before he could recover. She raced to the gate where the lounging guards came to surprised attention. She had come within a few steps of the gate when Carleton's roaring bellow sounded behind her.

"Arrest that strumpet!"

Instantly the guards blocked her, their bayoneted crossed muskets forming a barrier she could not swing around or hurdle. She stopped and Carleton bellowed again.

"Bring her here! Now!"

She whipped around in defiance. He came striding to her. Soldiers appeared before their cabins and she heard a stir beyond the gate that told her her neighbors had heard the disturbance. Carleton came storming up, his face red except for the slightly white area on his cheek where her hand had struck.

"By God! you'll pay for this!"

"If I'm delayed one more minute—if you or one of your men touch me, I'll shout your insults at the top of my voice!"

"Colonel Carleton!" another voice thundered and Harris stepped between Abby and the commandant. "What is the meaning of this?"

"I'll have her stripped to the waist and dragged

behind a wagon around the post. She'll have bleeding stripes—"

"Colonel Carleton!"

"Shut up, sir! I'm in command here."

"Shut up yourself, sir. You're disgracing your uniform and yourself. I know Mistress Forny. Do I report this directly to Lord Amherst or do you return with me to your quarters and explain?"

Carleton's face turned a deeper, darker red and a vein jumped so violently in his temple that it threatened to burst. "You dare not, Harris."

"Oh, don't I, though! It would give me great pleasure, sir. I dislike to serve under a boor."

The two blocking gate guards, Carleton, Major Harris, Abby and the small knot of settlers remained unmoving as though carved in stone. Carleton and Harris locked eyes. Harris spoke first.

"Your quarters, Colonel?" he suggested coldly then threw a look at Abby. "You may go home, Mistress Forny. After I talk to Colonel Carleton—"

"She leaves Fort Pitt!" Carleton snapped. He had gained control of his voice but his nostrils flared wildly with each breath.

"I'll do no such—" Abby started.

"Mistress Forny!" Harris's tone now had a whip and snap Abby had never heard before. "Please to go home."

She glared at him then at Carleton and a modicum of reason cut through her anger. She flounced about and, as the guards stepped aside, strode through the stockade gate, checking her impulse to race to the house for a musket or a whip to use on Carleton. She had gone but a few feet when a sound behind her whirled her about.

The stockade gates had closed and she heard the heavy bars behind the barrier fall into place.

X

Abby raged and fumed within the limited space of her few cabin rooms. Her hands fairly itched to grab up the musket Edward had placed over the fireplace, storm the palisade of logs about the fort and end Carleton's arrogance once and for all. She knew that her time with Corn Dancer and the Onondagas had nurtured his savage anger. It had also made the arrogant Britisher's wound to her pride the more keen, but a great deal of that deep sense of insult had come from Edward's touchy Gascon temper. Both Indian and Frenchman had shaped her personal sense of worth along with the Brewster family sense of self-sufficiency.

If it had not been for tiny Henri's demands on her attention now and then she might have done something very, very foolish. She had in effect slammed the door in the curious faces of her neighbors, knowing she could not have told them a coherent story and it was more than an hour before she at last admitted Letitia. The woman listened to Abby's story with growing shock and anger. She could no longer contain herself when Abby finished telling of her interview with Carleton.

"That bastard! Really, that bastard!" She saw Abby's shocked, rounded eyes but only tossed her head. "That's what he is. That's all he is! I know I ain't ladylike in my language but why was he talking to you like that? He had no call for a single word."

"I know, but there's nothing we can do about it," Abby answered in resigned anger. "We're part of England and under its rule—"

"And of soldiers like Carleton," Letty added, a snap to her voice. "Oh, they're high and mighty now but the time's not far off when we'll take 'em down a peg."

"Careful," Abby warned. "Your talk's getting close to treason."

"And his was pure gutter dirt, pure insult. Do they think they can treat us all—"

"Not all, Letty. Just me."

"Today just you." Letty jumped up and paced

back and forth across the room. "But my Dean and some of the other men in the settlement have been treated like scum or barnyard shit on their fine boots."

"Letty!"

"I mean it. Maybe we're all 'Colonials,' as they call us, but we're most all English descent—like they are. Just happens we don't live across the ocean on their fine little island in their big fancy stone houses and castles. Does that make us any the worse!"

Before Abby could answer a startling tattoo of knuckles on the door swung both women around. The knock came again and Abby flung open the door. Major Harris faced her and she read both deep anger and great embarrassment in his eyes and demeanor. He started to speak, saw Letty and his lips snapped closed. He swallowed deeply as he swept off his lace-trimmed tricorn hat.

"Mistress Forny, could we have a word? In private?"

"Of course, Major. Do come in."

The officer entered and stared hard at Letty, who flushed and managed a bobbing, awkward curtsy. She found her voice. "I'll be leaving, Abby. If ye have need of me—"

"I don't, Letty. Our fort doctor is not our fort commandant."

Harris's face turned beet red and he choked back a retort. He glared at Letty, who swung around him and fled the cabin. The doctor closed the door after her and turned to face Abby. She stood by the table in the center of the room, straight and tense with anger. She realized she had again clenched her fists and

133

knew it was the gold-trimmed, red uniform and not the man before her that had once more set her blood to boiling. She regained composure and her shoulder muscles loosened.

"Won't you be seated, Major?"

"Thank you, Mistress Forny. You make my task easier."

But he did not accept the chair she had indicated with a curt nod. He tucked his hat under his arm. "I have come to make amends, if I can."

"That will be hard, sir."

"Indeed, I am aware of that. But allow me to try." His gesture indicated the fort, only a portion of its high log walls visible through the window. "There was a contretemps and an altercation between you and Colonel Carleton?"

"That hardly describes it, sir. He was nasty and insulting beyond all reason."

"I witnessed a good deal of it, mistress, and it distressed me. No matter what provocation you may have committed—"

"*I* committed! *I?*"

Colonel Carleton said you presumed to tell him his military duty and—"

Her indignation fairly choked her. Then a modicum of reason returned. She understood that Carleton must have twisted the facts beyond all recognition and that Major Harris knew only what he had been told by the commandant. She held tight control of her voice, and once more indicated the chair.

"I beg you, Major, be seated. There is much to be said between us."

He studied her a second and then with a courtly

nod walked to the chair and sat down. Abby groped for her own chair beside Henri's crib and took a deal of time to settle herself in order to gain at least a semblance of control over her seething anger. It flashed through her mind that Letty was right. These boors in red and gold—she caught herself up. That had no direct bearing on what had happened.

"Did Colonel—did *he* tell you why I asked to see him, sir?"

"As I told you, you presumed to tell the Colonel his duty."

"I brought a warning, sir, and no more. There is Indian trouble brewing and it will soon be upon us."

"Was that it?" Harris exclaimed in a tone of relief. "But we have dispatches on that matter from our posts at Ligonier and further east."

"Do you have word that the couriers and *voyageurs* report that the chiefs have disappeared and the tribal villages are suddenly moving north and westward?"

Harris shook his head. "Nay, madam, we do not have that word—if it is true. Colonel Bouquet's dispatches say that the Indians are as peaceful as they have ever been."

"Does he say where they are?"

"Should he? I would presume they're either hunting north of the river as they usually do or killing one another south of the river, as they also usually do."

"Then your Colonel Bouquet is also misinformed, sir."

"But there's no sign of trouble anywhere!"

"It's a false peace, Major. I tried to tell your precious commandant what I have learned from the

135

couriers camped on the river and of what I learned of Indian ways and thinking when I was their prisoner. I was not only laughed at but insulted. At the very best he made me out a doxie."

"He went too far, Madam Forny. I told him as much."

"What insults did you get for your trouble?" she demanded.

"None, madam. I vowed to put him on official report to both Colonel Bouquet and General Lord Amherst if anything like this happens again."

"He had best stay inside the stockade for a long time to come, Major. My neighbors have heard a deal of it—"

"And you told your friend more," Harris added dryly.

Abby had the grace to flush. "I did, sir. Insult—anger—yes, I told her. She will spread the story. The people here about do not like his high-handed ways. They do not even like the manner of that fuzz-cheeked subaltern with his superior airs. The commandant could be in serious danger if—"

"Madam!" Major Harris's voice cracked in abrupt ire, "Do you or any of your friends dare threaten an officer of His Majesty's army!"

"If he's an oaf, a foul-mouth, an insulter of good decent women—yes."

Harris stood up with ominously slow movements and met her angry eyes directly with his own. His voice held a cold unemotional tone as ominous as his action. "The first to put a hand on Colonel Carleton or even the lowliest private in the king's uniform will be hanged higher than Haman, madam."

136

"It will happen, sir. If anyone is hanged, there will be blood because of it. We'll deal out English justice right here, sir, without the Royal Court's blessing if need be. We've all had quite enough of Colonel Carleton!"

"Treason, madam!" Harris thundered.

"Nay, Major, self-defense and self-pride." Abby suddenly realized how dangerously far her anger and the stiff military pride of the good doctor had led them. She took an impulsive step to him and placed her hand on his chest in conciliation. "Major! Please?"

He stood like a stone for long seconds, jaw outthrust and eyes shooting fire. Then he lost his stiffness and shook his head in wonder at what they had inadvertently said to one another.

"You're right, Madam Forny. I'm afraid all of us have injected too much bile into the day—deliberately or otherwise. I actually came to apologize."

"Carleton sent you!"

"No, I came on my own accord. I have suggested that the colonel stay within the post for the rest of the day." He smiled crookedly at her. "You see, I anticipated your thoughts. I have also suggested that early tomorrow he take a small hunting party north beyond the forks. Fresh air and game should cool him off."

"He accepted?"

"He had the report I threatened in mind. Will your friends cool off in a week of his absence?"

She shrugged. "A little, I suppose, as I will. It would be better if he happened to be transferred."

"That is hardly possible without reason, madam."

She almost snapped that the reason had already occurred but bit back the words. Instead she promised, "I will do what I can to allay any hard feelings in the settlement, Major. But the less any of us see of the colonel, the better."

"You really confine him to quarters, madam."

"For his own safety and for the general peace. He himself has done the confining." She shrugged again. "But we are on the edge of quarrel once more. I will do what I can."

"Thank you." He walked to the door, opened it, turned and bowed. To her surprise his old smile flashed out with all its warmth. "Madam Forny, I wish all Colonials had your good sense."

"Thank you, but I could lose it easily at the very sight of Carleton."

"You'll see little or nothing of him. Good day, madam. You do accept my apologies for needless and heedless insults?"

"I do, Major."

Abby made certain she would not see Carleton, keeping herself within the cabin, doing unnecessary cleaning, giving Henri a great deal of time and even starting with flour, water and yeast to batch bread for baking in the fireplace. She had visitors twice, women of the settlement who were angered by Letty's story of the incident. Abby knew that enough ill feeling had been created so she thanked her visitors, admitted the insults but hinted that Carleton, despite his birth, breeding and position, really could not help his basic crude personality. It sounded rather weak, even to herself, but the women somewhat dubiously accepted it. Abby turned from the door with relief when the visits ended.

Henri's cry of hunger awakened her early the next morning as it always did. She gave him her breast and rocked as he suckled. Contentment stole over her, contentment and love for both her men. Just then Henri burped and she laughed as she patted his plump little bottom.

"Now *that* was something only a big man would say," she told the baby and laughed in sheer delight. His lips eagerly sought her nipple again and his tiny fingers clutched her breast. She continued to rock and sing.

Henri fed and sleepily content, she took him to the table where she changed and washed him, then put him in his rocking crib. She crooned to him as her foot moved the crib in a lulling rhythm. Soon his eyes closed so she dared to check the bread dough in its pan on the work table. It had risen beautifully and she dropped the cloth back over it to stir up the hearth for the baking.

As she passed a window, movement and men's voices outside caught her attention. Carleton and two junior officers rode at an angle from the stockade to the Allegeway and along its south bank, around the first bend. They carried hunting muskets and game sacks slung over their shoulders. Abby's jaw hardened and her eyes flashed as she watched the small party take the river path to the northern woods and hills. Major Harris, she thought, had kept his promise and the obnoxious Carleton would not be seen for the remainder of the day. She only wished it could be forever.

She dismissed the thought and the man and went

about her baking and household chores. She wondered if there could be some means of living out of sight of the post. She would ask Edward—she stopped short, aghast at a new thought. What would Edward do when he learned of Carleton's actions and speech! It would be like her fire-eating Gascon to try to take a whip to the officer! A vivid picture of the result flashed through her mind—Edward shot out of hand, or hanged following a farcical court-martial in the post. At best, he would be placed in irons and sent to Ligonier or beyond for trial. No matter what the cause, no one struck one of His Majesty's officers with impunity.

She dropped into a chair, stunned by the impact of the new threat. She must get word to Edward, warning him to stay away. No, that wouldn't do. It would only bring him on all the faster. She had to go to him! How could she? What about Henri? He could not be left alone! She instantly thought of the Indian cradle boards. She could easily barter with the mission Indians for one at Gnadenhutten, put Henri in it and carry him on her back as she had seen many an Iroquois woman do. True, there was a tremendous risk but Henri needed her milk in order to live. One risk offset the other.

She thought of the courier encampment and her face instantly cleared. That was the answer. She understood this chief, Pontiac, hated the English but not the French. A courier or *voyageur* could move safely down the river to Edward. He could be told to make a wide circuit of the post and wait to join her to the east. She would explain what had happened and persuade him to go up the Allegeway with her to the

Lake of the Eries instead of returning to Fort Pitt.

She jumped up, ran to the door and jerked it open. She raced outside but stopped short after a step when a great shout of alarm riveted her attention toward the fort. Soldiers at the gate and atop the stockade pointed northward. Her neighbors streamed from their cabins and they, too, looked north.

She raced back around her own cabin to a point where the high fort stockade would not block her vision. She instantly saw a dense plume of smoke rising above the trees along the river. A cabin afire. Then a new shout whipped her about and she saw more smoke plumes and also a family in a careening wagon, the driver standing up, unmercifully plying the whip to his lathered beasts.

"Shawnee!"

"Seneca!"

"Injun raid!"

The shouts came from all directions. She heard another from the stockade walls. "The colonel! I saw 'em kill him! Right out there, beyond the river!"

Abby whirled about, raced to her cabin and grabbed up Henri. When she emerged with the baby, the racing wagon and its terrified passengers had reached the farthest cabin but pounded on to the fort, the whip ceaselessly cracking. Abby glimpsed the frightened faces of the children in the wagon bed back of the seat. The woman beside the man up on the seat screeched mad alarm.

"Injuns! Everywhere! Back o'us. They kilt at least a dozen I saw myself and—"

Her voice trailed off as the wagon shot through the stockade gate. Abby now saw several smoke spirals and then, down the road leading to Ligonier, she glimpsed crouching, racing red warriors. She screamed herself, unaware of it, and raced for the gate, clutching Henri. She became part of a small flood of men and women seeking sanctuary.

XI

The gates slammed shut on the very heels of the last fugitive and heavy bars thudded down into thick iron brackets. A milling crowd of men and women filled the once vacant parade ground but the red-uniformed soldiers moved with swift, controlled precision. Abby now understood the reason for the daily drills that had heretofore seemed so useless and boring.

All the storage, soldiers' and officers' cabins had been built against the walls so the structures themselves became part of the stockade. Short ladders led to their sloped roofs ending just at the wide firing platform encircling the walls. Where there were no cabins, longer ladders placed at regular intervals enabled the soldiers to scramble up them.

For all his age, Major Harris, now in full command, clambered up to the platform, saber swinging against his legs, two flintlock pistols in his wide sash, powder horn and box of pistol balls attached to a wide, heavy belt under his sash. He shouted orders and the junior officers jumped to the snap of his voice.

"Attach bayonets!" The order was repeated around the walls.

The heavy blades snapped out of their scabbards and soon each musket barrel was also a long, triangular-shaped sword, the sun glinting evilly off the metal. Abby watched in horrible fascination as men rolled out powder and bullet kegs, placing them to flank each ladder. Soldiers on the ground checked their muskets and flintlocks, rammed powder, patches and leaden balls down the musket barrels and then waited, like coiled springs, for further orders. Up on the firing platform, the soldiers aimed their muskets.

Harris's bellow lifted above the constant but controlled noise and activity.

"Hold fire! The red devils are beyond range. Hold fire until ordered to pull your trigger!"

The juniors repeated the order. Suddenly every-

144

thing and everyone within the post seemed to freeze, swords drawn, muskets leveled, the settlers waiting and looking on in wide-eyed fear.

Abby could see nothing but the tight and thick stockade walls. For a time there seemed to be only a deep, frightening silence beyond them. The war whoops and wild Indian firing had stopped but Abby knew it was a false, momentary calm. A sergeant at his post above the stockade broke it.

"They've crossed the rivers, Major. More of 'em have cut the road eastward."

"How many?" Harris shouted.

"How many leaves on the trees, sir! They're moving toward us slowly and canoeing across the rivers."

"Hold your fire. Give 'em time to get closer. They'll hit us hard. If we kill enough of 'em on the first sally, they will catch a bellyfull and could give us up as a bad idea."

"Not from the looks of this bunch, sir."

"I can see 'em from over here," Harris answered. "Don't let their war paint and screeches faze you."

"We're soldiers, sir."

"Thank God for that!"

Silence again except for an unfamiliar sound, something like a whisper from beyond the walls. It shattered abruptly. A small, round object like a cannonball arched over the walls against the clear sky and landed with a thud on the parade ground. A woman screamed. A man cried, "Oh, my God!"

A subaltern shouted. "Colonel Carleton's head, Major! less the hair."

145

That was to be only the first of the horrors that would come. A bone-chilling, savage yell sounded. Abby didn't hear the order but Harris must have passed it on in some manner. Muskets and rifles crashed outside the walls. The soldiers on the platform fired in return, dropping their empty muskets to seize freshly loaded ones passed up to them by the men below the platform. The fired muskets were instantly reloaded even as the second volley crashed. Powder smoke filled the area within the walls, choking and blinding. More volleys crashed and Abby heard answering fire from the attackers. A flaming brand sailed over the walls to fall harmlessly by the flagpole but others instantly followed. One struck the shingled roof of a supply cabin and began to smolder on the thin shakes.

"Watermen!" a voice bellowed. "Cover the powder kegs!

A bucket line of soldiers formed from the post's well to the endangered cabin. At the same moment the gates suddenly shook from a mighty blow from without. The inner bars, slammed against the iron brackets, angrily puffed wood powder and splinters but the gate held. Another blow struck it but the men on the firing platforms now concentrated their fire on the Indians trying to shatter the gates.

Major Harris seemed to be everywhere at once, meeting each attack as it struck, even anticipating some. Abby heard his shouted orders from first one direction then another.

More firebrands sailed over the walls. One struck a tightly closed keg of powder, bouncing high up and

146

away. A subaltern yelled from the platform.

"They're bringing up ladders!"

"Gun loaders!" Harris ordered. "Up on the walls! With muskets and bayonets! Settler men! Load muskets!"

Letitia's husband raced by Abby to the wall, grabbed up a musket dropped from above and rammed powder and shot down the barrel. At the same instant painted dark faces topped the walls. Tomahawks and lances flashed. Muskets made a constant roar. Bayonets flashed, first bright steel then crimson as they sank deep into bronze bodies. A lance whipped by Abby's head to bury itself deep in the ground just beyond her. The women huddled about her came closer as though to find shelter and protection by the touch of the others.

"Mistress Forny!" Harris yelled. Through the swirling fog of powder smoke, she saw him on the platform atop the commandant's cabin. "Mistress Forny!"

"Here, Major!"

He pointed to another building far down the line. "Hospital! Take your women there! Nurses for the wounded. Hurry!"

The battle for the stockade walls raged. Muskets flashed and roared, swords, bayonets and tomahawks made deadly, bloody havoc. The townsmen did the loading below, while more soldiers manned the walls but still it was touch and go. A soldier did a spinning fall to the ground inside the stockade, an Indian musket ball between his eyes. Somehow Abby, amidst the pandemonium, managed to gather the

147

women and lead them to the cabin Harris had indicated. She looked over her shoulder to see a knot of soldiers using long bayonets to drop the attackers. One man swept up a dropped tomahawk and buried it deep in a red skull. The ladders were pushed away from the ramparts and Abby heard wild yells of anger and hate interlacing the barking, fearful war whoops.

Then she plunged through the door of the cabin. It took her a moment to adjust her eyes to the comparative darkness of the interior. Then she saw a sanded, bare floor on which pallets lay in orderly rows. She saw water kegs, stacks of cloth of all colors and sizes to be used as bandages.

She had little time to take stock or to organize the women, who looked more stunned than frightened. She had a fleeting thought of thankfulness for the harsh way the stern wilderness had trained her aides. They were only momentarily confused by the suddenness and power of the attack.

"Letty!" Her friend stepped instantly to her side. Abby indicated the far wall and handed over Henri. "The babies and children over there, out of the way. An older girl to guard them. Hurry! We'll be swamped in a few minutes!"

As Abby turned to another woman, she heard Letty's crisp orders. She herself assigned women to various stations around the room between the pallets.

Letty reappeared beside her. "The young'n's as safe as they'll ever be in this blazing hell."

"How about the bandages? How many?"

"Like usual—rags of all shapes and sizes, some

148

clean and some dirty, parts of old shirts and dresses and things like that. How many? Who knows until we use 'em?"

Abby lifted her voice to catch the attention of all the women. "Off with your petticoats! They make bandages. Hurry! Don't forget pantaloons! They make bandages, too. No man in here will care where they came from."

She followed her own orders. Her underskirts and garments fell on the pile with the rest. Their coarse skirts once more secure around their waists, the women resumed their stations between the pallets.

Abby stood in the doorway. She first saw a new, dense cloud of smoke rising beyond the palisade to the east. The blue fog swirling within the post now smelled of wood rather than gunpowder. Abby instantly knew what had happened. She gripped the frame of the doorway and tightly closed her eyes. Her home would be going up in flames along with the rest.

"The second time in my life," she said, not knowing she spoke aloud.

"What'd you say?" Letty asked at her shoulder and then gasped as she, too, saw the lowering cloud of destruction. "Our homes! Everything's gone!"

"Except our lives. We can thank the Good Lord for that."

"But not for much else."

"That's enough. Everything else we can rebuild or replace." She pointed out across the parade ground to the far wall. "Here come the first of the poor boys. Are we ready?"

149

"As much as your Good Lord will let us be."

Furious firing broke out anew all along the walls. Yells and shouts arose as men came toward the cabin, carrying or supporting sagging wounded between them. Abby spoke swiftly over her shoulder. "If the wounds are not serious, bandage them and send them back. We need pallets and space. Put the badly hurt ones in the far back row and work forward."

"How about Major Harris? He's the doctor."

"Now he's the commandant, too. We'll make do without him until he can help."

"If he can. Injuns can kill or hurt him as quick as another."

Abby did not say that was exactly what she feared but stepped aside as the first man was brought in. A tomahawk blade had slashed into his upper arm, almost severing it and Abby felt certain the bone had been cut through. Blood streamed out the sleeve of his dangling arm. The flow had to be stopped immediately otherwise the man would die. Before Abby could give an order, Letty took charge.

"Take him back there. Rag about the arm and twisted tight with a stick."

Abby turned to meet the second casualty, a soldier with an arrow protruding from his shoulder. He spoke in a sibilant whisper through tightly set lips. "Broke off, mu'um. Head's still in there. I can feel it."

Abby whirled him about and he cried out in pain as she jerked his red jacket off his shoulders, ripped the shirt beneath to look at the wound. She saw the splintered end of an arrow shaft, a slow welling of blood about it. The head must come out or it would infect, she knew, but not immediately. Surgeon Harris, if *he* lived, would have time enough to cut out the wicked, triangular barbed metal head.

"Can you use the arm?"

"Hardly, m'um. It's stiff. Hurts like hell."

"Your other arm?"

He moved it easily. "Ain't hurted, mu'um."

"That's to the good." She signaled one of the women. "Bandage that arm. Soldier, they need you out there to pass up muskets. Can you do it?"

"Sure—but not easy like."

"Enough to save all our scalps!" She spoke to the woman. "Send him back out when he's bandaged. Work fast."

They were the first two of a procession that, although not steady, seemed to last forever. The pallets slowly filled, though the women sent more men back to the walls than they allowed to remain. Blood flowed across the floor and the women's clothing became a dark, dull repellent red. Abby herself now worked with the wounded. She saw a larger boy among the children, and put him to carrying out filled buckets of soaked bandages and to scattering dirt over the floor to soak up the snaking rivulets of red that covered it and made it slippery.

Outside, the attack continued its fury without let-up. More men came in, some pallet cases, more to be bandaged and sent back to help hold the firing platform and the stockade at all costs. Now and then a woman would become sickened by all the blood. She would empty her stomach in the nearest pail of red-stained bandages and return to the task at hand. Abby, cold sweat on her forehead and her body shaking had to retch two or three times. But she would recover in a moment, attend to the wounded at hand and swiftly turn to the next. There was always one waiting.

Her hands and forearms were stained, her dress becoming saturated, but she worked on. She finished an arm sling for a soldier with a bullet-smashed shoulder and turned to the next. She froze and her eyes widened and rounded. Major Harris, using a bullet-smashed musket as a crutch, hobbled in. His left hip bled profusely from a long, deep gash. His haggard face had paled but he held tight control of his voice.

"Mistress Forny, attend this cut."

Abby hurried by him as he dropped on a stool and extended the wounded leg. "Slash the cloth to get to the cut, madam. Bandage it."

Abby worked fast while Harris looked around the room. He gritted his teeth as Abby touched the raw flesh of his wound and kept them clenched as he spoke. "My surgical apron . . . just inside the door over there."

His quick, painful nod indicated a closed door at a far end of the room that Abby had not noticed before. "My kit of tools and knives inside . . . on a shelf. Bring it. On shelf—bottles of laudanum . . . whiskey jugs . . . bring 'em."

"Be quiet, major," Abby cut in. "You bleed the more."

"Hell's bells, madam! I'm a surgeon! You tell me

my business!''

"No, Major.''

"Then get on with the bandage. Twist rag on a
stick tight above the slash. Stop bleeding. Send
someone for apron . . . tools.''

Abby sent the boy who threw out the bandages and
scattered dirt on the floor for Major Harris's tools and
medicines. The old man looked around the cabin
once more. "I'm needed here—badly. Look smart to
my things, madam.''

"They'll be here in a minute. Who directs outside?''

"Captain Blaine. Good man. Knows what he's
doing about those devils out there.''

The raging fight for the stockade walls continued
and the sound raged and roared through the open
door. The boy came up and Harris snapped a heavy
cloth gown out of his arms and tossed it to Abby.

"Help me into it, madam. Tie it—in back.''

She helped him stand up as he worked himself to
his feet. The gown was stiff with ancient, clotted
blood, some of which must have dated back to his
student days. Each stain was like a medal, a certificate
of his experience and knowledge, Abby knew, but she
forgot the whole business as the boy shoved a satchel
of medicine in her hand and another, heavier one,
filled with instruments.

Harris gave each a swift but thorough inspection.
"The saw—the surgical saw,'' he snapped. "Kegs of
whiskey? Blast your eyes! roll 'em out! Irons back
there. Put 'em in fireplace. Red hot to cauterize!
Damn it! Move!''

153

His voice roared and the boy jumped to follow orders.

Harris spoke evenly to Abby, pointing down a row of pallets. "The fourth man . . . arm shredded . . . has to . . . come off."

The man heard Harris and he screamed in terror. "No! My God, no! Can't go through with it. Let me die!"

"Mistress Forny," Harris gritted. "Force whiskey down his gullet until he's dead drunk. Come with me. Bring laudanum. Send boy outside for a bit of wood the man can chew on. He'll need it."

Fighting pain himself with every move, Major Harris attended the soldiers. The first man finally became unconscious from the fiery frontier whiskey and drops of laudanum. Harris started to work. He first forced the small block of wood between the man's teeth, had the boy hold it and then his scalpel cut deep through flesh down to the bone. The man screamed, the wood fell and Harris swung his open hand at the boy, rocking his head to one side.

"The wood! Idiot! Get it back in his teeth. Mistress, another man in here—now!"

Abby halted a man with a bandaged head who was about to leave. In a moment, under Harris's direction, the man knelt on the screaming soldier with his full weight, holding his arms out and on the floor by brute strength. The surgical saw sounded "burr-har" through the arm bone. Abby, her senses fading, grimly held on despite the whirling room, the screams in her ears. The arm finally fell away.

"Hot iron!" Harris shouted.

154

The smell of burning flesh filled the room as Harris used the dull red iron to cauterize the stump and seal the arteries and veins. The soldier sagged limp on his bloody mattress, completely unconscious if not dead. Abby again tried to vomit but her stomach only heaved painfully, spasmodically. It had long ago completely emptied.

She did not know that Harris looked at her sharply and snapped to another woman, "Take her place."

"I can't! Afore God, I can't!"

"Afore God, you will!"

The yells, curses, war whoops and screams outside mingled with the steady blasting of muskets, could hardly be heard above the din in the hospital cabin. Abby lost all ability to think. She would have remained standing or seated, frozen in a near catatonic state if it had not been for her instinctive need to follow Harris's roaring orders, moving from pallet to pallet with him with weaving, uncertain steps.

She did not know that the light slowly faded. She was not aware that the Indian yells steadily lessened as had the musket fire. Candles flamed bright feathers of flame throughout the cabin but they were only spots of eye-smarting pain to Abby, an added small horror among all the greater ones she had endured.

Fear suddenly lanced through her brain-fog and she whirled about to run to the rear of the cabin. "Henri! Henri! Lord Above, Henri!"

A strange woman stood before her, holding up a blanket-wrapped small bundle. "Here he is, Mistress

Forny. He's yelled and screamed himself to sleep."

"Sleep? Sure? Just sleep?"

"Hiccuped, too, Mistress. He's a strong young'un, that baby."

The release from panic fear proved too much. Abby fell in a dead faint.

XII

On the third day of the siege, Harris and Abby, Letitia and their children transferred from the hospital cabin to that of a subaltern who had caught an Indian arrow in his throat the previous day. Although before the attack the fuzz-cheeked sub-lieutenant had treated the settlers with disdain, frequently using snuff in delicate pinches, he had died with pistol in one hand, saber in the other, fighting off the Indians, tipping over their scaling ladders with the bravery of the most seasoned soldier. He now lay beneath one of the increasing number of dirt mounds around the flagpole.

The morning after her move to new quarters, Abby awakened at first dawn. Faint gray outlined the closed and bolted door and the windows along the front of the cabin. The rear wall was solid, forming part of the stockade, its thick logs a sure barrier against the Indians who constantly prowled around the walls seeking a weak spot or a momentarily unguarded area whereby entry might be made.

For several moments Abby lay without moving, ears strained for any slight sound from the other side of that all-important wall. None came. For an unbelievably short period the whole world was wrapped in a wonderful, silent peace. A single shot shattered the illusion and then renewed muffled shouts and curses, Indian whoops, signaled the start of another day of bloodshed and death.

Two young subalterns had shared this cabin. Now one was dead; the other lay on a pallet in the hospital cabin, leaving the bunks for Abby and Letitia. The single room was narrow but long, a fieldstone fireplace at one end, now black and ash-filled. A table dominated the center, chairs pushed back from it as the former tenants had hastily left them. Two heavy, brass-bound trunks sat along one wall, their rounded lids closed. The door of a corner cupboard stood open revealing red uniform dress coats and lace-trimmed tricorn hats hanging desolately within.

Henri made a fussing sound and Abby instantly returned to the blanket-bundled baby. He made more hungry sounds, urgent and impatient. Abby started to unbutton her blouse to feed him and then saw Letty's twin boys watching her from the barred doorway. She hastily closed her blouse against their curiosity.

"They've seen tits before," Letty spoke from her bunk. "They've watched me feed my youngest time and again. Pay 'em no mind unless it fashes you."

"I'm not used to it," Abby said apologetically.

"Shoo! you will be come your third or fourth'n!" She cocked her head to listen to sounds from outside. "Them devils ain't yelling and shooting as much this morning. Reckon they're gettin' tired?"

"No—at least not yet."

Letty swung out of her bunk, her blood-stained skirt twisting up and aside to reveal dirty bare legs and thick thighs. "Them boys'll do more good toting water buckets to the sojers out there. Go ahead, boys. Scoot!"

The boys lifted the bar and flung open the door. Bright sunlight streamed in and the bare room became transformed. Fresh air stirred Abby's hair as she opened her blouse and held Henri to her breast. He made hungry, sucking sounds and she felt relief at the tug of his lips on her nipple and the slow easing of the pressure of her milk. A sudden fusillade from the walls made her jerk up her head. But silence fell again and she eased back in her bunk and made crooning sounds to Henri.

Letty spoke from her bunk as she shifted her own baby to her swollen white breast. "Ain't this one hell of a time and place to be a mother!"

Abby managed a wispy smile. "We're not the first

159

wilderness women to nurse like this."

"Too bad we won't be the last." Letty drew several deep breaths. "Lord! that morning air's good to smell!"

"I wish we could leave the door and windows open all night," Abby nodded.

"And let that poison night air in!" Letty gasped. "It'd kill us. Why you think they close up tight over at the hospital!"

"I know . . . but somehow . . ."

"What?"

"I don't know, Letty. All that stink trapped inside! Every morning before they open up, seems like the men feel worse—and one or two have died."

"Of arrows, bullets and knives, not the night miasma. You get funny ideas sometimes, Abby."

"I guess so."

"I know so! Why, look what even the daytime air can do to a lance cut or a bullet hole! They do fine while the bandage's on to stop the bleeding. But let the air hit it after, and watch the pus come! Air can be plumb poison then."

"Maybe some day we'll find out."

"Until then," Letty said curtly, "don't take chances with air, particularly at night. It's cursed. Ask Major Harris or any other doctor. Evil things use night vapors, especially at full moon time."

"I know," Abby agreed and both women fell silent.

The babies fed and cleaned of their night soil, Abby and Letty straightened their wrinkled, filthy dresses as best they could, combed their hair and ventured out into the fort compound. The Indians had abandoned their attempts to storm the high stockade, contenting themselves with shooting arrows, some with flaming tips, over the pointed stake walls. A degree of safety now existed in the palisade ground. Still, Abby and Letty almost ran to the cabin that served as officers' mess.

Captain Blaine rose and bowed when they entered. "A fine morning, my ladies, if not a cheery one."

"It is not your fault, Captain," Abby curtsied and accepted the chair a batman with a bandaged hand and dirt-smeared face held for her. "Our visitors out there are not the best of company."

"Indeed not, mistress!"

Blaine resumed his seat. Before the Indian attack he had been a darkly handsome man in his late thirties with long grooved cheeks and deep-set eyes. Now his face resembled a skull and weariness had scored his forehead, deepened the lines in his face and had seemingly pushed his eyes deeper under craggy brows. He merely picked at the food in his platter, pulling deeply from the pewter mug of wine at his hand.

"Are they still out there in full force?" Abby asked.

"Yes—as usual and—as always."

"You're discouraged, Captain. I don't blame you. But this will not last forever."

"Thank you for the thought, mistress. It is bright and hopeful but—"

He made a small gesture that swept away the idea as a chimera, a tale of a nonexistent promised land. The batman placed bowls of hot porridge before Abby and Letty.

"I know Indians, Captain. They're fierce and deadly fighters but they grow impatient at prolonged

161

attacks—especially sieges. I'm surprised this has lasted as long as it has."

"I've been told by Major Harris and some of the settlers of your amazing life, mistress."

"And also from Colonel Carleton?"

The captain flushed as he nodded. "Yes, but *told* in a manner that shamed us all. He was a good officer but left much to be desired as a gentleman. That ended when we buried his head."

"I am sorry for that," Abby conceded.

"But to my point, mistress. You knew but one tribe of the Iroquois Nations, the Onondaga. Our post is attacked by every tribe from here to the Spanish Mississippi and north to old New France. There are the Seneca—"

"An Iroquois Nation," Abby cut in.

Blaine impatiently nodded and continued. "—*And* the Shawnee, Piankashaw, Delaware, Miami, Wea, Potawatomi, Kickapoo, Kankakee and some we haven't identified yet. I think this whole western land is one large Indian battleground. When has ever one chief controlled and directed all the tribes like this Pontiac?"

"I have never heard of one, Captain. You know it to be a fact?" Abby asked sharply.

Blaine finished the last of his wine and pushed his empty mug aside. "No, mistress. We have no proof or even news of anything. Pitt is completely surrounded. We can't break out, no one can break in. God knows what hell has been turned loose elsewhere! For a time we saw smoke from burning cabins east, west and north, but that has long since gone. We can only guess."

A knock on the door interrupted and the batman answered. "Mistress Smith, it's your husband."

"Dean!" Letty jumped up. "Thank God! I worry every morning until I see him."

She hurried out. Abby sighed and pushed back from the table. "Dean helps at the hospital so this means they've opened it for the day."

"For more wounded and more dead, I'm afraid, mistress. Major Harris does wonders over there."

"So he does, Captain, and wounded himself. Be thankful the fort has such a surgeon."

"With every breath, mistress. He *does* improve? I talk with him but I'm no doctor to judge his limp with that damned musket crutch he uses."

"He improves—all but his temper."

"Like mine, mistress. I hope no more died over there last night."

"Amen to that!" she breathed. She had started to leave but mention of the doctor brought up a puzzle that had annoyed her since that horrible, insulting meeting with Carleton. "Captain, what authority does Major Harris have here?"

"Somewhat mixed, mistress. As surgeon and doctor, he outranks every other officer in matters of medicine. But as a fighting soldier, I am in command, except in the hospital and so far as the general health of the post is concerned."

"*That* explains it!"

"Explains what, mistress?"

"I wondered how Major Harris could order Colonel Carleton to go hunting and be obeyed."

"Harris acted as medical officer then. His order was not military, mistress. Carleton had to obey in

163

that instance, just as I would have to obey him in the hospital this morning."

"Thank you, Captain, and right now I must be over to help the major however I can."

The door and the windows of the hospital stood open as Abby hurried to the cabin. While still several yards from the building the sickening odor of putrescence, blood and sweat brought her up short. Gulping and gasping to find her breath she was finally able to continue on her mission. Major Harris, using the bayonet point of his broken musket crutch as a pivot, swung about as she walked in. He was haggard, unkempt, his beard an uncombed tangle as was his iron gray hair. He still wore his bloody apron.

"Mistress, you're a God's blessing to my eyes this morning—you and all the ladies."

"Thank you, Major." She looked around the room. "No one died last night?"

"Not one!" His face fell as he indicated a limp, unconscious form nearby. "But that one slips steadily. He might last the day, but not tomorrow."

"The others, sir?"

"Some improve but most hold their own. I don't know what I'd do without all the ladies."

"We don't know what we'd do without you, Major. You worry us considerably."

"I? How?"

"You don't take care of yourself. Right now you need food and rest."

"No time!"

"Nonsense. Take it now. Get out of that apron, wash your hands and face and get over to the officers' mess. Captain Blaine has food and wine. You haven't been out of your clothing in days and days."

"Be ye daft, woman! These men—"

"Have us women to nurse them the short time you'll be gone, Major. Everyone on the post needs you, so don't be a fool. Stay alive. Prop up that wounded leg for an hour or two—though heaven knows it needs days and weeks!"

"Mistress, I am the one who gives the orders—"

"Up to now. You will again, as soon as you've food and wine in your stomach, fresh clothing on your body."

"Blast your eyes! do ye think—"

"Blast your eyes!" she came back at him, "you can give orders but not take them! Is that it? If something untoward happens here, you'll know in an instant, sir. Now do as I say!"

He glared, ready to order her out. But his weariness and strain suddenly plainly showed as his shoulders sagged and he passed his hand over his eyes, lowering his head.

She spoke gently. "Please, Major? If you kill yourself, you kill all of us."

"Food? Wine?" he asked in a small voice.

"And bunks in empty cabins to roll up in for half an hour's sleep, sir. If aught goes wrong here, I'll come for you myself. Here, let me untie your apron and you can slip out of it. You'll feel all the better."

His weariness sapped his will and he turned about so she could loosen the apron strings. Holding the soggy, dirty garment, Abby watched Harris almost stagger to the door and out. As she turned, one of the bedraggled women tugged at the hem of her skirt.

"Mistress Forny, bless ye for what ye've done. That man's been going on plain nerves, guts and stubbornness. He ain't snatched more'n a quarter hour sleep at a time since we been here."

"I can tell." Abby again surveyed the pallets. "Is just the one man in bad shape?"

"Ain't none so close to going as he," the woman agreed. "But one or two ain't much further behind him to crossin' over." She smiled grimly. "But we'll manage to hold 'em all until Major Harris gets rest."

Time slowly passed. Now and then one of the wounded would groan, moan or try to move, only to desist with a painful half-cry or garbled curse. For some reason, the Indians beyond the stockade restricted their attacks to musket shots, or an occasional flying arrow. Letty came in and Abby worriedly questioned her about the abnormal quiet.

"Ain't no one can really figure it out," Letty answered. "Oh, there's redskins out there all right. There ain't a chance of us breaking free. They're thicker 'n fleas on a cur dog's back. We see 'em all the time, moving about through the trees and bushes. But most times they keep well out of musket range. For some reason they're leaving us just to sit and shit."

"Letty!"

"True—and that's what all of us're doing, knowing they're planning some new devilment."

"How's Henri and the babies?"

"Fine, fed and sleeping. Better off'n most of us."

Time dragged on. Except for needed attention to a wounded man to bring him water, gently turn him on his pallet or help him through spasms of pain by

166

tightly holding his hand or shoulders, there was little to do. Major Harris did not return and Abby asked Letty to make sure the old man rested. Letty returned with a reassuring message from Captain Blaine, along with his thanks for making the major take a necessary rest. Letty had other news.

"My Dean says they slipped Joe Harlan out last night when it was pitch dark. With luck, him being a wilderness man from Carolina, he can slip through to Carlisle, where that Colonel Bouquet is camped as far as we know."

"What can Joe do?"

"Find out why Bouquet ain't moving. Might be he ain't got enough men and he's waiting for more. Might be he just don't know how bad off we are here, so Joe could stir him up."

"It's lack of soldiers," Abby said flatly.

"Whatever, we'll find out when Joe gets back."

Letty relieved one of the weary women and once again time moved slowly. Now and then the Indians fired at the men on the walls or sent a flight of arrows arching high to fall harmlessly into the parade ground. They served to warn that Fort Pitt stood ringed with besiegers. An occasional musket shot or warning shot from the men at the stockade only accented the unusual silence, making it all the more threatening.

The sun stood at the nooning when Major Harris hobbled through the door. His rest had been shorter than Abby liked but, even so, he showed improvement. His eyes looked a bit brighter and less strained. Obviously Captain Blaine's batman had helped him in and out of a tub for a bath of sorts, combed his hair and loaned him a clean shirt with ruffled white cuffs, a startling touch in this room of pain, blood, dirt and filthy dresses.

Abby instantly left the pallet of the fitfully sleeping man she had been attending and helped the doctor hobble to his cubbyhole. She held his blood-stiffened surgical gown and he worked his way into it.

"Mistress Forny, I'm thankful to you."

"You needed relief, Major."

"I didn't have sense enough to know it."

"Nonsense, sir! You cared more for the men on those pallets out there than for yourself!" She tied the gown's strings at his back as she asked, "You ate as well as slept?"

"Indeed! What I could. It's done wonders."

"What are the Indians doing, Major?"

"Sniping at us when they glimpse us so's to keep our heads down." Harris managed a surprising smile. "But we just might catch *them* napping. Captain Blaine lowered a messenger over the walls in the dead dark of night."

"I heard of it."

"Pray he reaches Colonel Bouquet, who ought to be somewhere around Carlisle."

"Could he break through to us?"

"If he has enough men. He needs militia besides his regular soldiers, Captain Blaine says. The captain sent Joe Harlan to hurry him on—without the militia, if need be. Come pitch dark tonight Harlan should be able to slip back in to let us know. But right now, what about our patients?"

"Little change, sir."

168

Harris hobbled along the rows between the pallets, stopping to examine each man, making certain for himself that nothing had really changed, as Abby had told him.

He had just finished the second row when Abby heard a roar from the stockade, a blast of muskets and then frenetic, bloody cursing. Beneath it all, she thought she heard a distant screaming but a fresh burst of firing from both the stockade and the Indians beyond drowned the sound. She rushed to the door to see Captain Blaine and every man in the post running toward the walls. A woman came to Abby, stumbling and weaving. Her face was white with terror, her eyes almost popping from her head. When Abby grabbed her, she saw the streams of sweat on her forehead and face. The woman's fingers sank deep in Abby's arms.

"It's Joe Harlan. They caught him. They . . . they burned him alive at the stake—out there where . . . Awww!"

She collapsed, a dead weight in Abby's arms.

XIII

That night Abby, like the others, ate horror and despair along with the mouthful or two of food she could choke down. She could still hear Joe Harlan's screams as, long ago, she had heard those of the tortured merchant the Onondaga had captured and burned. That had driven her to flight and escape but here at Fort Pitt there could not be such relief.

The smooth bore muskets of the soldiers could not

throw merciful bullets far enough. The Indians had set up the torture stake and ring of burning fire just beyond range. Letty's husband had quickly grasped the situation and seen the writhing pain of his neighbor whose face had been painted black and whose body sparked from small flaming resinous splinters the Indians had viciously needled into his flesh.

He had watched for a long moment from the firing platform, jaw clenched and a muscle jumping in his cheek. Then he slid down one of the ladders and raced for the cabin where the men had been quartered. He reappeared with his long rifle, powder horn and bullet pouch. He used a ramrod to set patches on the powder he poured down the rifle muzzle and then moistened a bullet in his mouth, solidly tamping it down before climbing up to the platform again.

He knelt, placing the muzzle securely between two of the palisade stakes and, disregarding whizzing Indian bullets and seeking arrows, checked the flint, the firing pan and then pulled back the heavy hammer. Silence fell on the platform as the men crouched below the parapet, watching him, the expression in each grim face a prayer.

Dean took his time aiming though every scream jarred along the nerves of the men. Abby, standing at the foot of the ladder just below Dean, finally had to plunge her fingers in her ears to lessen the horrible sounds that no longer seemed of human origin. Then Dean pulled the trigger. Powder flashed, a tongue of flame lanced far out the muzzle. The screams cut off on the instant. The rifle had carried farther than the smooth bore muskets could. Dean dropped from a crouch to a sitting position on the platform, rifle sagging in his arms, head hanging low. A moaning sigh made a sorrowing string of sound along the stockade.

Now, at the mess table, all of them still heard the ghostly screams, shuddered and silently blessed Dean Smith and his marksmanship. Abby asked herself the question she knew was in the minds of all at the table and throughout the post. Had Joe Harlan reached Colonel Bouquet? Was relief on its way?

Captain Blaine, as though he had read her thoughts, answered her question as his chair made a harsh scraping sound when he pushed back from the table and looked around at the women and the haggard bedraggled lieutenant who was the remaining officer.

"We have to face stark cold facts. It's my opinion Joe Harlan never had a chance and we can expect no help from Carlisle or anywhere else."

"Be ye saying he never got through at all?" a woman asked. There was no surprise in her question, only a fatal acceptance of a fear she had not voiced until now.

"But wasn't he coming back when they caught him?" another woman asked.

"I don't think so. He wouldn't have had time to slip through the Indians to Bouquet and come back. If any of us thought so, it was only blind hope. I think Mister Harlan was caught not long after we lowered him over the stockade."

"We'd have heard something, some kind of noise. Joe wasn't one to be easy taken," another woman disagreed.

Blaine looked the length of the table at Abby. "Mistress Forny, what is your thought?"

"Like yours, Captain."

"How do you know?" a third woman demanded.

Blaine looked over at her. "Didn't you and your family reach us just ahead of the first Indian attack?"

"That's right. We barely made it."

"Then you don't know that Mistress Forny was an Iroquois captive for some time before she escaped."

"You was?" the woman directly asked Abby, who nodded. "You lived with them savages! But—but I heard your husband is a French courier."

"He is. I married him right here in the fort settlement."

"Well then, I reckon you'd know. Is the captain right?"

"We've been surrounded every day, every hour and every minute after you and yours were lucky enough to get through. No one has come in since."

"But after we stopped 'em trying to break through the gate or come over the walls time and again, we ain't heard much of 'em."

"Give them credit for brains," Abby snapped and then curbed her impatience and spoke more evenly. "They've failed to get inside the fort. None of us will ever know how many warriors they lost trying. Indians carry off their dead so an enemy never knows. But the point is, why risk more dead and wounded warriors if starvation will do what bullets, arrows and lances won't? They just wait."

"And cut us down one by one," Blaine added. "Lieutenant, what's our fighting force now?"

"Less than twenty regular soldiers unwounded, sir."

"And other men?"

"About as many, Captain."

"Fighting wounded—soldiers and all?"

"Fifteen, sir."

"Forty fit," Blaine summarized. "Fifteen more who can hobble about but couldn't stand up to an all-out fight if the Indians managed to storm the stockade. We have you women—and a few of you have wounds. There are the children."

He stopped and slowly looked around the table. "Every day we dig another grave or use another pallet in the hospital. Each time that happens, we are one fighter weaker. Our supplies are low. Mistress Forny is correct. Our red friends have only to wait."

"Maybe someone else would have more luck than poor Joe Harlan," someone suggested. "Ain't I heard Indians don't like night and sort of pull off from fighting?"

"But not from watching," Abby answered. "I agree with Captain Blaine. They saw us lower Joe but made no move or sound until he was out of earshot of the fort. Then they grabbed him. It would be the same for anyone else."

"Lord God! then we just sit here until . . . ?"

"Until," Blaine echoed grimly. "Or Colonel Bouquet can attack the Indians from the rear and break through."

"I reckon then," the woman said slowly, "we'd best start making our peace with the Lord."

"If prayer will help," Blaine nodded, "use it. Frankly, I do—every day and every night."

174

The lieutenant growled, "Better use someone—man or woman—with more luck than Master Harlan."

"There ain't no such person," a woman snapped and the meal finished on that final, despairing note.

Abby walked outside. Half of the parade ground stood in deep shadow, the setting sun blocked by the palisade. The hospital had already been tightly closed against the poisonous night air and Abby turned from it, wandering aimlessly to the stockade gate. She stood listening, hearing only the scuffle of a soldier's feet on the platform walk above her. The besiegers had become quiet again. She looked up, startled, when the soldier above her softly called down.

"Mum, best not linger near that gate."

"But it's solid barred."

"Yes, mum, but I ain't trustful of anything around the post these days."

She smiled wryly up at him. "I understand how you feel. But if there's no Indian near—?"

"There ain't. They don't risk a musket ball anymore these days. They keep their distance."

"Where are they now?"

The soldier glanced over the stockade before he answered. "Clean out beyond the first burned cabin, mum, and some down at the river bank."

"Then it's safe enough down here."

"And up here for the minute, mum."

Abby saw a ladder just beyond the gate but near at hand. She spoke impulsively. "I'm coming up. I've never had a look."

"Oh, no, mum!" came the horrified protest.

175

But she had already sped halfway up the ladder and in another second stood on the platform beside the soldier. He stared at her, aghast.

"Mum! This ain't safe! Get back down. Them savages—"

"I see them," Abby cut him off.

She had carefully placed herself so that only a portion of her head showed in the narrow space between two of the sharpened logs forming the palisade. She first looked to where her cabin had stood and saw an ugly heap of black ashes, one side of the charred door frame broken off short. She tightly closed her eyes for a moment and then, partially recovered, looked at the ruins of the rest of the village. Letty and Dean's cabin had not been spared even a single partial door frame as hers had been. The rest of the houses had also been torched.

Far out and along the Allegeway and Monongahela river banks she saw an almost solid row of Indian cooking fires, temporary round-roofed shelters of bark over logs, canoes pulled up on the shore. Straight out from the gate stood the ugly circle of fire and the stub of the black stake where Joe Harlan had been burned. She had a sudden vivid, ugly picture of the torture circle back in Onondaga Town. Indians, almost row on row of them, squatted with weapons at hand, all watching the fort. As the soldier had said, they were beyond musket range.

She lifted her eyes, following the dirt road that led eastward into Pennsylvania Colony, the way to Carlisle, and all the hamlets and towns eastward to invisible, afar-off Philadelphia. It plunged into the forest and disappeared beyond the barricade of lithe,

176

living bronze red bodies. She noticed the painted faces, the leggings, moccasins and headdresses of the Indians, identifying each tribe by its distinctive garbs, tribal marks, clan symbols. As Captain Blaine had said, every tribe she had ever heard of—and some she had not—awaited bloody opportunity out there.

An insistent, impatient and hard tugging on her sleeve brought her attention back to the soldier. "Please, mum! Please! The captain'll have me cat tailed around the post for this."

"He will not. I'll see to it."

"All the same, I'd feel better if you was safe back down there on the ground."

"I want to look first," Abby remonstrated.

"Mum, Injuns is Injuns no matter how they paint up or dress."

"But of different tribes. Where are the Seneca?"

"I don't know one kind of devil from another, mum. Now please get down out of danger."

"No danger, but you needn't worry about me any longer."

Remaining crouched, she turned and scurried northward along the platform away from the gate. The soldier squawked, "Mum! Mum!" but he couldn't stop her and the next sentinel along the wall could only watch her rapid approach. He moved so that he completely blocked her and lowered his musket so that its bayonet pointed directly at her.

"You ain't going no farther."

He wore the red uniform of the British king but had a face that could only be Irish. It was hard, all jaw, steel green eyes, beetling brows as shaggy as hedgerows. A white crooked scar ran from his left ear

177

diagonally along his cheek to his throat. His voice was a growl as menacing and filled with steel as his face. Abby tried to push the bayonet aside but it swung back to within an inch of her nose.

"Get that out of my way," she demanded.

He did not budge. "There's a ladder right behind you. Get down it."

"I'm staying here until I get a look at the Allegeway."

"You ain't sightseeing up here. If you ain't down that ladder in a minute, bedamn! I'll carry you down."

"I dare you to touch me."

Admiration touched his hard green eyes. "Bejasus! ye've got brass and guts, me lass! like ye came direct from the Auld Sod. But down ye go—by your own feet or by my help."

Authority and arrogance in tone or plain female stubbornness would not work with this man. Abby looked up at him from her crouched position and gave him a wide smile as her voice softened. "Sure, and can't a lass take just a tiny peek between the posts?"

"For what? They's nothing but Injuns out there."

"Seneca perhaps?"

"Arrah! I can't tell one red devil from another!"

"I can."

He blinked, looked down at her with new interest. "Can ye now?"

"Certain. Just one small peek?"

Suspicion darkened his face again. "And what would Seneca be to you?"

She answered truthfully enough. "They're Iro-

178

quois and the Iroquois murdered my mother, my father and my man years ago back in Connecticut."

"Then why d'ye want to see 'em again?"

"To curse them for murderers, if for nothing else."

"Ye can tell them—Seneca—from the others?"

"Couldn't you if their kind had killed your people? Just one quick look?"

The bayonet point no longer menaced her face and the soldier moved back and made a swift sign to the palisade with his musket barrel. "No more'n a minute, mind ye, and be damned if I know why I'm doing this."

The northern corner of the fort was a few yards beyond and Abby would have preferred to take her quick survey over there. But she knew she dare not try to get around this man or she'd get no look at all. So once more she crouched at the stockade wall and slowly lifted her head to look out between another pair of pointed stakes.

"Only a minute, mind ye," the soldier hissed.

She nodded, inched herself up, expecting disappointment. But when she could see out beyond the walls, her heart jumped with excitement. She could see a long stretch of the Allegeway and its gravelly beach to the point where it curved northward. The waters made white froth around the submerged rocks where the river came out of the mountains in its haste to meet the Ohio.

Canoes thickly covered the far bank, one after the other. Just beyond them she saw the warriors, armed with every imaginable savage weapon as well as muskets and an occasional long barrel rifle. Most of them sat or crouched, watching the post. From their

179

number she understood Captain Blaine's despair. Beyond them, other Indians relieved cramped muscles by stalking back and forth, some smoking short calumet pipes, some talking and gesticulating. Abby's attention centered on their war paint, metal upper arm bands, their moccasins and bead work, even on decorative war bows. Seneca!

"Muldoon!" a heavy voice roared.

Captain Blaine stood just below the platform, fists on his hips. He glared up. "What is that woman doing up—Mistress Forny!"

She spoke quickly. "Captain, I came up here before anyone could stop me. Private Muldoon ordered me down, even threatened me with a bayonet. He did his duty, sir."

Blaine's eyes moved in a searching question to Muldoon, who waited reprimand, his scarred face looking harder and tighter than ever. Abby hurried on before the captain could vent further anger.

"Blame me, sir. Truly, your men did what they could to get me off the platform."

"Mistress, you endanger yourself and distract my men. Why?"

Abby did not answer but scurried to the nearest ladder and climbed down. Blaine lifted her off the last step and placed her solidly on her feet with a thud that jarred along her spine. He looked up to the platform.

"Carry on, Muldoon."

"Yes, sir."

"I'd march you off to the guardhouse if I could spare you. But don't think you won't answer to me eventually."

180

Abby touched his sleeve. "Please, Captain. He tried to follow orders. I wouldn't let him."

"Come with me, mistress."

He took her elbow in none too gentle a grasp and led her across the parade ground to his office cabin. He slammed his hat on the table that served as his desk and pointed to an uncomfortable straight chair. Abby sat down, nervously smoothing her skirts.

"Well, mistress? I wait explanation!"

"Woman's curiosity, Captain."

"At this place! At this time!" his roaring voice fairly bounced of the walls.

"Yes, Captain. I wanted to know what had happened to my house. I haven't seen anything but stockade wall since we were all driven inside."

"Damme! no woman has. It's too dangerous."

"Risky, I admit, Captain, but dangerous only if I'd been careless." She folded her hands uncertainly, fingers tightly interlaced. "All the women feel like I do, sir. We're cooped up, uncertain. We need to see what it's like to be out there."

"You've been told by everyone from me to your husbands to my soldiers."

"Yes, sir."

"So what good was the risk you took!"

She made a small gesture. "Seeing for myself is worth a thousand reports, sir. We believe our eyes—"

"But not my plain statement of facts?"

"Oh, yes, sir. But there's always a tiny little bit of doubt—like I couldn't quite believe my home was destroyed. It's like death, sir. It always comes to someone else, not you."

He started a retort but blinked instead. He had

placed his hands on the table before him and now he watched his own thumbs making flying circles about one another as though his brain had nothing to do with the motion. He suddenly caught himself up, fell back in his chair and placed his palms flat on the table.

"You make your point, mistress. But I'd be remiss to allow the others to take your liberty."

"I understand, Captain. I'll not put you to that worry again."

"Thank you, mistress. I have enough as it is."

They both started when a knock sounded on the door. It immediately opened and Major Harris entered on his improvised crutch. He hobbled to a chair and dropped into it. The weariness had returned to his face and he spoke with a hopeless voice and with a despairing look at Abby.

"What is it, Major?" Blaine asked.

"Burial detail, Captain, I lost another man not ten minutes ago."

"Another?" Blaine hardly made it a question but more an acceptance.

"Another, Captain. The string runs out. Sorry, Mistress Forny but—" His sigh finished his apology and he looked back at Blaine. "What with Harlan captured and burned by those fiends, we've no chance, Captain. It's last stand and it's not long to the last man."

Blaine's shoulders made an expressive lift and fall that was answer enough. "Wrap the poor devil up, Major. We'll last as long as we can."

"I'll have the women do it," Harris said. "He'll be ready to join the others around the flag."

He pulled himself back up on his crutch and limped to the door and out of the dead silence that held the room. Blaine called his orderly and named off the burial detail then slumped even further down in his chair, eyes on the open door. Abby plainly saw that he looked at a black future rather than the grave-pocked parade ground and the stockade. He caught himself and his eyes lifted slowly and heavily to her.

"Mistress Forny, I've dreaded this moment but I can no longer put it off."

"If I can help—"

"Mistress, just give me an honest answer. You heard what Harris said and what all of us face."

"Yes, Captain."

"Women and children," he said dully. "When there are no fighting men left in the fort and the savages outside will come over the stockade without hindrance, I can't leave you to that fate—none of you."

The blood left Abby's face and she tightly gripped the arms of her chair, leaning forward. Blaine's eyes held hers and he spoke slowly, carefully.

"How do you women want to die? How do you want your children killed?"

"Captain!"

"Mistress, please! It will be our last act of mercy. Every man would want it that way. Please ask the ladies and let me know."

"But—can't we hold out for a little time yet!"

"Not long, mistress, and it's best I know now, to prepare the men for the task. Ask your ladies." He pulled himself to his feet. "If you'll excuse me, mistress, I must see to what few defenses remain to us."

He picked up his hat, gave her a short bob of his head instead of a bow and walked out the door with a heavy step. Abby sat unmoving. A shot sounded from the stockade but it only accented the silence and underlined the futility of the defense. She again saw the row on row of waiting Indians across the Allegeway and knew they also lined the Monongahela. She saw the row on row of canoes that could speed the warriors across the rivers to the final attack.

She saw Henri, kicking and cooing in his crib, small arms making jerking motions as he gave her his toothless smile. She saw Letty's babies and her older children, those of the other women. She saw the weary women beside the pallets in the hospital. Some of them had not been out of their dresses in days and the dresses themselves were stiff with blood, pus and vomit from the wounded.

She closed her eyes tightly.

How could she answer Captain Blaine!

XIV

Abby knew that Captain Blaine's "immediate answer" was rhetorical and that "soon" would have been a better word. He no more wanted an answer than she wanted to give him one but both of them knew that time was running out. Unless something was done or rescue came, death had only to patiently wait a short while longer. But not today, she told herself after Blaine walked out. No need to put the question today—to the other ladies or to herself.

She had no idea how long she sat frozen in the chair, even her thoughts numbed, but suddenly the paralysis broke. Returning full awareness sent a shock along her nerves and she could not sit still. She jumped up, then froze again. She could not face the women, the children or anyone else. She had to find a balance, check her final despairing whirling thoughts.

She hurried outside, pulling up short when she saw two men appear around the corner of the tool cabin. They carried spades over their shoulders and walked to the flagpole. They stood there for long moments, looking about the circle of new mounds, then one pointed to his left and the other nodded. They plodded beyond the outer ring of graves, looked at one another and then bent to the task. The spades bit into the earth and Abby thought she could hear the dull sound even at this distance.

She whipped around and looked along the line of soldiers' cabins, many of them already emptied by death. She almost hurried blindly to the nearest and plunged inside. She stood in a long room, empty except for a table and a double tier of bunks along one wall. Some of them still held rumpled blankets, cast aside as the occupant sprang out to answer the last alarm he would ever hear. There were encrusted platters on the table, with benches along each side. She dropped onto the nearest, listened for a moment or two. She heard no approaching step and knew she had not been seen. Only then did she bury her face in her hands and cry—for Henri, for Edward, for her

186

doomed neighbors and for herself. It took a long time for the last sob to shake her and the last tear to streak down her face. She felt washed out and weak. Certainly, the outbreak had solved nothing, but it had brought her a new balance and cleared her mind. She could slowly, very slowly bring herself to truly face the situation.

Death—from a mercy bullet or from a hate-filled enemy who would use knife or tomahawk with relish. How would infant Henri die? Her eyes misted again but she angrily, frantically knuckled them away. There must be some other way. She must think more clearly than ever before in her life.

No man could slip through the Indian besiegers. Joe Harlan had proved that. What would happen if Edward tried to get back through to her? and she knew her man well enough to know he would try it. The Indians would accept him and Simeon as *voyageurs* and the odds stood that they would not be killed. On the other hand, Abby knew they would not be permitted to get through to Fort Pitt itself. She felt thankful for the slight edge of safety Edward had.

Her main responsibility remained Henri and all those within the stockade. She lifted her hand and looked at the peculiarly cut scar on her wrist made by the knife of the Keeper of the Faith. That made her Onondaga, Iroquois. The Seneca would recognize it. If she could get over the stockade walls without her dress and in Indian garb, the scar would be her passport.

She would have to work out that problem somehow but, first, she must think of Henri. Who

187

would take care of him, who feed him if she left the post? The two problems of escape and of Henri's well-being stood intertwined, the solution of one dependent on the solution of the other. She had to find the answer, not only for Henri but for the other babies—

Her thoughts pulled up short. Letty Smith suckled a baby! She jumped up and raced out of the cabin to the hospital where Letty and the babies were. The women still held to their heartbreaking vigil and tasks between the pallets and the children remained in a group at the rear of the room. Letty nursed her baby and looked up with a wan smile when Abby picked up Henri.

"You suckled him not two hours ago," Letty said, puzzled. "Be your tits making too much milk and aching?"

"No, but—can we talk outside a few minutes?"

"Reckon so, but what's to talk about?"

Abby dropped her voice to a whisper. "More than enough, but only for your ears. Outside? Please!"

When they stepped out of the hospital cabin, the diggers had moved sod and now their spades turned the first foot or so of repellent brown dirt and clods. Letty watched a moment and sighed. "Poor devil! We thought he might pull through. He died at dawn light." She turned away from the burial preparations and directed her attention to Abby. "What would ye tell me?"

"Will you promise to say nothing to the others?"

"What about?"

"Promise first, Letty."

188

"You sound like you know when the end of the world is coming," Letty commented skeptically.

"It's almost that bad. Letty, we waste time! Promise?"

"If it's as bad as that, I promise."

Abby then told her of her talk with Captain Blaine. Letty listened in silence, face turning more and more gray, eyes rounding. She now suckled her child quite automatically, unaware of the pulls on her nipple. Abby finished and Letty could say nothing. She looked sick with fear. Abby dropped her hand on Letty's shoulder and shook it.

"Do you understand, Letty? Do you know what this means to all of us?"

Letty could only gulp convulsively and nod but her arms tightened about her baby. Abby hastened on.

"Do you have enough milk to suckle Henri for days or even a week or two?" Letty faintly nodded. "Will you?" Letty gulped and nodded again then found her voice. It came out weak and quivering.

"But—what good's—that?"

Abby turned her wrist to show the scar her friend had seen many times before. "I'm a blood adopted Onondaga—Iroquois. The Seneca will know the sign of the cut and will honor it."

"But—they're—out there! How you gonna reach 'em afore they kill you?"

"Your Dean's my size. I want his clothes and moccasins. Can I have 'em?"

"He'd be jay-ass naked."

"Better that than the rest of us jay-ass dead, Letty.

189

That's what we'll be. Maybe some other man . . . ?"

"Yeah, sure . . ." she answered in a frightened daze, then suddenly snapped fully alert. "But the captain won't let you!"

"He'll have to. He must. First, let me talk to Dean."

Dean listened to Abby's request for his clothes with growing indignation and flatly refused. "Why, I couldn't stir out of the cabin! Besides, how do we know they'll fit ye?"

"Trying them on," Abby answered. "If yours won't fit, we'll find someone else more my size."

"How you gonna try 'em on? When and where?"

"Here and now," Abby snapped. "Letty, get him a blanket to wrap up in."

"Be damned if I do."

"You'll eventually be dead if you don't, and so will all of us."

"Just because of my clothes? Be ye daft, Abby Forny!"

She looked a question at Letty, who said, "You can trust him like ye can trust me."

She told Dean of Captain Blaine's plans when the Indians finally took the post. He listened, his face growing more and more pale, his eyes moving from Abby to Letty and her baby then out the door to the hospital cabin where the twin boys made a poor business of their forced captivity. Abby finished the story and the outline of her plan with a final plea.

"Don't you see, Dean! I can't be slipped over the stockade and try to reach the river in skirts and petticoats! I'd be seen in a minute and, besides, I have to move fast if I have any chance at all."

"You have to get the captain's say-so," Dean added.

"I'll get it—or go without it if some of you men will help. But right now, let's see how I size to your shirt and pants."

Letty pulled a worn blanket from an abandoned bunk and held it as a curtain. She passed Dean's moccasins first and Abby examined them with approval. Some courier had fashioned them and followed the Indian way of cutting the soft skin, lacing the ankle thongs and doing the decoration in red, black, white and green beads. Then she grabbed the trousers Letty tossed to her, dropped her skirt and petticoats and pulled on the pants. The long-tailed shirt slipped over her head and her hips, hanging down below her knees. It was slightly loose, like the trousers, but the wide leather belt bearing an empty hunting knife sheath tightened them both to her waist. She made final tugging adjustments and then stood for inspection.

Dean peered over the top of the blanket. "Sort of fits, Abby. You're a bigger woman than I figured from just looking."

"And I'll bet ye've done more'n enough of that!" Letty said in a heavy attempt to lighten the load of fear all of them bore.

"How about my hat?" Dean offered.

"No squaw wears a hat. I'll braid my hair Indian style. Could I get by in the dark of night?" Both nodded and Abby said, "All right. Now for the captain after I change back to a lady again. Hold up

191

the blanket, Letty."

An hour later she again sat across the table from Captain Blaine. He listened to her with growing astonishment, shock and disbelief.

He blurted his answer. "I can't permit it, mistress. You'd be killed within five steps from the stockade wall if they didn't murder you before you reached the ground."

"Better just one dead than all the post, Captain."

He jumped up, leaned over the table on the knuckles of his fisted hands. "It can't be done. No man could do it, so why—"

"Could a woman, Captain? I showed you the mark on my wrist."

"That means nothing!"

"It means everything if I get a chance to show it to the first Seneca. They honor blood adoption in a tribe more than family birth. They believe that once the blood is mingled, the rite done, the adopted one forgets his own blood and family, tribe, race and people. I'm an adopted Onondaga so no matter what my past or the color of my skin, I am always Onondaga—Iroquois—blood kin to the Seneca who are also Iroquois."

"Primitive balderdash!"

"Mayhap, Captain, but certain Iroquois safe passage for me. I could move freely, reach this Colonel Bouquet and tell him how ill we fare."

Blaine, still supported by his stiff arms, leaned over and glared. But she saw a change deep in his eyes, a touch of uncertainty and she hastened to take advantage of it. "If you are so concerned for one

192

person you'd allow all the others to die, you would be a dolt, Captain."

He flinched as though she had actually slapped him. "You are loose with your tongue, mistress."

"And you're loose with your thinking, sir. Consider the children, the women, your men. Am I worth more than all of them?"

He straightened slowly and she watched the play of conflicting thoughts and emotions in his eyes and facial muscles. She pressed her point. "You asked me not long ago to face cold facts, Captain. I have. Can't you?"

He turned from the table and paced from one end of the room to the other, his hands clasped behind his back, deep furrows in his forehead. Abby watched him. He suddenly halted across the table, looking hard at her. Without a word, she extended her arm, turning it so her scarred wrist inexorably pulled his eyes down to the sign. Then she dropped her arm and waited.

His mouth writhed with indecision as he fought a lifetime training as to the duties and responsibilities of a gentleman and an officer of the king. He groped for the back of his chair, found it and slowly eased down to a seat. Then he abruptly shook his head.

"I can't do it, mistress."

"You have no choice, Captain. Both of us know it."

After a moment he heavily asked, "What would you have me do? Mind you! I don't say I will."

"I know Captain, but could you first take me up to the western platform?"

"The one overlooking the point?"

"Where the rivers join and the Ohio begins? Yes, Captain, that one."

Shortly afterward, they crouched side by side just below the stakes of the palisades. Guards on the platform and a small crowd of soldiers and settlers below at the foot of the ladders looked curiously at them. Blaine growled, "Take your look, mistress. With care. I'll be at the next post."

They both slowly lifted themselves so they could peer out on the comparatively few yards to the joining of the rivers. "There's little room for warriors and canoes, Captain," Abby said without turning her head. In daylight no one could move out there but what a soldier up here could bring him down."

"That's why it's empty now. But look just across the Allegeway where it flows into the Ohio. It's thick with warriors just out of musket range. See those canoes? At full dark they cross the river and the point is as well and closely watched as our stockade gate."

She looked across the river, confirming the view she had earlier stolen from this lookout post. "Seneca over there."

"Mistress, I would not know the signs of the differing tribes. There are too many of them around us and all seeking our scalps."

"But I do, Captain. I've seen what I want. We can go down now."

"At least you cut your risk, mistress."

"This time, Captain. Let's go back to your cabin and plan."

Back in his headquarters, Blaine dropped heavily

into his chair after Abby was seated. "Now, mistress, do ye see how daft ye be?" he asked.

"Yes, Captain, if you put it that way. But only a daft person and plan has a chance. Everyone in the post knows we can't break out."

"Nor can we."

"Every Indian outside the stockade knows we can't. They have only to wait."

"I have said as much over and over but—"

"I won't listen, will I?" she smiled crookedly.

"You listen," he growled, "but either you don't hear or the sound doesn't reach your brain."

"We waste time, Captain."

"Nay, mistress, you waste time with whatever mad scheme you have in mind. But I'll listen at least."

"That's a small gain for me." She hitched forward and rested her arms on the captain's table. "What would the Indians least expect, sir?"

"You've said it—the impossible. A break-out."

"Then that's what we'll give them, Captain."

"Good blazing God! You are demented! You need to be chained so you won't hurt yourself."

She disregarded his explosion and tapped her finger on the table as she outlined her scheme. At first he hardly listened and she had to repeat herself time and again. But slowly he began to comprehend and he stared at her as she continued without interruption. She finished, dropping back in her chair.

"Well, Captain?"

He pulled at his chin, pinched his lip as he studied her, but his mind swiftly weighed the steps she had outlined. Finally he dropped his hands on the table and puffed out his cheeks.

"Mistress, I still think you're demented. But your plan's just crazy enough it might work. If it does, you will have the epaulettes of a general, so help me!"

XV

By nightfall, Dean Smith had obtained other clothing as good as his own except for a jagged patch over an arrow hole in the back of the long shirt. So he could unabashedly examine Abby in his own clothing as she stood in the light from the fireplace. Letty, her children along with Henri, under the care of the women in the tightly closed hospital cabin, critically studied Abby.

"You sure look Injun even to them two braids," she admitted. "At least you'll pass in a black night like this'n. Where'd you get that headband?"

"Made it this afternoon." Abby touched the cloth and the bead design she had sewn on the front. It duplicated the Onondaga symbol of her *ohwachira*. She accepted the heavy hunting knife Dean handed her and slid it into her belt sheath. The knife's owner now lay under one of the mounds out in the parade ground.

"Honey!" Letty suddenly bawled. "You cain't do this! We won't see you never no more!"

Tears streamed as she suddenly pulled Abby tightly against her. The woman's whole body shook with deep sobs and Abby, her nose suddenly buried deep in the rough cloth of Letty's dress, could hardly breathe. She managed to work her arms up between herself and Letty and, using them for leverage, freed herself, forcing Letty to stumble back against Dean.

"You'll see me," Abby said with more hope than promise as she shook Letty's shoulders. "You'll see me, back here or in Carlisle, I promise you." She looked over to Dean. "We best be about the night. The captain will be waiting."

Letty's tears finally stopped flowing but sobs shook her. She accompanied Abby and Dean out of the cabin and walked with them to the western wall, where Captain Blaine waited. He moved agitatedly about and wheeled around when Abby and her friends came up.

"Mistress, I still think this is such a long chance—"

"One we have to take," she finished. She stood at

198

the foot of the ladder and looked up to the firing platform. She made out the dim shapes of two crouching figures just below the stockade rim. She looked across the dark parade ground toward the wide gates that the black night hid. "Are you ready over there, Captain?"

"As we'll ever be, mistress."

He stepped back, came to stiff military posture and saluted her.

"What was that for, Captain?"

"For your bravery, mistress."

"Thank you," she said dryly, "but I have no intention of dying, sir, only of being found over across the river. When next you see Dean you can start your part."

She turned to the ladder and hurriedly ascended, Dean scurrying up behind her. She came to the firing platform and the two soldiers pulled her to a crouch beside them. Her hand instantly touched a coil of thick rope between them. She peered over the stakes and instantly saw moving shadowy forms on the small point of land between the palisade and the rivers. Then, with a slight thrill of excitement, she saw the line of canoes on the near bank. With luck . . . but she stopped that thought knowing she could not depend on it.

She took a deep breath. "All right, Dean. Over to the gate."

He squeezed her arm and then slid back down the ladder. She hissed to the soldiers. "Ready with the rope?"

"Yes, mum."

"Minutes, maybe seconds, count," she warned.

"Give me the rope."

She made a sliding hitch around her waist and waited. It seemed to her time dragged and dragged. Would Dean never reach the stockade gate! The thought had no more than flashed through her mind than the dark, peaceful silence of the night shattered. She still peered between the pointed stakes as muskets and rifles roared above the distant stockade gates. It sounded like a battle.

For a tense moment nothing happened below. Then the Indians shouted alarm as the firing and racket continued. It sounded as though the soldiers and settlers had burst open the gate and charged out toward escape. Below her, Indians raced for the canoes. Some of them ran at a crouch around the corner of the stockade and within less than a minute the point of land stood clear and open. She jumped up.

"Now!"

The rope sailed out over the wall and down. Strong arms lifted her and she grabbed the rope above her head. The soldiers paid out the rope so quickly that the logs of the stockade dimly blurred by her face. She swung in against the stakes but her braced feet saved her from a full body crash. She struck the ground, threw off the rope, whipped around, her hand at her sheathed knife.

The ruse had worked. No one was near her. Then she saw three or four canoes still pulled up on the point. She raced for them, a prayer of thanks flashing through her mind. It took only a second to push the light bark craft into the water and swing into it as she snatched up a paddle below the narrow seat onto which she had thudded. The canoe shot out and away as though propelled from a cannon.

The fake battle continued behind her, and it had even lured the Indians on the far bank of the Allegeway around to the front of the post. She could plainly see the cooking fires all along the fringe of the forest. The women would be there if they had not also raced to see what might be happening at the fort's gate.

The current gripped the canoe, too strong to fight against but she could direct the craft at an angle across it with her frantic paddle strokes. She struck the far bank below the junction of the Ohio. She jumped out. With a kick of her foot she sent the canoe back into the full grip of the current. It disappeared westward into the dark.

She scrambled for the screen of bushes and trees on the slim chance she had not been seen in the excitement and so might delay immediate discovery. But she heard shouts behind her across the stream and more on this side of the river. She heard the deadly whisper of an arrow a few feet from her head and she instantly halted.

"Hai! I am Onondaga!" she shouted in the Iroquois tongue. "I have escaped."

Rough hands seized her and warriors packed around her. A painted face came close, trying to see her clearly in the dark. "You're white!" he growled in the Seneca dialect.

"White," she agreed. "But the Keepers washed it away. The blood ceremony made me Onondaga. I am Strong Woman of Moon Willow's *ohwachira*. Take me to the fires and I will show you."

The Indian's cruel fingers in her shoulders wheeled her around and she was hurried to the fires so fast that she stumbled. She was jerked back to her feet and at last she stood beside a cooking fire. Scowling, painted warriors stood about her. She recognized the markings of a war leader and then of a Sachem. Women, as fiercely suspicious as their men, glared at her, tugged at her shirt.

"You speak the tongue," the Sachem said.

"And I speak true. See."

She held out her arm, turned so the flickering fire light clearly showed her wrist scar. A woman grabbed her hand, tugged her closer to the light and bent to examine the scar. The warriors waited her verdict and Abby held her breath. Though the men fought the battles and hunted, became war leaders and Sachems, Abby knew they did so only with the permission of the women. Family lines were traced through the mothers in all the Six Nations so now the stalwart warriors awaited the verdict of the woman who studied Abby's scar.

Finally she looked up at Abby. "Strong Woman, eh? What is your true name?"

Abby shook her head. "Mother, you know I can't tell you or anyone. The Owl Society gave me that in secret. I keep it in secret."

"Why?" the woman demanded.

Abby disregarded her harsh voice, knowing this was a test question. "My true name gives my head, my heart and my body over to whoever knows it, Mother." She bent close to the woman and saw the small tattoo on her cheek just below her ear. "You are

202

of the Doe Society, Mother. Are there Owls among the Seneca?"

The woman straightened, looked around at the warriors. "She speaks with a straight tongue." She returned to Abby, swung her arm to the fort across the river. "But why do you return to the white skins?"

"They caught me far up the Allegeway, Mother. They still think I am white skin and they do not let me go back to my people. But I waited my chance." She held up her fingers. "Two years I wait. It came tonight."

"Hah! The white skins are fools! If you were made Iroquois, you are always Iroquois. Are any of their tribes greater than ours!"

"No, Mother. They do not believe me when I tell them. So tonight at last I slipped away."

"Hai! You are among your own people again."

"My people but not my Nation, Mother. I want to return to the Onondaga towns and my own *ohwa-chira."*

The woman looked around at the ring of warriors and spoke to a war leader. "We'll call a council and pick warriors to take her on her journey."

"Mother," Abby put in quickly, "I can travel alone. I know the forest ways."

"The paths have changed in two years."

"But the Seneca are still Keepers of the Western Door?"

"For the Six Nations," the woman agreed. "But now we fight with many tribes against the white skins. Some would let you pass, perhaps some would not."

"I don't understand, Mother. Who but Seneca Sachems tell Seneca what to do?"

"Pontiac."

Abby pretended ignorance. "That is not a Seneca name."

"It is Ottawa."

"An enemy!"

"Once, Daughter, but you will learn at the council." The woman turned back to the leader and with a move of her hand indicated the fort across the river. "They are silent now."

"We kept them from breaking out, Mother. They shiver like rabbits behind their log walls. They will not try again."

"*Hai!* We will watch close until first light. The white skins are cousins of the night ghosts, who help them. Tomorrow we will hold the council to decide who will go with our Daughter and by what path. Strong Woman, we will make a place for you. Come with me."

The tight ring of painted warriors parted and Abby followed the Seneca woman along the path formed for them. She crossed the gravelly, sandy beach and entered the bushes and trees that formed a wall just beyond the sentinel fires. Now she walked along a winding path between trees. Brush and high grass swished constantly against her leggings and everywhere she heard faint sounds, movement, guttural voices. She began to fully realize the size of the force that had attacked the post. No wonder Captain Blaine had known hopeless despair!

They broke through what must have been a nar-

204

row band of forest into an open space where many fires had recently flamed high under pots of meat or turning spits of deer, buffalo and bear but now had subsided to mere flickers of ruby spots in black circles of ash. No order passed, but women threw fresh fuel on the fires and the flames instantly writhed up around them.

The bright, wavering light revealed a portion of the camp. It was temporary, so Abby did not see the high walls and rounded roofs of the Long Houses. Instead, stout poles supported coverings of leafy boughs, thick enough to turn all but the hardest rains or deflect the direct bright rays of the sun during the day. Though only skeletal, the shelters followed the pattern of the Long Houses, outlining the central hall, the small rooms to either side of the central family fires.

For the first time Abby saw the Keepers of the Faith drawn up before what would have been a doorway for one of the structures. The three men and three stately women with their high ceremonial headdresses stood as unmoving and aloof as carven figures. When Abby and the woman approached, one of the priestesses took a half step forward and lifted her hand high, palm out. Familiar with the ceremony, Abby halted even before her woman guide stopped.

"Night Star," the tall Keeper commanded. "who is this one?"

"She says she is Strong Woman, adopted by the blood ceremony into the Onondaga."

"By the blood?" The priestess put the question directly to Abby.

"Here is the mark." Abby held out her wrist.

The Keeper held Abby's arm in an iron grip as she examined the scar. Then she gave way to one of the men who also carefully traced the mark with his finger. One by one the six made sure and at last Abby could drop her arm and step back, awaiting a verdict. None of the six spoke but merely looked one to the other.

"She is Onondaga," the tall priestess said at last and, as if she had asked them a question, the others nodded an affirmative answer. The tall priestess turned to Abby.

"You are one with us, Strong Woman, though we are Seneca. Night Star, see she has food. She can stay at a fireside in the *ohwachira*."

The six turned and walked away. Abby very slowly and carefully expelled her breath through faintly pursed lips. Her second and most critical test had been passed and, for the first time since leaving the fort, she felt safe. She suddenly thought of an Indian phrase, "My path opens before me."

The Council the next evening was not a gathering of the whole tribe but only of the Keepers, most of the women and several war leaders. By its make-up and few numbers, Abby could read the relative unimportance of her own problem to the group. She was strongly reminded of the small, short staff meetings that Captain Blaine held with the subaltern officers of the post. A routine matter or small problem would be discussed, then Captain Blaine would make his decision almost out of hand.

So the relatively small problem of seeing to it that

Strong Woman reached her nation, town and *ohwachira* could be quickly decided. Though the Indians held the matter to be unimportant, time and again Abby had to hold back her gasps of stunned surprise.

She learned that every British fort, post and settlement in the western country had been overrun, most of them destroyed. Downstream, Fort Vincennes was a burned-out hulk. Ouitenon, far up the Oubache River, was destroyed. Settlers' cabins had been burned and the settlers themselves killed, made captive or had fled. Pontiac had in some manner welded all the tribes into an overwhelming fighting machine, so successful that now only Fort Niagara, Fort Detroit and Fort Pitt held out. The whole of the western lands to the bounds of the Spanish Territories along the Mississippi and in Florida had been seized and were firmly in Indian hands.

She used the Iroquois respect for the women as their true leaders to dare question the matter. She looked around at the war leaders and then turned to the Keepers, particularly their aloof, hard-eyed leader. Abby bent her head in respect to the woman.

"I have been a prisoner behind the log walls across the river so I do not understand many things."

"Ask."

"Pontiac is Ottawa. They have long been allies of the French. We are Iroquois—Seneca—and since our father's fathers we have been friends of the English."

"That is right, Strong Woman."

"When I lived in the Onondaga towns, *all* the Six Nations counted the Hurons, Tiontah, Ottawa and

207

Pottawatami as enemies. Yet we are now allied with them. I do not understand."

"The British are themselves to blame. They have a new Great Sachem across the wide waters. They have conquered the French and driven them from the land and now they believe that the new British Great Sachem rules us as well as all white skins. We are no longer allies, Strong Woman. They make us captive dogs to do their bidding."

"But I can't believe the Seneca follow the lead of the Ottawa!"

"Because they are also treated as captive dogs. That is true of all the tribes north of the Ohio. They hunt and trap where they are told by the British Great Sachem. They move their villages as they are told and when they are permitted. They are given few trade goods and little wampum belts for their pelts. They can do nothing, the British traders and chiefs tell us because—" The proud woman leaned forward, her handsome face working with hate and scorn. "—because they say *we* are *their* people and *must* obey."

"They are wrong to treat their ancient friends, the Iroquois, that way. But their new Great Sachem is young and will soon listen to his Council. He will send a new pipe of peace to the Six Nations."

"It will be too late for him. We will have driven them from the land when we have taken these last three forts."

"They will not be taken, Great Mother. This Pontiac is like the wind—strong and powerful one minute, then gone the next, forgotten the minute

208

after that. He sheds Seneca blood for his own purpose."

"And for ours." The Keeper's eyes flashed but Abby had caught a faint stir of approval in the women and warriors who had gathered around. Bold and fearsome fighters who could strike hard, the Seneca needed immediate victory to sustain them, like all Indians, and Abby wondered that they had besieged Fort Pitt for so long a time. Pontiac's personal power of persuasion and fervor must be great. But Abby sensed even now that the Seneca around the post had grown restless and uncertain. She wondered if it would take very much to bring their impatience to an end.

She again pointed in the direction of the fort. "They hold out, yet how many of our warriors have died over there? They still have soldiers and guns. You say two other pale skin forts hold out against this Ottawa chief himself. Do you know how many pale skins are beyond the mountains and forests to the east? More than leaves on the trees or water drops in the rivers."

"Hai!"

The word came as a single, long soft breath from the assembly seated around her and the Keepers. She pressed the point. "Do the Seneca fight alone out here with strange allies? or do the other Five Nations of our people help?"

Now even the Keepers and the war leaders showed uncertainty. No one spoke. No one moved except to look questioningly one to another. Abby pressed on. "Have the Seneca gone to the Council of the Nations

209

in the Onondaga town?" She pointed to the dark sky. "Isn't the moon of the yearly meeting close?"

"Hai!"

The priestess finally stirred. "The Council moon is near, Strong Woman. The Onondaga have sent a Sachem. He waits to the east of the pale skin fort to announce the Great Council. He has sent a messenger to us."

"An Onondaga Sachem!" Abby exclaimed. "I could go with you to meet him and then to my town and *ohwachira*. I could tell the Council Mothers and Sachems how bravely the Seneca have fought even though the pale skin fort still stands."

The priestess studied her and then looked to the other Keepers, to the Mothers of the tribe who sat close, waiting for decision. The Keepers gave the priestess slight finger signals and she stood up.

"Strong Woman, you will go with one of our leaders and his warriors to the Onondaga Sachem. Tell him what you know of the British here and tell him we will send Sachems and leaders to the Great Council. Go with him to the Onondaga town of the Council and be present so that all the Iroquois will know why we have fought for Pontiac, who is not our enemy but the ally and friend of all Indian tribes."

The meeting broke up and Abby followed Night Star to the skeletal Long House and dropped wearily on the pile of leaves and furs that was her bed in this temporary fireside. But she could not sleep though she lay full length with her eyes closed, breathing long and evenly. Her mind raced with increased hope.

She had completed another step! Tomorrow she

would start on a journey eastward through the Indian besiegers. The Onondaga Sachem, whoever he was, would be waiting well behind the fighting Indians and that meant the way to Colonel Bouquet and his rescuing soldiers would be open.

She silently prayed her luck would hold for that final small journey.

XVI

The journey eastward was made as swiftly as circumstances and the land would permit. Abby's stalwart bronze guardians led her into the high hills lining the northern bank of the Allegeway so she did not have so much as a parting glimpse of the fort. Well beyond the point where the river turned toward far distant Lake of the Eries, they came again to the stream and launched canoes. They paddled along the west bank against the current until they came opposite a river flowing in from the east, then they angled to ascend the lesser stream. Its current was not as strong as the Allegeway and their progress speeded.

On the second day the Indians beached the canoes, hid them in thick bushes and underbrush and took to a narrow trail still leading east but at a long southern angle. Abby knew they had circled about the fort's besiegers and she must now be somewhere near the outer ring of Seneca warriors. Her guides moved with less caution and the camp fires were now much further apart. These would be the fighters who acted as a rear guard should the British attempt to break through to Fort Pitt.

As her escorts hurried her on and encountered many more of the fires, Abby began to understand why help had not come before. Colonel Bouquet would need more than just a few men, whether British Regulars or colonial militia. She began to wonder how she herself could slip through.

They came at last to a large camp and once again Abby saw the skeletal Long Houses. She also saw, with a shudder, the ceremonial ring of ashes and the charred post in its center. How many white prisoners with painted black faces writhing in agony had died there under torture of the flames? She turned her head until they had passed the platform and stopped before one of the Long Houses. Her warriors pushed her forward to stand before another group of Keepers. She swiftly explained how she had escaped her white captors and now claimed her right as an Onondaga. She answered innumerable questions and again displayed her adoption scar. She named her town and *ohwachira*.

"I am of the Owl Society and my Mother is Moon Willow. I had my own fireside and my man, a war leader. I have heard of a Sachem of the Onondaga somewhere among you who calls for the annual meeting of the Nations."

"That is true," a Keeper answered, "but now he inspects the pale skin fort."

Abby saw an opportunity to help Captain Blaine and she spoke in quick, feigned alarm. "Your Sachem should keep well out of range of the many long rifles in the fort. They are well armed, well stocked with food and can hold out for a long time."

"But there ain't many of 'em," a harsh voice spoke behind her. "I'm damned certain of that."

She wheeled about to face the most filthy white man she had ever seen. He wore the typical long shirt and thick leggings of the courier but his clothing was stiff with caked grease and dirt. His beard looked to be a thick tangle of hair as packed with bits of food as a buzzard's nest, stained about the mouth with dribblings of fluid, probably whiskey and, judging from the lump in his scaly, dirty jaw, tobacco spittle. Long tangled hair as matted and dirty as his beard fell below his wide-brimmed hat and hung about his shoulders in a ragged uneven line as though the man now and then used the heavy hunting knife at his belt to cut it. Dark, muddy eyes peered at her from deep beneath the hat brim and traveled slowly over her as he gnawed gristle and fat from what appeared to be a joint of an Indian delicacy—cooked dog.

He threw it aside as he examined her and wiped his

214

hands on his shirt front. Abby felt her skin crawl under his scrutiny and she wanted to cross her arms before her body because the man's very look seemed to undress her. A gaping shadow appeared in his beard as though somewhere deep in the greasy hair he grinned.

"Well, now, I ain't seen a woman-piece as purty as you in years! Who be ye and where do ye come from?"

She could not get her voice for the moment but only helplessly looked at the Keeper. The priestess said, "He was pale skin but now, by their blood ritual, he is Shawnee. His people camp over there, beyond the Seneca."

"Name's George Girty," the creature said in his harsh, rasping voice. "You're white, too."

"Not your kind!" Abby blurted.

"Ho, now! Hoity-toity, eh? No call for it. I bet you've bedded every big-pricked Injun brave between here'n the Mississippi from the looks of you. Ain't that right?"

He reached out, grinning, to hold her chin. His black grimed fingers looked like writhing snakes to Abby and she slapped them aside. Instantly his eyes blazed and he jerked his knife free of its scabbard. The Keeper stepped between them, facing Girty. The Indians standing about surged toward them but the Keeper's imperative signal stopped them. Girty held the wicked knife blade out from his hip ready to swing in and slash or stab but the priestess stood firm, statuesque and unharmed. She pointed beyond him.

"Your camp is over there. Go."

"Not until I teach that snotty bitch a lesson,

by God!"

"Go! Keep with the Shawnee where you belong. This woman is Seneca."

Girty still crouched, his knife ready. The priestess uttered the single-word warning of the Iroquois. Warriors moved forward and Girty was encircled by knives as wicked as his own, poised lances and lifted tomahawks.

The renegade remained crouched, not a muscle moving, and Abby wondered frantically if the man's evil brain was so twisted that he could not control the murderous rage that she could almost see emanating from him. If the Keeper saw it, she gave no sign.

"Go!" she repeated. "Now! Or your face will be blackened and we'll tie you to the stake." Girty still did not move. She ordered, "Take him—alive. He is for the—"

"Wait now," Girty cut in abruptly with a slight whine under his defiance. He spoke the Seneca tongue, but awkwardly as though not fully familiar with it. "How was I to know she's one of yours?"

The priestess threw a sidelong glance at Abby who now stepped up beside her and faced Girty and his knife. "I am Strong Woman of the Onondaga."

He grinned with that unpleasant writhing of his tangled beard about his mouth. He looked left and right at the threatening warriors, then sheathed his knife. He deliberately made a sickening throaty sound and then spat a great globule of phlegm, just missing the foot of one of the Seneca warriors. The man lifted his lance and took a step forward. The Keeper's quick, sharp word halted him in midstride.

Girty's muddy eyes cut to Abby. "There'll come a

time, bitch, when you ain't gonna have friends around you. You best figure I'll be close, huh?"

He turned on his heel and walked away, using shoulders and elbows to make a path through the crowd. Abby stood unmoving until Girty had disappeared, then let her shoulders sag in relief.

"He is gone, Strong Woman."

"I hadn't expected to see such as him with the Seneca, Great Mother. He is more animal than man."

"Pontiac has given us strange allies, Daughter. Some of them we do not like but we must accept them."

"I will watch him closely."

"We all will, Daughter. I will speak of him to our Sachem when he returns." The priestess allowed herself a slow smile, as dignified in its way as the rest of her and certainly as reassuring. "You can rest now. The Sachem will start for the Onondaga Towns in a day or two. Have you eaten?"

The Keeper led Abby to a skeletal Long House and established her among a Seneca family who made her welcome. Downy Feather, the Mother of the *fireside*, gave her a clay bowl of rabbit stew and an ear of roasted maize that Abby hungrily devoured. Then she gratefully accepted the small pile of fur and trade blankets spread over leaves. With all the daylight activity going on about her, Abby made no attempt to sleep but it felt good to curl up on her side atop the soft bed.

She thought of Henri, longing for him. She would feel better if she had the baby beside her though she knew Letty would take good care of him. She realized then that her breasts had stopped aching somewhere along the path she had traveled. She wondered about it for they had been swollen with milk each day that she nursed Henri. Surely her body should be providing milk even now. She had heard that it took a week and sometimes more to adjust when a baby stopped feeding. Then she wondered if the constant danger, tension and movement of her journey had caused the change.

Downy Feather came up and turned Abby's attention from her own body. The *fireside* mother plied her with friendly questions about the fort, the pale skin defenders. "I heard you escaped from them," she said. "Why did they keep you? Don't they know now you are Onondaga by the blood?"

"Yes, but they do not know our ways, Mother. They believe I am still pale skin."

"They are fools. The blood ceremony changes all that. Besides, don't they know the Indian way—especially Iroquois—is free and good? We are not behind walls all of our lives. We move from place to place in season to hunt. Our men are strong and good to us. They hunt, fish and fight for us and plant the seed of babies in our stomachs."

"Some the pale skin understand, Mother. But not much."

"What is your society?"

"The Owl, Mother."

"Mine is the Heron. Who is the mother of your *ohwachira?*"

"Moon Willow. She has a son who is a war leader and he was my man. Perhaps I will soon be with him again." As Abby answered, she wondered how she could work her way eastward to Carlisle and

218

Colonel Bouquet.

"The Onondaga sent a Sachem to us. We approach the moon of the annual meeting of the Six Nations in their towns. He will be back soon and we will meet him. He will take you to your man."

"If my *orenda* is good."

Downy Feather smiled. "Trust your *orenda*, Strong Woman. It leads you steady and straight along the path your life is to travel."

Downy Feather rose and walked off as Abby gratefully sank back on the furs. She feigned sleep, stretching out and closing her eyes to mere slits, undetectable a step or two away. She studied that small part of the camp she could see without moving and fought back discouragement. Wherever she looked, Indians surrounded the makeshift Long House. None paid attention to her but went about the normal life of any large encampment. Women cleaned game for the cooking pots or scraped flesh from the inner side of animal hides, cleaning them for the stretchers to dry in the sun.

Warriors strolled here and there or squatted around fires, smoking pipes and talking. Some fashioned feathers for arrows, others flaked musket flints or pounded copper into wicked, barbed arrowheads. She could not determine how far the encampment extended but, somehow, she had to work through it without discovery. She saw only Seneca about her but she knew there were other tribes, for the Shawnee had taken muddy-eyed, filthy George Girty as one of theirs. But only proud and lordly Seneca around her. Like all the Iroquois people, they bowed their heads to no one.

With a perverse sense of pride she thought that at least her blood adoption had been into the Onondaga, the leading Nation of the Indian lords of the eastern forest lands as well as of this western Ohio country. With that thought and a sense of pride she had a sudden flash of inspiration. Boldness would take her where evasion could not. Who would question an Onondaga woman whom even a Keeper had befriended and defended. She came up on an elbow and her view of the camp enlarged. She saw Downy Feather mending a moccasin a few yards away and called to her.

The woman readily answered. "Seneca all around us. Shawnee over there." She pointed and then swung her finger in another direction. "Miami there."

"And toward the rising sun?"

"Delaware. We Iroquois call them 'Lenni Lenape.'" Beyond *them* is empty pale skin country. But our warriors closely watch it should the pale skin try to help the soldiers behind the log walls where the rivers meet."

Abby forced a mocking laugh. "They will never break through!"

"Never," Downy Feather agreed. "We are too many for them. My man has told me that even if they tried, we have a surprise waiting for them. The pale skins are blind and fools. We have many warriors hidden in a deep, wide ravine filled with trees and bushes."

"Don't the pale skins send out scouts?" Abby asked.

Downy Feather chuckled, placed her finger beside

her nose and winked. "Yes—very close to the ravine. But they look westward toward our camp and think only of how many of us are out here. They never think of the ravine. Oh, we are safe enough there."

"I will go look," Abby said and rose.

Downy Feather spoke in agitation. "Just to the edge of the camp, Sister. The ravine is far beyond so you'll not see it. No warrior goes to the ravine except at night. We do not risk its discovery."

"I understand," Abby reassured her.

She walked away, leaving Downy Feather looking after her doubtfully. At first she covertly watched the Indians about her as she walked aimlessly about, fearful that her idea of boldness might not stand full testing. She had many curious, sharp scutinies but no one challenged her and she became more confident as she progressed. Apparently word of her had passed through the camp and she was accepted as Onondaga. She knew she could traverse the whole camp with only small risk of challenge that a bold answer would allay.

She made a wide circuit of the area that Downy Feather said the Shawnee occupied. The very thought of George Girty sent a shudder of disgust through her. She could not help looking back over her shoulder a time or two, half expecting to see the filthy renegade. She knew if he saw her moving along unguarded through the camp, he would trail her. But she had no glimpse of him.

Gradually the black, ashen circles marking the campfires grew farther and farther apart. The temporary Long Houses no longer blocked her way. Tepees of the other tribes and small bark houses lessened and at last Abby stood at the edge of the camp. Ahead of her, the fighting men of half a dozen tribes formed a thin, long line of sentries.

One of them glanced over his shoulder, quickly said something to a companion and jumped up. He came striding to her. He wore the war paint, leggings and moccasins of the Seneca and he carried a musket. His powder horn and bullet bag hung on thongs that crossed his chest. His hand lightly touched a knife and a flintlock pistol at his belt.

He stopped, blocking her way. "You are pale skin but wear Iroquois clothing. How did you come so far? Who are you?"

She held out her wrist. "Onondaga by the blood. I escaped from the pale skins in the fort. The Keepers acknowledge me and I hope to return to my own *ohwachira* and fireside."

He gestured behind him. "There is nothing beyond but the pale skins. We watch for them should they be fools enough to attack us. You can go no farther."

"I do not want to—only look."

He moved slightly so that she could see ahead. The trees had given way to an open area. High grass bowed under a small breeze up over the curve of the low mound. She saw the deep green of forest beyond the ridge, half a mile or more away. No enemy could approach without crossing that open space and making clear target for the Seneca sentries. Abby gazed slowly over the hillock. Somewhere in those distant trees, or just beyond, Colonel Bouquet camped. More to the point and an ever present danger, somewhere out there a great number of warriors lay hidden in ambush. She could not see any sign of the ravine, so she knew it must be in those distant trees or even beyond. So near! So distant and impossible! Frustration threatened to choke her—all this way to final failure at the very end of the gamut of risks she had run!

"Where are the pale skins?"

He pointed to the trees over the crest of the hill. "There is another, larger open glade beyond them and the pale skins camp there."

"Many of them?"

The warrior laughed. "Not enough to frighten us. There are maybe three hundred redcoats who stay day in and day out. There are bluecoat warriors who come and go. Sometimes there are enough that we prepare for battle. But then many of them leave and hardly more than the redcoats remain. Other blue-coats march in—sometimes few, sometimes so many that we are ready to fight again. But they also leave." The Indian shrugged. "The pale skins have a strange way of gathering their warriors."

Abby then knew why Colonel Bouquet had not relieved Fort Pitt. He did not have enough regular soldiers of the king's army. The "bluecoats" would be militia, called up by different colonies to fight but impatient at waiting and swift to leave for their families and farms. She wondered, biting at her lower lip as she studied the windswept hillock, how much she had risked for nothing.

A voice behind her echoed her thoughts. "White scalps will hang from Iroquois town walls and from the lodge poles of all the other tribes, Strong Woman."

The familiar voice sent a galvanic shock along her nerves. She whipped about.

Corn Dancer, in the regalia of an Onondaga Sachem, stood stern and proud behind her, his bronze face a scowling mask.

XVII

Many times in the past since she had fled the Onondaga town Abby had wondered what she would do if she should ever meet Corn Dancer again. She never dreamed that she would face him with such mixed emotions and churning feelings as she felt now. There before her was the first man ever to possess her, long before she had met Edward. Those muscular arms had held her close and tenderly.

Suddenly, vividly, she remembered how he had filled her body and how she had flamed in response.

Fragmented memories, thoughts, emotions flooded her mind. Edward—how she loved him! Like Corn Dancer? How safe and warm she had felt lying beside him in the Onondaga Long House, part of the *ohwachira* of Moon Willow and Abby Mother herself of her own fireside—Corn Dancer her man.

How safe and sure she had felt lying beside Edward in their cabin at Fort Pitt, her body opening to his thrust and bearing his child. Henri! She stood in this savage encampment in order to save them—her husband and her son. But she faced a man and a love she believed had long been behind her, yet despite herself, she thrilled to the sight of him. What kind of a woman was Abby Brewster? To her horror she realized she didn't know—at least in all this inner storm and turmoil that prevented clear thinking but opened wide the floodgates of sheer, naked emotion and passion.

Corn Dancer's deep, harsh voice cut through the miasma of confusion. "Strong Woman, you will come with me."

He turned on his heel and stalked off, knowing she would follow. This was a new Corn Dancer—no longer a war leader who needed to prove himself but a man of power and authority, a proud man who could make any woman proud of herself to know him as her man. But Edward also . . . Abby dug her fingers into her hair on each side of her head.

Corn Dancer halted, sensing she had not followed, turned and his blazing eyes held the authority of his voice. "Strong Woman! Come!"

He wheeled around again to stalk ahead. Abby, barely aware of the Seneca warrior who had questioned her, stared at Corn Dancer's retreating broad bare back. She hardly knew that she stepped out, following Corn Dancer to whatever place or crisis he might take her.

As she moved, her mind slowly began to clear. Second by second she became more and more a thinking woman, more and more able to distinguish one emotion from another. She became less a female animal guided wholly by passion and one who began to know right from wrong, duty from desire. The Onondaga would say she could begin to tell the Dark from the Light Path and sense what her *orenda* whispered in her mind.

Yet she felt strange, confused. She looked about as though seeing objects for the first time. She glanced back over her shoulder and with her gasp of repugnance, her mind became clear. That filthy horror of a man who claimed to be white stood beside the Seneca warrior, questioning as he looked her way. She hurried to lessen the distance between herself and Corn Dancer.

He strode ahead like a man who knew exactly where he would go. He did not look back and Abby could examine him closely without embarrassment. He wore the headband and feathers of a sachem and his proud head bore the stiff single line of black hair along an otherwise bald skull. She caught the golden glint of a chain across the back of his neck. He wore long trousers of Indian weave, ending in short leggings laced halfway up his shins. His bare back rippled with muscles and he had grown wider across his shoulders. Abby could tell his legs, thighs and arms would be hard as rocks, probably far more powerful than Edward's.

He led her away from the line of rearguard sentries but avoided the crowd and activities of the main camp itself. They now entered the trees but Corn Dancer did not slacken pace. Camp noise diminished almost step by step and finally only the sounds of the deep forest remained—the whisper of wind in the boughs, a chattering of squirrels, varied bird songs and notes. He continued on and Abby felt more and more isolated.

They abruptly entered one end of a long glade formed as the close pressing trees fell aside and greensward covered the ground. The sun worked its way through the leaves, whose constant movement made dappled shadows on the ground. Corn Dancer continued along it almost to the far end. Then he abruptly halted and wheeled about.

Now Abby saw that his chest had broadened and was as muscular as his back. His cheeks seemed more hollow than she remembered but that might be caused by the typical high bones and long jaw of the Indian. A large bronze pendant hung from the chain about his neck and swung back and forth with his slightest movement. He folded his arms and muscles rippled beneath his bronze skin.

"You left my fireside," he accused her in a deep voice so devoid of emotion that it frightened Abby.

She had been unable to think of what to say or do as she had followed him, though she knew she would live or die dependent on the direction of his questions. Now his flat statement gave her no clue and he

228

waited an answer. She knew she must keep the faintest note of fear from her voice. A plea would be an equal sign of weakness and arouse contempt instead of understanding and mercy. She knew she had to meet his flat statement with an answer as flat and factual as his own.

"I left your fireside, Corn Dancer. I did not want to, and I planned to return."

"Why did you leave?"

"I am a blood Onondaga, made one in your own town by your own Keepers. But I had been a pale skin but a short time before."

"You speak but say nothing."

"I say much to explain, Corn Dancer. I had never before seen the ritual of the fire and the sacrifice. I watched as long as I could and then had to put it behind me. I dare not show pale skin weakness to my sisters of the *ohwachira* and the Owls."

His dark eyes seemed to flick back and forth as he searched her face, weighed her words. She thought she saw a faint lessening of their angry lights but could not be sure because of the shadow his brows threw over them. Pictures of Henri, Edward, Blaine and Letty flashed through her mind and she knew she must go to every length for them. Her question threw a challenge directly at him.

"Did you think I ran from you? from Moon Willow?"

"You did not return."

"I tried but could not."

"Why?"

"My weakness did not leave for a long time and I dared not look on the charred stake in the circle.

When I could at last think of turning back, I was near the Allegeway. The pale skins caught me."

Corn Dancer's expression did not change and Abby could not tell what he thought. He suddenly asked, "They saw you were Onondaga, eh? Why should they want an Indian—what they call it—squaw?"

"They saw I was pale skin. I showed them my blood sign but they said I had been captured by the Onondaga."

"That is true. I myself captured and claimed you in your pale skin village east of the great river called Hudson."

"At the fort, they could not believe that I wanted to return to the Onondaga. They cannot understand anyone wanting to live with Indians."

Her mind raced frantically as she talked. Just this one magnificent man stood between her and the end of her mission, between life and death for the fort, for Henri and for Edward. Corn Dancer still stood aloof with folded arms, accusing, but she had an instinctive knowledge that he looked on her with much the same feeling as she had on him after all this time. Could she appease him, lessen his suspicion so that she would have even the smallest chance of slipping away? Her body and her sex were added weapons in this tense situation and she must consider them as nothing more.

She held her arms out wide and then toward him in invitation. She caught a quickly suppressed response in his eyes but he did not move.

"What did they do to you?"

She told as much of the truth as she knew she

dared. "They welcomed me. They made a home for me in one of their firesides until they could build a house of my own. They treated me well."

"Did you tell them about Corn Dancer?"

"I told them how you and Moon Willow protected me and that I became part of your *ohwachira*, yes."

"Did you tell them I was your man and you were the Mother of our fireside?"

Abby knew what a dangerously thin line she walked between Onondaga and white man's ethics. She inwardly prayed to find the right words. His present question could be truthfully answered. Corn Dancer, a warrior himself, would understand what could happen to a captive.

"I told them that a brave Onondaga war leader and chief had taken me and that I was part of your fireside."

"Did they honor that?"

She took a step toward him. He did not rebuff her by gesture or word and she grew more confident. She could still answer him truthfully and he would at least partially understand.

"The pale skins called me 'captive woman slave.' They said they understood I had to do as you demanded." She took another step. "But they could not understand that I had become Onondaga and that I *wanted* to be of your fireside. They pitied me! But I was proud to belong to Corn Dancer. I could not tell them so. They would have spit on me, maybe beaten or killed me. At best I would be no more than a filthy animal in a woman's body. I could not do that to the memory of Corn Dancer."

She stood very close now. His face softened and she

sensed his pride respond to her words. Yet he was not wholly convinced. His sudden question was the one she had feared all along.

"Did a pale skin warrior take you as his woman?"

The Indian punishment of an unfaithful woman could be fearful, death the most merciful, her face as often knife-gashed, the wounds filled with dirt so that horrible scars remained the rest of her life. Sometimes her nose was cut off. If she did not bleed to death she was made an outcast, one to be kicked and cursed, merely allowed to live on the scraps and offal that she might wrest from the camp dogs.

"I was given to one," she answered without hesitation but hurried on when she saw the thunder gather in his darkening, angry face. "But I refused him. He wanted me but I would not have him. What did your warriors do with such women when you attacked my town and carried me off with my friends?"

He glared at her for a long, long fear-filled moment. She came closer, touching his arm as she spoke. "You took them by force or you killed them, Corn Dancer. Do I speak straight and true?"

He slowly nodded. She dared to grasp his muscular forearm. "They did that to me. I tried to knife myself but they would not let me. I became woman of a pale skin fireside but all the time I thought of you and Moon Willow in the Onondaga town. I was 'captive woman,' Corn Dancer, to the pale skins, though they always thought of me as someone who had escaped the Onondaga. Could I have done anything else?"

She added after a moment, "Could you take me back to Moon Willow and the *ohwachira* when you

232

return? Am I soiled—dirty?"

Abby was not prepared for her triumph. One moment Corn Dancer stood tall and aloof, apparently unaware of her touch. The next moment, he suddenly swept her close. She was slammed against a rock of muscle and flesh as his lips smashed down on hers. One arm held her tightly while his free hand plunged up under her skirt, grasped the top of her leggings and with a single sweeping tug stripped them below her knees. Then he whirled her around and down. Her skirt swept up and his hands cupped her breasts so tightly that she cried out. She lay on the ground, Corn Dancer looming over her.

She looked up into his handsome, passion-filled face that she had so often seen before. Despite herself, Abby's desire and body betrayed her. But it would have made no difference if she had resisted. Her legs were wrenched apart and his hand swept over her stomach, down into her hair to touch and press her lips, move between them.

He guided himself and his muscle filled her, lunging deep and unmercifully into her. Before she became fully aware her body arched and fell away in rhythm to Corn Dancer's flaming, hard desire. She cried out. Her arms circled his neck. She could not think, she could only want, and want, demand and demand. A flicker of sanity asked what kind of woman—and then coherent thought left her. She heard her own avid cries as though at a far distance, not at all in her voice.

She felt the warm gush of his explosion as she strained and ground against him. Heat and desire rolled wave on wave through her body. She did not

233

know her fingernails clawed his back. She could not let him go. His thrusts continued and great tremors threatened to tear her body apart.

A woman's voice somewhere near exclaimed, "Edward! O Edward! God! Corn Dancer!"

The red haze and turmoil of passion abruptly vanished in the midst of his deep, throbbing penetration. His body stiffened in a strange way that made her gasp even as her senses returned to full life.

Her eyes snapped open. Corn Dancer still pinned her down, but his torso had arched high in a galvanic spasm. She looked up into a bronze face no longer passion-filled. His eyes bulged in amazed terror and his mouth sprang open. An instant later blood spewed out between his lips and over her. Corn Dancer fell limply to one side.

When his body fell off her, Abby looked in frozen, stunned horror on George Girty's dirty, scabrous face and matted hair. He held a hunting knife, the blade red with blood. Before she could move Girty dropped onto her, ripping at his trousers. His voice came in panting animal gasps.

"Now, handle a white man!"

XVIII

Abby screamed, trying to push off his weight. She beat at his face but his battering arm knocked her fists aside. He still clawed at her and tried to free himself from his trousers. Her blindly groping hands hooked into his belt and touched metal. She clawed at his eyes but again with curses he battered her down.

She tried to twist free. Once more her fingers blindly wrapped about a metallic object wedged between her body and his. In a flash of clarity she knew she had grabbed the handle of a flintlock pistol. At the same instant Girty lifted himself, his pants gaping, his muscle free. The lifting of his weight enabled Abby to yank the pistol from his belt. She blindly turned the muzzle to him and pulled the trigger.

The thundering explosion, flash of fire and Girty's ripping scream of pain all came in an instant. He fell from her as Corn Dancer had. He continued to scream as he held his left side just above his hip. Blood gushed from between his fingers. Abby threw away the empty, useless pistol, struggling to work her feet and legs under her and jump up.

She saw Corn Dancer on the ground just before her. His chest was a mass of blood and his breath came in burbling, bloody gasps. His own pistol had fallen when Girty's knife had plunged into his back. He looked up. Abby could not recognize his agonized, red streaming mask of a face. Only his eyes had pleading for her but they began to film. He pulled himself forward on his elbow, found his pistol. He lifted it, muzzle pointed at Girty who still screamed and clutched his side, moving blindly, heedlessly in a weaving, faltering step.

Corn Dancer's pistol spit flame and lead. The heavy ball caught Girty in his chest just to the right of his neck. He spun around with the force of the impact and fell. Corn Dancer shuddered, dropped his weapon. His hands splayed out before him, fingers digging into the ground. Another spasm shook him and then he went completely limp, face falling onto the ground. His body twitched and then lay slack.

Abby threw herself beside him, tried to turn him over but succeeded only in moving his head. His eyes had closed, his mouth hung open, filled with blood from the deep knife wound in his chest that must have ripped his lung. He did not breathe.

Abby sobbed and prayed, slapping his slack face in a vain attempt to force life back into him, her terrified mind refusing to realize that she looked upon death. She looked about in desperation for help that would never come in time. She then saw Girty sprawled on the ground several yards away. He tried to lift himself, moaning, and succeeded in partially coming up on one hand and elbow. Then life flowed out of him as it had from Corn Dancer and he dropped in a limp heap of dirty rags and carrion flesh.

Too much had happened too quickly. Abby tried to come to her feet but without warning the whole world whirled madly around her and then merciful darkness swept away all consciousness.

Some time must have passed before she awakened. Her eyes slowly opened on a rapidly darkening world as shadows filled the forest glade. She first saw Girty's sprawled shape and stared at it without comprehension. Then her memory returned with full, horrid impact. Her eyes rested on Corn Dancer's still form. She had tried to bring him to life but had not succeeded. Maybe now . . . he could not be dead! She stood up, swayed a moment before she could step to Corn Dancer's body. He lay face up, as she remembered she had turned him. Her tiny flicker of hope vanished.

She sat down beside him. The pistol still lay in his splayed lifeless hand. He had died for her. Pictures of the past flashed through her mind—the raid on Westover where Corn Dancer had taken her prisoner; the never-ending flight to and across the Hudson into the land of the Six Nations; the Onondaga town and the fireside; her adoption; the flight down that minor stream to the Allegeway. She touched his cold cheek, started crying and could not stop. Savage Indian some might have called him, but Corn Dancer had loved her. She knew it as she knew she had loved him. What would have happened if she had not been found on the Allegeway and taken to Fort Pitt and met Edward?

Edward! The fort! Henri! Colonel Bouquet!

Full knowledge of her mission and her danger swept in on her. She dared not be found here by the Seneca or any of the Indians. A murdered Onondaga Sachem and a murdered Shawnee by adoption lay in the glade with her. If any Indian found her, a pale skin even though Onondaga by the blood rite, out of hand she would be found guilty of double murder. She would be dead herself within minutes of her discovery.

She picked up Corn Dancer's pistol and used his powder horn and bullet pouch to reload it. She checked the flint, refilled the firing pan and shoved the weapon under her own belt. She found Girty's weapon where she had dropped it after shooting him. She reprimed and loaded it. Overcoming repugnance, she recovered Girty's knife.

She stood over Corn Dancer again, looked down at him and said a silent prayer for his travels in the eternal unknown into which he had gone. She knew that both her God and the Great Mysterious of the

Onondaga would listen to a plea for such a man as he.

She swung powder horn and bullet pouch over her shoulder, checked the pistols and knife in her belt. By now the forest literally melted moment by moment into the darkness. She looked about, recalling the direction Corn Dancer had taken to bring her here and she knew she could find her way around the Seneca rearguard. She started off but moved with the silent caution of the wilderness born.

Now and then, looking up through leafy branches, she saw the bright winking of the stars. She had but brief, restricted views of them but enough that she thought she traveled in the right direction. She prayed for the forest to end but it seemed to continue forever and ever. Then it thinned suddenly and she stopped at the edge of a great open field of high grass that whispered softly but sorrowfully in the night breeze. Now she could plainly see the whole sweep of the sky and the lore of the pioneer and the Indian enabled her to definitely set her direction. She had traveled north rather than east and now she knew she stood far beyond the Indian rearguard. If she continued in her wide circle, she would avoid the Seneca. She remained in the shadows of the last trees as she tried to pierce the darkness with her eyes and almost sniff the air for any aura of nearby danger. After a moment, she stepped out into the open and continued her journey.

Before dawn, she came on another wall of dark trees. She had no idea how far this new area of forest would extend. The thick shadows beneath the trees offered concealment and protection so she unhesitatingly plunged into the grove. Less than an hour later, she suddenly halted, listening. She heard the gurgle and murmur of flowing water somewhere ahead and off to her right. She turned toward the sound.

The stream was hardly more than a brook but she gratefully kneeled on the bank and cupped cool water into her mouth with her hands. Then she rested back on heels and knees and tried to think out her position and situation.

The small stream flowed south and she knew there was no larger creek in that direction. So this brook must join with a westward flowing, larger stream that, in turn, must flow into the Allegeway or perhaps that other branch of the Ohio, the Monongahela. From what the Seneca had told her, she was well north and east of the ravine where the Indians hid in ambush should the pale skins dare attack.

She stood up then, crossed the brook and headed east and south. She traveled on and on under trees, occasionally resting briefly. She could tell by the increased intensity of light through the high leafy boughs that the sun climbed higher and higher in the sky. Sometime around nooning she heard the chatter and bark of squirrels and realized that her body craved food. She became the huntress, drawing one of the flintlocks from her belt and holding it ready. She moved slowly and silently, pausing at every tree and looking up, her sharp eyes cutting from limb to limb. She heard the barks again and her step became a slow, slow stalking prowl. Then a swift blur of brown and gray caught her eye and she froze beside a huge oak. She pulled back the heavy, brass pistol hammer and held her breath when its clicking sounded like slamming thunder. It surely must have warned her quarry.

Silence except for a bird call off somewhere among the trees. But she heard no chatter. Well aware of the caution of wilderness creatures, including the human, she did not move. Minutes passed. She waited, her eyes moving to search from branch to branch. Then she saw a flick of brown and black high up in a tree a few yards away. A second later a fat squirrel suddenly popped into sight and stood up on its haunches, sniffing the wind as its bushy tail flicked. She suppressed her impulse to move, for the animal did not yet offer a good target.

It scampered further out on the limb, made a chattering sound that was answered from another tree. Now she could fully see the animal. She slowly lifted her pistol, fearful that her slightest movement would catch the keen eyes of the squirrel. But it remained erect on its hind feet. She made a mental prayer, lined the pistol muzzle and pulled the trigger. The flash of powder and the explosion of the shot came simultaneously. The squirrel dropped to the ground with a solid, heavy and final thud.

Abby did not immediately move from the shelter of the oak but waited for the echoes of the shot to die. Full, almost tangible, forest silence followed. She constantly searched the grove as far as she could see in all directions but nothing moved. She continued to wait until she could honestly assure herself that no human ear, red or white, had heard the shot. But as she waited and listened, she reloaded the pistol, tamping the heavy leaden ball down its muzzle, setting it with a patch of wadding. Then she pressed

241

against the oak and waited.

Minutes later she heard a tentative bird whistle deep among the trees. Another answered after a moment. A third in another direction seemed to call a question, an answering call coming from yet another direction. As though an "all clear" had been signaled, the forest sounds abruptly returned to full life. Abby eased out her breath and boldly moved away from the oak to retrieve her catch.

As the women of the Onondaga had so well taught her, she skinned and cleaned the squirrel where it had fallen. Then she moved on for several minutes before she stopped to cut a stout stick from a fallen tree limb and skewer the squirrel. It took but a moment to build a small fire and, feeling at least momentarily safe, she squatted before the fire, restraining her hunger until her meal had been cooked.

When she finished eating, only picked bones remained. She wiped her hands on the grass and then on her shirt as the Indians did. Hunger gone and strength restored, she rose and continued her journey, not stopping until once more day faded. As the light diminished, she searched the trees and finally found what she wanted. She grabbed a low-hanging tree limb and pulled herself up. This was the first of a series of steps to a place where several limbs branched out from the main trunk in a cluster. She could brace herself against the main trunk, sink down in the crotch the branches formed and be supported on every side. She had found her bed for the night well above the ground from prowling beasts or humans.

Abby really did not sleep. She would find a somewhat comfortable position, close her eyes and lose

242

consciousness until rough tree bark on arm, leg or body awakened her, or she would feel herself slipping and snap awake just in time to keep herself from falling. When dawn came, she felt stiff in every muscle and she doubted if there was an inch of her body that did not ache or twinge.

Her eyes felt grainy, strained, and she wanted nothing more than to be out of her torture-bed and down on the ground. But she held onto one of the limbs that had supported her during the night and searched the ground below in all directions. Nothing threatened and the normal bird and small animal sounds of the forest told her that nothing disturbed the wilderness about her. She at last swung out of the crotch and dropped to the soft grass below.

She recalled that clear, cold brook she had crossed the day before and wished that she could drink and wash the weary sleepless hours from her eyes and face. She instantly dismissed the useless thought and set herself to her journey. She had traveled little more than an hour when a rabbit suddenly popped out of a hole a few yards ahead. She instantly pulled her pistol, took quick aim and fired. The unscathed rabbit popped back into its hole and Abby spoke some unladylike curses under her breath as she reloaded.

She set her course by the sun and moss that she knew grew only on the north side of trees. She refused to wonder how much farther she had to travel, the answer to that being much too definite—until she found the British camp. It might be anywhere, near or far. In fact, each step she took might take her a step farther from it. She grimly set her jaw. She had to risk it. She would only confound confusion by changing course as one uncertainty replaced another. She traveled east, the one direction sure to bring her eventually to army camp, cabin clearing or walled village this far beyond the Indians.

It seemed to her that light became brighter far ahead and a new hope sprang to life. She lengthened her stride. This stretch of forest must be ending! Light increased and when she swung around a thicket of bushes to enter another glade, she saw a clearing at its end. She almost shouted in relief. She would soon be at another of the many grassy fields that broke the rulership of the trees.

Her vision widened as she approached the far end of the glade. She could see grass broken by nothing larger than bushes. She faced a sloping hill, its grassy, sunny crest hiding whatever lay beyond. She took a step out into unbroken sunlight and a sound stopped her short. From beyond the hill crest came the brazen sound of a bugle call!

Camp! Soldiers! It could only be—

Fiery streaks filled her eyes and a hammer slammed her head. She did not feel her body strike the ground.

XIX

She dreamed in a world of crushing pain. Something had a vise around her head and slowly tightened it. She tried to escape but there was no escape, and something even punished her for the attempt. The pressure of the vise increased. She threshed helplessly and then . . . black nothing.

Pain again. But this was not a vise. It had been removed. Now something steadily beat a hammer against the right side of her skull, broke a jagged hole in the bone and the hammering entered deep in her brain. Why is pain red? something deep inside her asked. Why does the world spin around and around and around? The all-important answer almost came and . . . black nothing.

Pain once more, steady and unrelenting, continual. No vise, no hammer—just pain, but also more. What? She had the sensation of moving upward, upward through layers of dark, at first pitch black and then, as seeming eternities passed, growing less dense. A faint, faint sense of a dim, dim glow afar off. Always the steady pain but something more and she groped for what that might be.

Suddenly she knew! an infinitely small grain of consciousness, an awareness that she lay enwrapped in something like a cocoon. More grains of consciousness came and with each one a peculiar expansion in her head—or somewhere up around that continuing agony. Suddenly she escaped the pain, floated freely above it and could almost see it—tangible! Real and solid! Her awareness detached like a bright cloud around a golden center of vibrating light, which attracted more grains of consciousness.

Abruptly the bright cloud, the center of gold, the grains of consciousness and the enwrapping cocoon burst apart in a silent explosion. She felt yanked across infinite space, and slammed into an unidentifiable substance. The cocoon! and now a sound—a voice.

"The delirium is gone," it said quite clearly. "Thank God! We nearly lost her."

The words had no relation to anything she knew or

246

felt. The sounds were only added barbs of the arrows of pain that repeatedly plunged into her head. She had to understand! She struggled to know.

Her eyes snapped open. She stared, uncomprehendingly upward into the worried face of a woman with iron gray hair and clear blue eyes filled with concerned pity and care.

Abby started to ask, "Who—" and whirled off into darkness again. But a ghostly voice seemed to echo from afar off behind her.

"The fever is broken. Now she has a chance."

Nothing more.

Her eyes opened as naturally and easily as if she had awakened from sleep and, for an instant, she felt soothed and lulled. The pain struck without warning, annihilating her feeling of peace. She cried out. Instantly the woman she had glimpsed before stood above her. Strong hands held her down but the restraint was not harsh.

"Easy, little lady, easy! You'll start bleeding all over again."

"Bleeding? Me? Was I hurt?"

The woman lifted Abby's hand and her fingers touched a thick turbanlike wrapping of cloth around her head. "Shot! You came in a hairline of being killed! A soldier saw you at the edge of the woods and thought you was Injun. Certain sure you was dressed like one. He just up and shot. You're lucky the ball grooved your skull and no more. Still, you've been out of your head and close to dying for a week."

More of Abby's surroundings came into focus. She lay on a bed in a room! She saw a cupboard, a chiffonier of many drawers, a window through which sunlight streamed. Then she looked up at the woman.

"Where am I? Who are you?"

"I'm Betty Gray—Mistress Gray. You're in the settlement of Carlisle."

"Carlisle! Then Colonel Bouquet—"

Again splayed, firm but gentle fingers pushed her back onto her pillow. "You cain't dare twist about like you do! Colonel Bouquet's camp is right at the edge of the settlement, little lady."

"I have to see him. I'm from Fort Pitt."

"Through all them Injuns! You couldn't of made it."

"I did. The fort is—"

The world started spinning and Abby with it, around and around and right out of her senses.

When she awakened, the room was dark except for the wavering, uncertain light of a single candle in a stubby holder whose broad base caught the hot dripping wax from the flame. Abby still lay in bed and her head ached like a throbbing tooth, though the pain had eased so she could manage to order her thoughts. She turned her head and saw a heavy form lying under a blanket on a nearby cot. Abby freed her arm from the blanket that covered her and touched her head. The thick cloth wrapping was still there.

Her movement awakened the sleeper on the cot, who threw aside her cover and sat up. Mistress Gray swung around to place her feet on the floor and in two steps stood beside Abby.

"Be ye all right?"

Abby nodded. The motion sent lances of pain through her head. The woman ordered, "Don't ye

248

move until I can get a good look at ye."

She swiftly crossed the room and took the candle holder from the table against the far wall. She returned, cupped hand shielding the wavering flame from the small breeze her movement had created. She bent over Abby and peered closely at her.

"Aye," she said grudgingly. "Ye can now focus your eyes, I can tell. Can ye see me clear, and hear me?"

"Yes," Abby answered impatiently. "But I must see Colonel Bouquet."

"Time enough in the morning. He's been asking of ye each day."

"Not time enough," Abby gasped. "Men and women and children die at the fort. There's few of them left. Please—the colonel?"

"Who are you? How did you get through them savages being a woman and all?"

"Please! The colonel!"

The woman looked down at her a moment longer and then crossed to a door that she flung open. "Abner! She's come around. Wants Bouquet right away and won't lay still until she sees him."

A heavy male voice replied, "Well, thank the Lord it's yet early enough."

A door slammed in another room and the woman returned to Abby. "The colonel will be here directly, anxious as he's been to talk to you. Now, can you tell me who you are?"

"Mistress Abigail Forny. I got through the Indians because the Onondaga adopted me into their nation. Mistress, can't we wait until the colonel comes?"

The woman's face instantly melted in deep

concern and she eased herself down on the edge of the bed. She smoothed Abby's cheek and hair, careful not to touch the bandage. Abby closed her eyes, responding gratefully to Betty Gray's palm and fingers despite the throbbing pain pounding in her head. A door slammed and male voices filled the room. Abby's eyes snapped open and Mistress Gray abruptly arose from the bed.

Then a slender, tall figure in the red uniform of the king's army, stood framed in the doorway. Abby pulled herself up as the officer, laced tricorn hat under his arm, came to her cot.

"I'm Colonel Bouquet, mistress, commanding His Majesty's troops stationed in Carlisle."

"Praise God!" Abby breathed. "At last!"

"Praise God, indeed, mistress, that you're alive. You were taken for Indian and I'm told you've somehow reached us from Fort Pitt. That itself is a miracle. Can you—" His face and the room swirled before Abby's eyes and she heard the clipped voice exclaim, "She's fainting!"

She thought her eyes instantly snapped open and into focus. She realized some time had elapsed when she saw Mistress Gray seated beside her, applying a wet cloth to her face. The officer also stood near and there were now several candles alight in the room. Betty Gray studied Abby a moment and then looked up over her shoulder at the officer.

"She's come around again, Colonel."

"Can she talk?"

"I think—"

"I can talk," Abby falteringly cut in. "Colonel, listen! Captain Blaine can barely hold out. Food . . .

bullets . . . powder . . . men dead . . . and—"

Bouquet took Betty Gray's place on the edge of the bed and he placed his finger over Abby's lips. But his smile belied his abrupt action.

"*Ma foi! madame!* You stumble over your words. You are safe. There is time. I will not leave until I know what you have to tell me. So . . . slowly, *ma chere*, slowly, eh?"

She stared, not believing her ears. "You're French!"

"Swiss. Formerly of the Berne Guards but now in the service of His English Majesty. Tell me of Fort Pitt." He looked around at Betty and her husband. "If you please to leave us, eh? Her message will be for me alone."

"Well, I'll be damned—" Abner started but Betty grabbed his arm, whirled him about and marched him across the room and out the door. She closed it firmly after her.

Bouquet turned about to face Abby directly. He reminded her somewhat of Edward. True, his skin was more fair and his hair a light brown rather than dark, his cheekbones not quite so high and pronounced. He had hazel eyes, golden-flecked and as direct and penetrating as twin sword blades.

For a moment Abby could not fully collect her thoughts and she babbled the first thing that came to her mind. "My husband is Gascon, Edouard Fournet, Colonel, but I had him change it to Forny and—"

"Gascon! You are fortunate, madame, and have excellent taste. But—" his smile flashed again. "But we need to know first of Captain Blaine and Fort Pitt, eh?"

His words brought her up short and she could

251

think again. He had placed a strengthening hand over hers and she held it in a tight grip, clinging to him. Even as she spoke, her mind raced with the knowledge that her goal had been accomplished, all effort behind her. This man in the red and gold uniform now bore her burden and she knew she could not have endured flight, dodging, fear and strain much longer.

She started talking, hesitantly at first but gradually her tongue loosened and she could speak easily and answer the sharp, pointed questions he threw at her from time to time. His face darkened with worry when she described the conditions within Fort Pitt. She told of Major Harris and the crowded, stinking, blood-soaked hospital cabin and of the women who tended the wounded and watched the children sheltered there. She spared no detail in answering Colonel Bouquet's painful questions.

She had to explain, wearily hoping it was for the last time, how she had become an Onondaga captive and of her escape to the Allegeway, which the settlers called the Allegheny. A few times the colonel's brow arched in surprise and near disbelief. But he now had explanation of her ability to work her way through the red besiegers and finally find an open path to Carlisle, this cabin and he himself.

He told her of his problem in gathering enough troops to attack the Indians. There had never been trouble with the regular British soldiers, he said. It was always the colonial militia. Pennsylvania, Virginia, New York had up until now sent hardly enough to risk a useless attack that would end in defeat.

"This Pontiac would welcome such an event," he told her. "It would strengthen his control on all the tribes he had somehow managed to bring together and encourage to greater attacks and atrocities. This whole western country would be lost to us."

"Then you can't help?" Abby asked in despair.

"Up until now I haven't been able to," he corrected. "Colonial militiamen are farmers and merchants, not soldiers. They'll fight willingly enough if there's fighting to be done immediately. That is the whole point—immediately. They will not submit to rigorous drilling and training. They will not wait until I can bring in more men. They think of their homes, their families, their farms. They want to fight today, this week, this month at the most or not at all. They melt away, go home. There is nothing I can do."

"But what is the difference now?"

"Virginia and Pennsylvania have sent new volunteers less than a week ago. They are at a fine fighting pitch—for perhaps the next two weeks. Then . . . pouf! . . . gone like the rest. If I knew the strength of the Indians or if they plan battle—"

"Colonel," Abby's fingers tightened on his hand, "the Indians are like your militia. I wonder Pontiac has held them together so long."

"Nothing like victories, *ma cherie*, and that's all our red friends have had except for three places."

"But the three hold out, Colonel. The Seneca and the Shawnee grow restless and weary. They do not like long sieges. If you could work them into a trap such as they plan for you, then—"

"Trap for me?"

253

She told him then of the Indians who waited in ambush in a wide and deep ravine who would strike when they saw the British were unprepared. Bouquet listened, absently rubbing his jaw, his hazel eyes beginning to spark.

"That would be a place we call Bushy Run," he said when she had finished. "Ah, if we could only ambush the ambushers!"

At times Abby had to close her eyes tightly against the stabbing pain in her head but she fought it off. She instantly grasped the possibilities in Bouquet's wish. "You can, Colonel!"

"How? Tell me, and I'll make you a general here and now."

"Have you seen our quail, Colonel?"

"Comment?" he asked blankly.

"If the chicks are hatched and an animal or man comes near the nest hidden in the thick grass or bushes, what happens?" She hurried on when she saw he had not grasped the idea. "The hen or the cock instantly leaves the nest with a racket. They flutter about as though crippled by a broken wing. They lead the hunter away from the chicks. Even though the hen or the cock is killed or captured, the chicks are saved."

"But we speak of Indians—not quail."

"But the trick can work, Colonel. You are watched day and night, be sure of it. Suppose you move out with only a few men—an almost hopeless force to break through to Fort Pitt? The hidden Indians see you and tell themselves you move to defeat and death. They fill this Bushy Run. Others back toward Fort Pitt await the signal to rush in to finish you

254

off. But—"

"My main force is waiting!" he broke in with a crowing triumphant laugh. "You are now Madame General Forny and I would give you medals to wear if I had them. But no mind, eh? I will send men to scout this Bushy Run and—"

"No, Colonel! The Seneca would know then—"

His fingers once more closed her lips and he smiled. "Leave fighting battles and wars to those who fight battles and wars, *ma petite*. My scouts will only report where this ravine starts and where it ends. I will question the Carlisle settlers, who will also know about it. Ah, but I plan a surprise for our red friends and perhaps even for you, Madame General. But now I had best—how do you say it in America— start the ball rolling."

He gave her hand a tight pressure and then stood up. His military ardor gave way to concern when he looked down at her. His voice grew soft with sympathy. "Ah, but you need rest. I will send our doctor to look at your head again and give you something to ease the pain."

"But Fort Pitt—?"

"It is my concern. You have done all you can—and far more than even most men. *Bonne nuit*, madame."

He wheeled about and left the room. After a few moments, Betty Gray hurried into the room and critically inspected Abby. "The colonel fairly whirled out so fast me nor Abner could hardly say a word let alone bid him good night. Did he wear you down?"

"Almost," Abby managed to say through a sudden, rising wave of pain. "It was worth it. He said he'd send someone to help me and—"

255

The pain swept over her and she could only surrender to it. The reaction to all she had experienced since leaving Fort Pitt came on the heels of the pain. She couldn't fight it as much as she wanted to. Then, finally, she knew she did not have to fight it. She need no longer be Strong Woman of the Onondaga, cunning, poised each second to fight, needing to be alert to the least sound of danger.

Vivid memory of her home and mother back in Westover flashed through her mind. She thought she sank back in her bunk and her mother came to sit beside her. Life had returned to an even, peaceful flow and she allowed herself to be swept with it into exhausted sleep.

XX

Sometime in the night she briefly awakened, if Abby could really call it a return to consciousness. It was more like a groggy nightmare of pain, light and great shadowy figures looming over her. She felt her mouth forced open and some sort of thick liquid forced down her throat. She vaguely knew she swallowed spasmodically several times to keep from choking. Voices said unintelligible things from afar off and then she plunged into sleep again.

When her eyes opened once more, sunlight streamed through a window into the room and touched the foot of her bed. Its brightness hurt her eyes and she tried to turn from it. Instantly a hand touched her.

"You've come around!" a voice said.

Abby tried to move away from the touch but only further aroused her dazed brain. She tried to return to blessed, wonderful unconsciousness. But the thing that gripped her shoulder tightened and could not be thrown off. The darkness she sought lessened and then wholly evaporated. She looked up at Betty Gray but the woman's face was not quite in focus.

"Wake up, honey!" the woman urged. "Wake up!"

"Don't . . . want to . . . wake. Sleep."

"I swan, Girl! Here you set the colonel off to fighting at last and you don't want to hear it?"

Abby stared, something alarming gnawing at her brain. Then it slowly penetrated. Colonel . . . Bouquet! Fighting? . . . Seneca? . . . Shawnee! . . . Miami! Fort Pitt! Henri and Edward! Her lassitude vanished. She suddenly struggled to sit up. But her body revolted and Betty Gray had to catch her to keep her from falling out of the bed. Though held firmly, she still clung to Betty's strong shoulder.

"Fighting?" Abby had difficulty forming the words around a tongue that seemed partially paralyzed. "We can't—hold off—Captain Blaine lost too many—"

"Colonel Bouquet, honey!" Betty gently shook her and Abby's mind threw off its haze. The older woman

258

still held her, lifting her chin so Abby looked directly into her eyes. Betty slowly formed her words as though she could physically force their meaning into Abby.

"This ain't Fort Pitt, honey. This is Carlisle. No Indians around here and won't be if sounds way out yonder mean anything. Listen!"

She held Abby by each shoulder and turned her toward the open window across the room. Abby druggedly heard sounds so faint they must be coming from a great, great distance. They were constant cracklings and poppings that continued on and on. Abby turned questioning eyes on Betty.

"Rifles and muskets, honey! Hundreds of 'em. The colonel must've kicked over a regular beehive of red skins and they're fighting mad."

The meaning slowly penetrated and Abby's face paled. "You mean they're . . . beating . . . the colonel?"

"I'd say the other way 'round. Two hours ago it sounded like the battle was right on the edge of town but now it's drifted off and back—way back."

"They caught him in their ambush—in the big ravine."

"Where? Oh, you must mean Bushy Run." Betty nodded. "Yep, the first sounds come from close around there. But now they're far west of it. The colonel's fighting in the woods beyond the Run, I'd say. Them red killers is falling back if they ain't running."

Abby sucked in her breath. "You think so? Do you really think so!" She grasped the bed covers and started to throw them back. "I have to go see. I—"

"You stay right where you are!" Betty's voice became a harsh command and she grabbed Abby's wrists. "Ain't nothing you can do out there. We both sit and listen. The sojers are doing the fighting—and pretty good, it sounds to me. We'll know soon enough."

Abby struggled unsuccessfully to free herself. "Fighting out there. Bullets, arrows and tomahawks. Wounded. They'll be coming in and—"

"We women have made things ready for 'em. Now calm yourself if you want to get back to Fort Pitt once the colonel has whopped the Indians."

"Will he? Do you really think he will!"

"I sure do. If the colonel can't do it, no one can and you can depend on it."

Much as she disliked the idea, Abby knew Betty had the right of it. She could only listen to those distant, fateful sounds. At times they seemed to increase but then they would diminish, only to momentarily come loud again. She strained to read their message but could not. Her head pounded under the bandage and from time to time she had to close her eyes. She thought of Edward. Where would he be? Somewhere west of the fort seeking a way through the Indian besiegers? Or had the Indians caught him and Simeon? The thought caused her to sit up with a cry of fear. Was Edward dead? Betty Gray rushed in the room, saw Abby sitting erect and almost pushed her down, pulling the covers over her. Anger edged her patient voice.

"I told you to stay quiet, girl!"

"Edward! My husband! They have maybe killed him!"

Betty's ire evaporated and she held Abby tightly in her arms, rocking her. She spoke softly. "Your man can take care of himself, honey, from what you've told me about him. He'll manage to live to see you and his son just like you're going to see him. Rest easy. Nothing any of us can do."

They both heard a pounding on the door in the other room and it opened. A strange male voice called, "Mistress Gray!"

"Who's there?"

"Jake Smith, mistress. They're bringing in the wounded from Bushy Run."

"My neighbor," Betty said hurriedly to Abby and then called to the other room. "Be right out. Where they taking 'em?"

"Camp hospital, mistress. Hurry!"

"Is the colonel whipping—" But the outer door slammed before she could finish the question. She looked around at Abby. "I can't nurse here and there, too."

"The men!" Abby gasped. "They need help more'n me."

"Carlisle has a heap of women who can nurse and bandage and dose. You'd be likely to try to get up while I'm gone and I'd find you on the floor fresh bleeding. I'll go out to see how the women do and find out what's happening. I'll be right back. Don't you want to know how the battle goes?"

Abby nodded and Betty's voice softened. "Abner's likely to come any minute with news and he'll want

261

to know where I am. You wait here for him. That's the one thing you can do for all of us. I'll be back as soon as I can. Keep Abner here instead of flying around looking for me."

She left and silence settled on the house. Abby wanted to revolt against just remaining there doing nothing but gradually she understood Betty's wisdom. The distant sounds diminished even as she fought her battle with herself. She heard the sound of carts in the street and painfully pulled herself up. The carts would be bringing in the first of the wounded from the battle.

Suddenly the front door slammed back against the wall. An instant later Abner Gray plunged into the room, looking around wildly. "Where's Betty?"

"She's rounding up the women to help," Abby said blurting the first thing that popped into her head. "She'll be back any minute. She wants you to stay."

"I can't. Too much going on. Got to see about them that's shot and hurt and—"

"Betty said to stay," Abby cut in. Abner started to turn and leave but Abby cried out, "Stay! What's happening out there? Is the colonel trapped?"

"Trapped!" Abner stopped short and whirled about, his face alight. "Trapped! The colonel? Not him! He's got them red devils running ever' which way—scattered to hell and gone. Pardon the word, mistress, but—"

"It's all right. The Indians are running?"

Abner stepped into the room, filled with news and eager to tell it. He had a confused story of night

262

battle, a trap that shattered the Indian ambush and then a complete rout, so far as Abby could tell. It hardly made sense except in one glorious, wonderful certainty. Colonel Bouquet had somehow overcome the red warriors pitted against him.

Betty returned and Abner repeated his story but Abby remained confused as to details. Later in the day more news trickled into Carlisle. Colonel Bouquet had now penetrated deep into the forest toward Pitt and continued to advance. Surely, Abby thought and prayed, Captain Blaine would soon be rescued and Henri safe. Still, Edward's fate remained a gnawing worry and fear.

All day long Abby heard the passage of carts along the street before the house. No matter how great his victory, Colonel Bouquet paid for it in dead and wounded, Abby knew. Or is it a victory? she admonished herself. Were all the wild tales only hopeful fantasies? Mistress Betty went out several times to return with little scraps of news that held no real answer. The increase in the wounded in the camp hospital was the only certainty—and that could mean anything.

At nightfall the passage of the carts continued but the far-off sound of muskets and rifles had long since stopped. Yet no troops marched back into Carlisle in either victory or defeat. Mistress Betty brought Abby supper and unwrapped the turban about her head and examined the wound.

"It heals, I think. Certain sure, the bleeding's stopped. But from the looks of it, you'll always have a raggedy scar up there."

"It will be ugly?"

Betty again studied the wound that Abby, of course, could not see. When she had come in, Betty had placed a clay jar of Indian make on the table and now she plunged her finger down its narrow neck and hooked out a thick jellylike substance.

"They say Injun balm heals anything. Much as I dislike them red devils, I give 'em credit for knowing salves and herbs that we whites never heard of. So I've been using this on your head along with the army doctor's laudanum. He ain't noticed and I ain't telling so—"

Whatever the balm, it felt cool and soothing so Abby had no wish to be curious about it. The salve applied, Betty again examined the wound and pursed her lips.

"No telling right now how it might heal—ugly or no. But if worse comes to worse, you could comb your hair in a low swirl just afore your ear and no one'd see the scar. We just wait and see."

A cart wheeled by, the sound loud in the early night. "Any news?" Abby asked.

"From all them poor fellows tell, the colonel is doing himself proud a'fighting. But there's not likely to be real news until daylight, I reckon. Tonight, get yourself rested. One way or another, I figure you'll be on your feet and ready to move afore long if you do what you should."

She replaced the turban bandage, blew out the candle and walked to the door. The light behind her outlined her ample, motherly figure for a moment and then she softly closed the door.

Dawn light awakened Abby and for long minutes she did not know where she was. Then she recognized the familiar room and heard street sounds, muted by the walls of the house. She did not hear the sounds of passing carts. Had all the wounded been brought in? Or was the battle over—won or lost? Her head did not ache and throb as it had the day before and she wondered if she could sit up without the world spinning about her.

She moved slowly. Now and then pain stabbed through her head but her senses did not reel. The room remained stationary and the bed did not swing crazily like a canoe to the rippling of a strong river current. At last she sat erect, carefully moved her head to look about. She wondered if she dared stand. But suppose she could? Other than proving her increased strength and ability, what would it accomplish? She probably could not walk across the room. She decided to defer the test until tomorrow—or the day after that. She leaned back against her pillow.

Abby discovered that although her body might rest and the throbbing in her head ease a bit, her thoughts would not. What happened at Fort Pitt? Was Henri safe? He would be, she knew, so long as Letty had care of him. But what of Edward? Dead or alive? If alive—where? Her thoughts went around in an endless fret.

The door suddenly opened and Betty entered carrying a tray holding the clay jar of Indian balm alongside a pot, a cup and a plate covered with a cloth.

"Well!" Betty exclaimed when she saw Abby.

"You're sitting up!" She placed the tray on a table by the bed. "Let's look at your head and then get some tea and food down ye."

"Any news?" Abby demanded.

"Nothing for sure but signs if there is, it will be good. The colonel sent sojers for medical stores last night. He's set up a new hospital somewhere out in the woods and there ain't any new wounded coming into Carlisle."

"That means—"

"He's fighting too far away to use Carlisle as a hospital anymore. That's what everybody's saying, at least. Now let's look at your head. A few moments later she said with satisfaction, "Them Injuns know their balms, I'll vouch. You're healing up fast."

"But no word from the colonel himself?"

"He's too mighty busy to waste time reporting to us settlers." Betty applied fresh, cool, healing salve to Abby's head and rewrapped the turban. "Next time I'll bring a clean cloth. This'n is getting sort of stiff-like. But first we get the tea in you."

She held a steaming cup to Abby's lips and the first swallow of the brew sent wonderful streams of warmth throughout her body. She eagerly took the cup herself, nearly scorching her lips and throat in her eagerness. Betty uncovered the plate and Abby reached for hot corn pone swimming in melted butter. She had not known how hungry she was. It took effort to keep from gulping everything down.

An authoritative rapping on the street door stopped Abby's gorging. She and Betty exchanged blank looks and the older woman said, "Who can that be! It ain't Abner. He left at first light."

The rapping was repeated and Betty hurriedly left the room. Abby heard her raised voice. "Coming! No need to split the door. Coming!" A second later, she exclaimed, "Left'nt Fowler! I swan! How come you ain't out in the woods—"

"Mistress Gray," a man's voice cut in, "Is Mistress Forny here? Colonel Bouquet sent me with a message for her."

"Abby? 'Course she's here! Come in the other room."

Instinctively, Abby touched her hair and encountered the bandage. She had a panic wondering about her appearance and then Betty filled the doorway. Abby glimpsed a red uniform behind her. Betty and the officer crowded into the room. Lieutenant Fowler was a slender blond young Englishman with a wisp of mustache, blue eyes that lost military hauteur the second he saw Abby and the blood-soaked turban she wore. He carried his hat under his arm and his sword swung at his side. He showed marks of a long and strenuous ride, red uniform coat wrinkled, black boots dusty, a smudge on one cheek. A long strand of golden hair escaped the black ribbon that held it at the back of his neck and the lock swung down along one cheek. He brushed it aside impatiently.

"Madam Forny? I am Lieutenant Fowler, aide to Colonel Bouquet. I've come to Carlisle for more supplies and also with a message for you from the colonel."

Abby held her breath in fearsome expectancy and bent forward, rounded eyes locking with the officer's.

She finally gulped and swallowed. Her voice sounded strange. "What—? What—?"

"I don't understand the colonel's meaning, mistress, but I am to tell you he has again promoted you."

Abby's face lighted. "He's won! Oh, thank God, he's won!"

XXI

Abby fired her questions at Fowler so fast she fairly stumbled over her words. He tried to answer them as speedily but everything was disconnected, a gabble without meaning until Betty abruptly smacked her hand down on the table. The sharp slap of her palm on the wood was like a sword cut through the noise.

"We're not learning nothing," Betty said flatly. She placed a chair beside Abby's bed. "Left'n't, you sit down. Abby, you wait until I bring the left'n't some whiskey to clear his throat and brains of travel dust. Ye'd like that, sir?"

"I would. Thank you, mistress."

Betty glared at Abby. "Girl, I'm as anxious to know what's happening as you and I don't aim to miss a thing. So both of ye hold your tongues till I bring the whiskey. If ye can't, the left'n't comes back later. What'll it be?"

Abby managed to look contrite and impatient all in the same instant. She sympathized with Betty and saw Fowler's weariness. She answered Betty in a small voice. "I'll wait. So will Lieutenant Fowler, I'm sure. A few minutes more will make no difference, sir?"

"It will help me sort out all I'm to tell you, mistress, and catch my breath. The news will keep that long." His eyes flashed proudly. "It's a glorious day for us, mistress."

Betty grunted as though she had known that all along and left the room. Abby and the officer sat facing each other. He broke the silence.

"If you'll permit me, mistress, I can well understand the colonel's praise of you. He gives you credit for the key to our battle and he also said you are as charming as you are intelligent. I heartily agree."

"Thank you, sir." She touched her bandage. "This does me no favors, however."

"An honorable wound. The colonel told me about it. You are very brave."

"I have a son and a husband to make me brave, sir."

"Someday I hope to find a wife like you, mistress."

Betty returned then with a mug that Fowler gratefully accepted. He took a long pull, then dropped back in his chair and expelled his breath in a deep relieved sigh. He caught himself up and smiled at Abby.

"And now the news I've been ordered to bring you."

Within minutes it became evident that the telling would take time so Abby interrupted sharply. "The main thing, Lieutenant. The details can follow. Is Fort Pitt saved?"

"By now, the colonel will be in sight of its walls, mistress. Count the fort saved."

"But west of it, sir? along the Ohio? Do the Indians still block that way?"

"Mistress, the river is open to safe travel from Pitt to the Spanish Mississippi. Just a few Seneca stand between the Colonel and the fort here on the east side, but they only fight so their tribesmen can escape."

Abby closed her eyes in a silent prayer of thanksgiving. If Edward had avoided capture and death, he was safe and probably with Letty and Henri this very moment. Abby felt a heavy invisible burden lift from her mind.

"Mistress?" Fowler said, "are you well?"

She looked at the young man's concerned face and worried eyes and smiled. "Well? Lieutenant, I have not been so well in a long, long time! But you were to bring me news!"

"Yes, mistress. The colonel ordered me first to thank you for your story of the quail, whatever that means, and that he used the idea to great advantage."

"I understand his meaning, Lieutenant. Tell me

271

what happened from the moment Colonel Bouquet left Carlisle."

The story was long but Fowler had a way of recounting events in logical order. Abby had only to remember the country through which she had fled and she understood what had happened.

Bouquet had first called in the settlers of Carlisle and had them draw maps of the country as far as Fort Pitt. The location and importance of the long, wide finger of Bushy Run, the ravine, became instantly clear. He discovered from the crude maps that the western end of the Run ended about a mile this side of the Shawnee and Seneca camps. The brook emerged there into bright sunlight and coursed along an open meadow before plunging into the forest.

Fowler explained, "Bushy Run is more than a ravine, mistress. It's a wide gorge or defile running generally east and west. It is filled with bushes, trees and all sorts of vegetation—small animals and birds, too. It had no military value to us or to the Indians until Fort Pitt was surrounded. The Carlisle folk paid it little attention except for a likely place to set rabbit traps, bag a squirrel or fish now and then."

"But then the Indians struck."

"Correct, Mistress Forny, so many of them that the Carlisle folk never ventured into the Run, fearing a chance encounter with a redskin." Fowler shrugged his chagrin. "But I'm afraid the Indians proved better tacticians than the settlers, particularly after Colonel Bouquet moved here, hoping to march on Fort Pitt. He never had enough militia that would stay and fight until now."

"Did he scout the Run?"

"Using Carlisle men," Fowler nodded, "but they gave it little notice. As I said, only an Indian hunting for game or an unwary settler with hair enough on his head to make a good scalp ever went down into it. They reported that it was no threat to the colonel, but they obviously never risked their hides going into it."

"Lieutenant, don't blame our people for not being soldiers. Too many of them have lost scalps to Indians wandering the woods. Our women have been raped, murdered or kidnapped. Too many children have been stolen and never seen again. We live alone without brave soldiers like you to guard us. So perhaps we're over-careful. Can't you understand how we feel?"

Fowler had the grace to flush. "Thank you, mistress. I've not been fair."

"Because you haven't understood, sir. But we've strayed from the news."

"If it hadn't been for you, mistress, the colonel would never have known what the Seneca were doing. Under cover of night, they filled the Run with warriors. They watched our scouts. They watched the colonel but we did not know it. He wonders now how in the many times when he moved toward Fort Pitt with a few regulars and militia they didn't destroy him."

"I've been forced to know Indians, Lieutenant. They prefer to strike with all the odds on their side, even from ambush. I'd say if the colonel had a few less militia, they would have. But they knew their main band was much stronger, so they kept concealed."

"That may well be, mistress. In any case, when you told the colonel about the Run, he made his own plans. He moved almost his entire force out of Carlisle, but northward instead of westward—and they marched by night. He left a few soldiers here in Carlisle. Here's where he put to use your incomprehensible story about the quail and its young."

"Decoys—small enough to tempt them."

"Yes, mistress, but he did not tempt them, he attacked."

"What! Down in the Run?"

"He moved troops out of Carlisle in broad daylight to make certain the Indians would see them, then turned west and south in the night. He concealed them in the woods along the whole northern bank of the woods, but especially strong at the west end."

"But that's all open country between the Run and the main Seneca camp!"

"Exactly." Fowler smiled, anticipating the surprise his news would bring. "He left me in command of a company of regulars in Carlisle. We sent out a small band of militia and settlers—your quail, mistress. It worked. There were so few the Indians thought this was the time to spring their ambush."

"You mean you sacrificed—"

"Nay, mistress. When the Indians struck, I attacked with my regulars at this eastern end. The colonel threw all his fighting men into the Run from the north and cut across that open mile between the Run and the Indian camp. We had the ambushers trapped! They tried to escape but had no chance. I think two Carlisle men were wounded in the five or ten minutes before the Indians realized what had hit them. They broke up, every man for himself."

"Only to join the main camp—"

"No. Colonel Bouquet wheeled west and hit the main camp straight on. Hundreds of Indians were killed, the rest scattered and the colonel captured war chiefs and Sachems. He has driven the rest north of the Allegheny and the Ohio. Most of them are trapped along the Muskingum River. Mistress, I believe that by now Colonel Bouquet and Captain Blaine are shaking hands inside the Fort Pitt stockade." He grew alarmed. "Mistress! are you all right!"

She had bent over, face buried in her hands, crying in sheer relief and joy. Her body shook as the tears streamed between her fingers. She managed to answer with a word at a time.

"Lieutenant . . . I can't help . . . crying for . . . my son and . . . my friends at Pitt . . . my husband . . . somewhere west . . . Maybe alive. I have . . . to find out."

"Mistress Gray!" Fowler flung open the door to the other room.

Betty rushed in. Abby blindly reached for her, needing those warm, wonderful arms about her. They would indeed prove that the world and all Fowler had told her were real. Holding Abby close, Betty crooned soft reassurance.

"I know. My Abner told me. No more blood and scalps on the lodge poles. No more murdering Injuns! It's finished. Honey, just tell yourself that over and over. It's all finished!"

Abby's fingers had taloned and her nails sank deep into Betty's fleshy arms. The understanding woman made no attempt to ease the torture or free herself. She stroked Abby's face below the bandage and looked over her shoulder at the young officer.

"Is there aught more to tell, Left'n't?"

"Not of the fighting. But the colonel has ordered an escort for Mistress Forny as soon as she is able to travel. He knows she wants to return to Fort Pitt as soon as possible."

"That will be weeks, mayhap a month," Betty answered.

Abby's head jerked up. "No! Only days. Only days!"

Lieutenant Fowler smiled and stood up. "Knowing you, Mistress Forny, it will be within a miraculously short time. I understand why the colonel spoke so highly of you. I will take my leave and you can rest for the day."

"You're not leaving Carlisle!" Abby asked in fright.

"I have much to do here, mistress, so, I will not leave immediately. I'll ask for your health and to see you each day, if you'll permit."

"Permit! I'll expect you!"

She had not known how much physical and emotional stress she had undergone during Fowler's visit. Fright, then elation, new hope, then increased elation and the knowledge that the threat of Indian destruction and death no longer cast a long shadow over the land had drained her. Though her brain whirled with myriad plans for return to Fort Pitt, for holding Henri and rocking him in his crib, for some means of discovering Edward's whereabouts and safety, she could not fight off the deep lassitude that swept over her.

She did not know when her eyes closed and sleep mercifully enwrapped her.

She awakened with a start. Betty gently shook her and looked relieved when Abby opened her eyes. "Lord! I'd begun to think only Gabriel's last trumpet could wake you."

Abby looked confused. "Did I sleep? It must've been only for a minute."

"It was the clock around and then some. That nice young Leftn'n't Fowler come asking about you and—"

"But he just left!"

"Yesterday afternoon, honey. He was here this morning and he'll call again late this afternoon. Me'n Abner asked him to stay for sup after he's talked to you."

Abby looked blankly around the room and then to the window where she saw the long slant of a setting sun. Betty considered her critically.

"Ye look better, though mighty frowzled. Hungry?"

Abby realized she was ravenous and badly in need of a hot liquid, like tea. When she nodded, Betty smiled. "Thought as much. You need sponging and combing, too, and I want to look at that bullet gouge along your head. Can ye sit up?"

"Of course!"

Abby quickly moved to a sitting position. As before, the bed, room and all went spinning around and around. Betty grabbed her.

"Steady! Steady! Girl, you gotta learn your noodle ain't ready for full work yet a time. All right now?"

When Abby nodded. Betty cautiously eased her back on the pillow and tentatively released Abby's shoulders.

"There now! You're steady. Sit still but lean against me if ye have need."

She sat on the bed, close enough that Abby had no chance of even swaying without instant support. Betty unwrapped the turban and reported, "It looks to be healing fine. Does it still hurt? Does your head feel all busted up?"

"My head feels fine. The skin and bone is sore above my ear all along the side of my head."

"No wonder. I still don't know why that musket ball didn't kill you. A scant whisper deeper and it would've. Let's salve it again and then get you fed and cleaned up."

Betty left the bed to return with a mug of hot soup as well as the Indian ointment. By the time Lieutenant Fowler appeared, Abby felt renewed and presentable except for her bandaged head. She greeted him with a question.

"Is there more news from Fort Pitt?"

XXII

Abby still could not quite believe it even as she held Henri, watching him kick, crow, giving her his toothless smile and groping for her with plump little hands and arms. Even at high noon, it could be dark in the tepee, though the flap of the triangular entrance had been thrown back. How wonderful it would be to have a real house once more!

How wonderful to be back at Fort Pitt settlement

and hear the constant pound of hammers, axes and saws that shaped newly cut logs to build up the walls of cabins. How wonderful to know that when she carried Henri out into the sun, she would undoubtedly see Edward, working with others to restore what had been so ruthlessly destroyed.

In the last month she had lived through a miracle. She could remember all too clearly those long, torturing days that she lay recuperating in Carlisle, of waiting and waiting for definite news from Fort Pitt. She could even now vividly remember the morning Lieutenant Fowler had burst into Betty Gray's cabin. She had by then freed herself from the bed in the inner room and was seated in a straight-back, sturdy chair by the fireplace where she could watch a bubbling pot of stew hanging from a crane over the flames.

"Mistress Forny! a messenger from Fort Pitt! He's one of those French couriers. He rode out of the forest less than five minutes ago."

"A messenger a'horse? Then he's not a courier."

"But he is garbed in their manner. One of the town boys saw him just as I started to rap on your door. I saw him myself."

She had heard an increasing heavy beat of racing hooves along the street, a shout that made her jump up, eyes rounded in disbelief. She had taken only a step to the door Fowler had left open when its frame filled with a form that only her constant dreams and hopes could have conjured up.

"Edward!"

They held one another close, tightly as though each knew the other would vanish as soon as this

280

sudden, amazing dream ended.

But neither vanished and the dream did not end.

Colonel Bouquet had not sent one of his own men as a messenger but Edward Forny.

Betty and Abner appeared a few moments later, having heard the news, and they made Edward welcome to their cabin as well as to Carlisle. Then they discreetly withdrew, Abner giving Edward a signal to follow them outside. Abby impatiently waited the few moments it took Edward to return. He kicked the door closed behind him and once more gathered her in his arms. This time their kiss was long, lingering and passionate. His hand traveled along her shoulder and down her side to her hip as he pulled her in tightly against him.

She responded hungrily, starved for this moment, this actual bodily contact with the man she had often fearfully thought she would never see again. She brought his hand up to cup her breast beneath the coarse cloth of her dress and gave a small gasp of delight when his fingers tightened around it. Her tongue parted his lips, making little caressing movements.

He broke their embrace and, strong hands on her shoulders, held her at a slight distance. He searched her face concernedly fixing on the narrow strip of white cloth that had recently replaced the cumbersome turban about her head. She saw her own desire mirrored in his face and could see that he held it in tight control.

"J'ai malade d'amour pour vous, ma coeur."

"And I'm also love-sick for you," she whispered.

"Mais alors, you have been shot and—"

"It heals. See!"

Before he could prevent it, she snatched off the bandage, exposing the wound along her head. He sucked in his breath as he saw the long gash, lumpy and angry as it healed.

"*Mon Dieu!* you came close to death!"

"The army doctor and Betty told me. But I would not die, my love. I had to live for you."

She pulled him back into a tight embrace and kiss, his body pressed close against her so that she could feel his increasing strength. She spoke low and rapidly in his ear, "There is a bed—next room. Take me! It will be better medicine than—"

He bent and his strong arms swung her up to carry her through the door. He eased her to a seat on the bed but she literally bounced up and whirled about. "Undress me. I can't release the catches. Hurry. Oh, hurry!"

Her dress and coarse petticoats fell about her ankles. She stepped out of them as her fingers hooked in the drawstring of her pantalets. She turned to face him, completely naked. He almost tore off his own clothing and they fell on the bed, clutching one another. She spread her legs and opened herself, guiding him, feeling his great, warm, thrusting entrance. She threw her head back on the corn-husk pillow and moaned in a delight that, but an hour ago, she doubted she would ever know again. Nothing in the whole universe existed but the sensations of her body, his weight upon her, his power within her. Now, weeks later and miles away from Carlisle, the time that followed was still only a blur of feeling, ecstasy, completion. She would not want it any other way, she knew.

A sudden black shadow blocking the tepee entrance shattered the vivid memories engulfing her. She came back to the present with a start. Edward half crawled through the low opening and straightened to stand tall and wonderful, towering over her. She felt his excitement but his first concern was for Henri. He crouched down and put his hand over the baby's bald head. Henri cooed in delight.

"Eh, *mon petit chevalier!* How many giants have you killed—a dozen or more, perhaps?"

"Your 'little knight' won't kill one," Abby replied with a laugh, "so long as you weigh him down with all that hand and those fingers."

"*Pardieu!* You liked it well enough!"

She flushed, then pertly tossed her head. "But I am *demoiselle*, not knight." She sobered. "Does the building go well?"

"We will soon have a chateau again."

"I'll settle for a cabin."

"*Paysan!* But Lieutenant Fowler has come from Colonel Bouquet and asks to see you."

"Of course! Has something happened?"

"The lieutenant will tell you," Edward answered, returning to the open flap as he called out, "My good wife and son will see you, sir."

Fowler crawled in, came to his feet and bowed to Abby. "It is good to see you again, Mistress Forny. I have renewed acquaintance with your husband. Ah, this must be your son."

"Henri Forny, Lieutenant."

"His father's strength and his mother's charm, I'd say."

283

"Said like a Gascon, Lieutenant," Edward chuckled. "But tell her the news and the colonel's request."

The tepee held no furniture except for Henri's crib that she had brought from Carlisle. Indian-style, blankets and furs thrown over piles of boughs and leaves formed the bed. The blackened fire circle in the center of the floor was substitute for a fieldstone cabin fireplace. It had been placed so that smoke would be drawn directly upward and out through the open vent formed where the tepee poles came to a point high above.

Abby indicated the nearest mound of furs. "That's all I can offer for the time being, Lieutenant."

"Far better than many a pallet I've known since Carlisle, mistress. Thank you." He sat down, cross-legged, looked over at Edward, then at tiny Henri. "Can the Forny's, baby and all, make a short journey to the Muskingum and the colonel's camp?"

"All of us?"

Edward exclaimed, "Henri is much too small!"

Abby's slight gesture checked his concern as she asked Fowler, "How would we travel, Lieutenant? Is it important?"

"Mistress, the Ohio flows just beyond the fort. The Muskingum River enters it not far to the west and Colonel Bouquet is encamped not far up that stream. I came the distance by canoe, expert *voyageurs* at the paddles. All of us would go by river."

"*Les bateaux* are not for *les enfants*," Edward objected.

"Why does the colonel want us particularly at this time?" Abby asked.

"To be present at a treaty powwow with all the

Ohio tribes. He thinks it is truly fitting that you be present since, without you, it would not have been possible. He sends word your presence would honor and please him as much as a commendation from General Gage."

"Who is General Gage?"

"Lord Amherst has been recalled to England and Sir Thomas Gage takes his place, mistress. Perhaps I should not comment, but I think Lord Pitt has made a wise change in the command of North America. But, can you make the journey?"

Edward shook his head. "I would not endanger my son."

Abby considered a long moment before asking, "Edward, you know the river and the canoes. Couldn't you and Simeon take us safely through?"

"*Certainement!* But there is the question of how you carry our son. There can be rain and hot sun—night camps—"

"Only two or three, Mr. Forny."

"*Eh bien,* but I still do not like it."

"Nor would I," Abby agreed, "except that Colonel Bouquet has done so much for us. We should accept his invitation if at all possible." Her slight frown abruptly vanished. "Is there an Indian woman in Fort Pitt?"

"Not one!" Edward answered. "They fled with their men so quickly they left much of their camp behind."

Abby clapped her hands. "Good! I have the answer once I see Letty."

That evening a much battered Indian cradle board leaned against a side of the tepee and Dean Smith

285

assured her he could have one built before midday sun tomorrow. Letty promised to line it under Abby's directions and Abby looked triumphantly at Edward, then turned to Fowler.

"We could be ready the day after tomorrow if that is not too much delay."

"I know Colonel Bouquet would be happy for me to wait, mistress. Mr. Forny and his Simeon would wield the paddles?"

"If it pleases you."

"But it does not please me," Edward snapped. "I have but one son and one wife. "I'll not risk them to the rivers."

"Mon coeur," Abby pleaded, "wait until Dean comes tomorrow with the cradle board. He will make the necessary changes on it. Our son will be comfortable and safe. You will see. If you're still afraid for him and for me, we won't go. Is that fair enough—just to wait and see what Dean does?" When he still hesitated, frowning darkly, she added, "Please?"

"Eh bien," he surrendered. "I'll wait."

"There it is, Lieutenant," she turned to Fowler. "We will decide by tomorrow afternoon."

The young officer came to his feet, tucked his hat under his arm, smiled at her and gave Edward a short, military bow. "I'll spend the time in hope."

Edward also rose to leave with him but Abby said quickly, "I need you to help measure our Henri before Dean takes the cradle."

Edward was puzzled but said nothing. Measuring the baby proved to be a difficult task because Henri thought it all great fun. He kicked and squirmed, threshed his arms about and drooled, smiled and cooed. But at last Abby and Edward were able to determine his girth and length. Edward brought the battered cradle board and held it as she indicated the changes she wanted made. When she had finished, Edward thoughtfully turned the board over and over, inspecting it anew.

"*Oui*, it might be as you say," he reluctantly conceded. "But let us see how it is when Dean and Letty have finished with it. Until then—"

His fingers briefly caressed her cheek and then he too left the tepee to return to their unfinished cabin.

The next day right after nooning, the tepee filled to bursting with visitors. Letty came, holding her baby while her two boys clung to her long, ample skirt. Dean carried the rebuilt cradle board. Edward and Simeon followed them into the tepee and a moment later they heard Fowler's voice at the entrance flap.

"Am I welcome, mistress?"

"Of course! I hoped you'd come."

None of them could believe the cradle board was the same battered, dirty object Dean had taken with him the day before. It was longer and rounder, according to Abby's specifications. Dean had neatly cut away the front from the back and then rejoined them along one side with cleverly carved and fitted small hinges. The top could now swing completely open, be closed and tightly latched. Letty had lined the interior with layer on layer of alternating thick moss and feathers, topped by a final covering of soft flannel. The once filthy back and cover had been scrubbed clean and Letty had redecorated it with bands of color from boiled berries, bark and roots. A discarded soldier's belt made stout straps into which

Abby could easily slip her arms and swing the whole contraption, Henri and all, onto her back. She swiftly changed Henri into a warm buckskin wrap, placed him on the padded board, closed the lid and latched it. She stood up and the baby, confused by the snug new cradle, looked around round-eyed.

"There! How could I lose him! How could he fall from a canoe!"

"Tonerre! Vous avez raison," Edward marveled. "He will be safe." Then he frowned. "But he cannot stay in so tight and small a crib night and day!"

"Only in the canoe," Abby assured him.

Then Henri ruined the whole triumphant effect. He could not move his arms freely and his kicking legs were tightly confined. He realized it just as Abby shifted him to a more comfortable position on her back. His protesting howls filled the tepee and echoed from the walls. Edward clapped his hands over his ears.

"Sacre bleu! he is tortured!"

Abby lifted her voice over the howls and cries. "No, he is mad because he can't move in the cradle board. He will become used to it."

"Or our ear drums will split," Edward almost shouted.

Abby opened the crib and relieved Henri's temporary restraint. Instantly the howls and cries subsided to an occasional deep sob. He thrashed his arms and kicked his legs. Edward looked at his son and scratched his head.

"Eh, but I have seen Indian babies in those things. They make no sound."

"Because they're placed in even tighter confinement from almost the moment they are born. They stay in those boards from morning until night if their mothers are busy. They foul themselves time and again and remain in it until their mothers have time to take care of them."

"Do you mean *our* son—!"

"I mean no such thing! With latches and hinges he is easily removed in a minute or two. That's why I changed the design."

Letty shuddered. "I wondered how them Injun babies was taken care of. Now I wish I hadn't learned."

Abby hardly heard, her attention centered on Edward. "Darling, can't we go with Lieutenant Fowler?"

She caught his instant impulse to refuse but the hard light left his eyes. "It is important to you, eh?"

Those days and nights that she spent working her way through the Indian ring around Fort Pitt rolled through her memory in one instant. She saw, with an inward shudder, the murder of Corn Dancer and the killing of George Girty. Her head still bore, under the roll of hair combed over it, the scarred gouge of the musket ball that had nearly killed her when she was in sight of Carlisle and so near Colonel Bouquet.

"Isn't it only my right and due that I see the final end of all my work?"

"I have never once thought differently," he answered, "but *notre enfant*—"

"Our child should be present even if he won't understand, *mon cher*. It is his right and due also— and yours—because I did everything for both of you as well as for our friends and the brave soldiers here at

Fort Pitt."

He rubbed his hands over his knees for long, thoughtful moments. He looked at Fowler, around at Letty and Dean, then cocked his head as though listening to the sound of life and activity outside. At that moment a bugle within the fort sounded a call. Edward's fingers tightened atop his knees.

"We will go, *ma femme brave*. It is your right and due, as you put it."

XXIII

Edward took the bow of the long canoe when he and Simeon had made sure that Abby and Henri sat securely on the wide seat athwart the center of the craft. The current caught the canoe, sweeping it beyond the fort into the grip of the mighty Ohio. Though his eyes and attention were cast ahead of the prow down the river, each second Edward could picture his wife in her Indian garb once more, the cradle with Henri on her back as safe as in his crib at home. *Le Bon Dieu* blessed me, he thought, when he brought us together.

His chest swelled with pride when he recalled her bravery. He had learned of it the moment he entered Fort Pitt after the Indians had fled before the smashing, slashing attacks of Colonel Bouquet. That Swiss officer in the service of the British crown had nothing but praise for Madame Abby Forny when he spoke of her to Edward. Bouquet had insisted that Edward be the courier to bring the good news of the complete Indian defeat to Carlisle.

"Ride fast and hard," Bouquet had ordered as Edward mounted the horse provided for him. "Your good wife barely came through alive and she is wounded, but she thinks only of you and hopes beyond hope that you are alive. Tell her what we did at Bushy Run, thanks to her. Now—ride!"

Quelle Marvellieux their reunion had been. How wonderful to find her alive and vibrant in his arms once more despite the bandage about her head and the ugly, healing scar beneath it. Ah! there had been so much for each to tell the other when, at long last, their mutual physical hunger had been appeased. They had fairly babbled in their eagerness to recount all that had happened.

He forced her to tell her story first. He had inwardly quailed at times in the telling of it and would hardly believe that she had come through it all and was still alive and beautiful. He shook with hatred when she told him of George Girty's attack. He had known of Corn Dancer long before, of course, and had instinctively feared Abby's reaction should that handsome Onondaga warrior come back into her life. But when he heard how Corn Dancer had died saving Abby, Edward breathed a prayer for his soul and sent silent, heartfelt thanks to the spirit of the man for his sacrifice. Loving Abby so much himself, Edward fully understood why the Indian had sacrificed himself. Edward could have done no more.

He told Abby of his own hectic, desperate days and weeks. He and Simeon had left Fort Pitt at a time of peace that must have shattered soon after they started to survey the great river for prospects of trade. He diplomatically omitted that unexpected and utterly mad interlude with Pearl and Hank Jonas, but told her with regret of the many destroyed cabins and settlements all along the river and up many of its tributaries.

"The French are still there," he told Abby, "even now after the English have won the whole of the country. Ah, but you and I would have a trading empire, *ma petite*, had it not been for that damnable Pontiac stirring up the tribes."

He and Simeon had no warning of it until they came to the Falls of the Ohio. They had been camping there when they were attacked without warning and barely escaped with their lives. They had tried to fight the Ohio's current going back upstream. Its power might have been overcome had it not been for the constant attacks on them from the north bank. Cabins and settlements they had once passed had been reduced to ashes. On the second day, Edward had turned to the south bank, abandoned the canoe and struck out in that hunting and fighting area that no tribe claimed and where none settled except for widely separated, temporary camps such as the one near the Great Salt Lick.

They soon discovered that even south of the river there was no real safety until they fled further inland. They often came on ancient camps, long since abandoned by either of those traditional enemies, the Shawnee or Choctaw, after some long-ago attack. They met settlers, couriers and *voyageurs* like themselves, who had fled for their lives into this Dark and Bloody Ground.

Only then did they learn of the vast devastation the Indians had made, of a little known Indian chief, Pontiac, who had welded the tribes into a hitherto unheard of Indian alliance. Nothing had stood against them but three forts—Detroit, Niagara and, most important, Fort Pitt. Edward's blood had turned to ice in fear for Abby and Henri.

New desperation dogged Edward's feet and drove him eastward. He and Simeon became as wary as hunted animals traversing the long, torturing miles. Several times they came close to discovery but at long last the increasingly hilly country told them they approached their destination. At last they broke out of the forest and looked down on open grassy fields that formed the banks of the Monongahela. Edward judged that they were perhaps thirty miles south of the fort. They stood not far from where not many years back the French with their Indian allies had annihilated proud but stupid Braddock.

Now Edward and Simeon progressed with extreme

caution, moving back into the forest, working northward along the west bank of the river. At one time being French had been a passport through Indian country but Edward had learned hundreds of miles back that Pontiac's allies saw only white skins and did not hear language or recognize the old camaraderie they had known with the *voyageurs*. Now the Indians attacked and killed on sight.

Soon they encountered signs that the Indians could not be far ahead. Though Edward wanted to rush into the fort and be at Abby's side, he had to progress with painful, straining caution. They often hid for hours as hunting bands threaded the woods around them. Once they had been forced to hide a whole day in a thicket while Senecas camped within a stone's throw, sending out hunters, some of whom came so close Edward could have touched them with his long arms. They slept cold that night while a warm fire blazed not fifty yards away.

Thankfully, their imprisonment ended the next day when the Seneca gathered up their kill and moved back toward the river. Even so, Edward and Simeon remained concealed the whole morning, finally venturing from their hiding place to scavenge what scraps of food the Indians had left. Hunger at least partially appeased, they plunged northward back into the forest.

At break of dawn two mornings later, they lay flat side by side atop a great finger of rock, a small mountain projected out over a sheer cliff that dropped a hundred feet below into treetops so thick Edward could not see through their covering of leaves.

But he could look afar out and see the silver, crooked course of the river threading the mountains to the north. That would be the Allegheny, as the settlers called it, or the Allegeway as Abby had named it. Directly below him, the Monongahela flowed to join it, forming the broad, westward moving Ohio. But it was the small point of land afar down out there on which his eyes riveted.

As morning mist cleared, tiny objects down there began to take shape. He saw circle on circle of red-glowing Indian fires, little pits of light in the morning gray. They completely surrounded the joining of the rivers and his heart grew heavy before the small mound that was the stockade of Fort Pitt could at long last be seen.

That projecting shelf of rock so high above and so far away from Abby would be as close as he would come to her for a long time. He and Simeon could not stay there long. It was too exposed and dangerous, for at almost any moment they would be discovered. They retreated to the forest and worked their way down steep slopes to the open valley of the Monongahela. They dared not venture out in broad daylight.

So they had skulked along the forest glades toward the junction of the rivers. Within less than half a dozen miles of the Ohio, Edward began to understand the hopelessness of the task. He and Simeon had to move slower and slower and spend more time hidden in thickets as the number of Indians increased. The warriors constantly moved on all sides of their

296

various hiding places and finally Edward cautiously peered out on a solid encampment extending as far as he could see in either direction. Somewhere beyond, out of his sight and certainly beyond his reach, Fort Pitt stood on its point of land across the Monongahela.

He began a slow probing circuit of the encampment, spending days in hiding, nights moving in a great circle with what speed he could. First he and Simeon worked eastward but the ring of death around the forest grew more dense and wide. The Indians knew that any attempt to relieve the fort would come from that direction and prepared for it. He came almost in sight of Carlisle but he knew Abby would not be there, nor need he plead with the commander of whatever militia or regular troops were there to relieve the fort. The officer would already be doing everything possible.

Only after the siege was lifted did Edward learn how Abby had worked her way through the Indian camps as he vainly circled them, hoping against hope to find some unguarded spot that would open a path to the fort. Time and again he heard distant sounds of firing, angry and frightening outbursts of fighting that drove him frantic with fear for Abby. He had to use an iron will to hold himself back from some foolish, hopeless attempt to dash to the stockade.

He had almost completed his circuit, crossing the Allegheny and the Ohio itself and approaching the Monongahela once more when, without warning, the Indian ring of camps, canoes and warriors dissipated in frantic, desperate flight in all directions; some north and west into the country they had so recently devastated, down the Ohio in canoes, flashing paddles adding speed to that which the great river current gave them. Others dashed west and south into the Dark and Bloody Ground that they normally shunned. Every single warrior vanished like the remnants of a horrible nightmare.

Neither Edward nor Simeon could believe the brassy, triumphant sound of bugles within the battered fort, nor the roar of muskets and rifles fired in jubilation. They watched from their hiding place as red-uniformed regulars and blue-clad colonial militia marched into the fort over ground occupied by savage hordes now scattering to the winds.

One nightmare had ended but an unreal dream remained for surely none of what they witnessed was true! They remained hidden, uncertain until they saw soldiers and settlers emerge from the stockade. They saw women and children come down to the river bank and wade ankle deep as though they, too, moved through a dream and not reality. A day later, he rode as Bouquet's courier to Carlisle and to Abby with the news that Henri was safe.

Henri's sudden cry shook Edward out of his memories and he looked over his shoulder. Abby smiled at his concern. "Your son needs a cleaning, a rest and a feeding. Do we have the time?"

"For as long as he needs!"

He guided the canoe to the bank. It was good for the adults to be free of the canoe and to walk back and forth while Abby busied herself taking care of Henri.

How wonderful it must be for him to be free of that confining cradle board, Edward thought. *Eh, bien!* He reminded himself that without that contraption the baby and his wonderful wife could not be with him. *Ah, prend patience, mon ami!* Have patience, for Henri will grow to be a strong, proud man and I will be an equally proud father.

Soon they were on their way downstream again. Toward dusk they turned into the mouth of the Muskingum and made camp for the night. Edward and Fowler fished while Abby and Simeon gathered driftwood to make a fire on the bank. They ate in comfort, and the blaze of the fire set aglow in the darkness without fear of attracting enemies was proof in itself of the return of peace to the country after so long a time. Strangely, all of them except the baby felt uneasy and wary. How long, Edward wondered, would it take them to adjust to a world without war?

The next morning they breakfasted on freshly caught fish and then worked their slow way against the current of the winding Muskingum, first through high rough and broken hills called "knobs" in this country and then coming into open, rolling grassy prairie broken here and there by rounded hills that were hardly more than mounds.

Edward first saw the large cloud of blue smudge against the clear sky far ahead and called attention to it over his shoulder. "Smoke—from many fires."

Fowler answered with satisfaction, "That will be the colonel's camp and conference grounds."

Simeon called skeptically, *"Parbleu!* he must

have hundreds or thousands camped around him!"

"You'll see," Fowler laughed, "and be ready to face more Indians." He chuckled at their alarm. "These are tamed—by Bouquet's bullets and bayonets."

They rounded several curves, the river now and then threading patches of woodland, then suddenly came out on a seemingly endless plain. They came in sight of the camp and all but Fowler could hardly believe their eyes. Edward and Abby would have sworn they looked once more on a besieged Fort Pitt. Then, as they came close, they saw what Fowler had meant.

The Indian huts, tepees and fires were surrounded by soldiers, Royal Regulars and militias of York, Virginia and Pennsylvania. Soldiers instead of warriors came to the river bank to help them land and carefully help Abby out of the canoe. Fowler sent one of them as a messenger to Colonel Bouquet's headquarters, hidden somewhere ahead amidst the forest of shelters.

Edward and Abby marched deep into the camp between a double file of soldiers. He saw the dress and markings of practically every tribe north of the Ohio. But how the once arrogant males had changed! They sat hunched in dejected attitudes before their fires. The few pipes he saw were not painted with the bands of war, nor did they bear belligerent eagles and hawk feathers. The smokers puffed on them as though the tobacco exhumed the taste of bitterness, so they found no true satisfaction in it.

They came at last to Colonel Bouquet's large tent on the rim of a huge, cleared circle of ground.

Directly across from it stood a structure of leafy tree boughs, one side completely opened on the empty circle. Edward had time for hardly more than a glance when Colonel Bouquet came out of his tent to welcome them.

Face alight, he walked directly to Abby, grasped her hands, held them tightly as he smiled at her and then around at Edward.

"Your wife, sir, is the bravest woman in all this western land if not in all the American colonies. Would you take it amiss if I kissed her?"

"He would not, Colonel," Abby said quickly, "nor if I kissed you. We both owe everything to you."

"*C'est vrai et juste*, Edward agreed. "She speaks true, Colonel."

"And tomorrow you will see what His Majesty and I owe to you, Mistress Forny. If I had my way, you would be dubbed a Lady of the Kingdom."

The colonel had amply prepared for their coming. A spacious officer's tent awaited them, complete with field furnishings of cots, chairs, benches and tables, even to a rough woven covering for the smoothed dirt floor. Two regular soldiers served as batmen for heavy tasks and Colonel Bouquet sent over squaws to help Abby with the few household tasks to be done. Like the other Indians in the huge encampment, the women moved with an almost hangdog air.

After watching them for a time, Abby commented to Edward, "They act as though their men had beaten them to within an inch of their lives. It is not like an Indian woman to be so cowed."

"I think they only show the fright their men must

301

feel. Our good colonel has somehow placed the fear of le *Bon Dieu* on this whole country. He has some *acte magnifique* planned for tomorrow." He made a gesture of sniffing for an odor and smiled. "I can smell it in the air, *ma petite.*"

Just then Fowler appeared to invite them to dine with the colonel in his tent.

XXIV

Edward proved to be a true prophet. Fowler arrived the next morning when the sun was more than three hours to nooning. The colonel again requested their presence but Edward sensed an order beneath the polite words. Fowler acted impatient and on edge as he waited for Abby to take care of Henri and reluctantly hand him over to one of the Indian women.

All morning Edward had heard stirrings outside the tent and he investigated now and then. Each time, he saw the Indians moving slowly into the great area between his tent and the open-sided one far across the way. He called Abby, who joined him to watch the assembling of the tribes. Then Fowler came with the colonel's request and instructions.

"You will be seated on the colonel's left. I will be with the other officers to his right."

"What is to happen, *mon ami?*" Edward asked.

"History," Fowler answered laconically. "Our Swiss commander knows how to make it. There'll not be another conference—powwow, as the Indians say it—so important in this country for many a year, if ever."

When he led them from the tent, the Indians still moved into the area in a turgid, milling stream. They found places to sit or squat, packing close together so they formed one great mass of red humanity. Once more Edward noted the hunched shoulders and lowered heads that bespoke unmistakable defeat.

Colonel Bouquet had made one almost shocking change. A line of redcoat regulars, bayonets affixed to their muskets, made a menacing triple line before the main pavilion. Just behind them stood a double line of tightly bound Indian captives. Abby sucked in her breath when she saw them.

"The war chiefs and Sachems! Prisoners!"

Fowler added grimly with a gesture to the assembled Indians, "And hostages. But we'd best hurry before Colonel Bouquet is ready to make his entrance."

They worked a circuitous way to the open side

pavilion and found that a long platform had been built upon which canvas officers' field chairs were placed. Fowler seated them and then joined the regu.ar and militia officers beyond the central, vacant chair. Their entrance had created a faint stirring among the packed Indians for a moment, after which they subsided. A long, strained silence ensued, broken now and then by a woman's wail here and there among the crowd. Each abruptly broke off as though silenced by an unseen blow.

A bugle from the colonel's tent brazenly broke the silence. Instantly, the soldiers came to attention, the officers rose. Looking over the dark heads of the seated Indians, Edward saw Colonel Bouquet in full dress uniform emerge from the tent and walk with deliberate, proud and conquering stride around the circle to the pavilion. Bayonet-tipped muskets snapped to Present Arms and a redcoat regular sergeant stepped to a tree trimmed of all branches to allow the English standard to be raised. It snapped loudly as the breeze caught and unfolded it. Every soldier, including the colonel, came to full attention and salute. Then Bouquet continued his march to his seat of command.

He looked to be a completely different man to both Edward and Abby. His face had frozen in stern lines and his body moved with forbidding, ramrod stiffness. Edward thought he saw a ghost of a smile on the forbidding lips when the colonel looked at Abby for a second, but could not be sure.

Bouquet took his seat, murmured a low word permitting his officers and men to be seated or come to Parade Rest. Bouquet sat unmoving, giving every single Indian in the mass before him time to study him.

"Are the translators ready?" he demanded.

Several Indians standing just before the first line of soldiers stepped forward as an aide answered, "They are ready, sir."

"Good. Have each tell his tribesmen to look on their head chief, Sachem or war leader who stands bound before me."

The order was repeated in a chatter of a dozen or more tongues. A low moaning sound swept the assembly then silence returned. Bouquet looked slowly from left to right and back again. Edward thought, *parbleu*, our colonel is an actor as well as a soldier!

Bouquet suddenly leaned forward, his hands balled into fists on the arms of his chair. "Tell them that everyone before me is my prisoner. I may do as I please with everyone of them," he added after the translation and the repeated wave of low moaning. "I may destroy their towns and villages. I may burn their fields, give their women to my soldiers and take their children to slave for others somewhere afar off where they will never be seen again. Tell them!"

The answering moan became a loud wail that was promptly silenced when Bouquet lifted his hand, palm out, in a gesture commanding silence. "Ask them if they still believe Pontiac's medicine is powerful and good."

The denial came in a dozen tongues. Bouquet rested back in his chair but the frown of the conqueror did not leave his face. "Tell them that it is not only Fort Pitt that is in our hands again and that

Bushy Run is not their only defeat. We have news Pontiac has forsaken his warriors around Fort Niagara and it, too, is free."

This time the reply did not come as moan or wail. Edward could see from the way each Indian looked at his neighbors that the news of complete collapse had stunned them. Edward corrected his thought—not quite complete, perhaps, for Bouquet had not spoken of Detroit. Yet what did that matter? It would certainly soon be relieved.

Bouquet leaned forward once more and with a sweeping gesture indicated all the land about. "Everything from the mountains to the east as far as the great river to the west belongs to the mighty English chief across the waters. Tell them."

He waited for the translations then continued. "All this land from north of the wide waters of the lake belongs to the English and not the French as it was before . . . Tell them that the lands south of the Ohio, that of the Choctaw, the Creeks and the Cherokee is also English . . . Tell them there is no place they can go from the Spanish country beyond the Mississippi and south to the Floridas except by the rule and pleasure of the English chief. Tell them."

Edward and Abby exchanged surprised looks as the translators spoke. Colonel Bouquet outlined an empire! Bushy Run and the relief of Fort Pitt were far more than battles won; it signified the collapse of Indian domination and rule, not only along the Ohio but along all the streams that flowed into it. The babble of Indian voices arising from the assembly bespoke their stunned understanding of what had happened. The colonel had still more to reveal.

He had once more eased back in his chair and his eyes moved over the assembly, drinking in the effect of his sweeping pronouncement. He again leaned forward, lifted his hand for attention and instantly had it—complete silence. No one moved. He pointed to the captive chiefs, slowly, one by one, saying nothing. But every eye followed his finger as it indicated a bound, defeated and sullen Sachem.

"They led you to war upon us," Bouquet spoke abruptly. "Because of them, you murdered, raped, burned and killed. Do I speak true?"

"Hai!" came the low growling answer when the translators finished.

"Your hands are stained with our blood. White scalps hang from the lodge poles in all your villages and towns—scalps not only of *our* warriors but of our women. Do I still speak true?"

"Hai!"

"Shouldn't the scalps of *your* warriors and women hang from *our* lodge poles? That is only just. Do I still speak true?"

This time there was no answer when the translators finished and Bouquet smiled icily. He indicated a Kickapoo war chief at the end of the line to the left and ordered the red-coated soldier standing near, "Strip him."

In a matter of minutes the chief stood naked, the ropes retied tightly about his body and arms. Edward heard a deep angry growl from the assembly and braced for trouble. He would grab Abby and wheel about to the rear of the tent. His knife would rip the canvas and they could escape the rush of avenging tribesmen. Then he realized Bouquet had control of the situation. A full company of regulars swung around the corner of the structure, muskets and bayonets forming a deadly barricade to the Indians. The growling subsided.

"Bring the dress," Bouquet ordered.

Edward blinked in surprise. Another soldier appeared holding a linsey-woolsey dress. The chief stared blankly a second and then realized what was intended. He struggled to free himself, to twist out of restraining hands. He could not succeed but he tried to squirm away from the dress as it was dropped over his head and jerked down to his ankles. The soldiers stepped back. The war chief made a ridiculous figure now and he struggled even more violently to wrench free but failed. The fight suddenly went out of him and he stood unmoving, head hanging so low that no one could see his face.

His tribesmen jumped angrily to their feet but on Bouquet's sharp order the soldiers' muskets leveled on them and Edward heard the hammers click back, ready to strike sparks into the powder pans. The Kickapoo slowly sat down. On a subaltern's barked order, the hammers slowly lowered and the muskets came to Order Arms.

Bouquet smiled tightly at the assembly. "He is no longer a chief but a woman. He should be paraded in every town of my people to be seen and mocked. 'Such are the Kickapoo!' will be said of him."

A tortured moan answered. When at last it died off

309

into silence, Bouquet indicated the other captives. "I will take them to the fort and put dresses on them, too."

His answer came in a great wave of protest. Bouquet allowed it to fade into silence before he spoke. "But I do not want to shame you before all the world unless you force me. I will not shame you or your chiefs if you will make a solemn treaty with me that will never be broken in our lifetime. Do you agree? Or shall your sachems be turned into women?"

"HAI!"

The shout thundered against the sky but Bouquet shook his head. "It is not enough. You may speak with forked tongues and take the warpath against us. Do your chiefs and sachems make your talk straight so that I can trust a treaty with you? Ask them!"

Edward swore that a thousand or more red arms lifted and extended toward the captives. Certainly the roar of voices nearly deafened him. He could not hear Abby but only see her lips move as she spoke to him. He leaned down to her, yet even so close she had to almost shout a few words at a time in his ear to be understood.

"Colonel Bouquet . . . somehow . . . understands Indian pride. He uses it . . . with skill . . . to his purpose . . . the British for once . . . have the right man in . . . the right place."

"Je tombe de nues—completely amazed," he replied.

The captives shouted answers to their tribesmen but for a long time the questions and answers swung back and forth. Finally the noise lessened and Bouquet commanded the guards, "Turn the captives to face me."

That done, he indicated the Seneca sachem. "What is your answer?"

"My people will speak straight," the translation came clearly.

One by one, Bouquet questioned each chief and finally pursed his lips as he studied the Kickapoo in the woman's dress. "If I make a man of you once more, would your people obey you? Could I trust them?"

After a long, long moment, the man lifted his head. Edward had to strain to hear his low reply. *"Hai."*

"Remove the dress," Bouquet ordered and in a moment the man was again naked. Still, his pride had not returned. He edged away from his companions, his stance that of complete defeat. Bouquet's hard eyes traveled along the line of captives and then lifted to the throng beyond.

He outlined the terms of the proposed treaty and the translators enumerated them one by one. The warriors of each tribe would return to the camps and towns of their people. There would never again be war between them and the whites—British or French. Each tribe would collect pelts, prime skins, that would be collected a year hence by officials of the king. These would be payment for the destruction their adherence to Pontiac had caused. There were more terms to be met but they were secondary.

Item by item, the chiefs and sachems agreed, thereby binding their tribesmen to honor each particular term. Bouquet would then look above the particular chief to his men and demand their obedience to the treaty point. Finally he nodded his satisfaction, edged forward in his seat and the cold look returned to his face, his jaw hard and tight. He spoke slowly, giving the translators ample time with every phrase.

"You and your chiefs have bound your people to the agreement made this day here on the Muskingum between your tribe and the great British sachem. How shall we put certainty to its execution?"

He allowed the question to hang in the air unanswered. He watched the constant uncertain stir in the red assembly, heard the constant murmur of voices. A Piankashaw chief finally rose and spoke swiftly. His words were as quickly translated.

"What would give you certainty that we speak true?"

"Your sachems, your war chiefs and tribal headsmen."

One of the captives, a Miami, looked up at the colonel. "We have given our word for our people. I will speak again for the Miami. We will keep the peace. We will abide by the treaty. What more do you ask?"

A grim smile played about Bouquet's lips as he listened to the translation. His short laugh was more like a savage bark.

"You—every one of you. I will take you to Fort Pitt and then on to Carlisle, perhaps move you even beyond to Lancaster or somewhere deep in Pennsylvania Colony. You will still be my prisoners—

312

hostages for your people and their acts." He held up his hand, stopping the rising protest of the chiefs and the general assembly. "You will not be prisoners forever."

"For how long?" a Wea chieftain demanded.

"Until such time as I am satisfied that your people will truly fulfill each word and each point of the pact. I will hold you a year, two years, maybe more. Then you will be free."

"My people will abide with that," the Wea agreed through the translators.

"But this minute you scheme, knowing a year or so will not be long. Then you can hunt our scalps again, eh?"

"Our word is our word—sacred and true."

"But only for the time you are bound unless—" Bouquet paused and then spoke slowly in brief phrases that the translators passed on. "While you are my captives, your tribesmen will send your families to me. I demand your sons, young warriors who will be chiefs in their time. I plan to hold *them* as hostages as I will hold you. Then I will be sure."

"But you yourself might not be chief for the Great Sachem across the waters."

"True . . . but another chief will take my place wearing the red war coat and bearing the same weapons I do. He will honor my word as his own."

It was an idea hard for the Indian throng to grasp and Bouquet patiently allowed the buzz of discussion and argument to continue for a quarter of an hour or more. Then he raised his commanding hand and had instant silence. He indicated the captives.

"You know the terms of the treaty. I take these captives with me to Fort Pitt and then on to Carlisle. I will wait a reasonable time there for your messengers to bring your tribal marks of agreement to the treaty. There is no more to be said."

A protesting clamor rose but Bouquet quickly silenced it when he rose and gave orders to the soldiers guarding the chiefs. "Take them to their stockade."

He stood unmoving and unmoved by the anguish of the massed Indians as the chiefs, prodded now and then by a bayonet, turned and marched out of sight around the pavilion tent. Then he raised his hand high, palm up.

"The powwow is finished. Go to your villages— all of you. Begin to fulfill the treaty."

He turned his back on the Indians. The steel and iron left his face when he smiled at Abby and took her hands.

"What are your thoughts, Mistress Forny?"

She shook her head in amazement and Edward laughed. "For once, my good wife *est sans voix*."

"Mistress Forny speechless!" Bouquet snorted and then his eyebrow arched high. "Ah, perhaps in this case. She has just seen what her journey accomplished, eh?"

"There is but one other thing, Colonel," Abby said.

"And that?"

"You put a dress on that poor Kickapoo chief to shame him."

"And it did!" Bouquet laughed.

"Should I be shamed, Colonel? I am proud to be

a woman."

His jaw dropped and his face turned beet red. He finally found words. "You have a right to be, Mistress Forny."

"And so does every other woman."

"But, mistress . . . it is the way of our world and time."

XXV

On his return to Fort Pitt after the conference, Edward reluctantly settled Abby and Henri in their large tepee. She appeared content to "make do until something better can be done" but Edward only knew impatience. He constantly pictured the cabin they had once occupied when Henri was born, where they had planned a full life based on trade along the Ohio and all its streams.

The ashes of the cabins that had once stood about the stockaded fort repelled him. One of those oblong piles of black charcoal symbolized his home and *par le Bon Dieu* he would have it again! His wife and his son deserved no less. Actually, they deserved much better and he swore they would have it!

Rebuilding the settlement instantly became a community affair, neighbor helping neighbor. Once before, Edward had taken crews up the Allegheny to cut logs for the high stockade of Fort Prince George, as Pitt had then been called. He once more took command to find trees and set his men to cutting and shaping logs to be formed into large, cumbersome rafts. They floated them downstream to the junction with the Ohio, where other settlers gave them final trim and notches. Walls went up quickly, the drafty chinks between them plastered and sealed with clay that soon dried thick and hard, wind and water repellent.

Each cabin had its great fireplace, formed of field-stone. No one, man, woman or child had much relief from house raising and furnishing. Every night saw each structure a bit nearer to completion but what a slow task it became!

Even so, the cabins in themselves were not the end of the task. As the builders labored, others who had skill with saw, hammer and plane, shaped tables, chairs, bedsteads and built tiers of bunks to hold the settlement's children. Women found clay along the river bank and shaped it into rough but efficient pitchers, plates and mugs, hardening them in fire. Some used berry and bark juices to mix colors and to bake them into the clay in stripes, slashes and spirals.

Edward's long-planned trading venture started before he really became aware of it. Later he would always say that this was because he did not go by canoe with trade goods westward down the river, but rode eastward overland on a nag purchased from Captain Blaine. He found a cart for his purpose in Ligonier and loaded it with necessities for Fort Pitt.

His merchandise vanished almost as soon as he rolled his cart into Pitt settlement, and he made a substantial profit. He would have to go east again if he hoped to have goods of any kind to trade westward down the river but the second trip must wait, he decided, until he could spend a few days with his family in the spacious new cabin that now covered the ashes of the old one.

He could not get his fill of the place. He stood before the great maw of the fireplace where flames licked and curled about thick logs, heating great kettles of water, stews and soups hanging from cranes. Abby half buried pans of bread to bake in hot ashes to one side of the curved fieldstone lip.

She sat on one of the long table benches, her moccasined foot working a curved wooden support of Henri's crib. The baby slept soundly, lulled by the rocking movement. She wore a colorful new dress Edward had brought from Ligonier. Its prim, wide scarf crossed over the front, pinned by a brooch he had also found back east. She looked so proper, he thought with a grin, but she dared not stand between anyone and light from either fireplace, doorway or window. Every curve and line of her delightful body would be clearly silhouetted, for as he had asked, she did not wear a stitch beneath the dress.

"We would waste precious time shedding folderol before getting into bed, *ma petite*."

Just then she looked up from the curtain material she was sewing and read the message on his face. "Darling! So soon! The bed must still be warm from the last time."

"*Pas du tout!* It grows cool. It should not be."

With a single long stride he was beside her, lifting her to her feet. She came readily, pressed against him and he marveled at her rich, soft curves. Ah, he would never have enough of her. Never! A glance at the crib assured them that Henri still slept soundly, so they hurried to the great sturdy bed that had been built for them. Abby unpinned the brooch and her white collar floated away. Her dress dropped to the floor. Edward pulled his shirt over his head and it with his trousers formed a second pile of clothes beside Abby's dress. She looked down at him in amazement.

"Is he always at attention?"

"Always a good soldier, *ma petite*."

"Trained for invasion, I swear."

"*Vous avez raison*—as you see."

They fell into bed and rolled over so that she straddled him. The invasion commenced in a fierce attack that left them both breathless. When she fell over to his side, Edward contentedly asked himself who had won the battle. Ah, but there would be yet another time to find an answer. He pulled the coarse sheet up over them as she snuggled her curves to his angles of bone and muscle. She spoke sleepily.

"Darling, we will need another crib if we keep this up."

His eyes snapped open and he lunged up on his

319

elbow to look down at her, surprised that the thought had not come to him.

"Vraiment? But yes, and it will be a boy!"

She placed her palm against his chest and pushed him down again. *"If* it happens, I hope it won't be until Henri is older." She frowned. "Must it be a boy? Do you need an army of Fornys? I would like a girl."

"Then you shall have one."

She deliberately removed his arm from across her body and firmly placed it beside him. "Later, Mister Forny—much later."

"C'est triste—very sad." Then he chuckled. "But we have had a very good—how is it said?—house-warming."

"We nearly burned the place down." Her voice sounded angry but her smile belied it. "Now go to sleep after a yeoman job."

"Yeoman—what is that?"

"Later—sleep now."

For the next two days, Edward and Simeon worked on the canoe that would take them down the Ohio. It needed fresh patches of birch along its sides, so pine resin was used as glue to hold the bark in place. The ribbing of the structure proved sound but Edward did not like the looks of one of the paddles. A new one was soon carved, smoothed and shaped. They gathered supplies of powder, shot and patches for their rifles, condiments for food. Both knew their moccasins could not withstand the long and hard wilderness journey and Abby shaped new ones from deerskins long before softened for use.

As he worked, Edward thought of his eastward journey. He could buy the goods needed for his trade only in that direction. Calico, needles, knives, muskets and rifle parts could not be found along the river nor in the settlements. Yet who else could deal with the lone settlers, the inhabitants of the little posts and towns if not him? How could he travel the waterways and at the same time replenish his goods in the eastern towns?

The problem gnawed at him for a long time, growing more and more troublesome as the answer eluded him. His nag and cart waited. His canoe, so swiftly taking shape, would soon be waiting. It came to a head one night when Dean Smith rapped on the door just as Abby placed supper on the table.

In the frontier way, Dean made no apology for his interruption but came directly to the reason for his visit. "When be ye going east again, Edward?"

"Qui sait? Not before I need to. I look to the Ohio now."

"It's not a very long journey to Lancaster, Edward. Many of us need such things as woolen goods, what with winter not too far away. Some could use needles and pins—there's always call for them. Dress goods, plain and fancy, to hear the womenfolk complain. They also speak of ribbons but, of course, such fancies can wait."

"But—" Edward made a helpless gesture westward. "—I need to know how many have returned to the Ohio country since Pontiac's trouble."

"I reckon you've heard Pontiac finally gave up on Detroit? Word has it that he was recently killed by a drunken Indian somewhere in the Illinois country."

"I heard," Edward answered impatiently. "But if everyone rebuilds in the Ohio country, there will be more need of goods out there than in Pitt settlement."

"Sure, but you could be gone out there a long time. We in Pitt can't wait until you get back—whenever that will be."

Edward growled disgustedly. "Split me in half, part to go east and part to go west, eh?"

Dean started a reply but Abby cut in before he could utter a word. "Can you come back later, Dean, or early on the morrow?"

He scratched his head. "Letty's sure a'fit for needed geegaws."

"I understand." Abby's face lighted, "Come after sup and bring her with you."

"That means the whole Smith tribe, Mistress," Dean warned, "babies, kids and all."

"There's room enough."

Edward stared at her until Dean left and then he asked, "What have you in mind?"

"Dean Smith," she answered.

When she elaborated on her idea Edward sat hunched forward, elbows on the table, his plate of food forgotten. He dropped back in his chair when she finished. "Will he do it?"

"It depends on Letty. That's why I asked her to come with him. But let's finish sup and have things cleaned up before they come."

"Can you persuade him?"

"Nay, that will be your task."

They cleared the table and put more logs on the fire. The flames danced high, red and cheerful when the Smiths returned. As Dean had warned, the whole tribe trooped in after him and Letty—a new baby at

322

her breast, a toddler in Dean's arms and the half-grown coltish boys. Abby seated them about the room. Edward had long since learned the custom of the country when guests came and he had a squat jug, plugged with a corncob, placed on the table, drinking mugs about it. He filled one for Dean, another for Letty, a little more than a dollop for Abby, slightly more for himself. He passed them around and had started to lift his own in a salute when Letty checked him in mid-gesture.

"Ain't my tads to git some?"

"Whiskey? But they're just boys!" Abby exclaimed when Edward looked at her, brow arched in question.

"They already come thirteen," Letty answered. "That means where we come from they're nigh grown men. They carry their load in work, they can carry it in whiskey—and they have for close on a year. They'd take it strange wasn't they to get their mugs."

"*Mon Dieu!* How soon a boy becomes a man out here!"

"A boy has to or he won't keep his scalp on his head."

Edward shrugged and filled two more mugs that the boys accepted as a matter of course. The preliminary social duties thus disposed of, Abby took Letty over to Henri's crib and entered a long discussion of infant problems and news of the settlement women. The boys sat at one end of the long table with their mugs while Edward and Dean conferred at the opposite end.

"The house building is soon ending?" Edward asked.

"The week should see it done, and that will be a God's blessing. The men have land to clear to make ready for planting. The women start sewing dresses, shirts and things and there's the quilts."

"Always work, eh?" Edward chuckled.

"Never stops, that's for sure. It's one reason Letty's all fired anxious for the trade goods you could bring."

"*Je comprends.* I can certainly understand."

"I would rather head west, *mon ami.*" Edward laughed as Dean's expectancy vanished. "Eh, but sometimes there can be more than one answer to a problem."

"Not this one. Like you said, you can't be two places at once."

Edward rocked heel and toe after he moved to the fireplace and turned to face the room and his guests. He emptied his mug and tossed it to one of the boys who skillfully caught and placed it on the table. Edward had the attention of all of them and he read approval in Abby's expression. He spoke to Dean but looked over and beyond him to Letty.

"You have your land to clear, too?"

"Sure. I ain't no different than the others."

"I think you are."

Dean looked blank. "But—but if it ain't cleared I don't get any crop in. How does that make me any different!"

"Do you really want to pull stumps, hoe to clear the fields then plant, plow and hoe some more?"

"How else do you farm!"

"*Certainement*—truly there is no other way that I have seen. But do you want to be a farmer—you?"

"That is all I know. My father farmed—his father farmed and—"

"Does that mean you're forced to farm?"

Letty jumped to her feet and glared. "You keep talking around and around and around! What else is there for Dean? If he don't farm—"

"He can work for me, eh?"

"—we'll starve," she finished and then caught herself up. "What do you mean?"

"It is very simple, *ma cherie*. I have a horse and wagon, *non?*" When she nodded, Edward continued. "I will go east with him. I will introduce him to merchants so they will know he is my man, eh? They will show him the trade goods he is to buy. He will bring them here and sell them or store them until they are needed—either in Pitt settlement or as I should have call for them along the rivers. This will be what you call—what you call—?"

"Transfer point?" Abby suggested. "Factory?"

"Ah, factory! That is what it is called in New France, *non!*"

"Yes, but there ain't a New France no more. It is all English."

"Pouf! French—English—what matter? This idea will work, eh?"

Letty dropped down to her seat, stunned for a moment. Dean could only stand with gaping jaw and stare. Letty recovered her voice.

"But trade goods cost money—"

"My money," Edward answered. "Nothing out of Dean's pockets. In fact, I shall put his wages in each month to the amount that we agree."

Dean shook his head. "But my land? My farm?"

"It just can't sit out there," Letty echoed his consternation. "Someone has to work it or there ain't gonna be food on our table come winter. Besides, if we don't plow or plant, someone'll grab it for themselves."

Edward lifted his finger high to make his point. "Eh, but that can happen whether you plant or not. Do you have deed and title? None of us do."

"It's free for the taking," Dean protested. "Like the very land this house—or mine—sits on."

"Someday—and soon—Pennsylvania Colony, or Virginia or mayhap even New York will lay claim to everything about us. Then all of us will have to pay good pence, farthings and pounds for every square inch of earth around Pitt and everywhere else, for that matter. There will be land companies and surveys and colonial agents who will see to it, *parbleu!* They will say, and not very nicely, that you pay the price they set or get off. The royal governors and the king himself love the sound of jingling coins and will have their due. I will be able to hand over whatever money is demanded when the time comes. Will you?"

Dean and Letty pulled their eyes from Edward with an effort and stared at one another. Edward knew that they, like most settlers in the western country, had never given a moment's thought to ownership. They only saw the vacant land lying about ready to be freely taken by anyone at any time. Kingdoms, colonies, governors, land offices and agents, deeds and titles had long ago been left behind. Edward's few words swept away their hitherto unquestioned illusions as the wind sweeps away fine sand.

Dean managed to answer from a dry throat. "We've got only what we build or grow ourselves—except for what little the sale of a bit of our crops we can spare brings in."

"It will always be that way?"

"How else can it be?"

Edward walked to the table and sat down on the bench facing Edward. "Working for me."

"But the fields?" Letty protested with a croak.

"Count them as yours until some official makes demand for payment or surrender. But let someone else do the clearing and planting, eh? Share the crop with him for a bit of profit until this year, or next, or the next, a colony's agent lays claim. By then, if you and I do well, it might be you will still be able to purchase title, eh?"

"But damn my eyes, I've already stumped and cleared a lot of it! No one can take away what's mine!"

"The point is," Abby put in softly, her voice filled with sympathy, "It *can* be taken away. You have no proof it was ever yours. Edward and I have no proof this house has ever been ours although we built it log by log, board by board, stone by stone."

"*C'est vrai, mon ami,*" Edward echoed. "Let us both be ready so that it will never happen. I need you and you need me. The land? It will always be there, eh? nor will it care who works it, you or someone else. Which is best—sweat and muscle in the hot sun behind a plow or swinging a hoe or scythe . . . or driving wagons loaded with trade goods back and forth between here and the eastern towns? The plow

327

and the hoe will pay a pence or a farthing. The horse and the wagon will pay shillings and pounds. Which would you have?"

Letty, completely confused by this departure from all she had ever known or been taught, looked at Abby. "Is he right? Will he pay more'n a farthing?"

Abby's hand on her arm gave added assurance to her words. "He's right—and he will."

"I never heard of such a thing!"

"Nor had I until I met Edward and he made a journey down the Ohio just before the Indians went on the warpath. I was like you. All my people and I knew was farming, so it takes getting used to."

Edward turned back to Dean. "All my life and everywhere I have seen that the world pays far less for muscles than it does for brains. A peasant in my Gascon homeland seldom had a coin in his smock pocket. But the tavern host, the storekeeper and his clerk could jingle them most of the time. Eh, it is true here in this country as well."

Dean studied Edward, frowning, and then slowly nodded. "You have the right on it." He turned to face Letty. "You'n me have seen it all our lives but why ain't we known it?"

"Because we're born to be farmers?" She made the statement a half question.

"Ah, there you are wrong," Edward disagreed. "You are born to be what you can become in this new country. That is even more certain here at Pitt settlement and in your American colonies than in New France. I give you a chance to prove it."

Dean sat unmoving and Edward could sense the swirl of the man's thoughts—accepting, rejecting, accepting again. Edward waited patiently, not wanting his eagerness to show. There were other men, of course, even here in the settlement, but Edward knew and trusted Dean. However, the decision must be made by him, with Letty concurring.

Dean looked at his sons, judging their strength and ability, then back at Letty, and once more at the boys. He spoke slowly to them. "If I left the farming to you, could ye meet the hard work of it all alone?"

"I can," the oldest answered instantly and proudly.

"Ye heard Dave," Dean turned to the second boy. "How about you, Obed?"

"If'n he can, I can, Paw."

"Letty, be ye agreed?"

"Ye've made up your mind, Dean," she answered. "I reckon if they cain't handle the work we could always share it out like Edward says. Let 'em try."

Dean swung back to Edward. "So be it. I'll drive your cart and do your buying east once you've taught me how it's done. When do we start?"

Edward clapped Dean on the back. He swept up the mugs. "Another round to seal your words, *mon ami!*"

He refilled the mugs, adding to the portions he had first given Abby and himself. They all jumped up as he did. The empty mugs thudded down on the table and Edward dropped to his seat on the bench across from Dean.

"Is there aught to keep you in the settlement?"

"No more'n seeing Letty's fixed secure and then showing the boys where to start clearing and stumping the fields—say a couple of days."

"Excellent! Then we will leave for Carlisle in three days. I can set Simeon to framing another canoe against the time we'll need it. That'll come soon now."

He laughed again in sheer delight and turned to the boys. "Ah, now you *are* farmers!"

XXVI

Edward's voice broke the wilderness silence of the Ohio as he sang a Gascon tune of love and happiness. He and Simeon kept perfect rhythm in the strokes of their paddles and Edward looked constantly ahead for landmarks he remembered from the voyage made so long ago before Pontiac's bloody shadow had fallen on the land.

Fort Pitt and the settlement lay more than a day's

journey behind them. Somewhere east of Pitt, Dean Smith would be driving his empty cart to Carlisle and Lancaster for its second load of trade goods. To be free of the settlement confines and to have Dean proving out so well on his work was reason enough to be happy. Yet Abby's news of three weeks before was cause for even greater happiness.

She thought she was pregnant! Soon there would be another Fournet—*Non!* Forny—besides Henri who crawled everywhere and was constantly being pulled from under bed, table and benches or scooped up before he tumbled out the cabin door. Another son!—no, daughter. That was what Abby wanted and *merci à Dieu* she would have one.

They rounded another turn and a long stretch of tree-lined river flowed ahead to a far bend. Around it would be the Muskingum River and Edward vividly remembered Colonel Bouquet and his tribal pow-wow. Ah, there was truly a soldier of the proud tradition, a professional who knew command but also knew how to shape it to the circumstances of the moment. Colonel Bouquet now ruled all this Ohio country and had the respect of General Gage. Edward briefly wondered what might be happening to that arrogant and stupid Lord Amherst. If anything had brought on Pontiac's blood bath, Jeffrey Amherst's treatment of the Indians as animals, or even less, had. The pompous oaf had not realized that Indians had a pride equal to and certainly more deserving than his own.

Simeon broke in on his thoughts, calling from the stern of the canoe. "Beyond the Muskingum is that island where so much happened to us."

The Jonases! Edward recalled with a start what a tempestuous time Pearl had given him in the barn loft. Simeon called again, "Do we portage around it? Madame Jonas might be even more eager than ever to see you, *mon ami.*"

Edward placed his paddle across the thwarts and let the canoe float ahead with the current, guided by Simeon's skill at the stern. Edward pursed his lips, and then silently mocked himself. Had he lost so much courage he could not face her?

"We go straight down the river, *mon ami.* If our friends are still there, we will wave and give a 'haloo!' as we pass. That is much easier than unloading all we carry, packing it several miles and then loading it all up again, eh?"

"*C'est vrai*—and you forget we also will carry the canoe. It is true—much easier to salute Monsieur Jonas and his redoubtable Pearl as we skim by."

Beyond the Muskingum, the Ohio turned almost directly south but Edward was not fooled. He remembered from his previous trip that a series of turns and bends actually angled the river westward. They neared the Little Kanawha's mouth and, despite his bold resolution, Edward slowed the rhythm of his paddle. After another turn he saw the eastward spit of the island straight ahead.

Narrowed into two channels by the island, the Ohio's current grew so strong a paddle was needed only to guide the speeding birchbark. The wooded shores whipped by. Edward glanced at the south bank where the warring tribes had met to fight their battles but never to settle. Colonel Bouquet's harsh treaty terms held sway even here. Then he gave his attention to the island again and frowned.

Hadn't Hank Jonas cleared the land over there? There had been open fields ready for the plow. Now he saw high grass, gently bending to the wind. Everywhere saplings grew. He looked ahead but a wooded spur of the island hid the area where the cabins and barn stood.

Simeon called forward, "Did our friends also run from Pontiac's warriors?"

Edward replied, "In a few minutes we'll see their place and I wager they'll hail us."

Just then they rounded the spur.

"Mon Dieu!" Simeon exclaimed, and steered the canoe to the shore.

He and Edward jumped into ankle deep water just before the canoe scraped on river sand. They looked on what had once been a wilderness farm area of buildings, fences and gates. The crooked rail fences remained here and there. A sagging gate stood open, one end buried in earth. Edward could barely trace the road under the high grass.

The house had been burned to the ground and the capacious barn had been reduced to a few charred posts pointing skyward like elongated grave markers. The winds had left the rest a pile of black ashes. Edward and Simeon exchanged questioning looks. Edward cupped his hands about his mouth and shouted.

"Haloo!! Hank! Pearl!"

No answer save for the whisper of wind in the trees. Edward called again and so did Simeon. No answer. Even bird calls had ceased. Edward tried once more.

"Haloo!! Jonas! We are friends. Pearl? Hank?

Show yourselves!"

After a long moment of silence, Simeon suddenly whirled around to face the tree-filled western end of the island. "Do you hear?" he asked.

Edward listened but heard nothing. Then, he heard a distant, muffled metallic sound. He waited. It came again. Cow bell? As though to answer his question, he heard a distant "moo!" coming from deep within the trees. Holding his long rifle ready, Edward signaled Simeon to follow as he crossed the weed-grown farm lot to walk through the gate and start up the grass-choked road.

Edward had no very clear idea of the extent of the island. The river current shot a canoe too quickly along its length to be able to judge the time it would take to actually walk along it. Now he began to understand why Pearl could send her husband off chasing a stray cow and feel safe enough to come to Edward in the barn loft with amorous intent. Only the good God could tell how many acres of trees, inlets, grassy fields and grazing land comprised the island.

He and Simeon moved cautiously, ready for sudden attack or to come on Hank Jonas, or Pearl, or both. The intermittent sound of the cow bell, now near, now far, lured them on. They both whirled about, rifles lifted and ready to fire when a thick wall of bushes nearby suddenly threshed wildly. A wild-eyed cow burst into the open, the bell about its neck clanking loudly.

Edward lowered his rifle and expelled his breath. Simeon eased down the hammer of his rifle and swiped the back of his hand across his mouth. The animal looked to be well fed, so Edward knew it had not lacked for forage. However, its udders were badly swollen and in need of milking. The animal and the two men eyed each other, the cow ready to bolt back into its bushy cover.

Edward made the sound he had so often heard the peasants use in his boyhood Gascon countryside and the animal's ears swiveled forward as it looked at him.

"Eh, there is the cow," Simeon said. "Where are the Jonases?"

"They must be close about if they are on the island at all. *Certainement*, we should not leave the place until we find them."

Simeon lifted his voice in a resounding shout. "Haloo! Haloo! We are friends. Do not fear us, Haloo!"

The cow tossed its head and bolted back into cover. Its flight drowned out all other sounds for several minutes. Then everything became quiet. They heard no answer to the hail.

"They have long since taken to their heels, probably but two, three steps ahead of the Indians," Simeon ventured.

"We make certain," Edward grimly decided.

"How?"

Edward visualized the island. "We go to the western tip. If this road goes that far, we use it as a dividing line between us. You search north of it. I'll search south. We'll go slowly, missing nothing, eh? If either of us comes on a sign of the Jonases, a gunshot will bring the other."

The faint roadway wound erratically through

brush and trees to finally bring them to the western tip and once more the broad expanse of the Ohio sparkled and rippled westward to disappear around a far bend. Edward turned south, Simeon north.

Before he plunged into the bush, Simeon commented dubiously, "I think the cow is the only Jonas we'll find, my friend."

"It may be," Edward agreed. "But can we do less?"

"*Eh, bien*, let's go about it then."

Edward found the task slow, laborious and probably useless. He was inclined to agree with Simeon. Time passed in tedious search. At first, he listened for a gunshot signal and then gradually forgot it. He worked back and forth from south bank to the road and to south bank again, so his eastern progress was at a snail's pace. The sun reached nooning and then slowly began to drop behind his back. He knew that he slowly approached the site of the burned structures but still had seen nothing.

A minute move in the high grass off toward the road caught his eye. He stopped short. The movement came again, a small flutter of something that did not belong over there. It was gone again and Edward realized that vagrant breezes had caused the movements, for they ceased the moment the puff of wind had passed.

He strode across the field and entered knee high grass that resisted his steps like an equal depth of water. Though nothing moved, he kept his eyes on the approximate place where he had seen the flutter. A current of air touched his cheek and in the same instant he saw the movement not ten feet ahead, just where he had expected it. He took two long steps and stopped short.

The flutter he had seen had been caused by a long, ragged and faded strip of cloth. Wind, rain, sun and time had partially loosened it from what had once been a calico dress. There were other strips of it but none of them long enough to appear above the grass. What was left of the dress covered a body. Edward saw a brown arch of boney rib cage here and there through the worn fabric. Skeletal arms did not fill but held down the sleeves. He looked into vacant eye sockets, a jagged shape of cartilage and bare, brown deteriorating remains of a nose bridge above teeth making a death-head grin. Scraps of desiccated skin still clung here and there to the skull except for a circle atop the dome where the scalp had been cut away.

The remaining hair lay entwined in the grass. Edward, choking back nausea, knelt beside the skeleton. The legs, like the rib cage, were no more than bones covered by desiccated skin. Worn moccasins hid the skeletal feet.

He forced himself to touch the skull, still attached to the knuckled spinal bones of the neck, and turn it over. He immediately saw the great jagged hole between the temple and the ear, the bone crushed by a heavy, blunt instrument, obviously a tomahawk. Pontiac's allies had not passed by this island. Pearl lay unburied where the Indians had caught up with her. Edward wondered if she had been raped before the war hatchet had killed her but the pitiful collection of bones would always keep that secret.

Edward rose and, still looking down at her, pointed his rifle to the sky and pulled the trigger. A moment later he heard Simeon's shot in reply. Edward pulled the long metal ramrod from below the barrel of his rifle and plunged its tip in the ground beside the skeleton as a marker. Then he moved slowly in an ever-widening circle. Surely Hank would be somewhere close.

But he had found nothing when Simeon hurried out from the trees bordering the road. Edward pointed to the thin black line of the ramrod and continued his search as Simeon waded through the high grass to Pearl's side. After a moment he joined Edward.

"C'est l'imprinte des diables rouges. The red devils left their sign. Ah, the poor woman! Perhaps her murder was quick, eh?"

Edward shook his head. "We both know better. Everywhere in war no woman is safe from enemy warrior or soldier."

"I wonder how many—?"

"Qui sait? More than enough before she died, I'd guess." Edward ran his knuckles thoughtfully along his lower jaw. "We will have to bury her. We'll probably find a spade near the building ashes."

"How about Hank?"

"You're right. We'll try to find him first. *Le Bon Dieu* knows Pearl will not be lost again. *Eh, bien,* back to your side of the road and we start looking once more."

Late in the afternoon they found Hank's bones, partially clothed in weather-worn rags as Pearl's had been. Hank's skull was missing but Simeon had an explanation. Hank must have put up a stout battle for his life, killing several of the attackers.

"There is no sign of that," Edward objected.

"*Oui*, because the Indians never leave their dead to be counted if they can help. Still, Hank must have made them pay heavily, so they considered him a brave enemy warrior. They cut off his head and carried it on a pole as a trophy of their own prowess. We'll not find it on the island."

Edward considered the explanation for long minutes and then made a typical gallic shrug.

"Let us find spades, then."

XXVII

The fate of the Jonases preyed on Edward's mind long after he and Simeon left the island. Hank and Pearl were decently buried and the cow forced to swim the narrow northern channel. That in itself was a task of no small dimensions since the brute tried time and again to turn back, nearly upset the canoe half a dozen times and twice tried to gore its birchbark hull. Edward and Simeon had armed themselves with long pointed poles which they used as goads. At long last, the cow splashed ashore and faced only the Good God knew how many thousand acres of grazing land. At first it would have none of it and tried to plunge back into the river to swim to the island.

In desperation, Edward stumbled onto the solution. His frayed patience at an end, he cursed when the brute made a final turn and attempted a dash for the river. Edward grabbed up his rifle, pointed the muzzle in the general direction of the animal and pulled the trigger. He had not taken aim though he wanted to end the futile business once and for all. The bullet scorched along the cow's back. Flame from the rifle's muzzle and the roar of the shot finished the job. The cow bawled in terror, turned and fled inland, its boney back streaming a line of blood.

Edward lowered the rifle and stared in disbelief as the terror-crazed animal raced away, tail crookedly lifted in panic flight. He looked back over his shoulder just as Simeon recovered from his own surprise. He lifted his paddle from across the thwarts and dipped the blade deep into the river current.

"Ma foi! It is time we disappeared ourselves."

They shot away down the river. For years after, Edward would now and then see that stupid, fleeing bovine and wonder whatever had become of it. Not that he cared—just an occasional tickle of vivid, exasperating memory.

Beyond the island and in the wide, full expanse of

the Ohio, Edward once more felt the peace and wonder of this western country. Each turn and bend opened new vistas of beauty. There would be long stretches of calm water where only the ripple of the current disturbed and beautifully distorted the reversed images of the oaks, birch, elms and evergreens along the banks. Sometimes as they camped on a beach, the tipped canoe their shelter and only their fire, a glowing, dancing little red circle of flames to break the blue-black dusk, he would watch the fairy dance of the fireflies. Or he would hear a splash and barely catch a flick of movement as a fish broke surface to catch an unwary insect that had skimmed too close to the ripples. Mornings dawned bright and golden with sun that soon evaporated little diamond drops of dew from the grass. Fishing lines and hooks would quickly pull breakfast from the river and, shortly after, they would launch out on the waters.

Peace had returned to the land although the signs of recent violence still remained here and there. More than once, they found ashes or charred walls of fire-gutted cabins. Now and then a chimney crowned the ruins, pointing a stick-and-mud or fieldstone finger to the sky. Occasionally Edward glimpsed untended horses or cattle, their pasture extending from the Ohio northward over the horizon.

Their freedom would last only until nearby settlers would gather them up, for the animals were there for the taking. Their owners, like Hank Jonas, were dead or had long ago fled to safety. Edward silently cursed himself for not foreseeing this opportunity to accumulate riches on the hoof.

He and Simeon found new cabins and clearings, for already the more venturesome of the frontier pushed slowly out into this empty land. Their number was small, however, since the English king had prohibited settlement in the "Indian lands west of the mountains" and had drawn a demarcation line beyond which no new towns or farms could be established. This was to be Indian country, a vast breeding ground of animals for pelts and furs. Only trappers and those who served them would be allowed.

It might be easy in a London palace for a monarch to draw such a line and make such a decree but it was sheer impossibility to enforce such a decree in these thousands on thousands of miles so far away. Despite all that General Thomas Gage and the redoubtable Colonel Bouquet could do, a small but steady trickle of pioneer families slipped eastward by Carlisle and Fort Pitt, southward through the passes and "gaps" from the Carolinas and Virginia, far to the north by way of the Lakes, Fort Detroit and even from New France.

Edward and Simeon encountered many settlers, although not a single cabin had been boldly built in plain sight of the Ohio or its main tributaries. Rather, the French settlements, posts and camps occupied the promontories or snuggled in river coves. Simeon, the third generation of his family to be born in this country, took them as a matter of course, normal, the buildings and inhabitants shaped to this country and its life.

But time and again Edward felt disgust almost to the point of nausea. As a rule the sagging, poorly constructed cabins were so filthy that he preferred to sleep outdoors under the shelter of the canoe. Often, however, the mere hint on his part of such an intention could start a hulking courier with lice-filled hair and beard to growling about insults, accusing Edward of being *très élégant*, too superior to understand and accept the hospitality of *La Belle Rivière*.

There would be much spitting, growling and fingering of sheathed belt knives. If there were others of his like about, they would also glower at Edward and sometimes he believed even the cur dogs snarled a warning, even though they slinked about underfoot with their tails between their legs. The slovenly Indian women who lived with the trappers would stare at him with beady black eyes, and the half breed children of all ages and both sexes would mutter half-heard threats.

So Edward would choke down and hide his dislike, for it was these very people who would trade with him in the days to come. In fact, they welcomed him even now although he had nothing but promises to offer. They demanded that he bring them everything, on his next trip downstream, from new rifles and traps to lead that they would melt and mold into bullets for their muskets and rifles. Clothes of all kinds for the women, pins, needles, awls—a million and one things that would quickly fill up a trade canoe.

In return, they offered prime fur pelts, now and then a long-saved louis d'or. Once a bearded man grinned at Edward through his tangled beard and winked, placing his finger knowingly beside his nose.

"Eh, I have a piece of pelfry better than most to offer you over and over."

"*C'est impossible*," Edward replied. "We trade this item for that item and it is finished."

"But suppose my pelt is always here and ready, *mon ami?*" He laughed at Edward's puzzled look, scanning his brood of Indian women and half-breed children. "Debora!"

A slender girl instantly turned from her chattering companions in a far corner of the cabin. As she approached, Edward appreciatively looked at her pretty face, framed by two braids of coal black hair. The hair, her high cheekbones and the slightly Oriental slant of her eyes marked her Indian blood. She had a slender body, its curves barely concealed by the dress she wore. Her breasts were small but rounded, promising full and desirable development. Already her nipples made little projecting points under her dress.

"She is my second daughter," the man said. "*Elle est jolie, non?*"

"Pretty? *Oui.*"

"Take off your dress," the father ordered.

Debora appeared neither surprised nor disconcerted. As Edward and Simeon watched, she pulled her dress up over her head and held it at her side. She wore nothing under it. Her skin had a smooth coppery tone and, as Edward surmised, her body was supple, well formed, the legs full at thigh, tapering to the knees, slender and shapely to delicate but strong ankles. The black hair between her legs would grow and become thicker but now it only partially concealed what lay within it. Her stomach was flat and muscular. Her breasts lifted and fell with her breathing, bold, outthrust and tipped with dark cherry-colored nipples.

"*Ma foi!*" Simeon exclaimed, his eyes bulging.

The father chuckled and patted the girl lightly on her groin. "Now that bit of pelfry can be traded over and over, *n'est-ce pas?* It will always be here for you when you come with goods we need."

Debora stood without moving under their inspection, as unperturbed as though she were fully clothed. In fact, Edward thought, she enjoyed showing her charms and even moved slightly to allow them to see her at a different angle.

"You have made your point," Edward said. "I have seen enough."

"Dress yourself," the father said and dismissed his daughter when he spoke to Edward. "Have you had a better offer?"

"Not so far," Edward admitted.

"And you'll not have one later. Do we have a deal?"

"We will bargain when the time comes," Edward evaded.

"You'll trade," the father said with assurance. "There's no one so young and delectable the whole course of the river. Ah, you'll trade."

"We will see when I have goods to trade." Edward said, quickly changing the direction of the talk. "Is there a settler building among the trees behind your landing?"

"*Oui*—two of them. Follow the creek upstream

347

about two miles and you will come on Monsieur Fair. Then, beyond him another three miles is Monsieur Zane. Will you visit them?"

"In the morning," Edward nodded. "They will be in need of goods like everyone else."

The man spat on the dirt floor and agreed. "All of us out here have no seats to our trousers, *mon ami*. And when you next call on them, you will stop to dally with Debora. The Good God was kind when He made women for men, eh?"

"He was kind."

As he expected, Edward found the Fair and the Zane farms far back from the river, their clearings on the banks of a creek that flowed into it. Both men proved to be young and clean, their modest wives, neatly dressed and retiring, a far cry from the Indian women of the French settlement.

Edward and Simeon could not escape the hospitality of Warren Fair and his wife, nor did Edward want to. The cabin had a single long room, fireplace, cupboards and table at one end, a wide bed neatly made with a crazy-quilt cover smoothed over it at the other. Just beside it, pegs on the wall held hats, bonnets, a powder horn, bullet pouch and a long rifle.

Everything appeared spotless. The floor was only dirt tamped smooth and firm but Edward saw that Anne Fair had probably swept and sprinkled it the night before. Her copper cooking utensils gleamed. Iron kettles looked to have been sand-scoured before being turned bottoms up in a neat line by the fireplace. Edward had to admit reluctantly that his own countrymen could not meet comparison.

For the first time in days he ate food without a preliminary inspection. It was well cooked, plain but savory, lacking only the flavor of herbs and wines so dear to the Gallic palate. Warren and Anne insisted that their visitors stay the night and helped them carry their packs up a wall ladder to a storage and sleeping loft, long and spacious as the room below.

"Different faces ain't too common in these parts," Warren said. "Me 'n Anne is right suited to one another and all, but still it's good to hear a different voice now and then."

His wife added, "Luvelle Zane and me get along like sisters and I see her ever' chance I get when her Jeremy and my Warren give a help at work to one another. But outlanders like you bring news and different kind of talk."

"You have neighbors down by the river," Edward suggested.

Anne hesitated, flushed and then blurted, "Then you know what they're like. They ain't our kind of folk. I don't mean 'cause they're French with a lot of Indian mix, what with their wives 'n kids 'n all. But it's the way they live that fashes me 'n Warren—the Zanes, too."

Warren cautioned, "Anne, might be Mr. Forny's French too, like Simeon."

"Might be," she admitted. "But they're clean and not a'crawl with bugs."

Simeon grinned widely and Edward laughed, "Madame, you have the right of it. Neither of us could stay the night in their cabin. We preferred the

349

riverbank and the shelter of our canoe."

The meal finished, Anne cleared the table, refusing Simeon's proffered help. "You men folk got a heap to jaw over and catch up with. I can scrub and scour the pots and pans and listen at the same time. There ain't much more 'n Warren and me would use no how."

Edward luxuriated in stretching his legs along the table bench. Warren did not produce the indispensable squat jug with the corncob stopper before dinner. Surely it would appear now. It did not. Though Edward believed he completely hid his surprise, Warren was sharp of eye and wits.

"Be ye looking for whiskey to smooth your gullet to talk, best you don't. Most about think us mean that we don't take to strong drink nor allow it in the house. Me 'n Anne use the powerful strong and clean drink of the Lord's own words each night afore we a'bed."

Simeon's eyes shadowed but Edward answered quickly, "We respect what any man feels directed to do." He smiled. "And to be even more honest, I have never really learned to like the fiery liquor of these parts. Wine is more to my taste."

"As it was to the Lord's, we have read in the Good Book. But me 'n Anne think of wine only for meeting house communion like it was back in Connecticut."

"Connecticut! My wife is from that colony."

Anne whirled, her face alight. "Where?"

"Westover."

She looked puzzled, probed her memory but Warren came up with the answer. "Westover was attacked and burned clean to the ground by the

Iroquois many years ago. My cousin lived near there and he said there was no one left alive."

Edward told him what had happened, repeating Abby's story of the terrible day and of the events that followed. Anne and Warren listened, gasping now and then as Edward recounted incidents in Abby's adventures and the strange path by which she had finally come to him.

He finished at last and a long silence ensued. Warren broke it with a whispered question. "She's alive in Fort Pitt after all of that?"

"And has borne me a son!"

"Sure as sure," Anne said, "you've thanked the sweet Lord over and over for His mercy and His gift of her to you."

"Time again in my mind and heart," Edward agreed.

"But ain't you come down to your knees and said your thanks aloud to Him!" she demanded.

"A prayer in the heart—"

"Ain't enough, is it, Warren?"

"Not the way we see it, Mr. Forny. The Good Book says 'In the beginning was the Word'—and that's an out-loud word. Here your wife who should be dead is alive and has given you a son."

"Yes, but—"

"But you ain't said a word of thanks. We're gonna do that right now!"

Before Edward and Simeon could exchange looks of surprise and dismay, Warren had walked the length of the room to return with a thick, heavy bible he took from a cupboard by the bed. He brought it to the table, opened it at random and looked sternly around at his wife as well as Edward and Simeon.

"Down on your knees while we lift our voices in praise and thanksgiving."

There could be no argument except stalking out. Edward rejected that. Warren was too good a man, too sincere, too willing to give spiritual as well as material help. His help might be too narrow and backwoods orthodox for Edward's taste but it flowed from a deep reservoir of sympathy and understanding. Warren could not be faulted for intent—merely for method.

Edward passed a signal to Simeon, rose from the bench and sank to his knees on the clean dirt floor. He had to make a second fierce signal to Simeon before the *voyageur* also knelt. Warren started to pray—one of those partial sermons, partial spiel, partial demands mixed with pleadings that Edward occasionally heard in this strange land south of what had been New France.

Time, interminable time, passed but still the words flowed out as Warren knelt, face lifted to the low ceiling, eyes tightly closed, hands clasped knuckle-tight. Now and then Anne would intone a vibrant "Amen" like an altar boy making a response. Edward knew the comparison would shock her but still it was apt. He ventured to peek at Simeon. The man knelt uncomfortably, head down so his face was hidden but Edward did not miss that, though his hands steepled in prayer, two fingers of each hand were crossed.

"Ah!" Edward thought. "God is God, so who is to

shape or define?''

Ages past had not answered that question so Edward surrendered it to the ages to come.

Unbelievably, the prayer of thanks for Abby's escape from Indian captivity ended. A moment later it was as though a fervent hour or more had never been. Warren replaced the Bible, Anne returned to her pots and pans while male conversation resumed. The frontier had too little time to dwell on a finished task of faith as it had on a finished task of farming when either were fully and satisfactorily completed.

In the short period of conversation that could be spared before early bedtime, the Fairs confirmed Edward's belief that they had simply moved out to the most likely looking land and started farming after building their cabin, stable and barn.

"Own it?" Warren echoed Edward's question. "No one but the Lord owns it and He made it for farming."

"*Your* farming?"

"Somebody's. I figure it might as well be me."

"Nothing's free in this world except the air we breathe," Edward commented, "and we have to work our lungs to get it. Someday, someone will come along with a solid legal claim and title."

"Not likely and right now it's getting late to argue about something that ain't likely to happen. The Sweet Lord led us to this land, he'll see we'll keep it. So let's thank Him for the day, for watching over us while we sleep and giving us new life and strength come dawn light."

It took more than a quarter hour on bended knees

to be sufficiently grateful.

Jeremy and Luvelle Zane, like the Fairs, had found land they liked and made it their own. Unlike Warren Fair, Jeremy Zane did not appeal to the "Sweet Lord" or the "Good Book" for approval. He readily admitted that someday he might have to pay rental, title or filing fee to keep whatever acres he might then have.

Also unlike the Fairs, he produced the traditional squat jug and Edward inwardly winced until he tasted its contents, a sweeter fluid than the frontier whiskey. He openly showed his pleased surprise and refilled the mug.

"Hard cider," Jeremy answered his question. "Made from apples. Don't let the taste fool ye. It's tricky. Drink enough and ye'll find it has a kick as hard as a mule's hoof. It can addle ye as bad as whiskey and the next morning ye'll feel twice as Gawd-awful. You'll swear you're gonna die but the hell of it is, ye don't. Drink it slow and with respect, my friend."

Edward could already feel a subtle, surprising warmth spreading up into his chest from even the little he had imbibed, so he recognized good advice. He cautiously sipped as he talked or listened to Jeremy or Luvelle.

They were tall and slender with coal black hair and dark eyes but had the white, fair skin of Northern Europe. They said their families had come from England and Ireland generations back. Edward guessed they inherited Spanish blood from the survivors of the devastated Spanish Armada of two

354

hundred years ago. Luvelle herself had not only inherited the Spanish coloring but also the feminine allure. Hints of her undoubtedly delectable figure appeared time and again beneath her shapeless frontier dress. As she placed dishes on the long table, or watched the meal cooking over the fireplace flames, she often ogled Edward. When she refilled the mugs of the three men, she inevitably stood across the table from Edward, bending over time and again, the loose neck of her dress falling forward to reveal the curves of rich white breasts. Then she would give Edward a brief, covert upward look that was invitation in itself.

Simeon openly stared but Edward looked quickly away, very much aware that Jeremy sat within arm's length across the table, his lips thinning slightly now and then. He abruptly looked up at his wife as she turned from the fireplace and approached the table to join in the conversation. Fireplace heat had formed small beads of moisture along her full lips and she brushed aside a wisp of gleaming black hair.

"Bring another cider jug," Jeremy ordered.

"But they's already a'plenty afore ye now."

"Bring another jug from that good batch we made late last summer."

"It's in the barn!" she protested.

"I know. Bring it."

He waited until she had lighted a candle from the fireplace flames, secured it in a bull's-eye lantern and left the room. When the door closed behind her, Jeremy smiled at his guests as his thumb indicated the door. "Ain't often Luvelle has furriners for company."

"Foreigners?" Edward took exception.

"Outlanders then. Anyhow, she ain't used to 'em, especially a fine gent'man like you, Mr. Forny."

"She's a lovely woman, *Monsieur* Zane."

"I know it. She knows it. Luvelle cain't help what she is and she's getting all flustered with you folks."

"She needn't be," Edward smiled.

Jeremy did not. "That's how I figure, Mr. Forny. I'd take it hard if she got upset by something, if you get my meaning."

Edward understood. "I get your meaning. Have no worry."

After several seconds, Jeremy eased back into his slouch. "Your word eases me considerable."

In a few moments, Luvelle returned with another jug that she placed on the table. She sensed a change, though nothing had been said. Edward gave her a fleeting smile and then turned his full attention to Jeremy. Luvelle's eyes swung to Simeon, back to Edward and then over to Jeremy. Without a word she turned back to the fireplace and took a seat on a high-backed chair facing the flames.

Edward learned that the Zanes, mountain people for generations, had come into the country from the Carolinas. Jeremy's speech, like Luvelle's, was soft and slurring, a contrast to the sharp, nasal quality that Edward ordinarily heard. They took daily problems almost as a matter of course, unlike the Fairs, never in a hurry or a strain. Yet, Edward noted, they worked as hard, accomplished as much and never seemed the least bit concerned that the Lord stood eternally over their shoulders giving them good marks or bad marks in some sort of heavenly record book. The sun came up or it didn't. Neither Zane thought much about it except in faint annoyance now and then. Neither of them prayed to the sweet Lord to change His mind once the dawn came.

Only one thing bothered Jeremy and, like the weather, he could do nothing about it except work up a surprising anger for one so ordinarily placid. Edward had heard the same complaint many times before in the few years since the French had been driven out. It only took a chance word to make Jeremy slam his fist on the table and his eyes to flash.

"Tell me how in hell a damned Britisher clean across an ocean can know what we need here in America? You tell me!"

"I can't." Edward answered. "Can you?"

"Of course not! They say do this and do that, move here, don't move there. Why, they ain't supposed to be no one but animals, Indians and trappers out in this country! You 'n me are sitting where we ain't supposed to according to all their fine laws."

"We're British subjects," Edward suggested.

"We ain't. We're colonists—I'm a Carolinian, you're a Pennsylvanian. The Fairs are Connecticuters—we're all American. It ain't right for hoity-toity dukes and lords thousands of miles away to make our laws."

"But it works out that way, *mon ami.*"

"Not for long."

"You come close to treason, some would say."

"I come close to common sense and naught else.

357

Look how they tax us for this and tax us for that! Look how they send their sojers over when each colony has plenty of its own to keep us safe from Injuns or anyone else."

"The king has sent over his royal governor, Jeremy."

"Thomas Gage—*Sir* Thomas, and don't forget that 'Sir' makes him better 'n us. God's socks! *How* does it! And look at them red-coated cocks'o'-the-walk with their noses in the air. Why, they's a good American right in Pennsylvania as has more sojer'n all of 'em put together. They know it, too. Didn't they make our Ben Franklin a member of one of their brainy London gaggle of scientists! Yet I bet there ain't a grog-drinking iggerent British sailor as would give him a 'Howdo, sir.' I bet you."

"What can we do about it at this distance?"

Jeremy subsided into a series of frustrated growls and then wagged his finger under Edward's nose to accent his prediction.

"Do what Ben Franklin had in mind when we went to war with the Frenchies. He wanted all the colonies to work together like one. Remember, he even designed a flag of a snake cut up in thirteen parts, each named for one of the colonies, and the flag warned, 'Join, or Die' to the colonists. The colonies even called a meeting but nothing came of it."

"I remember. Each colony feared another would get more than its rightful share of credit in conquest or more business—jealousy. They might feel the same way now—so you're still left with thirteen separate parts."

Jeremy squirmed, angered that he must admit Edward's argument no matter how much he disliked it. Yet he would not wholly surrender.

"Ye have the right of it when we was fighting the Frenchies. Every colony was sending its sojers to help the British, according to our bounden duty. They figured then that French land, like up along the St. Lawrence and the Ohio, would be divided up among us, we being right here and all. Then there was seatrade to be divided along with the land, since colony ships already sailed the whole coast and to the French islands like Haiti and Martinique. That wasn't the way them Londoners figured it. Everything is theirs and we ain't got a say."

"Colonies never do," Edward tried to explain. "British, French or Spanish, they exist to bring wealth to the mother country, only keeping a little bit for themselves. The Americas were treated no worse nor better than Mexico, Brazil, or any of the others."

"Not for much longer, I can tell you. We can't trade with no one but England. We can't ship our own goods in colonial ships—only British. The king rakes off the cream and leaves us with the blue skimmed milk—and then taxes that every way possible. That ain't fair."

"No, but so long as the colonies are almost thirteen separate nations, each jealous of the others, what can be done about it?"

"Throw out the British."

"Jeremy, you're not making sense. No one colony is strong enough and they won't combine."

"They'll combine and they'll be strong enough, you mark me good."

"Combine—and then quarrel? Will Massachusetts agree to a Pennsylvania militia general leading its own troops? Will Rhode Island agree to laws and needed wartime acts passed by Virginia, Delaware or Georgia? I don't think so."

"Ye'd be wrong. Them kings and lords and prime ministers will make some damn-fool move or add some tax that'll be just enough to set all hell blazing over here. You'll see how quick all of us get together—even if only long enough to kick the whole kit and caboodle of 'em out."

"Afterward?"

Jeremy laughed. "Afterward! Who cares? The job'll be done and we'll all be free Americans as we ought to be."

"Thirteen nations—not one."

"That don't sound too bad to me."

The jug of hard cider that Jeremy called "applejack" went around two or three times more and Edward began to feel quite warm and mellow. Simeon's cheeks now held a high color and his words slurred. Edward realized what was happening and, despite protests, dragged Simeon off to bed in the upstairs room.

They had breakfast at dawn-break the next morning, loaded the canoe and prepared for the day's journey. Luvelle had hot cornpone that she topped with a thick, dark and sweet liquid called "black-strap" that had found its way up the Ohio from the Spanish lands. Edward knew it to be one of the intermediate products as raw sugar cane was processed into thin syrups and sugar. They were far too costly to transport over the mountains from the east. But the farther west the Ohio settlement extended, the more blackstrap was used since it was almost right to hand and far cheaper. Edward made a mental note to consider it as a possible future trade item.

He felt relief when, at last, they shook hands with the Zanes before launching their canoe downstream on the return journey. Luvelle had worn the same scanty dress she had the day before and the bright morning light appeared to accent her shapely body more alluringly than had the flames of the fireplace. Jeremy kept a sharp eye on her but she still managed underbrow looks at Edward. The meaning was clear enough.

The canoe was almost packed when Jeremy learned Simeon's skinning knife had been left in the loft. The two of them hurried into the house to get it. The moment they disappeared through the door, Luvelle stepped close enough to Edward for him to see little flames deep in her dark eyes.

"Jeremy ain't let you 'n me hardly look to one another let alone speak," she said.

"It's my loss," Edward smiled uneasily.

"Sure is. I ain't seen a man I've wanted to bed so much." Before he knew what she intended, she grabbed his trousers in a swift, investigating grip, stepped back and grinned. "I knowed you'd be one to have all your wife or any woman would want."

He threw an alarmed look over her shoulder to the cabin. Jeremy and Simeon had not yet appeared. She

361

stepped back, lifted her skirt above her groin revealing the black mass of hair between her legs. "You 'n me could've set this whole damn creek afire if'n we'd had the chance. But Jeremy knowed it." She dropped her dress and shrugged. "Well, we both have an idea what we missed, huh?"

Just then Jeremy and Simeon emerged. Luvelle's smile vanished and her face became almost dull as she casually adjusted a paddle and pack in the canoe.

"You come see us again sometime, y'all hear?"

"She's speaking true," Jeremy echoed as he came up. Edward had caught the flick of his hard, sharp look at Luvelle that had apparently satisfied him nothing unseeming had occurred between his visitor and his wife.

"Next time we're this way," Edward answered quickly and swung to Simeon. "The time gets on, eh? We best be downstream."

They shoved off. The current caught them, bore them gently the length of the clearing, around a bend of the stream and out of sight. Edward answered Luvelle's small farewell gesture by lifting his paddle shoulder high. Then they were gone.

Edward wondered how much longer Jeremy would be a successful guardian of his sensuous wife's wiles and lusts. Someone else will find out, not me, he decided and increased his rhythmic paddle stroke.

XXVIII

Abby would always remember that wonderful autumn of 1763 as an interlude of love, peace and contentment. She knew once more the joy a woman experiences when the man she loves returns after a long absence spent in a dangerous and nearly unknown country. He and Simeon had appeared at the doorway without warning one warm, golden morning. She never knew how she had crossed the room in a rush after her surprised cry of delight. She could only remember his strong arms tight about her, his muscular body pressed against hers in a crushing hug and his lips on hers.

They had no idea how long they had remained unmoving, clinging to one another. They had not heard Simeon back out of the cabin and close the door behind him. Oh, the wonderful feel of him! the smooth caress of his beard on her cheeks, the masculine aroma of woodsmoke, wilderness, the aura of beloved manhood that enwrapped her!

Henri's sudden loud bawling shocked them into awareness that there was far more in the world than just the two of them. Edward released Abby and swept up the toddler, paying no attention to his frightened cries. He held the baby high, eyes alight with pride while Henri's cries increased in volume.

"Put him down! He's afraid!" Abby exclaimed but Edward only waggled the baby from side to side while his delighted booming laughter filled the room.

"*Pardieu!* He'll become used to me. He will become a giant, this one."

"Not if you scare the growth out of him. Let him get used to you. You're a stranger to him."

Edward looked startled, then meekly handed the boy to Abby. "I had not thought of that, *ma petite.* Eh, take him and calm him. Will he stop crying?"

Henri grabbed Abby's dress and buried his face deep in her shoulder, sobbing his fear. She soothed him with words, stroking and gentle pats, smiling all the while at Edward.

"You do look a wild one. I've not seen you with a

beard before.''

He touched his whiskers as though they surprised him, then looked abashed. "I had forgotten it out in the woods and on the rivers. I wonder you knew me yourself. Off it comes.''

"It can wait until you meet someone else.''

"With my son working his lungs full power! I wager he's alarmed the whole settlement.''

"And more—listen,'' Abby pointed to the great bed and Henri's crib beside it. But someone else kicked and cried in the crib. "You haven't met your daughter.''

She thought his eyes would pop from his head. Still holding and soothing Henri, she led Edward to the crib. She had only to study the swiftly changing expressions on Edward's face to experience the wonder of the gift that only a woman can give her man. He knelt down as though at a shrine, studied the little monkey face, spasmodic moving arms and kicking legs, then looked up at her in pleased, speechless disbelief.

"Mary,'' she said. "Mayhap you would like Marie. Four months old come the tenth of the month. Are you happy with her?''

His lifting voice started Henri on a fresh burst of squalling. Edward paid no attention but held his finger to the baby. She blindly grasped it and held tightly. He looked around and up at her with a pride and emotion that brought a catch to her voice and a surge of love to her heart.

"Oh, Edward!'' she almost wailed to herself.

Had it not been for Henri, Edward would have postponed shaving but the boy started crying each time he saw his father. At last Abby herself lost patience though desire gnawed at her. She left the big bed and Edward's side to fill a basin with hot water from a kettle hanging on a fireplace crane. Edward watched her slender naked body move about the room from fireplace to a long bench under a mirror hanging from a wall peg. She poured hot water in a basin, placed shears and razor beside it and returned to bed, taking Henri under the covers with her.

"Cut off the whiskers and shave," she ordered in patient disgust and sighed. "Will your son always have his way with us?"

"Not always. I'll see to it."

"Shave now and see to it later. You and I have important things on our minds."

Under the covers where he could not see Edward, and snuggled against his mother's warm body, Henri stopped crying. He was sound asleep when the job was done and did not awaken when Abby put him in a trundle bed Dean Smith had built for him. At one point he stirred as though awakening when Abby cried out in ecstasy and her fists beat on Edward's bare back. She gained control of herself, though with some difficulty.

She and Edward were fully dressed and she had made up the badly rumpled bed when Henri awakened. He looked at Edward. Abby held her breath. But Henri did not cry. He eyed Edward curiously, as he would a stranger, certainly not the bearded monster who had sent him off into such tearful panic. By nightfall and supper he sat beside Edward in a high chair and allowed his father to spoon porridge into his mouth while Abby nursed

Marie. The four of them had smoothly and miraculously made the transition into a family after so much noise and fear.

After sup, the neighbors came to call, having wisely kept their distance during the first few hours of reunion. The Smiths came first. Letty had yet another baby, also a toddler clinging to her skirt while the two older boys moved awkwardly and diffidently behind her. Edward could hardly believe they had grown so tall and become so muscular.

"They make good farmers," Dean said with pride. "Edward, you had the right on that."

"Will they be traders?"

"Hard to say. But you've made one out of me. I know every inch of the road to Carlisle and beyond. The warehouse here is filled, waiting for your orders and I've sold everything from nutmeg to awls all over the settlement and down the Monongahela and the Allegheny. I keep traveling back and forth but can't keep up with all that our neighbors and the new settlers need. What've you found west down the Ohio?"

"People as hungry for goods as they are here. But we'll go over our business come the morrow." He indicated the sound of knocking on the door. "We'll be besieged by neighbors tonight."

To Abby's pleased surprise, Captain Blaine was the first to call. He did not stay long, knowing his presence would inhibit these frontier people. But Abby had reason to be grateful for his respect and unobtrusive kindness and care during Edward's absence. Blaine repaid as best he would the debt he and the post owed her for bringing Colonel Bouquet to their rescue. He asked Edward about conditions down the river, the amount of havoc Pontiac had wrought, the speed of recovery.

"They rebuild slowly," Edward answered. "It would go much faster if they could be sure what the king will finally decide."

"Then it may go slowly for yet a goodly time, Mr. Forny. I have orders from Colonel Bouquet in Detroit to discourage settlement. The colonel follows orders from General Gage in Boston, of course."

"Of course. Boston is a goodly distance from us and Parliament and His Majesty's palace in London even farther. How can they know our conditions and country along the Ohio or any eastern stream? They are like blind men making rules for a horse race, eh? How can they make such laws?"

"As an officer of the king, I'd say wisely and well."

"As one of the many who live in Pitt settlement or along the Ohio?"

The ghost of a smile touched Blaine's lips but he kept his face straight. "No comment, sir. However, I will comment on the beautiful addition to your family."

"Ah, Marie—lovely daughter of a lovely wife, if you'll pardon a proud husband's and father's bias."

"Bias? Nay—truth, 'pon my soul. Now, with your permission I'll take my leave. I've long since come to feel that a red uniform tends to dampen frontier sociables."

Edward smiled. "No comment, Captain. Understand, you are welcome."

"Officially understood. I would be pleased if you called at my headquarters tomorrow. There is much you could tell me of the Ohio country over some excellent wine I have just received. I believe it's a Bordeaux vintage."

"Bordeaux wine here at Pitt! I thought the army supply trains carried only rum for its soldiers." Then he caught the officer's underbrow look. "Ah, but perhaps there is another supply train that has no restrictions, eh?"

"No comment, sir. I bid you good e'en."

Blaine roughed Henri's dark head, smiled down at Marie asleep in her crib and then made his adieu to Abby. When he closed the door, Letty sighed in relief. "There's a man all of us could like if it wasn't for that damned red uniform. Lord knows he fought hard enough when there was nothing but Injuns around us."

"And several red uniforms are buried around the fort flagpole," Abby added. "They fought for us hardest of all."

"May their souls rest in peace!" Letty acknowledged. "Had ye heard Blaine's due to become a major afore long?"

"It's no more than a whisper," Abby replied and looked around to Edward. "I thought to tell you the settlement gossip tomorrow—that is, what you don't hear tonight."

"It may be more than gossip, *ma petite*. He wants to talk to me about the west reaches of the rivers tomorrow. I hope it's true. Blaine deserves a promotion."

"Long overdue," Abby agreed.

As though Blaine's departure had been awaited by the neighbors as a signal, the first knock at the door sounded but moments later. Soon the cabin was filled with guests and their children. Some brought jugs and even mugs to supplement Abby's supply. The rooms became so crowded it was hard to move about. Henri mingled with the other toddlers while little girls took turns tending to babies like Marie. Abby proudly observed how the men warmly welcomed Edward home. Once or twice she had touches of alarm when she noticed nubile, shapely older girls speculatively eyeing her husband. She laughed at herself, certain of her husband and his devotion.

He held the center of attention as he told of what he had seen and heard on his journeys. The men were the most curious. Abby knew they dreamed and planned of more land and greater opportunities beyond the confines of Pitt settlement. They are a restless breed, she thought, and rightly so for this time and place.

Her own father would have been at home among them, for it had been this same need to escape settled confinement and strike out to discover what lay downstream, or on the far side of the woods, the other side of the mountain that had brought him from Maine down into Massachusetts and finally into Westover, Connecticut. What colonist escaped the feverish need to move on? to establish a better or larger farm? find a country more to his liking? Not even the women were exempt. Abby herself envied Edward's journey into unknown lands among unknown people. She believed every American colonist had the fever to a greater or lesser degree.

Simeon appeared, bringing the French fur trappers who had now established something of a

370

permanent settlement of a few cabins south of the fort along the Monogahela. Edward saw them the moment they entered the cabin and jumped to his feet, arms spread in warm welcome. In the Gallic way, the men hugged one another, jabbering in their musical, strange tongue all the time. Abby understood most of it, thanks to Edward. She knew that these *voyageurs* and couriers, like their English neighbors, wanted nothing more than to explore the virgin wilderness, follow large and small streams, named and unnamed—wherever canoe and trap line would lead them.

She heard that Vevay and Versailles in the Illinois country had been rebuilt. The British had strengthened the military post at Vincennes up a river with the strange name, Oubache.

"Oui," Edward answered a newcomer to the local French settlement, "Ouitenon and Terre Haute gradually return to normal. There are pelts to be caught out there to satisfy the English king with enough left over to please the French Bourbon monarchs. But, of course, King George, through his ministers and laws, sees to it that the French will not see so much as a single hair from a skin."

The trappers accepted his statement with typical fatalistic shrugs but the news of so much land untouched by traps or hunters excited them. Abby knew they wanted the freedom of the woods and streams, the jingle of coins in their pockets above all else. After all, a Pine Tree Shilling or an English crown could be come by much more easily than French gold. If all else failed, the Spanish were now in St. Louis and New Orleans. They had good, spendable money. Eh, there was no worry!

Abby moved slowly among her guests, making sure the girls took care of the babies, that the women formed comfortable little gossip circles, that the mugs never lacked for whiskey. She kept a particularly sharp eye on that. Though a great socializer, too much could turn some men mean and some women sharp-tongued, shrewish and nasty. She wanted no quarrels or fights. Since most of her guests would be up at crack of dawn, they would not stay long. Even so, serious trouble could erupt in a second without warning. However, no one wanted to mar Edward's homecoming so she knew they put a bridle on their appetite for the powerful frontier brew.

Because the packed crowd increased the heat in the comparatively small rooms, she opened the cabin door to whatever night breeze dared to compete with the rush of talk, the clouds of tobacco smoke, all the coming and going. As she worked her slow way the third or fourth time among her guests, she again came to the open door.

Candle and firelight illuminated a few nearby yards of the dark night and she saw a man out there who had been asking for Edward a few days before. She stepped into the doorway and beckoned him forward.

"Mr. Cleary, why do you linger out in the dark! Come be with your neighbors."

He took a few steps forward. She could see his blond hair, stocky body and his gentle, diffident smile that belied his pugnacious, hard chin. A black and yellow dog moved with him, remaining close to his leg, whether in fear for itself or in defense of its master Abby could not tell. Cleary held a wadded felt hat in his strong hands.

"Sure, and I hardly know any of the lot of them, ma'am. Be'n't Pluto and me would not be welcome."

"Nonsense! You wanted to see my husband. He's here so now's the time. Come in."

She finally persuaded him to step into the filled room but Pluto remained in the doorway, alert and suspicious, obviously unhappy that his master had plunged into the crowd, temporarily abandoning him. Abby took Cleary's arm and he flushed beet red at her touch. She firmly guided him to Edward.

Now that Abby could see both man and dog much better by candle and fireplace light, she had to change her impression of both. Sean Cleary's nose had been flattened as though it had forcefully encountered a fist at some distant time in the past. Now she knew the reason for her impression of something awry with his face in their brief previous encounter. He had said he came from Boston but everything about him marked Ireland, from sky blue eyes to blond hair.

She looked back to the doorway where Pluto waited. The black and yellow dog was much larger than she had thought. The animal sat just inside and to one side of the threshold, unmoving, wary, its flank protected by the log wall and door frame. It eyed everyone, the ruff at its neck slightly raised, its tail unmoving. She could detect signs of tense, bunched muscles beneath the smooth hair of its coat. Frightened, she thought, and felt sorry for it.

She stepped toward it and extended her hand to pat its head. Its head swung as swiftly as a wild beast's and its ears flattened. Its lips drew back from white teeth and fangs. A deep, menacing growl shook its body. It came to its feet, ready to spring.

"Pluto!" Cleary's voice cracked over the noise and all talk instantly broke off. "Down, Pluto!"

He dropped Edward's hand, wheeled and jumped to Abby's side. "Heel, damn ye, Pluto! She be friend. Here . . . see? . . . friend."

He put his arm around Abby's shoulder. "Beggin' your pardon, ma'am, but Pluto can understand this. Mr. Forny, would ye be coming up beside us? Your lady come near losing a hand and maybe an arm."

"That be a vicious brute," Dean Smith commented as Edward strode up.

"Nay, Bucko," Cleary defended. "A dog trained to guard and defend me and mine against red or white skinned skulkers. Wilderness bred. Once he sees you're my friend, he's gentle as a fine lady's poodle."

"One hell of a poodle, if you ask me," someone said. "I'd as soon come on a wounded bear."

"Ye'd be right was ye alone. Mr. Forny, come close." He put his hand around Edward's shoulder, pulled him and Abby up beside him. "See, Pluto? Friends."

He took Edward's hand and held it out and down to the dog's muzzle. Pluto's lips lifted slightly from his fangs but he sniffed Edward's hand. Cleary repeated the process with Abby. She controlled her impulse to jerk her hand away when she felt the animal's moist breath on her fingers.

Pluto looked up into her face for a long moment, as though memorizing it and then sniffed her fingers once more. He swung his massive head to Edward, smelled his hand.

"Pet him," Cleary ordered and repeated when Abby looked at him in disbelief, "Pet him. Both you 'n Mr. Forny so's he'll never ever forget you."

"Should we?" Abby appealed to Edward.

"*Certainement.* We will see Monsieur Cleary and Pluto mayhap many times."

She reached out gingerly. Pluto grew rigid but he did not show his fangs. She felt him flinch slightly when she touched him and smoothed his head.

"Friend, Pluto," Cleary repeated.

Then the dog completely surprised her. He rubbed against her leg and his moist tongue kissed her palm as he pushed his muzzle deeper into her hand. His tail wagged. He turned to Edward and his tail continued wagging as he allowed Edward to pet him.

"He remembers you, Mr. Forny, from the time you 'n your friend came to my clearing. I told you he never forgets!"

When Abby turned to Edward in surprise, he explained, "Monsieur Cleary and I met on the river— rather he hailed Simeon and me to his landing. A most interesting visit and a profitable one, I think."

"Now that's a point I'd be taking up with ye, Mr. Forny. There be changes since we made our deal."

"Ah, Pontiac's friends didn't miss you, eh?"

"The spalpeens missed me 'n Pluto, but my house and all else is gone."

"Business," Abby said in sudden understanding and rested her hand on Edward's arm. "It should wait until a quieter time, love."

"Vous avez raison, ma petite." He looked at Cleary and added, "Unless you have some of that smooth brew—"

"Distilling, Mr. Forny. I told ye 'tis not of beer we speak." He sighed. "Little left. The redskins found most of the kegs and a fine—"

"Please," Abby begged. "Our friends came to welcome you home. They don't care about trade goods."

Edward and Cleary exchanged looks that puzzled her. Edward said enigmatically, "They'd care about the goods Mr. Cleary and I had in mind."

"Tomorrow," Abby said with finality and turned both men back into the room and the crowd.

Cleary and his dog came after nooning the next day. As Abby worked about the room, watched Henri and tended to Marie, she kept a wary eye on Pluto for a time, but the big dog, after accepting brief petting from her and Edward, gave its full attention to Henri. It needed no introduction as it had with her and Edward. At first sight it trotted to Henri, tail awag and its sloppy affectionate tongue in the boy's face, knocking him off his feet and thudding his bottom on the floor. He started to cry but Pluto's playful antics distracted him.

Cleary crowed with pleasure. "And would ye be after seeing that, Mistress Forny! I never knowed before Pluto takes to kids."

Boy and dog rolled about the floor, tugging at one another, Pluto crouching and making mock ferocious leaps, growls that held no danger in their sound, submitting to ear and tail pulling, barking in

376

delight now and then. Between boy, dog, housework and Marie she managed to garner an idea of the business between Cleary and Edward.

For the first time, she heard the term "sour mash." Cleary poured some of the beautifully clear amber fluid from a jug he had brought. She sipped it and reacted to its warm, smooth taste as Edward had.

"I drink but little and then mostly to be polite when callers come to deal with Edward or pass a few words of talk with me. But this is not the whiskey I have known anywhere in the colonies."

"And ye'll not be tasting it again for a time," Cleary said mournfully.

Edward told her of his encounter with the brew. "Eh, I knew it was something everyone in the Western Lands would want. So I bought up all his stock to be delivered as soon as it had aged to what he considers the proper time. But now—"

"Them Injuns chased me 'n Pluto to the Moravian Mission at Gnaddenhutten. They burned me house and barn, ruined me distilling works and then found and drank up all but a jug or two of me stock." He laughed with a bitter sound. "The spalpeens drank from jug and keg, not knowing green, raw likker from smooth, nigh finished whiskey fit for a king, I'd say."

"So would I," Edward added, "and French kings at that. This is fit for a Bourbon."

"Aye, but all gone. I have to start over again and I know ye'll not want to wait for the aging."

"There you're wrong. We still have our bargain whenever the time comes."

Cleary's wide grin showed his relief. Then he suddenly laughed and slapped his knee. "I wonder if me red friends could so much as see Fort Pitt after they left my place."

"All to the good," Abby commented, her eyes darkening with memories. "We had enough of them as it was."

XXIX

Although in America the last shot of the war with the French had been fired three years ago, there had been no peace treaty. As Abby knew herself, that fact had a peculiar effect on every settler. Though she, Edward and all their friends said the war was over, they still could not be quite certain. Who could tell when the French would send an invasion fleet across the Atlantic to attack the seaboard colonies? Or perhaps they would come up the Mississippi from New Orleans with the blessing of their Spanish allies and attack by way of the Ohio.

Louis XV had lost the Americas to his arch rival, George III, but the two monarchs fought for supremacy and possession of over half the world—in Europe, Africa and Asia. There could be no treaty for the Ohio country so long as guns roared elsewhere, but early in the spring of 1763 word came that the warring nations had agreed in Paris the fighting should cease. Seven years of war, turmoil, Indian depredations and general uncertainty ended. Abby knew it was an illusion of her own making, but it seemed the sky was a softer blue, the bright sun warmer and, perhaps, the spring more gentle and hopeful than any she had known in years.

March winds proved less blustery and quickly gave way to April's tender, budding days. Abby swore Henri added an inch a week if not more and Marie gave promise of outgrowing her crib. Edward acted as though invisible shackles had been stricken from his ankles and wrists and certainly from his mind. His cheerful whistle sounded all over the settlement as he impatiently awaited Dean Smith's return from eastern trips. The log warehouse threatened to burst with trade goods, so much so that even Abby questioned this apparent wild spree of purchases.

She brought up her concern one balmy night as she cleared the table of dishes, pausing to scrub gravy and meat stains from Henri's mouth and cheeks. Dean had left for Carlisle just that morning with an empty wagon and would soon return loaded.

"We spend money as though we had it to burn or

throw away," she suggested. "I begin to fear we'll not have enough for our own needs."

Edward laughed and made a wide gesture south toward the Monongahela. "Eh, and why do I build a stout boat instead of a canoe?"

"I know—trade. But are there truly enough people downstream who need as much as we have in the warehouse?"

"Indeed—and more will be coming now that peace is truly signed. We will have our money back and much more beside. You will see."

Marie needed attention and Abby had just finished changing her when Captain Blaine knocked. Edward admitted him. Abby stopped in mid-stride when she saw his smile and the excitement in his eyes.

"You have news, Captain?"

"Yes, mistress. Army dispatches came today." He pulled a parchment from his pocket. It was rolled and tied with a ribbon, but the official seal was broken. "You now speak to *Major* Blaine."

"Promotion!" Abby exclaimed in delight.

"*Pardieu!* you grow too big for Fort Pitt!" Edward jumped up and shook his hand. "This calls for wine, my friend. You will not be with us long."

"Oh, dear! I hadn't thought of that!" Abby said.

"You're wrong. I stay here. But my authority is extended to command all posts along the Ohio to the Spanish lands. Colonel Bouquet in Detroit remains in full command of everything west of the mountains and I report to him."

"*Très bien!* We would not want to lose you. But first the toast to your good fortune and then the details."

381

They drank to Major Blaine's good luck, good health and long life, Abby joining them in the little ceremony at the table. When they placed their empty mugs on the table, Blaine took a proud military stance before the fireplace, dark now except for a few embers remaining from the supper fire.

"I need your help, Edward."

"You have it, Major."

Blaine's military mask broke into a wide, pleased grin. "That pleases me—Major. It will take some time to become used to it."

"You've earned it over and over," Abby assured him. "No one here has forgotten the siege."

"Thank you, mistress. It was only line of duty. Still, it pleases me."

"How can I help?" Edward asked.

"Loan me Simeon and another good *voyageur* along with one of your canoes. I am ordered to immediately inspect the river posts' military condition and report."

Edward frowned in instant concern. "Not war again?—and so soon!"

"Nay, only in case of future trouble, I think. I also understand His Majesty's minister wants more information. When you say 'Ohio' in Westminster, you might as well say 'Far Cathay.' Both are equally little known to His Majesty, the prime minister and Parliament."

"And," Abby commented caustically, "so are his colonial subjects, as far as I can see."

Blaine lifted a warning finger but continued to smile. "Have a mind to a newly minted Royal Major in the room, mistress, whom *lèse-majesté* would

382

distress. Not that he's as yet heard aught seditious, understand." He turned back to Edward, "May I count on your men and canoe?"

"*Vraiment!* You have them. I would like to go with you."

"Could you?"

Abby held her breath until Edward regretfully sighed. "You tempt me, but I have much to do here. Perhaps another time when Abby and the children could go with us? Ah, but that will be years hence."

"Not the way your Henri grows and your Marie develops into a beautiful woman a little bit more each day." Blaine looked curiously at Edward. "I know you built a boat for the Ohio trade, but is there aught else on your mind?"

"Across the river and into the mountains to the east, I have heard, new people come through the passes—what do we call them here?"

"Gaps?"

"*Oui*—gaps."

"That's news, my friend," Blaine said in a tone that almost demanded more information.

"I have heard whispers of rivers that way—the Holston, the Clinch and there is one called, I believe, the Cumberland. They are just names to me now but if they are to be water paths people will take into this western country, then they promise trade, eh? I want to know."

Blaine spoke carefully, selecting his words. "His Majesty has already made certain tentative decisions about these western lands. His ministers have not been sure our Ohio is safe, so settlement has been more or less banned."

"Not a very wise decision, *mon ami*."

"Whatever His Majesty decides—" Blaine broke off. "But now full peace has come with the new treaty. Many dangers no longer exist. Colonel Bouquet broke Indian power at Bushy Run." Blaine smiled at Abby. "Though His Majesty does not know it, he owes that to you, mistress."

"Nay, Capt—pardon, Major—it is owed to Edward. I would not have him risking his life trying to break through to the fort."

"So you broke through to Bouquet and saved all of us. We are still in debt to you."

"It is nothing. Simeon will be glad to be out on the river again."

After Blaine had left, Abby finished her evening tasks and finally went to curl up beside Edward in bed. He nuzzled her bare neck and shoulders and his hands gently explored her body. She thrilled in response to it. But Henri still moved about in his trundle and she whispered regretfully in Edward's ear.

"Our son is much too awake, darling."

"*Sacre bleu!* Does he never sleep!"

"Of course," she chuckled, "but at all the wrong times."

"Eh, but he will not understand." His fingers gently squeezed a nipple but she firmly moved his hand.

"But he'll be curious—and how do we answer him? Have patience. We'll talk until he sleeps."

"About what?"

"About those rivers to the south and west. I never heard of them before."

"Nor had I." He fired to the question and sat up in bed beside her. "Dean had word of them on his last trip—no more than a rumor and I paid little attention. Then a courier wandering down along the mountain chain seeking bear skins and beaver streams, came on some of the new clearings down that way. He worked his way northward to the source of the Monongahela and came to Pitt settlement but three days ago. He told me of them."

"Strange he told no one else."

"He did, *ma petite*, we who are French."

"The peace is signed," Abby said dryly, "but the war goes on in our minds. Will it never end? Must we always be English or French and never Americans?"

"*Oui*, it will end."

"When?"

"Our Major Blaine gave a hint of the answer. If the British king continues to be the fool and treat Americans as serfs or villains, he will find his colonists all of one mind and one people, to his lasting regret." He bent over her and kissed her long and fervently, his hands again exploring until Abby firmly grasped his wrists.

"Henri is still awake if you haven't noticed. Now . . . about those rivers and settlers?"

He told her what he had learned, and that proved to be very little. For twenty years or more a bold man from one of the southern colonies had withstood the mysteries that might exist west of the low, jagged peaks of the Appalachians. Then he packed up and went to see for himself. Or another might have found it convenient to disappear into the western wilderness to avoid creditor, jail or gallows.

It had been a sporadic thing, a sprinkling of lonely clearings hidden in unknown coves and hollows. Once in a great while a man dared bring his family, but that was rare. The war with the French had brought it to an end. Now, with peace it had revived again.

"They have become *audacieux*, what you call 'bold,' eh? They dare Virginia Colony's claims, those men from the Carolinas and Georgia. What matter the claim of a colony—Virginia, Maryland, even Pennsylvania—when there is no way to enforce it? So now those daring ones move through the passes—"

"Gaps," Abby corrected him.

"*Oui.* I had forgotten the wilderness word. They move in small bands of families quite often, though the single cabin clearing is still more the rule."

Abby drew a mental map of what little she knew of the country down that way. "They enter the Dark and Bloody Ground, don't they?"

"No tribe claims the land," Edward reminded her. "They use it just for hunting and war. Yes, there is what is called 'The Great Warriors Path' but since that is traveled only at certain times of the year, it is of no great problem. So the people move down that way."

"Enough of them to be worth the risk and time?"

He spread his hands. "Eh, there is always time—and what risk?"

"Indians and outlaws."

He laughed. "After all we've known from my Gascony and your Connecticut, you call them risks! *Ma foi*, you dream like a child." He abruptly looked beyond Abby. "As our Henri dreams at long last."

In a moment Abby had been pulled under the covers, her naked legs intertwined with his, avidly returning his kisses, exploring his groin as he explored hers.

She heard nothing more about an immediate departure for the country to the south but Abby knew Edward had only deferred it for more pressing matters. He spent hours sketching designs for a different kind of boat to be used on the Ohio, but none of them satisfied him. When Simeon returned from his expedition with Major Blaine, he scoffed at Edward's ideas.

"What is wrong with a canoe, *mon ami?*" he demanded. "We have always used them. We can build one as we used to, sixty feet long and three feet wide. It carries all the trade good ever needed on the river."

"Now, perhaps, but not for long. There will be new settlements and towns in very few years. No canoe could carry enough cargo for that."

Simeon rapped a crumpled drawing with his hard knuckles. "But how could we use paddles on a boat with a hull this high, eh?"

"Sails—long oars—something like that."

"*Mon Dieu!* You make an ocean of our Ohio."

Edward stubbornly shook his head. "Not an ocean, *mon ami,* but I have a certainty of what the future holds for us in the west."

"Future—not present," Simeon insisted. "Besides, I have heard whispers that the English king may not permit trade in these western lands. Eh, have patience until we have a better idea of how things will work out."

Edward shrugged and momentarily surrendered, contenting himself with half a dozen short trading trips after building the huge canoe Simeon had suggested. He took along six canoemen besides himself and Simeon. Once more Abby found herself alone, her days empty except for the exactions of Henri and Marie. She no longer had to worry about Indian war and pillage, but she knew that not a day passed but that Edward might encounter a lone Indian who knew he could garner a white scalp and escape into the sanctuary of the forest. The same would be true of one of those wandering renegades, like that horrible George Girty whom Corn Dancer had killed to save her. In a way, they were more of a danger than Indians. They could commit their killing and robbing with as much impunity as the Indian. They could wait out a hue and cry if the crime was discovered and, when the turmoil passed, mingle in the settlements and posts and never be suspected.

So she prayed each night and morning and then forcefully closed her mind to further fear. She had her fair share of frontier fatalism mixed with a spiritual trust that the wilderness circuit riders would have applauded.

However, Edward returned from the short trips, each time more enthusiastic. His trade goods disappeared to be replaced by furs and small pouches of coins of many denominations, nations and colonies. The sight of an occasional Spanish doubloon no longer surprised her.

Two days after Edward returned from one of his westward trips, a stranger came to their door. He was a short, stocky man with a bright eye and high, intelligent forehead. The moment Abby opened the door, she knew this one was not of the usual frontier breed. He wore a great coat of heavy, serviceable cloth, topped by a stiff high collar to protect against the rain storm that had just ended.

He wore the usual broad-brimmed, low crown hat of the frontier but a glance told her he had paid more than a few pence for it. He pulled it off the moment Abby opened the door. It dripped water as he held it by his side onto the foot of one of his fine leather boots that reached almost to the kneebands of his tight woven woolen trousers.

"Would you be Mistress Forny?" he asked and continued when she nodded, "Is your husband home, madame? Tell him Mr. Croghan would have a word or two with him."

"He is not here, but will return at almost any moment. Please come in and be welcome, Mr. Croghan. It could start raining again at any moment."

"Nay, I drip water like a waterfall."

"That's of no matter. We have pegs by the fireplace where your cloak and hat can dry."

"You persuade me, Mistress Forny."

She moved out of the doorway and he entered the room, loosening the clasp of his greatcoat and swinging it off his shoulders as he hurried across the room to the wall pegs by the fireplace. Abby closed the door and turned to make the caller comfortable. He wore a dark blue dress coat of smooth, expensive wool trimmed in a thin white piping along the collar, deep pockets on each side, and its edge that hung almost to his knees. His high linen stock and ruffled white shirt front looked to be of a foreign make and cut, though Abby could not be certain. His wig bore long curls above each ear and was combed back to a queue tied by a small ribbon of the same bone white as his coat piping.

He looked regretfully at the wet tracks he had made along the floor as he loosened the buckle of a wide shiny leather belt about his waist that held a leather-pouched flintlock pistol and a sheathed knife, those mandatory weapons of frontier travel.

"I fear I have muddied your floor, Mistress Forny."

"We all do in rainy weather," she dismissed the apology and placed her finger on her chin beside her mouth. "Croghan? I seem to remember Edward saying your name."

He smiled and she liked the way his weather-toughened face lighted and grew years younger. "Aye, we met years back on the river. It was just before Pontiac. I had come up from the Choctaw and Cherokee lands on my way to visit the tribes north of the Ohio, trying to undo the harm Amherst had done when he stopped annual gifts to the Indians. I sensed even then that something like Pontiac would happen."

"You're not English, then? I would have sworn to it a moment ago."

"Nay, Pennsylvania Colony born and bred. I have just returned from England—and glad to be back in America, I can tell you."

Just then the street door swung open again. Edward bent within its frame to work off a muddy

390

boot and Abby hurried to help him as he placed the boot just within the door and bent to the other foot. But he had seen his visitor and jerked upright.

"Monsieur Croghan! The last I saw you—"

"The Jonas' island." Croghan laughed in delight. "I had hoped you would not forget."

"How could I!"

Abby reached his side. "Your other boot, darling, before you renew acquaintance." Just then the rain renewed, coming down in almost solid sheets.

Edward jerked off his other boot and jumped into the room. He immediately turned and thrust his head out into the downpour and commanded, "Inside—quickly. *Ma foi!* Would you drown yourself?"

He turned to Abby. "A jug of Cleary's fine whiskey, eh? for my old acquaintance, Monsieur Croghan, and for this poor devil who long ago came a'soak."

He spoke truth about the bewhiskered, tangled-haired man who shuffled into the room. Though obviously soaked through to the skin, his long frontier shirt still looked saturated with grease, dirt and a myriad mysterious stains. His leggings were equally filthy and his moccasins were no more than shapeless coverings of skin on his feet. The cracked leather belt about his waist carried a bare hunting knife, the long blade a wicked gleam in the subdued light of the room.

Abby felt a shock at the man's filth. She made an imperious gesture to the fireplace and almost snapped, "Take your mud and wet over there—and stay until you're dry. Understand?"

391

"Yes, ma'rm. And thank ye."

"Thank my husband. He found you."

She wheeled about and strode out of the room. She kept the few precious jugs lined on the floor of a high clothes cupboard in the next room. She bent over Marie in her crib for a moment, thankful that by sheer chance she had sent Henri to the Smiths before the storm to play with the brood over there.

She turned to the cupboard and thought with distaste of the odorous newcomer. Why did many men of the frontier lose all sense of cleanliness and pride? she wondered, and then sighed. It was not too uncommon out here, she knew. They lived with the Indians, took their women as mates and before long adopted the Indian way of living—even to the lice that often infested the tepees and villages.

She suddenly remembered the horrible travesty of a man whom Corn Dancer had killed so long ago, and shuddered. The man in the other room was of the same degraded type. Abby paused abruptly. Come to think of it, both had the same shifting, slate-gray eyes, pinched nose and thick lips. Did they all come to look like one another eventually? and die as violently as that man, George Girty, had?

She dismissed the thought. No matter. They would soon be rid of him. She hovered over Marie another moment before she left the room. Now Edward, Mr. Croghan and the noisome squawman stood at the fireplace, Edward and Mr. Croghan many paces away from their companion.

Abby placed the jug on the table just as Croghan turned to speak to Edward, indicating the newcomer. "He joined our party coming up from the Virginias.

I manage to bear his smell because he can tell me much I need to know about the mountains, settlers and Indians down that way."

"Has he a name?"

"That I do," the man growled. "I'm Simon Girty."

Abby caught herself before she fell across the table.

XXX

Afterward she never fully remembered how she had managed to right herself as Edward jumped to her side to support her. Croghan had also jumped forward but had stopped short when he saw that Edward had her safely supported. She could not keep her horrified eyes off the travesty of a man who remained by the fireplace.

"Does he frighten you, *ma petite?* We can send

him packing."

She managed to shake her head. Girty scowled at her. "What's about my name that fashes ye? It's a good American one."

She choked out the question, "Simon?—not George?"

His eyes flamed with what might have passed as pleased surprise. "He was my brother. The Injuns kilt him, though he lived with a Shawnee woman. Did ye know him?"

"I heard his name, during the Indian troubles."

"Aye. He was with the Injuns right here, close to Pitt. I told him to stay down south with me where he belonged but not George! He figured where there was trouble there'd be chances to pick up a heap of things."

Croghan said distastefully, "You mean loot."

"However you call it," Girty shrugged. "Anyhow, George caught his, proper like I warned he would. His Shawnee woman told me what happened—as much as she knew it. She be with me now."

"I thought you had, well—a wife of your own."

"If ye live with Injuns, there ain't nothing wrong in taking on their ways. So I have me own woman— and George's, along with a passel of kids. Seems like them cows is always dropping babies. Lord knows how many of mine is scattered all over the country."

Croghan eyed Girty with such cold anger and disgust that Abby expected him to pull his pistol and shoot the man on the spot. Edward, still supporting her, bobbed his head to the door and choked out his order.

"Leave the house, *cochon!* This minute!"

"But it's still pouring rain out there!"

"Out!" Edward roared. *"Vouz avez le diable en votre corps.* With the devil in you, you need more than rain to clean your filth. Not even holy water could do that. Out! Now!"

Girty's lips pulled back in a snarl and he looked to Croghan, who actually touched his pistol. "You heard Mr. Forny. Your welcome's over."

Girty mouthed an obscenity but cowered when Croghan pulled his pistol and Edward made a lunging step. "All right, you bastards! I'll go." He glared at Edward. "But you'll get none of my help with the Injuns—and I got heaps of friends among 'em."

"Forget I spoke of it. I can imagine the kind of Indian friends you have—cutthroats and murderers. Get out!"

Girty walked to the door and Abby shrank against Edward as he passed the table. The renegade made no threatening move. He walked out into the downpour, leaving the door swinging open behind him. Croghan crossed the room and closed the door with a slam that shook the cabin. Marie broke into startled crying and Abby darted to her.

When she returned to the main room, Edward and Croghan sat on the table benches across from one another. Both stood up and Edward smiled reassuringly when he saw her wary look at the closed outer door.

"Eh, he is gone and will not be back." He took her hand, pulled her to a seat beside him at the table, filled a mug and pushed it to her. "Drink, *ma pauvre cherie.* I should not have brought that one but he said he knew all the tribes to the south and east—the Choctaw, the Cherokee and even the Creek. I thought he might be of help. Forgive me, eh?"

"Of course." She clung tightly to his shirt sleeve as she took a sip of the hot, reviving whiskey. "You didn't know."

"But the other one—this brother—how did you know of him?"

Edward, like everyone at Fort Pitt, knew how she had changed into Onondaga-white-captive-turned-Indian in order to slip through the red besiegers in order to reach Colonel Bouquet, whose troops smashed and scattered the tribes that ringed the fort. He nodded when she spoke of it.

"I had almost cleared the Indian encampments when I came on a band of Shawnees. George Girty lived with them and he saw me. He tried to make me one of his women along with his other squaws but I escaped. It was the last I ever saw of him." She visibly shuddered. "Once was enough. This Simon Girty reminded me of him."

"The one is dead," Edward soothed her, "probably killed soon after he tried to molest you. This Simon lives for a time with his Indian family and friends on the river bank. They will move on in a day or a week—at most a month. They are a restless breed, not welcome anywhere and they know it. Have no fear or worry about him."

"I can make even the river uncomfortable for him if he causes trouble," Croghan said.

Abby had almost forgotten him in her upset state.

397

She hastened to make amends, leaving the circle of Edward's arms. "Forgive me, Mr. Croghan. I am a poor hostess."

"Nay, Mistress Forny, one of the best and certainly the prettiest."

"You flatter, but thank you. I know you and my husband have much to talk about so—"

"Stay with us, mistress. Your company pleases."

The men did have very much to talk about. She learned Edward had first met their guest on a large island well down the river, one farmed by a couple named Jonas. Edward said both the man and wife were dead, the farm destroyed by fire.

"It is beautiful, that place," Edward told Abby. "I have sometimes thought if we owned it and the Indian threat were truly gone, we could build a house there among the trees with the Beautiful River flowing on both sides."

"The babies are too small for the Ohio," she objected.

"Eh, but they grow. I will teach them to swim, to fish, to paddle a canoe."

"Buy it," Croghan suggested, "and wait for the right time. I'm sure the island is too large to float away."

"*Oui*, but buy it from whom?"

"Me."

Edward stared. "You! But what have you to do with that island, my friend?"

Croghan laughed. "The right to sell it, that's all. As much has happened to me as happened to you since last we met."

"Sur ma parole! You can sell it? You do not own it."

"Pennsylvania does now, by royal grant, and I am land agent for the colony. Yes, on your word, much has happened since the Indian troubles."

Abby listened with fascination to Croghan's account of his last few years. She knew or had heard about some of the facts he mentioned. When the Ohio country came into British hands, the treaty with France had not yet been signed. Lord Jeffrey Amherst had acted as royal governor not only for New France but also for this Ohio country.

Croghan made a distasteful face when he mentioned Amherst and then explained. "The crown should never have sent such a man to the Americas to govern land, least of all, deal with the Indians. The French had been cozzening all the tribes with gifts for a century but received in return furs three or four times more in value. Our Lord Amherst would have none of that. He swore he'd bring the 'bloody savages' to heel without the expenditure of a pence. Bayonets would control them if starvation did not."

"I met his kind long ago in the Onondaga Town," Abby nodded.

Croghan's lips quirked. "Then you know what little effect my arguments and those of the soldiers and governors had on him. The Huron and Lake Indians grew unhappy and restless. I made several of the usual gifts out of my own pocket since Amherst would not. He would not reimburse me nor allow my claim against the crown exchequer. He would not permit the colonial governors to contribute or help me foot the bill. I tried to quiet the chiefs of all the tribes from Spanish Florida to Quebec and Montreal, but Pontiac had their ears. Edward, you and I met on my final trip—a desperate and useless one."

"Lord Amherst did not last long," Abby said.

"Thank God General Sir Thomas Gage took his place!" Croghan agreed. "By then I had hardly one pence to rub against the other but General Gage readily saw the point of my argument. He not only permitted me to go to England but paid part of my expenses. I have been long in London. Do you realize how hard it is to see the prime minister or the guardian of the exchequer, let alone the king! Had it not been for powerful friends at court—" he broke off. "But I could spend a month telling you of my rebuffs until at last a duke or two, an earl or two came to my help."

"But now you're back and we're well met again," Edward smiled. "I had not known of Pennsylvania Colony."

"Also part of my doing while I was in London. Virginia claimed this area and Lord Dinwiddie certainly fought the French for it time and again. He also sent Christopher Gist and a Major Washington to explore and claim it for the colony."

"But we have always looked to Pennsylvania," Abby objected. "We trade in that colony and its western towns are our neighbors and friends. Carlisle men fought with Colonel Bouquet to break Pontiac's stranglehold."

"Aye, and so he did. I said as much over and over in London to the royal powers-that-be but at first they

400

could think of nothing but the oldest and most loyal of the English colonies, Virginia."

"I would wager the wonderful and wise Jeffrey Amherst backed the claim," Abby snapped.

"That he did and it gave me the devil's own time. One thing worked in my favor. Remember during the war with the French, it was by way of Forbes Road that this country was supplied after Braddock's massacre? That was built and maintained by Pennsylvanians. It still is the fastest and shortest road from here to the eastern cities and garrisons. I finally had several meetings with the present Lord Penn in England. That turned the tide for me and brought the royal grant."

Abby saw that his mug was empty and she refilled it. He thanked her with a smile but the bitter note returned to his voice as he waved his hand toward the east.

"Would you believe that, even with Lord Penn's letter in my pocket it was as hard to see the governor in Philadelphia as the king in London! The Friends care as little for change as the Royal Court, I can tell you."

"They pay us little attention out here," Abby added. "I have heard that many a commander at Pitt, even before Colonel Carleton, asked that militia be sent to help us beat off the Indians but none came—except a few companies from the frontier towns."

"That's understandable once you've been in the colony towns of the eastern shore and rivers. They're far removed from warwhoop and tomahawk so their devotion to peace and abhorrence of war is never

401

tested. They can't understand that out here it's a case of fight or die. It's enough that even now many a settler would like to see Virginia rule the western lands."

Edward stood up and stretched. *"Eh, bien,* but you have settled that once and for all, my friend."

"Not really. I just kept Virginia at a distance. We are still in need of defending ourselves." Croghan shrugged. "But it was done once and it can be done again. Besides, I can now call on Sir William Johnson for military aid if it's needed. The British army puts more trust in powder, shot and bayonet than in neighborly love."

"Sir Johnson!" Edward said in surprise. *"Pardieu!* You gained allies in England!"

Croghan laughed then, once more at ease. "Indeed—but grant me I worked for those allies. Now I travel the western lands to report to Sir William. I also survey while I travel as land agent for Pennsylvania—not those in Philadelphia but the lord-proprietors in London. We will have a new era on the river, if I can bring it about."

"You will—and it is high time for it," Edward clapped Croghan on the back. "Perhaps my dream of the Jonas' island is not too impossible after all."

"I'll not sell it," Croghan said, lifting a warning finger. "At least not for a time. But do not keep me waiting too long. Such a jewel of a place will attract many a buyer, you know."

Edward put his arm about Abby's waist. "She will have the final decision for the Forny family."

"Mistress Forny will agree with you and me," Croghan nodded. "So I will hold it for a time. In the meantime, as land agent for Pennsylvania, I know you do not have title to this cabin and your storehouse."

"I knew it!" Edward smacked his forehead with his palm. "I knew there'd come a day when it would take colonial title and deed and it might cost all of us out here a pretty penny."

Croghan nodded. "Do you have that pretty penny? If so I have the patent parchment in my saddlebags. Just a penny for the Fornys, mind you. But it must be polished and shining to be pretty."

Edward looked at Abby with both triumph and tenderness. *"Ma petite*, now our home is certain, sure and forever—or as long as we want it. Does that please you?"

She kissed him in answer and then turned about to take Croghan's hands. She kissed him squarely on the lips and his face turned a beet red. He spoke softly as he touched his lips, and his voice quivered slightly.

"It's been a long time since this ugly face was kissed by a beautiful woman, Mistress Forny."

"I? Beautiful? Thank you, sir."

"My pretty penny," he nodded.

- The downpour of rain ended sometime in the night but the wind blowing up the river from the west had little chance to dry the ground by dawn. So the settlement, cabins, fort, paths and roads were still ankle deep in mud when the sun came up. Edward had fixed a bed for Croghan in the loft and his horse remained dry and well fed in the stable Dean Smith had established as a combined travelers' accommodation and shelter for his own horse and the high bedded wagon that brought supplies from Carlisle, Lancaster and even Ligonier.

Fast-moving clouds hid the sun for minutes at a time and then the whole world would be bathed in gold, a'glitter with raindrops clinging to tree limbs, only to darken as the clouds scudded eastward in steady procession. The few people who dared the road leading eastward from the stockade gate—and now called a "street"—found each step a straining struggle to escape the gluelike mud. One man took only two steps from his doorway before the black gumbo literally sucked a shoe off his foot. It disappeared as though forever, and the man returned to his cabin, his stocking a casing of mud halfway to his knee. He slammed the door in defeat.

Abby had not slept well during the night. Simon Girty intruded in her dreams, his slate gray eyes a steady menace as his dream-image moved through her mind. She would snap wide awake, filled with fear, only to find she snuggled against Edward and that Henri slept securely in his trundle as Marie did in her crib. A falling ember in the fireplace would make a bright, reassuring red gleam. She would fall asleep only to see George Girty trying to mount her and hear Corn Dancer's gun spit flame and bullet. She would see him drop dead immediately afterward, even as he fell off her to one side. She would flee then, down a crazy nightmare lane of trees.

Once more she would snap awake, her vision and mind frozen with fright. Once Edward had snapped alert when she inadvertently struck him

404

in her tossing.

"Bad dreams, darling," she reassured him. "No more."

"Ah, it's the memory of that pig of a man I allowed in the house."

"Something like that," she admitted. "He did no harm but he was a walking horror."

"He's gone," Edward enfolded her.

"For good, I hope," she prayed as she pressed against Edward's muscled chest.

"I will see to it."

As always, she left the bed just before dawn light. She moved as quietly about the room as she could, first dressing and then preparing breakfast at the long table, readying it for the fire she'd build up when it was time to rouse the children. Now and then rain made a swift tattoo on the cabin roof but that was a pleasant sound. The thick log walls shut out the world, rain and all, but she knew that somewhere out there Simon Girty would probably be wondering about her. She should never have admitted to even having seen his brother so long ago.

She fed the children and roused the men after she built the fire so the flames hungrily licked at the wood branches and finally ignited the black coal in the heavy iron container the local blacksmith had built for them. She thought, as she so often had, how wonderful that the myriad hills about the settlement and post had almost inexhaustible veins of coal and deposits of crude iron ore everywhere, some of it so close to the surface that a single scrape of a spade would expose it. How much easier her mother's life would have been if there had been so much riches underfoot in Westover!

The brief morning shower stopped before Edward and Croghan finished eating. When Edward opened the door and looked out, the sky had completely cleared. Not a single cloud scudded along on the gentle west breeze. The sun beat down warm and golden, but the street mud looked more thick and gluesome.

Edward shrugged as he and Croghan peered out. "Eh, our business waits, *mon ami*, until the ground dries. Right now it is too wet to walk on and too thick to canoe."

"My thought exactly," Croghan agreed. "We're housebound."

"But not idle. There's much you can tell me about the country south and east since you're freshly come from that way. Also I'm curious as to what Pennsylvania Colony would ask, if anything at all, of a man who'd try a business venture here and along the Ohio."

He closed the door and the two men turned to the table benches and sat down. Abby remained frozen across the room, rounded eyes fastened on the door. Edward became aware of her, bounced to his feet and jumped to her side.

"What frightens you!"

She looked up at him blankly as though he had snapped her out of a daze. He grasped her shoulders. "Abby! What is it!"

"That man," she pointed to the door. "—out there."

"What man?"

"The one who—Girty."

"Sacre bleu!"

He whipped around the end of the table and jerked open the door. Then he looked back over his shoulder at Abby. "Where? I don't see him."

"He's there." She pointed to Letty's house. "He was standing right there. I saw him."

Her paralysis broke and she came up beside Edward. As he had said, Girty could not be seen. She could not believe it and she started to step out of the doorway but Edward checked her. *"Ma petite!* He is not there. I would have seen him, no?"

"My eyes do not trick me!"

He gently but firmly turned her about, closed the door and led her to the table. He sat beside her on the bench. Croghan sympathetically watched from across the table. Edward placed her head on his shoulder and smoothed her hair over and over.

"You had bad dreams of him all night. He is a foul and frightening man. We are well to be rid of him."

"But we're not!" she tried to lift her head in protest but he held her firmly.

"If not, I'll see that we are," he promised. "It was not your eyes that tricked you, gentle one, but your fear. It has happened to all of us at one time or another."

She tried to deny the thought but he would not be convinced. "Eh, I have played such tricks on myself. I have seen Indians where there were none, and that not so long ago. No, no, that *cochon* would not dare come near us."

"He's evil through and through," Abby met his argument. "He'd ambush, murder and he's in the mind for it. Once he's done his devil's work, he will disappear."

She had to act contented with that but she knew Simon Girty lurked somewhere close.

XXXI

Abby felt grateful that the deep mud took so long to dry and therefore kept Edward and Croghan near her and the children. That protection would not last, she knew, so what would happen when everyone, including the horrible Girty, could move about without hindrance? She told herself over and over that there was no way by which Girty could know that she had been present at his brother's violent death. Only she knew that secret.

She told herself Simon's anger was because of the way in which Edward had evicted him so unceremoniously into the pelting downpour and the mud. Still, for some reason, George Girty's ghost haunted her.

The next morning dawned clear and bright once more and now, though the ground was soft, the street was passable to foot and horse travel, though cart wheels had a tendency to sink deep and hold fast. Abby dreaded the time when Edward and Croghan would leave her alone. She wondered what had happened to all that courage that was once hers.

She assured herself over and over that she still had it. Really, it was the distressful memory of Corn Dancer's death at the hands of the scrofulous George Girty. It was the picture of Corn Dancer using his last breath of life and bit of strength to kill Girty even as the man clawed open his trousers as he straddled her own body. Simon Girty, here in Pitt settlement, brought those memories up all too vividly. When she looked at Simon, her memory made her see George. There lay the key to her weakness.

Even though her logic helped for a time, she still felt a touch of fear when, breakfast consumed, Edward and Croghan rose from the table. But Edward almost immediately reassured her when he dropped his pistol in his cloak pocket and touched the sheathed knife at his belt.

"It is time we make certain our unwanted friend has traveled on."

"I'll share that pleasure with you," Croghan said, then turned to Abby. "Mistress, I cannot thank you enough for your hospitality."

But won't you be coming back in a few hours?" Abby asked, disconcerted.

"I will be a time with Edward making sure Girty is gone. Then I hope to find a *voyageur* heading downstream. If I do, there will be only time to grab my pack and climb into his canoe."

She walked with them to the door which Edward opened as he turned to her. She tried to keep apprehension in check when she looked out on the street. By sheer chance Dave and Obed Smith passed by on their way to the fields and both boys smiled at her and Edward. They carried hoes, bags of seed and planting sticks, for the time to put in spring crops had come.

Dave called, "Good day, Mistress Forny, and to you, sir." Edward's nod and smile acknowledged the greeting. "We set a field out to corn."

"You have a buyer for as many bushels as you care to sell come autumn," Edward offered.

"That pleasures us and thank you, sir. We'll sell all but our own need."

Obed added, "There'll be pumpkin, squash and pole beans."

"We'll trade for those, too," Abby assured him. "How is your mother, and the children?"

"Maw's healthy as ever and so are the kids," Obed answered. "She misses Paw but he's likely back soon, ain't he, Mr. Forny?"

"He better be, what with all the things our neighbors need."

The tall, husky boys walked on. Abby swept the street with a single glance but did not see Girty. Perhaps the renegade had left the settlement? She

411

knew that hopeful thought was false, at least until Edward proved otherwise. He kissed her just then.

"*Il n'y a pas danger*. My dear, there's nothing to fear. Monsieur Croghan and I will see to it. Stay inside and pull the latch string in if you like."

She summoned up courage to laugh at him. "You say that to Strong Woman of the Onondaga!"

His eyes glowed and his smile flashed. "Nay, now that she has returned. But still, keep an eye to the door, eh? and make sure who seeks entrance."

He and Croghan left. She watched them walk slowly side by side toward the fort stockade. Both scanned the areas between the cabins as well as the street itself. She finally closed the door, touched the latch string but jerked her hand away. She couldn't deny her own boast.

There was always so much to be done about a house, no matter how small, she thought as she moved to the unmade bed. Dishes to be washed, food to be prepared, Marie to be changed and rocked for a short time, Henri to be watched so that he did not get into too much mischief. There would be stockings to be darned, water to be heated for laundry. She suddenly thought of Moon Willow in the Long House of the Onondaga and laughed at her own tally of a woman's household work. Moon Willow must have felt the same way, though actually she had far less to do. But less with which to do it. Abby shrugged and began her own tasks.

She did not think of Girty again until she dropped onto a stool by the fireplace to wait for the laundry water to boil in its cauldron over the fire. Well! if she could so easily forget him for so long a time, he

412

simply could not be as much a threat as she believed. She looked contentedly about the room.

A month or more ago Dean Smith, always clever with tools, and wood carving, had shaped a horse's head that he attached to one end of a broomstick and then used the remains of a worn-out mop as a tail that he attached to the other end. Now Henri pranced astraddle of it, hitting his leg with a little switch and hallooing "Gid-yap! Gid-Yap" as he raced about the room.

Abby watched in amusement that slowly merged into pride. How like Edward he would be! There was no doubt even now whose dark and handsome son he was. Although a child, he had a flowing grace where one would expect uncoordinated, awkward movements. Her mind idly turned to the future and what it would hold for the boy. Edward had already begun to build a little river kingdom of trade to hand on to his son. Abby vowed she would teach him and Marie as much as she knew about reading, figuring and writing. Someday they would get a teacher for Henri or send him to a school. Oh, it wouldn't be one of those village one-room things but perhaps back east in one of the colonies in a place like Boston, New York or Philadelphia. Marie—

A sudden noise at the door sent alarm racing along every nerve. She fairly vaulted off her stool and whirled about, blindly reaching for the long iron poker leaning against the fireplace.

Edward entered, seeing her defensive crouch and impromptu weapon. Henri continued to prance-ride his hobby horse as his father froze in consternation and then found his voice.

"Mon Dieu! I should have given you warning, *ma petite!* I did not think."

She lowered the poker and the pallor began to leave her face. "I daydreamed," she said lamely, "instead of properly attending to my work. I did not expect you back so soon."

"Daydreamed, eh?" Edward took her into his arms. *"C'est bien.* It is good that you can do it."

She realized then that George Croghan stood in the doorway. She broke away from Edward to welcome him. She became aware that she still held the poker and hastily tried to partially hide it in the folds of her voluminous skirt. "I'm glad you returned."

"Only for a moment. I found my canoe man and he's anxious to be on his way. I came for my pack." He hurried across the room to the loft.

Edward said, "We've looked everywhere in the settlement and well beyond. Monsieur Girty and his Indian squaws have left us for the woods. We'll not see him for some time to come if ever again."

Abby's arms tightened about him as she nestled her head on his chest. "That is good news, darling. Are you sure? I was told never to trust any devil."

"I don't trust this one," he chuckled. "So I looked everywhere and asked everybody. The tribe has disappeared. No one has seen or heard of them. The woods swallowed them and the woods can keep them."

Just then with his pack Croghan came down the ladder. He again thanked Abby, shook Edward's hand and swung the pack on his shoulder. He stepped to the door but stopped short. "Oh, how about the Jonas' island?"

414

"Abby has not seen it. How can I say?"

Relieved by the news about Girty and recalling her vague plans for the future as she had sat by the fireplace, Abby asked, "Mr. Croghan, is it as beautiful as Edward says?"

"It is indeed, mistress. Of course, there are only fire-charred buildings and an old rail fence on it now."

"That is no mind if it would in time make a place on the river roomy enough on which to live or to spend a summer with the children."

"Ah, *ma petite*," Edward cut in. "It is all of that."

"Then speak for it, darling. Buy it now."

Edward looked over her head at Croghan. "You have heard the *châtelaine*. Seal it for us."

Croghan said, "My *voyageur* can wait some moments, no matter how impatiently. This will take but a moment or two and I will be as pleasured as you to know you have it."

He opened his pack, found the blank colony land grant documents, a quill, and twisted open the cap of a horn of ink. He rapidly filled in a few lines, signed the paper with a flourish and affixed the colony seal.

"There! It is yours." He made an emphatic negative gesture when Edward pulled his leather coin purse from under the skirt of his cloak. "No! I pay the fees. It is little enough recompense for the warm welcome I've had and too small a gift to friends newly made but already held dear."

He stubbornly shook his head as both Abby and Edward tried to persuade him to accept a rightful fee. He closed his pack, secured it, swung it on his back and raced to the door.

"Mr. Croghan, please—" Abby called.

But he had darted out the door. Only a faint echo of his voice answered her. "Would you have me stranded in Pitt when I should be down the river?"

After Croghan left, Edward played with Henri for a time, though Abby was aware that he watched her covertly. She felt good about his concern for her even though they all knew Girty had left. Gradually her tension faded, but each time she passed the open street door she scanned the passersby and the few cabins she could see. She realized Edward remained only because of her when he would rather be at the warehouse or gathering news of the river from the *voyageurs*.

She finally threw a shawl about her shoulders and, ignoring Edward's surprised look, lifted Marie from her crib and took Henri's hand. She smiled at him as she walked to the door.

"It's high time I moved about. I'll visit with Letty. I know you have business, darling, so be about it. I'll be all right now."

"Certain?"

"Indeed I am."

"Eh, bien." She heard the relief in his tone. "I'll check the warehouse and then see how the new boat builds after I've had some news of the river. I'll not be far should you have need of me."

"I'll not, what with woman's talk. Letty will be surprised to know we've an island now."

"A generous gift from George," he agreed. "It comes to my mind Henri's large enough to enjoy a canoe, and there is the old cradleboard for Marie. Perhaps one of my *voyageurs* could take us all to see

416

our new property."

"Henri in a canoe?" she asked doubtfully.

Edward was enthusiastic. "By my side and firmly thonged to the seat. He would be safe, I promise you. We could go very fast with the current downstream and spend the day exploring. I have camped there before and I know you would enjoy it, especially if your son and your husband caught fine fish for the supper fire. The next day we'd come home."

"I'd like it," she agreed, "and I'm serious. I'm just not sure about the children."

"Think about it—talk it over with Letty, eh? We'll both be home before dusk and that would give me time to engage a *voyageur* and his canoe."

"I'll let you know come evening—or before," she promised.

She could not help her split second of hesitation and her swift, sharp search up and down the street before she stepped out the door. But Henri tugged at her skirt and she held Marie a bit tighter. Her first step onto the street, like a magician's wand, banished all uncertainty. She walked a bit more freely with each step and soon approached Letty's cabin. She exchanged greetings with those she met on the street and proudly watched Henri receive compliments as a lady bent to hug him.

Letty appeared in her open doorway as Abby came up. "Land sakes! It's high time you become neighborly again! I begun to think you'd pushed me clean out of your mind."

"You know better!" Abby laughed.

It took but a moment in the cabin to put Marie in one of the cribs that always stood about the Smith home and release Henri to the boisterous attention of the three tow headed boys. For once, Letty did not nurse a baby but admitted she was two months along with child.

"Kids in this family ain't news, Abby, you know. You're the one makes news. Your man sure keeps my Dean a'hustle and a'moving. I see ye had Mr. Croghan to your place. Saw him leave this morning."

"We've had our fill of visitors," Abby admitted.

"Even to that Simon Girty. Glad you flung him out, even in the rain. Not that it helped none. He's too filthy to clean up and his Injun women ain't much better."

"Edward and Mr. Croghan have seen to it they're gone for good."

"We be thankful for that. One of them lice-ridden women hung around like she was watching your house."

"What!"

"No mind, honey! I saw her skeedaddle into the woods late last night and there's no sign of her no more. They're all gone now and you can bet on it."

XXXII

Time passed swiftly. There was so much to talk about, as women always discovered. Letty Smith could not really be called a gossip, for she never spoke ill of anyone, nor made innuendoes. But she apparently saw and heard everything. Abby had often thought that if Letty could write, she would be the perfect historian of Pitt settlement, now more and more often being referred to as Pittsburg.

She knew of the Jonases when Abby mentioned their island and of their massacre by the Indians in the late uprising. She nodded in pleasure when Abby said Edward had purchased the island. "From all I hear, it's as pretty a place as anyone could want. Why don't you and Edward go see it, like he said?"

"I'll tell him we will when he comes home tonight."

Letty instantly caught Abby's sudden doubtful expression. "Something jiggled your brain then, honey?"

"Well—yes. Edward's with the men who built his boat and he said he'd hire a *voyageur* and his canoe for the trip tomorrow if he had time enough."

"Land sakes! no problem there. I'll show you."

She had Abby follow her outside and around the corner of the cabin. From that point they could see the Monongahela flowing northward to its joining with the Allegheny. Trees and bushes came almost to the water itself at one or two points but Letty pointed to a long spit of land where tall river reeds grew. They could not fully hide the hull of what promised to be the largest boat ever to sail on the Ohio.

"He'll be right there, honey," Letty said, "just a hop and three-four skips, all in plain sight of the settlement. I'll watch the young'ns if you want to go down there and tell him."

Abby considered a moment. "I would like to go and I'm curious about the kind of craft Edward builds."

Letty laughed. "So 'm I. You just sashay down there and tomorrow morning you 'n the little 'ns will be paddling to your new island."

Abby squeezed her friend's arm. "You're wonderful, Letty. I will go tell him."

"Not wonderful, just itchin' to know what your husband has in mind building such a contraption. Go see, then git back and tell me."

Abby checked Henri and Marie before walking down the street paralleling the high fort stockade to the beginning of the path along the Monongahela. The river current burbled and sang gently, and to her left she heard the sounds of the settlement. They began to die away as she passed the last cabin. She heard the ripple of the river, the whisper of a gentle wind in the trees and over the bending grass, the cheerful songs of birds.

The sun warmly bathed her in golden light. It was so good to be free, at peace again, secure as ever a woman with handsome husband, son and beautiful baby daughter could be. She strolled by the trees, now close to her left, the path a soft well-trodden wide strip of brown dust before her. The trees behind her, she could now see the high shape of Edward's boat even more clearly. Her pace slowed as she tried to puzzle out what he had in mind. The hull looked like a small ship but of what use would that be on the Ohio? She could now occasionally hear hammers and the lilting songs of the French builders as they musically narrated the naughty misbehaviors and adventures of Amoreux Angela, who apparently traveled as diligently as she made love.

Abby laughed at the silly fantasies as she came to another place where the river path curved away from the bank, and tree boughs overhead shadowed the path. A high wall of bushes suddenly threshed wildly. Her laugh broke off as she flinched at the alarming movement. She froze in horror as she looked directly into Simon Girty's slatey eyes. He grabbed her as she screamed. His hand clapped over her mouth, his dirty thumb half blinding her. She glimpsed the greasy squaws rush in to grab her. The bushes closed about her.

She was swept off her feet and held close against the fouled, stinking shirt covering Girty's muscular chest. Her mind whirled in flashing impressions. She tried to scream but could not. Then she bit down hard and Girty yelled in pain. He actually threw her down. Her head struck something hard and the world whirled about her. She heard a chatter of a woman's voice as though at a far distance and but half understood the Shawnee words.

"She Strong Woman, all right . . . George went after . . . never came back . . . He found dead . . . Onondaga Sachem. But it her—Strong Woman. I see . . . in paleskin town yesterday."

Her senses began to swim. But someone grabbed her blouse and jerked her half upright. Girty's beard held spittle and he mouthed curses at her.

"You killed my brother or helped that damned Injun do it. They call you Strong Woman at Pitt. You was the one as worked your way through to Carlisle for Bouquet. They talk of that at Pitt. Great, brave lady, they say!" He spat in her face. "My brother's killer! You 'n your fine Frenchie husband and dandified friends! Just a squaw woman like any Injun cow!"

He grabbed a wad of her hair and twisted her head about, pointing to one of the Indian women. "She was George's squaw. She saw you. She knowed George had the heats for you and wanted to rut. He tried. Now I know the whole truth. You're gonna pay for George, a knife cut at a time after I have all of your cunt George wanted but didn't get. You think on it until we reach a proper place deep in the woods."

He cuffed her so hard her head swam again. He slapped a thick, filthy rag over her mouth, forced open her lips and pushed it between her teeth. He whipped her about and pulled the gag tight, tying it. She gagged but it caught in her throat, choking her. Girty held his heavy, wicked knife before her eyes.

"You'll get this instead and damned quick if you cause any trouble."

He shoved the blade in his belt sheath and lifted her to her feet by her hair. Pain made her scream but only a strangled gurgle came through the gag. He whirled her around.

She saw Edward plunge through the thick wall of bushes, a pistol in his hand. A squaw threw herself at him as he fired at Girty. The shot went wild. Girty whipped up his own pistol and fired, Edward grabbed his shoulder and fell full length on his face, his useless weapon spilling out of his hand.

"I'll finish the bastard!" Girty yelled, starting to load his pistol. It took but a second to blow out the muzzle, tamp a wadding down the barrel and drop a ball atop it. Abby stood paralyzed, without mind, without thought but fear for Edward.

Girty leveled the pistol at Edward's prone form. His move snapped Abby into instinctive action. She saw the knife in Girty's belt. She snatched it free and plunged the blade deep between the renegade's shoulder blades. She felt it thud to the hilt. The gag prevented any sound, though her scream roared in her mouth and ears. Girty threw his arms up and wide, fell, his body twisting about. She stared down into the bearded devil's mask that passed as his face. Suddenly blood streamed out of his open mouth and over his chin. He twitched. One second his eyes stared at her in surprised horror but the next second they turned cold and blind.

She did not see the squaws close in on her with clubs and knives. The world suddenly became a pinpoint then snapped into complete darkness just as she heard men yelling in French.

XXXIII

She loved Jonas' Island, as Edward said she would, especially at that time of the day when the soft dusk of late summer seemed to softly creep down the river from the east while the last thin, narrow streaks of golden, red and mauve sunset slowly faded in the west. The fireflies came out and started their fairy dance of twinkling lights out over the rippling current. Frogs made a basso profundo to the high, thin squawking of darting, shadowy bats or the sleepy complaint of a bird not quite settled on its tree branch for the night.

Edward, his left arm still in a sling, sat beside her on the riverbank, always so close he could touch her hand resting on her chair arm. In the small temporary cabin Simeon had built, Henri and Marie would be sound asleep by now. Simeon sprawled at ease on the soft sand of the riverbank. His question to Edward broke the easy run of Abby's contented thoughts that were really more like waking dreams.

"When will Dean Smith be back this trip?"

"Eh, much too soon to suit me. I've grown lazy waiting for this bullet hole to heal. Besides, Major Blaine will take most of our wares for the downstream posts."

"The British strengthen all of them, I hear," Simeon agreed, "and mayhap rightly so. *Tout les habitants sont san repos* from what I saw and heard and the *voyageurs* say everyone grows restless, unhappy."

"Is trouble brewing?" Abby asked in sudden alarm.

Edward's hand tightened on hers. "Not now but perhaps in a few years, a decade—*qui sait?*—maybe never."

She sighed. "Yes, who knows? I hope it *is* never. You and I have had enough for our lifetimes, darling, and for our children's lives."

"*Il est pour sûr* you've had trouble."

"Indeed it is certain," Simeon echoed, pulled himself to a sitting position and hugged his knees.

Abby could barely see his admiring gaze upon her as he spoke. "You are the brave one to kill that *bête,* Simon Girty."

"I would be dead if she hadn't," Edward completed the thought. "This one, she is not called Strong Woman for nothing, Simeon."

"I still can't believe I screamed so loud when he grabbed me that you heard it at the boat," Abby marveled. "Maybe I'd best be called 'Strong Lungs,' eh?"

"Thank God we heard you, my men and I. Thank God they were right behind me, and scattered those Indian women when they attacked you."

She shuddered at the memory of those horrible few moments. "Let's just thank God and put it all behind us where finished things belong."

"And think on the morrow, eh?"

"Nay, more than think, darling. Let's dream and plan on it."

"For you and me," he nodded.

"For Henri and Marie, too. We must plan for them. The future years are theirs more than ours."

"Ah, for all of us an empire of trade along the rivers, *ma petite!* I also have mind for those great inland lakes to the north. It is but a short portage from the upper Allegheny to the Lake of the Eries. From there we could canoe to Detroit to the west, or Niagara to the east." His voice filled with enthusiasm. "Not a canoe! Those lakes are for ships. We will build a whole fleet—"

She placed her hand over his lips and laughed. "Ships later if and when there are settlements enough

427

along the lake shores to warrant trade."

"There will be."

"Speaking of ships, darling, what do you build for the Ohio? There are only a few settlers or posts and a village or two."

"There will soon be more. I build a cargo boat with a sail to travel downstream."

"Upstream?" Simeon asked.

"Eh, have you seen the platform along each side of the hull? Men will walk them from stem to stern with long poles to push our boat against the current."

Abby laughed again, pleased and contented, but with a soft note of mockery in her question. "But what of the country to the south and east, down toward those 'gaps' into the Carolinas?"

"Ah, I have not forgotten. As soon as this shoulder heals and the stiffness is gone from bone and muscle, I will look down that way."

She rose, bent over and kissed him. "I vow! you must even plan and dream in your sleep. Do you envision a dynasty of Fornys?"

"Pourquoi pas?"

"Indeed why not!" She kissed him again and turned to the cabin. "But to make sure, I had best see that the second generation sleeps well and safely. We must be sure of heirs, you know."

He called after her as she walked to the darkened cabin, "You can always be sure. They are the children of Edouard, Sieur de Fournet, and Abigail Brewster, known as Strong Woman in the Ohio country."

She breathed a prayer of thanks that he was alive to

make the boast. She had the thought that saving Edward had somehow repaid her debt to Corn Dancer for having saved her. Perhaps his spirit heard as he sat at the Great Council Fire up there among the stars.

FICTION FOR TODAY'S WOMAN

EMBRACES (666, $2.50)
by Sharon Wagner
Dr. Shelby Cole was an expert in the field of medicine and a novice at love. She wasn't willing to give up her career to get married— until she grew to want and need the child she was carrying.

MIRRORS (690, $2.75)
by Barbara Krasnoff
The compelling story of a woman seeking changes in life and love, and of her desperate struggle to give those changes impact—in the midst of tragedy.

THE LAST CARESS (722, $2.50)
by Dianna Booher
Since the tragic news that her teenaged daughter might die, Erin's husband had become distant, isolated. Was this simply his way of handling his grief, or was there more to it? If she was losing her child, would she lose her husband as well?

VISIONS (695, $2.95)
by Martin A. Grove
Caught up in the prime time world of power and lust, Jason and Gillian fought desperately for the top position at Parliament Television. Jason fought to keep it—Gillian, to take it away!

LONGINGS (706, $2.50)
by Sylvia W. Greene
Andrea was adored by her husband throughout their seven years of childless marriage. Now that she was finally pregnant, a haze of suspicion shrouded what should have been the happiest time of their lives.

Available wherever paperbacks are sold, or order direct from the Publisher. Send cover price plus 50¢ per copy for mailing and handling to Zebra Books, 21 East 40th Street, New York, N.Y. 10016. DO NOT SEND CASH!